Frostfire
Book One of The Dark Inbetween

Sam Thorne and Lauren Ivey

PUBLISHED BY THORNE & IVEY BOOKS

This is a work of fiction. Names, characters, places, and incidents are either the product of the authors' imagination, used in a ficticious manner, or in the public domain. Any resemblance to actual incidents or actual persons, living or dead, is coincidental.

WARNING
This work of fiction contains scenes of sexual abuse, graphic violence, and mutilation.

Copyright ©2021 Thorne & Ivey Books, LLC

This edition first published in 2021
by Thorne & Ivey Books
Augusta, Georgia
www.thorneandivey.com

All rights reserved. This publication may not be reproduced, stored or transmitted in any form or by any means.
First published in the United States of America in 2021.
Printed and bound in the United States of America
by Thorne and Ivey Books LLC.

Cover Design by Benjamin P. Roque
Author Photo by Jacqueline Aleace Photography

ISBN 978-1-955221-00-9

Other Formats:
ISBN 978-1-955221-01-6 (hardcover)
ASIN B08ZHZ8M27 (ebook)

Part One

Chapter One

Kyran jolted upright, his heart hammering in his chest. What had he...? His head snapped to the shuttered window as someone screamed in terror over the clamor of a bell. Kicking the quilted bed cover back, he threw the inn's shutters open.

The village was engulfed in flames. Bright orange light flared against the summer night as people scrambled from their homes and into the muddy streets, panicked, fleeing in every direction. And over it all, a bell was tolling.

He had to do something. Jamming his feet into his boots, Kyran raced out of his room and down the stairs. On the bottom floor, the inn's other occupants huddled about the fireplace, hands clenched in fervent prayer, their eyes trained on the firelight. Candles burned on nearly every horizontal surface, creamy streaks of their wax running across the tables and shelves.

"What's happening?" Kyran demanded, but they either did not hear him, or chose not to.

A scream outside cut abruptly short. The supplicants flinched, but did not cease their prayers. Kyran looked from them to the door, but not a soul moved. He shook his head at them, muttering a curse for their cowardice, and threw open the door, breaking into a run.

The air stung his nostrils and throat, and he struggled not to cough as he closed in on the burning building. A woman fled from it, eyes wide in utter terror. He started after her to ask what had happened, but another motion caught his attention, and he saw it. Whatever *it* was.

The dark *thing* was hard to see, backlit by the fire, but it was small—no larger than a hound—and crouched upon the burning thatch as if bathing in the flames licking its blackened skin.

The beast jerked on the rooftop, its head twitching sharply towards Kyran as if it had caught his scent. Kyran stared back in blank incomprehension, recalling the old tales of salamanders crawling from logs after they had been placed in a fire.

The creature threw its head back and let out an earsplitting shriek. Kyran clapped his hands over his ears, gritting his teeth against the piercing pain. The sound trailed into an excited chitter, but before he could even pull his hands from his ears, the beast launched from the rooftop. It smashed into his chest and knocked him flat, its claws biting through his shirt.

He shoved it. Its body was hard and oily like an insect, but it clung to him, digging its hooked toes into his skin. Its mouth opened wide to reveal double rows of serrated bone, so close to his face he could feel its breath, its burnt odor stinging his nostrils.

In a flash, light traced through Kyran's skin, pale blue lines that glowed like starlight as he let his control over the power in his blood slip just a fraction. The beast's carapace crackled hideously under his palms, and it recoiled with a pained squeal, fire erupting from the tips of its claws as it leapt off his chest.

Beating frantically at the flames, Kyran scrambled backwards, his breath coming in short, panicked gasps. The beast let out another chittering yowl, charging him again.

He loosened his control even further. The lines of light beneath his skin flared to almost blinding brilliance, and the muck on the ground let out a torturous scream as it froze in an instant, turning to hard, slick ice beneath him. The creature balked and skittered away, hissing as ice scrawled across the ground after it.

Kyran yanked his knife from his boot and brandished it as he regained his footing, at last getting a decent look at the beast in the light cast by his own blood. Its proportions were wrong for an animal—gangly, but far too alien to be human—and it wielded fire.

"Stars above," he whispered. "What are ye?"

It feinted towards him, and he thrust the tip of his knife forward. It shrank back in fear. He quashed the panicked sounds at the back of his throat with sheer force of will, tightening his grip of control again. It was a beast. A strange beast, but a beast no less. And he hunted beasts.

As the light of his magic dimmed, the creature lunged at his belly. He twisted out of its path, slicing at its hindquarters. His knife bit flesh.

The beast let out a high, keening wail that sent gooseflesh rippling over Kyran's skin as the monster skidded across the ice. Steam sizzled from the wound on its flank. He turned to follow it as it circled him, the ice crunching as each step sank through its thin veneer.

"Get back!" a man bellowed.

Kyran whipped his head around. A rider was bearing down on them, the roar of the fire and clamoring of the bell drowning out the hoofbeat. The horse's flanks were lathered and heaving, its muzzle frothing from exertion, and the rider was struggling to keep his seat, his feet bouncing, hands too wide on the reins. He would go over its neck the moment his steed changed directions.

There was a hiss behind him, and Kyran turned. The beast lunged at him, its jaws stretched wide.

Magic surged down his arm, lashing into the monster's hide with a crackle of freezing flesh. It squealed and fell back, clawing at its face and neck, only to be engulfed a moment later by a black and crimson ball of flame that hurtled past Kyran's shoulder. The ground popped as the heat flashed the ice to steam, and the blast knocked the creature from its feet, sending it skidding over the muck.

Kyran's eyes widened, his pulse nearly stopping as he whirled to look at the rider—on foot now, his horse pelting away with a terrified bray. Another mage? He had never seen one before. Stars, he had started to think he was the only one.

"That ice," the rider yelled, pulling his own dagger from his side. "Was that you?"

"What?" Kyran asked, dragging his eyes back to the beast as it began to circle, its attention switching between them.

"The ice," the man repeated. Black fire limned with crimson danced along the fingers of his empty hand. "You're a mage! Is that your magic?" He thrust his hand forward, and more fire erupted from his palm. But the creature leapt out of the way and sprang at Kyran again, coming in low. The moment he raised his knife, though, it balked, turning aside and running past him instead.

Kyran turned to follow it so it could not get behind him, keeping his knife raised. He cut a glance at the man, at the fire he wielded so openly, and swallowed the denial on his tongue. "Aye," he finally admitted, nearly choking on the word.

"Watch your back," the rider warned him, closing the gap between them and taking his side. "It's after you."

Kyran shot a glance at the man but couldn't make out much before the creature again scuttled towards him. As one, he and the rider thrust their hands forward, simultaneous blasts of freezing air and black fire surging towards the beast. It leapt back, but not far enough. The rider's fire caught its backside, setting it ablaze. It bucked wildly, shrieking in pain, then dropped to roll in the thick mud to smother the flames.

"Trap it!" the rider bellowed, circling out from Kyran's side, obviously aiming to hem the creature in between them.

But Kyran didn't quite grasp how—until he saw the water gathering in the furrows the creature had gouged into the earth.

With a cry, Kyran thrust the tip of his knife at the monster, shoving his power through the metal and towards the beast. The creature wailed in pain as frost splashed across its skin and the earth around it, enrobing it in a frozen cocoon. It twitched, trying to move, to run. But it was trapped, half frozen into the earth.

"Hold it!" the rider shouted, taking his dagger in both hands and falling on the beast. He drove the blade into its hide with an audible crunch. The thing screamed, its body going horribly rigid as something beneath the man's shirt glowed with iridescent light. Then its body began to simply fall apart, its limbs and skin and muscle dissolving before Kyran's eyes, as if consumed by some inner fire, until there was nothing left—not even ash.

The man sat back on his knees, letting out a short breath before looking up at Kyran. "Was that the only one?"

Kyran nodded, gathering his senses again, bringing his magic back to heel under his control. "Aye," he answered, his blood dimming beneath his skin. "I dinnae see another."

The man nodded and got to his feet, wiping his dagger on his trouser leg before sheathing it at his hip. "Good." The firelight cast deep shadows over the man's face, but Kyran thought he could make out that his eyes were blue. "You did good with that magic."

The compliment caught him off guard. "Ah, thank you," he said hesitantly.

"Does it work on fires?"

"Aye, it does."

"Good. We'll get these fires under control. Then...." The man looked him up and down, taking in his Isleish garb, no doubt. "You don't live here, do you?"

Kyran gave him a flat look. "No."

"Let me buy you a drink, then. As thanks. You know where the Drunken Wind is?"

Chapter Two

Even with the villagers helping to chain water from the local well, it took a long time to put out the smaller fires to prevent them from spreading any farther. They managed to save a few buildings from being completely engulfed, but some smoldered in the night air as the fire consumed them down to their foundations. When the fire was contained, however, much of the village was still unharmed.

The rider helped for a while, but when it became evident they had everything under control, he stepped out of the line and spoke with the villagers. Kyran couldn't hear what he was saying over the noise of the fire and grunts of exertion, but one after another, the villagers shook their heads no.

At least the bell had stopped ringing, though only after a curious ritual. The rider pulled the villager at the rope aside, relaying something to him. A moment later, the villager tang the village bell twice, paused, then rung it twice again. In the distance, a second bell echoed the same pair of tones back before falling silent.

Once the fires were controlled, Kyran could hardly believe his ears when the villagers thanked them profusely for their help, though they notably did not venture too close to Kyran. The rider made their excuses while Kyran stood dumbstruck, then ushered them to take their leave.

They started down the road, away from the noise and confusion of the village, and Kyran noted for the first time just how tall the man was. He was almost the same height as Kyran himself, but much more broadly built. He seemed near Kyran's age, too, though it was hard to make out in the dark.

"Can you whistle?" the man asked Kyran suddenly, interrupting his musing.

Kyran's brows piqued. "Aye."

"Good. I can't. Can you whistle my horse over? Mihai trained her to it, but doesn't do me much good, and I don't feel like chasing her down."

A rider that couldn't call his horse. Kyran could not imagine how poorly the man rode, then. The poor beastie. Pursing his lips, Kyran blew a sharp, two-toned whistle. He cocked his head and heard, with some satisfaction, hooves striking earth.

The rider grinned. "Perfect. Stay here a moment while I catch her. She can get a bit flighty around mages."

The man darted off into the night before Kyran could reply, leaving him waiting on the road. The other mage returned shortly astride a handsome mare, her golden coat set off by a thick, creamy mane and tail. She snorted as he guided her onto the road, her ears pricked starkly upright and nostrils wide as she stared at Kyran.

"It's alright, Sweetheart," the man murmured, bending to pat the horse's neck. "He's not going to bite you."

Kyran looked the horse over appreciatively. There was good breeding behind it, and it was well cared for. He doubted the rider had anything to do with that, given what he had seen of the man's horsemanship so far. Whoever Mihai was, Kyran would not mind having a chat with him. "I'll follow behind you. Horses dinnae take ta me."

"You don't have to walk behind us. Sweetheart will behave herself. Right, Sweetheart?"

The mare blew another loud snort, chomping at her bit.

It took some trial and error, but Kyran found he could walk on the opposite side of the beaten road without causing the animal undue stress.

"Sorry. She's not usually this finicky," the rider said after they had settled into a good rhythm. "Name's Barrett, by the way, if I never got around to saying it."

"Kyran," Kyran returned.

"Well, Kyran, it's nice to meet you. I have to say, it was a surprise to see you out here. You were holding your own pretty well with that magic. I 'ppreciate the help."

"Aye," Kyran murmured, stiffening at the word "magic." But Barrett didn't say it with the same disgust Kyran had heard so many times before. The man had even wielded his own magic against the grotesque beast, without a moment's hesitation.

"I've never met anyone with your...your...." Barrett waved his hand vaguely, mouth pursing as he groped for words. "Ah, that uses ice like you."

"Is that so?" Kyran asked, his curiosity piqued. "What other magic is there? I havena met another mage before now."

An uneasy look passed over Barrett's face. "You meanin' me?"

Kyran eyed the man's sudden change in disposition. "Aye," he said slowly.

"Oh, er, well, I've only met one other mage besides you. He was different. He could control water."

Kyran tried to picture his own magic doing such a thing—pulling water from a trough or river, or even the bottom of a dry well. It would be useful on the *ben*, where he'd had to carry water up from the river to his shelter, but not as capable against something like the beast they had fought.

"The creature we faced," Kyran said abruptly. "What was it?"

Barrett's eyes narrowed, taking him in again. "You mean the demon?"

"Demon?"

Stars above, but the creature in the village suddenly made terrible sense. Demons had not been sighted in the Northern Isles as long as any man had lived there. What the Isleish knew of them demons were only wild tales told over strong drink. They were precious little more than stories of entire villages decimated and, of course, the epic battles waged by those that could fight and kill the beasts: demon hunters.

"You can't tell me you've never seen one," Barrett snickered.

Kyran's jaw tightened with a flush of misplaced foolishness. "There are na any demons in the Isles."

Barrett blinked incredulously at him. "So the stories are true," he finally said. "I didn't think there was anywhere that plague didn't touch." He ran a hand over his hair, smoothing it back, and slouched deeper into his saddle. "How long've you been here, then?"

Kyran quickly measured the days since he'd stepped off the ship in port. "A few weeks."

"And this was your first experience with a demon?"

"Aye. It was."

The man let out a low chuckle, shaking his head. "You must have a lot of questions."

That was an understatement. There was so much he did not know, not just about demons, but the men and women who hunted them. He looked the man over again. "You are a demon hunter," he ventured.

"I thought that much was obvious," Barrett remarked, sounding more puzzled than smug. "But I suppose you don't have any of those up in the Isles, either, if there aren't any demons."

Kyran shook his head. He hardly knew more about the folk that made it their business to hunt demons than the beasts themselves. The hunters had formed a guild acknowledged the world over as a power in its own right, a force of men and women blessed by the Light itself with the power to slay demons. Kings bartered for their services. And here he was, walking next to one who was also a mage.

"Are the other hunters like us?" Kyran asked. The word felt strange on his tongue. *Us.* By all the Graces in the Isles, for the first time in his life, he wasn't alone.

"Like what?"

"Mages," Kyran said, keeping his voice low even though there was no one around to hear him but the other mage. It just felt so strange.

Barrett shrugged. "There are a few. I haven't met them."

Kyran's pulse quickened. He could not believe what he was hearing. There were more people like him, and they were a part of the hunter's guild.

"Have you made it into the city yet?" Barrett asked, abruptly changing the subject.

"No, na yet."

"Well, it's somethin'. Bigger than the lil' town I grew up in. But if you've made it to the capital, it won't be anythin'. I'd offer a tour, but I promised you a drink, and I'm rather thirsty myself."

They followed the road towards the city and its high stone wall, illuminated by lanterns blazing along its top. Barrett filled the time chatting about the city's features—mostly about where to drink and where to find the best food. The entrance to the city was closed as they approached, filled with enough light to illuminate an entire inn. A guard sat slumped on a stool, distinguishable from any other commoner only by the club at his hip. He was busy speaking with a young lad of maybe ten years of age, who caught sight of the approaching party first.

"Barrett!" the lad called, waving him down. "Finished already?"

"Yeah," Barrett replied brightly, swinging out of his saddle as the lad approached.

The lad stopped dead in his tracks, gawping. "Who is that?"

"A friend," Barrett said, handing him the reins.

"What's his name? Is he an Isleman?"

"Kyran, and yes. Now tell Mihai thanks again for me."

The lad blinked at them, then nodded. "I will!" He gaped at Kyran again, then spun around and took off ahead of them, leading Sweetheart through the gates the guard opened for them.

Barrett offered the guard a nod, which he returned, leaning into the gate.

"Sorry about Valen," Barrett remarked. "He just—"

"It's fine," Kyran said quietly. "He isna the first ta ask."

Inside the city gates, buildings crowded the street, their stone faces glowing with light between cracks in their shutters. Kyran still didn't understand it, this obsession with light. His first sight of the port when he came over the Isleish Sea had been of innumerable twinklings like landed stars on the horizon. The port's streets had been lined with tall lamps that young lads with long-handled wicks lit promptly at sunset every evening, and refilled the wells of oil every morning. He scarcely understood the effort, which had to have been costly—not simply the lamps, but the price of burning candles and fires all night long. Everywhere he had been, the people lit their homes and every dark crevice with lanterns, candles, and fireplaces, huddling in the light from the moment the sun dipped below the horizon.

In the Isles, he had spent much of his life outdoors, sleeping under the stars, exploring caves and woods. The idea of fearing the night was outlandish. How did this country function under the geas of such a powerful phobia?

Even as Barrett turned off the main path, leading them past smaller, more ragged tenements built where the roads narrowed, changing from cobbles to mud, the lights continued to brighten their way. Turning down another narrow side street, Barrett finally drew to a stop by a dead end.

"Ah, finally," Barrett sighed, gesturing grandly to the building before them. "Welcome to the Drunken Wind."

The Drunken Wind certainly looked a bit drunken—slouched, crooked, and ramshackle, as if a good wind *could* knock it over. Kyran had to wonder if it was built to accommodate the name, or if time had finally rendered it more accurate. The door had been propped open to catch any wayward draft of air in the heavy summer night, spilling the raucous noise of the rowdy drunkards onto the muddy street. Kyran wrinkled his nose at the prospect of being amongst them. But he did not want to relinquish the chance to talk to another mage, even if it meant bearing the crowd and noise of the tavern.

"Come on," Barrett encouraged him, ducking through the doorway. "I've got a spot they keep for me."

Allowing himself a heavy sigh, Kyran followed, careful to duck beneath the lintel. The inside was as disorderly as the outside, and louder. The tables and chairs were scattered about in haphazard clusters, all crowded with bodies. A bar took up the back corner, serving drinks and supper to its patrons. There was a raised stage with two very drunk men slurring along to some bawdy song. Some folk sang along or cheered, while others jeered. Most simply ignored them, engrossed in their own conversations.

Several of the carousers raised their drinks as Barrett passed, slurring greetings and fare-thee-wells, to which Barrett replied in kind. Kyran was dumbstruck. A mage called to like a friend? And here Kyran had only ever prayed to find one person that could see him past the tales. It had to be the influence of the hunter's title from the guild. Nothing else could be strong enough to make people forget the ugly lies about mages.

A table in the far corner stood waiting and empty, and Barrett led him straight to it.

"It doesn't look like much," he said, settling down with a heavy groan, "but the drink is the best you'll find this side of the river, and folks here know to leave us alone. Ah, but have a seat." He waved at the empty chair. "I'll order. What'll it be for you?"

"Ale," Kyran answered as he nudged the chair out with one booted foot and lowered into it with a quiet groan of relief. Stars above, he had not realized how tired he was.

"Ale it is!" Barrett waved down the nearest barmaid, a dour young Hassani woman carrying a tray stacked with dirty plates and bowls, but she seemed to brighten when she realized it was Barrett that had called her. "Your largest tankard of ale for my friend here, please, and a beer for me."

"Of course," she said, then turned to Kyran. Her eyes narrowed as she took him in, and he shifted in his seat, glancing at his sleeves to see if his lines were showing through the cloth, but he did not see anything. It was likely his Isleish garb that had attracted her scrutiny. "Anythin' to eat with that?"

He almost turned her down out of hand for the look she was giving him. Then he thought of his empty belly—and then his almost empty purse—and shook his head. He would be drinking his dinner.

"Awh, come on," Barrett said, smiling when Kyran looked his way. "You've got to be hungry. Order somethin'. Anythin' you want. I said I was buyin'."

Kyran was inclined to refuse, but as much as his pride demanded he not accept the charity, his stomach had other ideas: it let out a fearsome growl.

"What are you serving?" he asked the barmaid, pressing a hand to his belly in embarrassment as Barrett gave a low chuckle.

"There's a lamb stew on the fire, and I believe the keep's wife has been trying out a new recipe for hazelnut bread."

"That will do," Kyran told her. It would be his first hot meal in a while, far more substantial than the scraps he had been earning on the road doing odd jobs for bits of coin or cold soup.

The woman nodded, turning her attention and smile back to Barrett. "Anythin' else?"

Barrett shook his head. "Still full from earlier."

The woman nodded again and let them be, heading through the crowd towards the serving counter. Barrett watched her go, toying at something beneath his shirt, offering Kyran his first real chance to observe the man in the light. His age was still difficult to determine, his strong jaw softened by several days' growth of golden beard.

Kyran resisted touching his own hairless face. Despite being well past age, he had never needed to shave, nor had he ever grown a hair anywhere other than his head. It was well and good his clothing covered him.

"Thank you," he said at last in regard to the food and drink, bringing Barrett's attention back to the table.

"Ah, don't mention it," Barrett dismissed him, pulling his hand from his shirt. "You looked a mite hungry. Think of it as repayment for your help." He leaned forward, setting his elbows on the table. "But what brings an Isleman like yourself so far south?"

Kyran's fingers twitched at the question. "Traveling." It was the answer he had given every farmer and craftsman that had asked.

"Traveling?"

"Aye."

There was a pause before the man prompted further, "Anything else?"

"Aye. Why do you ask?"

"Curious," Barrett said with another smile. "Despite appearances, I didn't ask you to drink with me just because you're pretty in a skirt."

"It is a kilt," Kyran corrected him sourly, pinching his sleeve between his fingers. "And I dinnae appreciate your mocking me."

Barrett winced and lifted his free hand in supplication. "Kilt, then. Sorry, I didn't mean to offend. It's been a long night."

Kyran sniffed, inclining his head a fraction in acknowledgement of his apology. It was far from the first time he'd heard the insult, and it was not likely to be the last while he was here in Tennebrum.

"So, traveling," Barrett repeated, his expression chagrined, and Kyran nodded again. "Anywhere in particular?"

Kyran picked at the hem of his sleeve with one nail. "Just seeing the country."

"Ah."

He sounded far from convinced, but before Kyran could decide how to change the subject, the barmaid returned with their drinks. She set a brimming tankard before each of them without spilling a drop, pausing long enough to receive her thanks and ask if there was anything else they needed before hurrying away again.

Barrett grabbed his tankard and gulped down a long draught before coming up for air with a satisfied sigh. "Nowhere better," he declared, tipping his head to Kyran's drink. "You'll like it, I swear, or I'll buy you somethin' else."

"Aye. I'll hold you ta that." Kyran withdrew a handkerchief from his lap and used it to grasp his tankard by its handle, dragging it closer. "But why do you want ta know where I'm goin'?" he prompted Barrett when the hunter watched him carefully wipe off the drink's rim.

"Ah, well, I just thought it was odd seein' you here," Barrett explained. "Don't usually see Islemen this far south. I'd have thought you'd be in the capital, tryin' to join the guild."

Kyran's eyes narrowed. "The hunter's guild?"

"Well, I mean, you're welcome to join one of the trade guilds, but yes, I meant the hunter's guild."

Kyran's pulse leapt, but he schooled his expression, trying to make certain he was not misinterpreting the man. "They would have me?"

Barrett snorted, taking a drink before he replied, "All mages in Tennebrum become part of the guild," he said without any regard for the people around them.

Kyran quickly glanced at the nearest table, catching a few sideways looks, but none of them hostile—more full of curiosity.

"It's Crown decree," Barrett continued without pause. "You're not from here, so you'd have to apply, but I doubt they'd turn you down. Are you interested?"

"In joining your guild?"

"Well, it's not *mine*," Barrett smirked over the rim of his drink, "but I believe that's what I said."

A chance to become a demon hunter. It wasn't something Kyran had ever imagined, let alone considered—facing creatures like the one in the village, saving people, being hailed as a hero instead of a monster. Stars, it almost sounded too good to be true, but he had seen it. Barrett was a mage just like him, and people had thanked him, smiled at him, even cheered him. And if Kyran joined, they would offer him the same.

He imagined telling his da when he finally saw him again. It would be something he could be proud of. Finally.

"Aye. I am," he said at last, lifting his drink to finally take a sip. It was surprisingly good.

"Really?" Barrett seemed surprised.

"That is what I said."

Barrett rolled his eyes. "Alright, alright," he grumbled good-naturedly, slouching back in his seat and dragging his drink with him.

The barmaid reappeared a moment later and set a heavy bowl of stew in front of Kyran. Besides the sizeable hunks of meat, large slices of carrots and potatoes were lumped together in the thick broth. Even in the heat of the tavern, the bowl was steaming.

"Anythin' else?" the woman asked, looking to Barrett.

"That should be all. Thank you."

She bobbed her head, smiling sweetly before bustling away.

Kyran picked up the spoon with his kerchief and wiped down the handle, ever conscious of Barrett watching him.

"How old are you, if you don't mind me asking?" Barrett said.

Kyran paused at his work, unaccountably embarrassed. "I'll be nineteen next week," he said quietly, lifting his chin, daring the man to find fault.

Barrett's face fell, and he let out a soft, almost wistful sigh. "Well, isn't that something. I just turned nineteen myself not long ago, just before the turn of the season." He lifted his drink, looking at something Kyran could not see.

He didn't seem nineteen. He seemed older in that moment than even

Kyran's eldest brother. But who was Kyran to judge, after spending so long alone? It was a miracle sometimes he could recognize a *bairn* from his da.

When Barrett lowered the drink, though, he smiled at Kyran again. "If you are serious about wantin' to join, I can write you a letter of recommendation. It'll take a few weeks to hear back, but I don't doubt they'll be interested in you. You'll have to travel to the capital—that's where the guildhall is—and go through training and examinations before they decide if you are fit to join, but then they'll likely sign you on as an associate."

An associate with the hunter's guild. Respected, powerful, and no longer forced to hide. "When can you send it?"

Barrett blinked in surprise. A grin spread across his lips. "Tomorrow." He wiped a hand across his face, drawing it down over his beard as he shrugged. "I guess that answers that. I thought you'd have more questions first."

"I have plenty," Kyran assured him.

"You don't want to ask before I send the letter?"

"It willna change my mind."

Barrett inclined his head. "Fair enough. In that case, why don't we save it for tomorrow? It's getting late, even for me. You should tuck in before your supper gets cold."

Biting back his questions, Kyran bent his head to his stew. Though curiosity burned at the back of his tongue, the night's toll was beginning to lay heavy on him too, and he looked forward to finding a place to lie down.

Barrett remained quiet, sipping at his beer until Kyran pushed his empty bowl away. "Done?" he asked, seeming to pull himself back from someplace deep in his thoughts.

Kyran nodded. "Aye."

"Good." Barrett set his empty tankard down and gestured for Kyran to follow him. "I know you probably want to get goin' soon, but I've got a room you can use. It's got two beds, though I'm not always there."

Kyran's mouth went dry. Share a room? He swallowed thickly, trying to unglue his tongue from the roof of his mouth. "I dinnae have the coin," he replied quickly, rubbing the fabric of his kerchief between his fingers.

"I wasn't asking you to pay for it," Barrett chuckled. "I just meant if you don't have anywhere else to go, this place isn't bad. The room is clean, with the exception of my things, and I can tell the people here to treat you same as me. They won't bother you."

A bed with a roof over his head and the quiet indifference of the people around him. He could obtain the first easily enough outside of the city, but the second was harder to come by. And if he left, he would miss the opportunity to finally talk to another mage, to know if there was someone else who struggled with the same things he did.

Daft, Kyran chastised himself, his mind made up. He was being daft. "Aye, I'll take you up on that," he agreed at last. "So long as you keep ta yourself."

Barrett balked at the accusation, holding his hands up innocently. "I don't know who you think you're talkin' to, but I'm not that kind of man. I swear."

Kyran raised his gaze to meet Barrett's, looking for that feverish glint he knew all too well, but saw only sincerity. "I'll hold you ta that."

"Okay, then." Barrett motioned towards the stairs. "Just follow me up, and I'll show you where it is."

Chapter Three

"No. No—Raleigh!"

Barrett raced towards the pull of magic, arms pumping, heart hammering into his ribs. "Raleigh!" he shouted over the din of chaos, choking on smoke and heat as it closed in around him. Curse the Graces, but he should never have left him alone! This demon was not like the others.

"Raleigh!" He screamed this time, voice hoarse, and felt his heart rend in two when he heard a low, whimpering moan at his ear.

He stopped in his tracks, his eyes locking on the thing he could see in the dark, no more than moving shadow. It could not be. It could not. But somehow he knew it must. Someone was laughing. A deep, rasping laugh.

"Raleigh?"

The thing in the dark turned towards him, and he caught a flicker of teeth and blood and bone.

A scream split the air.

Barrett jerked against the bed, his eyes flashing open to the same ceiling he had fallen asleep beneath. Thankfully, it was just his room at the Drunken Wind. There was no fire, nor smoke, nor laughing shadows. He closed his eyes again and kneaded them with the heel of one hand, the other clutching his amulet to his chest. Graces, but the nightmares were as vivid as ever. How many times was he going to have to relive that night? How many times did he have to see his failure replayed? Hadn't he suffered enough already?

He peeled his hand away from his eyes, letting it drop back to his chest as the answer to his last question came to him: no. As guilty and hollow as that night had left him, he was still alive. If he had been faster, or even realized the trap before he'd fallen right into it, Raleigh might have still....

Barrett didn't let himself finish that thought. Saying those words would be the end of him. He forced himself to take in his surroundings instead, searching for any distraction. The House's bells were tolling outside, their chime sweeter than the guild's call to alarm, ringing in the morning crowd to their dawn prayer. Beneath their clanging was the patter of rain, and a soft voice. He frowned as he tried to pick out the words, then realized they were not spoken in Common, but the soft, foreign lilt of Isleish.

Rolling over in his bed, Barrett squinted through the grey morning light. Kyran was standing by the window next to him, his head bowed towards the open shutters in prayer. As he looked the mage over, Barrett was struck again by how much Kyran stood out from the crowd. First and foremost, he was tall, almost a full handspan taller than Barrett, who could easily tower over a room himself. But unlike Barrett, Kyran's build was slight, almost frail. His face had a delicate bone structure Barrett hadn't thought any of the Islemen possessed, and his limbs and neck were long and elegant. In the sunlight, Barrett could see that Kyran's hair wasn't brown, but bright copper, and hung in soft waves past the nape of his neck. It only made his nearly translucently pale skin stand out all the more.

And, of course, there was no forgetting the mage's outlandish clothing, most notably his kilt. The plaid fabric was forest green, striped through with red and a surprisingly rich blue. It hung longer in the back, and every movement Kyran made flashed a bit of pale skin. It was shockingly eccentric amongst men who all wore tunics and trousers. But Barrett found he could appreciate an aesthetic that showed off a man's legs, especially ones as long as those.

He almost laughed at his groggy train of thought. What he wouldn't give to simply shut his eyes and dream about some tavern boy or maid instead of bloody, demon-ridden nightmares. But there had been nothing but nightmares for him since that night except the rare evenings he drank himself into a stupor, but the headache the next day put him off resorting to that too often.

As the bells faded, Kyran's voice trailed off too. He raised his hands to his lips and slipped a small, wooden token into the purse at his hip. Barrett hadn't kept the traditions of Lumen in some time now, his faith long withered on the vine, but he had never heard anything quite like Kyran's devotion.

"You do that every mornin'?" he asked when the mage started to turn away from the window.

"Aye," Kyran answered, sparing him a passing glance before he settled onto the side of the bed across the room.

Barrett didn't remember the beds being so far apart before. He lifted his head, peering around the room to reaffirm he was correct. He must have been sleeping for at least a little while to have missed that happening.

He frowned at the wan light from the window. A very little while.

"Did you get any sleep?" Barrett asked.

"Some," the mage replied, rubbing at his eyes with one hand when his stomach let out a loud, rumbling growl.

Barrett laughed. "Hungry?" he teased between snickers, enjoying the way the mage's nose wrinkled with embarrassment.

"Aye, have your gaff," Kyran grumbled, drumming his fingers against his knee.

"My what?"

The mage gave him a pointed look.

Barrett couldn't help but snicker again. "If you want to get somethin' from the kitchen, you can tell 'em you're with me. They'll take care of you."

Kyran nodded, his shoulders moving in a silent sigh before he leaned over and grabbed his boots.

Barrett lay there a moment longer, debating again if he truly wanted to get up yet, but the idea of closing his eyes and sinking back into his nightmare more than put him off the temptation, even as tired as he was. Dragging himself out from under the quilt, he fumbled for his tunic at the end of his bed and pulled it over his head with an open-mouthed yawn before he bent to tug on his own boots. If he was awake, he might as well get something done.

"I'm goin' out," he told Kyran, who was still sitting on his bed, staring out the window at the rain. "Don't wait up for me."

The mage nodded, and Barrett let himself out. His shoulders eased as he went down to the main floor, even as he reached behind him to gather his hair into a tail and tie it up. It was good to be moving, to be doing something. If he were honest, he hated the waiting that came after he killed a demon. It might have been wrong to wish for another beast to ravage the city, but it was all he was good for. If there were no demons, there was nothing for him but idleness and drink, which did little to distract him. And the less he had to think, the better, which was just one more reason to get this letter sent and Kyran on his way to the guild.

The mage was clueless. How anyone knew so little about demons, especially growing up a mage, was utterly baffling. Barrett wasn't even certain Kyran knew exactly what he was. It made him a danger not only to himself, but anyone around him. But the guild could teach him, and it would put Kyran far, far away from Barrett before anything could happen. Again.

His heart ached at the word until he thought a hole might have opened in his middle. He pressed the heel of his hand to his chest, biting down until his teeth creaked.

Guild outpost. Report. Letter of recommendation. Then more work on the search he had been conducting in town. He repeated the list of things he had to do, running down the items over and over, fixing them in his mind until the pain faded again, never quite leaving, but easing enough to ignore it. He had to stay busy. He couldn't face that today.

The streets were mostly empty; anyone who wasn't in service at the House was likely hiding from the rain, or already at work in the guild outpost. The guild's work was never finished. The outpost served as one of the guild's many branches in its far-reaching influence, a place letters, reports, and information could flow into and out of before moving on to the guild, or other outposts. In larger cities, the outposts were manned by a guild captain, but here in Oareford, it was only couriers and associates, largely lower-level scholars that handled the reports Barrett turned in and disseminated information to the rest of the city to assuage their fears of any "demon plague."

The outpost itself stood opposite the House in the city's center, a modest building built of the same rough, grey stone hauled from the surrounding fields as the rest of the city. It stood at two stories, crowned by a bell tower. A stable was attached to it for the couriers' use and was where Sweetheart stayed.

Ducking through the front door, Barrett paused just inside the entryway, summoning the heat of his magic to dry his clothes, which had managed to get quite sodden in the short trip over. The outpost had been built much more practically than the formal guildhall in the capital. The first floor was dedicated mostly to the practical matters of running Tennebrum's largest and most successful courier service. The walls were lined with small cubbies with tiny labels attached beneath each. Two long tables divided the space, each scattered with papers, quills, ink, letters, and books, a podium with a ledger open on it standing between them.

An older Hassani woman was bent over the ledger, squinting at the entries as she murmured to herself. She glanced up as Barrett came in, offering him a quick smile before going back to her work.

"Alex," she called, her voice warm and low, "the hunter is back."

A door opened off to Barrett's left, and Alex poked her head out. "Mornin'," she chirped brightly.

Alex's height and build made her look younger than she was. She was lanky for a woman, all long, coltish limbs, though her height barely reached his chest. Her face was a perfect heart shape, which only added to the girlish appearance, with large, dark eyes and smooth, brown skin. Her dark hair was pulled back and twisted in a knot at the back of her head, though he had caught her a few times sporting it loose, its tight curls springing wildly in every direction. He had found her rather attractive since he had first met her. He still did, but the infatuation had vanished the moment he'd met Raleigh.

She looked him up and down, quirking a brow at him. "Did you even sleep after last night?"

"Eh, not really," Barrett admitted, touching the amulet beneath his shirt.

"Well, buck up," she encouraged him, pushing the door open so he could enter. "Your stipend arrived."

He snorted, stepping past her and into the smaller room. A writing desk took up much of the far wall, a row of shelves filling another, stacked with supplies for writing and sending letters and packages.

"You have a report for me on last night?" she asked, bending to pull a basket from the bottom shelf.

He pointed to the desk. "That's part of why I'm here."

"And the other part?"

"A recommendation."

Alex raised her brows again, straightening with the box and setting it on the topmost shelf. "A recommendation?"

"There was a mage there last night. Helped me take care of the demon."

Her eyes widened. "A child? Is that why the demons—"

Barrett cut her off with a shake of his head. "No, I don't think so. He's older. My age. From the Northern Isles. And he hasn't been in town long, so he couldn't be the reason for the demons."

"That's unfortunate," Alex sighed with a soft cluck of her tongue. She leaned against the shelves. "But this mage?"

"Well, I had a drink with him last night—"

"Did you?" she teased, her tone saucy.

Barrett's ears prickled hotly, and he rolled his eyes. "I had a drink with him last night," he continued, giving her a firm, half-hearted glare, "and we were talkin' about the guild. He seemed eager to join, especially since there are other mages."

"Not many of them up in the Isles?"

"Doesn't seem like it."

"And you're going to write him a letter of recommendation, with your aptitude for vocabulary?"

He would have been irritated with her remark if it weren't true. His handwriting was fine, *"pretty for a baker boy,"* but he had never been good with words. Not just in putting them down on paper, but even speaking. He just wasn't eloquent. Raleigh had teased him about it relentlessly.

The memory of the dark haired mage's sweet smile flashed unbidden from his thoughts, and Barrett's knees threatened to buckle under the blow it dealt him. He had been doing well lately, but already he could tell today was going to be one of those days.

He cleared his throat and shoved the image down until it was merely a black silhouette again, holding it there, beneath the knot of pain it caused him.

"I know," he told Alex, his jaw tight as he fought to control his reaction. "I was wondering if you could help me."

Alex gave him another up and down. "Tell you what," she said, folding her arms over her chest. "You write your report. I'll read over it, then sit down and help you with the recommendation."

He bowed his head. "Thank you," he said sincerely. "I'll get started right away."

"Don't forget to be specific," she reminded him, leaving her box as she went to the door. "You know it drives them crazy when you're vague."

"I remember last time," he sighed, taking a seat at the desk.

The report took longer than he'd expected, not because he was focusing on specifics, as Alex had cautioned, but because every time he wrote the word "mage" in the report, he thought of Raleigh.

Barrett set his quill down and pressed his fingers firmly against his eyes as they heated and swelled with tears. Why was he not over this? He tried to think of something else, and found his thoughts circling Kyran.

Other than being a mage, Kyran was nothing like Raleigh. He was quiet, reserved, and there was something mysterious about him. Barrett was certain he was not just *visiting* Tennebrum for pleasure or trade, but there was no denying his eagerness to help fight demons. He had not hesitated to fight the one they'd faced last night. He had jumped right in, not even fully understanding what he'd been up against.

There was so much he didn't know. Barrett only hoped Kyran didn't ask a question Barrett couldn't answer.

Near noon, Alex came to check on him, bringing bread and ham. Barrett accepted the food and let her pull up a chair to read his report. Then, as promised, she helped him write the recommendation. It hardly took her any time, stuffy, formal language and all.

"You're really good at this," Barrett commented, carefully adding his signature at the bottom. "You sure you wouldn't prefer bein' a scribe? You'd barely have to travel."

"I like traveling," Alex confessed, blowing gently on the ink. "And my mother was a scribe. I'm used to hearing how these things should be written." She held up the letter and nodded in satisfaction. "I'll get these sealed as soon as they're dry and take them to be delivered. It'll be a couple weeks before you hear back on that recommendation. Last I heard, Selah and the captains were getting worked up over something. Don't know what, though. The guildmaster is doing a good job of keeping everybody's lips tight."

She huffed a sigh, then locked her gaze on Barrett, pointing an accusing finger at him. "That does mean I won't be here to make sure you write those reports. I don't want to come back and find out you need to write five or six."

He grinned sheepishly at her. He had waited a few weeks once to write his reports and wasted two entire days at a desk working them out. "I'll try."

"And you should go see your sister," Alex added, setting the letter down again as she turned to the box she had left out and pulled out a heavy envelope. "You've been loitering at that tavern long enough."

His smile faltered, and he glanced down at his boots. "We'll see."

She didn't press the matter any further, handing him the thick envelope and shooing him out. Barrett winced at the bright afternoon sunlight and again remembered that he had done little more than drink the night before. And as much as he wanted to bury his face back into a mug after the circle of thoughts he had dealt with all morning, he felt more pressed to continue the search that had led him to drinking—the missing children. All taken at night from the city by a demon, or demons. Quicker than he could get to them.

It was not an uncommon occurrence in Tennebrum for demons to take children, but demons were not generally this practiced at remaining undetected, especially in a town with a local outpost and assigned hunter.

He needed to keep questioning folk. Searching suspect areas.

Anything to keep busy.

Chapter Four

Kyran turned the bit of wood over in his hands, eyeing where he needed to make his next cut, the lines beneath his skin casting a blue glow on the wood. He had picked the piece up on the road and stashed it in his purse for later. Finding his place, he set his knife back to whittling out the shape he had spied in the fine grain, an Isleish song an absentminded murmur at his lips.

He liked working with his hands. There was something soothing about the easy repetition, the feeling of doing something he knew well, whether it was whittling or hunting for his supper. Handling horses had been that way for him when he was young, before the beasts spooked to even look at him. What he would not give to go back to that. To be a wee lad again, without a care in the world. Before his blood had awoken and its curse had infiltrated every part of his life. Before every terrible thing that had come from it had happened.

A rap sounded at the door, and Kyran quickly staunched his power before Barrett's voice called through. "Kyran, can you get the door for me? My hands are full."

Kyran sighed, the knot between his shoulders loosening as he turned his project over in his hands. Sticking his knife back in his boot, he levered up from his chair and plucked his kerchief from his purse. He opened the door to Barrett, wet from head to toe, holding up two pewter tankards in his left hand and balancing a platter with two steaming bowls and a loaf of bread in his right.

"You haven't eaten, have you?" he asked with a bright grin.

"Na yet," Kyran assured him, holding the door open to admit the hunter.

"Good." Barrett carried the food to the small table and shoved the scattered papers left atop it aside with his drink arm before settling the tray down. "Here." He picked up one of the drinks, holding it out to Kyran. "It's mead," he added when Kyran carefully accepted it with his kerchief, peering into the tankard at the amber drink.

"Thank you."

Barrett shot him a smile over his shoulder before it turned to a quizzical frown. "You makin' something?"

"Oh, aye." Kyran held up the piece of wood. "It isna finished yet."

"What is it?"

Kyran allowed himself a sly grin. "A whistle."

Barrett gave him a rather arch look. "See if I bring you dinner again." He broke the loaf, took a bowl, and sat on his bed.

"Says the man who canna whistle in his mare," Kyran prodded. Barrett only scoffed and bit into his bread.

Approaching the table, Kyran nudged the chair out with his toe and seated himself, letting his long legs stretch out beneath the table as he finally took a sip of his drink. It was warm, with a lingering, almost sticky sweetness to it. He could drink a barrel of that.

"They got that in fresh this mornin' from one of the brewhouses not far from here," Barrett said, tearing off another piece of his bread and dunking it in his bowl. "I got your letter sent off. Alex said it might take longer to hear back right now. Said the guildmaster and captains are busy with somethin'. Probably more political stuff."

"Stuff?"

Barrett shrugged, tossing the chunk of bread in his mouth. "Yeah, there's always somethin' going on. I don't know. I don't keep up with any of it. But it could mean I don't get a response back for a while, if you were planning to leave for the capital before then." He took a noisy gulp of mead before quickly adding, "Not to say I want you to leave. You're welcome to stay as long as you want."

Kyran shifted in his seat, one nail tapping against the pewter of his tankard. "Aye, and thank you again for your hospitality."

"You don't need to keep thankin' me. I'm glad to be of help to someone." The hunter took another swig of his drink and let out a long, satisfied sigh. "So, you said you were travelling. Where were you headed before?"

The click of Kyran's nail grew louder against the tankard, his mind racing to invent an answer, anything halfway believable. "I was hoping to find others...like me."

"Mages?"

"Aye," Kyran forced out, tucking his legs beneath him and sitting up in his chair. The word still felt like a slap, even coming from another mage.

You're nothing more than a demon-blooded animal.

"Well, you'll have better luck in the capital, especially since you are headed to the guildha—" Barrett left his sentence dangling as his head snapped to the window. He swore, nearly knocking his bowl of soup over as he scrambled up. "What, by all the Graces?" He peered out the shutters into the early twilight, then yanked them shut and latched them. "I've got to go."

"What is it?" Kyran asked, rising from his seat.

"Another demon. You stay here. I'll be back as soon as it's dealt with."

He was out the door before Kyran could ask anything else.

Kyran stood there a moment, half-risen, drink still in his hand, before spitting a curse of his own. Smacking the tankard down on the table, he raced down the stairs after the hunter. "Barrett!"

Barrett whipped his head around, already halfway across the tavern. "Wha—You—"

"I can help," Kyran said, flicking a glance at the patrons around them, who were watching intently. He lowered his voice. "Like last night."

Barrett looked from him to the tavern door, running a hand over his face. "Look, Kyran, you were a lot of help, but you can't—" He caught himself, glancing towards the ceiling before saying in a low tone, "You're not a guild member yet."

"And? I can still help."

"And it's guild law. I don't have time to argue this. Just stay here. I'll be back soon as I've handled it." He turned, leaving Kyran standing in the middle of the tavern, hands clenched at his sides.

Stars, but Kyran felt useless. Another one of those beasts was loose somewhere in the city. He wanted to help, not sit in some room like a contented barn cat.

He considered going after Barrett anyway, but the hunter had claimed guild law. If he went anyway, it might cost him his admission to the guild, to the power and respect he needed if he wanted to go home again.

Careful not to meet anyone's eyes, Kyran slunk back to the room to wait, locking the door behind him. He picked up his drink, then set it down again and took up the half-finished whistle. If he had to wait, at least he could do something distracting.

Chapter Five

Barrett sprinted down the street through the rain as fast as his legs would carry him, following the prickle of someone—or something—else's magic. Kyran was in the opposite direction, the swell of his magic already familiar and distinct, and Barrett was the only hunter in Oareford.

But it wasn't even fully dark yet. The rainclouds were still faintly illuminated by the fading sun. It was technically possible for a demon to come through in less-than-full darkness, but the difficulty of the task meant none but the very strongest could accomplish it. He might very well be racing to meet a demon stronger than him.

He skidded around a corner, sucking down a breath as a faint boom echoed through the city streets. The orange glow of fire bloomed ahead of him, sending a coil of dread down into his belly. Graces help him, but he was sick of burning buildings.

He angled towards the glow, shouting for people to move as he ran, but as he got closer, the demon's presence began to fade, fleeing.

Abruptly, it disappeared. Strange. Very strange. Demons strong enough to slip through the darkness rarely ran. Had it sensed him coming? But that would mean it was one of the clever ones, the most dangerous kind.

One clever enough to steal children without getting caught.

He turned a last corner and came upon the fire. Two buildings, side by side. One was fully engulfed from roof to street, and the second's roof and front edifice were just beginning to catch up.

A crowd was gathering in the street, watching the fire with the empty rapture of moths.

"You need to clear the area!" he tried to shout over the roar of the fire. A few faces turned to look at him, their expressions mixed. "What happened?" he asked the nearest person.

"There's a demon inside," the man said, voice trembling. "You have to help them—they're still in there."

"Save them!" someone shouted, "Kill the demon!"

Shielding his face with one arm, Barrett dove through the open doorway into the second building.

He immediately regretted it. His tolerance for heat was high, but the smoke made his lungs ache and his eyes burn, running with tears, his nose dripping. He covered his mouth with his sleeve and headed for the first doorway he saw, but the room was vacant, so he hurried to another room. A figure lay on the ground, but as he drew near, it resolved into a headless corpse. The building gave a hideous groan, its walls shuddering around him. He had to hurry.

He went back to the hall and was headed for another doorway when the building shuddered again. A crash to bring the world down rang in his ears. Embers scattered like fireflies, and fresh flame licked along the floor above him.

This had been a bad idea. This place was coming down. He had to get out. *But the people....*

"Can anyone hear me?" he bellowed into the hall, straining for any reply. Only the building answered, rumbling threateningly as something gave way. "Can anyone—"

The end of the hall collapsed. His heart hammered into his ribs as fiery timbers folded like so much kindling into one another.

Barrett raced back out the entrance, gasping for fresh air as fire licked around the doorframe. He fell to his hands and knees in the street, heart racing at the close call. Before he could lift his head, two people grabbed his arms, helping him to his feet.

"It's coming down," he wheezed, coughing and blinking. "The demon escaped."

Then he felt it. Another surge of magic, this time from the way he'd come. But it was not Kyran.

"No," he breathed, turning and breaking into a run, racing back to the tavern. He could still sense Kyran's magic, but underneath it, separate, was something else. The same thing he had felt earlier, but stronger. It was just like that night. Just like his nightmare.

"Graces, please, no! Not again! Not Kyran!"

Chapter Six

Kyran dug the tip of his knife into the whistle. He was marking out the finger holes when both lanterns guttered out. He looked up from his work, blinking into the sudden darkness.

"Must have been a draft," he muttered, though he could not recall feeling one. He loosened his grip of control until his blood began to glow, casting wan starlight into the room just bright enough to make out his surroundings. It looked just as it had before, but the skin on the back of his neck prickled. Something was off.

Someone screamed in the tavern below, and Kyran leapt to his feet as other voices joined in. "Stars above," he swore, taking only enough time to stuff the whistle into his purse before running for the door.

But the moment he touched the latch, it flew open, smashing into him hard enough to throw him off his feet. He hit the ground with a pained wheeze as pain flared bright and hot in his side. A hot wind howled past him, and the wooden door banged against the wall.

No, not wind. A black smoke rushed into the room, rolling over him with a tangible weight. It pressed against his skin, nose, and mouth, filling his ears until he couldn't hear anything but his pounding pulse, filling the room until there was no light, no air. He was choking on it, crushed beneath it. Even the light of his blood could not alleviate it; his own limbs looked barely more than pale shapes.

Then, as suddenly as the gale had come, it ceased, lifting from his skin enough for him to suck down a ragged gasp, his sides burning. He staggered to his feet. The pain in his side sharpened, throbbing with each breath of hot, heavy air. Setting the heel of his hand to the pain, he willed it to stop, peering into the darkness and waiting to spot another chitinous beast charging at him.

But there was nothing. Not the room, or even a silhouette of the doorway he knew had to be right in front of him. Not even a sound. The silence lay nearly as thick and heavy as the darkness pressing against him. It was as if the world had disappeared.

He touched his face to be certain his eyes were open and working, only dimly making out the light of his blood. It had to be some sort of magic, something a demon was doing. It was the only thing that made sense, even if it made no sense at all. He stayed perfectly still, straining to hear over the silence, to catch the scratch of a nail on wood so the beast could not catch him by surprise. Then something else answered him from the dark—a deep, echoing laughter laced with a feline hiss.

"So, the hunter found a new mageling." The voice was low and rough, whispering into his ear as if the beast stood at his shoulder.

He flinched, lashing at the nothingness with his knife, but it did not connect with anything. He turned, holding his breath, straining to make out footsteps or breathing or the rustle of movement, but everything was muffled as if covered by a thick snowfall.

He backed towards where he thought the door was. Heat brushed across his back. Panic, icy and sickening, shot through his middle. He whirled around, magic held ready, to find a mouth grinning at him just inches from his face. Its long, pointed teeth crowded the lipless gash of a mouth like a thicket of sewing needles. A cloud of its foetid breath, stinking of rotten, burning things, rolled over him.

With a cry, he thrust his knife at the beast's throat, but the demon moved faster. Its skin burst into molten light, like metal still being shaped at a forge. It knocked his hand away, snatched the front of his shirt, and yanked him closer. Heat blasted through the cold aura of his magic, licking at his skin.

Kyran grabbed the beast's hand and slammed his knife through its wrist, his magic diving through the metal blade and into the demon's flesh. The light dimmed in the spidery limb. The demon snarled and drove its weight forward, throwing him onto the floor beneath it. He screamed as his side flared in agony, but the sound choked off as a long-nailed hand wrapped around his throat.

He clawed at its grip. Its skin was ashen and dry to the touch. His hand found his knife still in its flesh and ripped it free. He thrust the glowing tip at the beast's empty eye sockets.

It caught his wrist and pinned his arm to the ground, hissing through its too-many teeth as it leaned into its grip around his throat, cutting off his breath.

Panic, cold and twisting, rose through Kyran again as his chest heaved, struggling to suck down even a dreg of air, but the demon's hold on his throat was unfaltering. Kyran arched beneath it, ramming his knees into the beast, but it pressed its weight down on him, crushing him. It was far heavier than it should have been.

"Stop!" he mouthed between strangled gasps. "Don'!"

"If I were not toying with you," it laughed, leaning down to nuzzle his hair, "I would be feasting on you already."

Bright spots flashed before Kyran's eyes. It was going to kill him. He couldn't breathe. He had to get it off of him, or it was going to kill him.

But how? It had him pinned, helpless. His magic was doing nothing, but he had nothing else. His magic had to be enough. It had harmed the weaker demon. He would simply have to use more.

Forcing himself to let go of the beast, Kyran groped at his side with his free hand, feeling for the leather thongs that dangled there, strung with beads and stones and hidden in the folds of his kilt. His amulets.

The demon's breath was hot against his throat; it snuffled at him and let out a satisfied purr. "Yes. I recognize that smell. I was right. You are one of the Old One's. I did not think any of his thin blood was left."

Where were his amulets? Kyran's chest hitched, desperate for air, and he clawed at his side, feeling for smooth stone.

"Mmh, but you are so young. Barely more than a child." The demon's claws flexed against his throat, biting into his skin. "What a shame to kill you like this, so weak and frail. I think I will keep you. Let you grow until your blood comes into its own. It would make me that much stronger. What do you think of that idea, little mageling? Be my pet. You might grow to like your cage."

At last, Kyran's fingers pulled a round, smooth river stone from the folds of his kilt. He gripped it in his fist, the water-worn hole in the center where his leather thong was tied biting into his palm. He all but shoved his power into the stone, letting go of his control entirely.

The blood surged through his body, and his heart raced to keep up as the magic stored in his amulet poured into him. The air screamed as silver ice ate into the demon's flesh, extinguishing its fiery glow with a loud sizzle. The demon roared in agony, its claws digging into Kyran's throat and wrist. Kyran bared his teeth in a fierce grin, frozen spittle cracking at the corners of his mouth. He was hurting it.

It started to rear back, to retreat, but Kyran wrapped his legs around the demon, grabbed its face with his free hand, and forced every inch of warmth from its boiling flesh. Its throat pealed out a shrill, inhuman scream. It ripped itself from his hold, staggering backward. Kyran sucked down a fiercely cold breath, coughing and choking as he struggled to his hands and knees.

"You little half-blooded bastard!" the demon bellowed, dropping to all fours as the scream broke into a mad laugh. Dark, ugly flames, the same black and crimson fire he had seen Barrett wield, licked from its maw like a flickering tongue. In the strange half-light of the fire and his own glowing lines, Kyran could see its flesh had cracked and split, blood as black as its flames oozing over the surface.

"Good, good!" the demon howled, mouth split in what could only be a wide, toothy grin. "Now fight!"

It spat a black and crimson ball of fire after him, and then another, and Kyran barely evaded them.

"Fight! Show me how strong you are! Show me what power you are going to give me," the demon screeched.

Kyran snarled an Isleish curse in return and thrust his knife at the demon. The air shattered as his magic surged down his arm. But it threw its jaws open and vomited a stream of black fire just before the blast reached it.

The fire and cold met between them in an explosive gale. Kyran's power held the flames at bay, devouring their heat, but he could make no headway, the immense power and force of the demon's fire like a weight pushing back against him.

"Yes," the demon laughed over the roar of its fire, stealing forward a step. "Show me!" It took another step, its fire pressing harder against Kyran's magic until he was forced back a pace. "I can almost taste you!"

Kyran tried to shape his magic, to divert the fire instead of simply holding it back, but the effort was too much. It came inexorably, and he was forced back another pace. He needed more power.

He snatched at his hip, his fingers closing over a piece of carved bone.

"Kyran! Hold on!"

Kyran's concentration wavered at the familiar voice, and a searing wave of air blasted through his magic, scorching his eyes and face as the wall of black and crimson fire rushed towards him.

He splintered off a fragment of his magic to reach into the amulet, shielding his face. Fire licked at his sleeves, the smell of burnt hair stinging his nostrils.

He was too slow.

Chapter Seven

THE TAVERN WAS not on fire when Barrett turned and shot down the winding street that led past it, but it was dark. Not a light shone from its windows, and the door hung open to only yawning blackness. Magic seemed to radiate from the building, clawing at his attention. It was here. With Kyran.

"No," he pleaded, pumping his legs harder. "No—not again."

Another crowd had gathered in the street outside the tavern, burning anything they could find for light—garbage, twigs, even bits of clothing.

The first to recognize him cried out, pointing at the tavern. "It's in there!"

"All of the wicks went out! Even the fire!"

"I'll take care of it," Barrett shouted back without slowing, parting the crowd. They scrambled to get out of his way as he called fire into his hands. "Just get away from the building, and don't come in 'til I tell you it's safe!"

But as he crossed the threshold of the tavern, the magic he felt vanished again, leaving only the barest pulse, and his stomach dropped to his boots. "No. Graces, no!"

Knocking blindly into tables and chairs, he raced for the stairs, his dark flames casting only the barest light. He took the stairs three at a time, stretching his legs, muscles burning, mind empty of all but the terrible anticipation of what he would find.

But when Barrett threw open the door to his room, there was nothing. Nothing but the smell of smoldered wicks and a darkness so thick that even his fire could not penetrate it.

This....Small, weak demons could not do this. It took enormous power to tear the barriers between realms this much in a place where there had been light. He had been right. This demon....It had to be old. Powerful.

"Kyran!"

Only silence answered him. He swore again, pushing into the room against the heavy blackness. He had felt this before, in the places demons had come through to this world, a tangible mark from where the beast had torn its way out of its realm and into the human one. It had been here. Right here, in his room. With Kyran.

"Kyran!" he called again, voice cracking. Barrett frantically searched the room, turning over the table, the chairs, even shoving the beds aside to look beneath them. Nothing. He was alone.

"He was just here," he panted, circling the room again. "He was just here. I felt him downstairs. I know he was here."

He is close, something whispered at the edge of his mind. The hair on Barrett's neck stood on end. *If you will listen, I can help you find him.*

That voice. It had been six years since he'd heard that low, gravelly voice. It had not said a peep since he had taken the pact to become a hunter.

"Shut up," he whispered, his fingers finding the amulet beneath his shirt. *Never talk to it.* That's what Kat had warned him of after she'd found out he had taken the amulet. *Never speak to it, and never deal with it.*

But guilt twisted thick and black in his gut. This was his fault. He should never have let another mage get involved with him. He should have learned the first time. Now someone else was dead because of him.

He is not dead, the voice at the edge of his awareness murmured. Barrett rolled his neck against the intrusive feeling. *But he will be if you do not let me help.*

"You're lying," Barrett snapped. "How can you help?"

I can show you how to reach him. He is falling deeper into the place you call the Inbetween even as we speak.

Barrett sucked down a breath. He had learned plenty about the Inbetween at the guildhall. It was a ripple between the realms, the place the demon and human realms touched and overlapped, but he had only been there once before, chasing after another demon, and he had been lucky to find his way out again.

But his demon would know. That was how it had come to this world in the first place, before being forged into his amulet so many generations ago to serve the guild. It would know how to return there. But it was not likely to offer information for free. What would it cost to learn how to save Kyran?

Never talk to it.

Run!

Barrett gritted his teeth. "Please," he begged softly. "Please help me save him. I can't leave him there."

It stirred languidly within him. The sensation sent a shudder through him. *There is no bargain, here, Kristopher. Only knowledge. I willingly offer my help. Is that not why you made this pact?*

Another sharp spear of guilt pierced through Barrett's middle. He hadn't joined the guild for any noble cause. He had simply wanted what he thought he deserved. Graces above, had he ever been a fool.

I will tell you how to get to your mage. How to get out. But the closer you come to our realm, the more of my power you will need to go deeper.

And the more wakeful the demon would be. Barrett swallowed thickly. If he was not careful, he could very well be handing the demon the perfect opportunity to overthrow his control for good. He would become an abomination—a walking horror that would cause even more destruction than he had already managed in his life. But he had to do this. He'd just have to find a way to remain in control.

He waited for the voice again, for it to whisper the secret to this travel into his ear, but it never came. Instead, as he looked around the room, he suddenly had words for what he was feeling and seeing. He knew that what he was sensing was the fractures in reality the demon had caused when it tore its way through into the human realm. A hole, so to speak. And one he could use to follow it.

There was no walking in, though. It took a peculiar application of magic to move between realms, one Barrett could not readily explain, despite understanding now *how* to do it. It was so much more nuanced than anything he had ever done. His magic had only ever been a means to summon and wield fire.

Taking a slow breath, he reached out mentally, following his demon's guidance. He pictured a shadowed hand slipping into the black tear and grasping something. He pulled.

It was strange. He felt himself shift, the skin of the world sliding over him as he descended. He reached out again, taking hold of the skein of darkness, and pulled himself deeper. With every inch he drew farther downward, the presence of his demon swelled in his awareness until it nearly filled him, crowding his thoughts. Not taking control, but pressing itself on him. It was strangely intimate, almost obscene, but the closer it came, the more strongly its power welled up in him, a bottomless fire burning at his fingertips.

Downward he crept, until a bright pinpoint of light cut through the darkness a split second before an overwhelming surge of magic crashed into him. He blinked away the darkness caught in his vision, and his eyes went wide. Before him was a tidal wave of witch fire, its deep crimson and black raging impossibly high as it surged towards the small, fey light that stood before it.

Your mage, his demon purred proudly.

They had done it. He wasn't too late. But....

"Kyran!" he shouted, fire leaping into his hands as he broke into a dead run. If he could just get in front of him before...."Hold on!"

Chapter Eight

KYRAN BRACED AGAINST the fire, the ridges of his amulet digging into his hand as the lines of light beneath his skin flared to almost blinding brilliance. His magic surged out of his blood, and the air screamed as it flashed from boiling to frigid in the span of a blink. The wall of fire's advance slowed, wavering not an arm's length away, so towering and vast it could swallow him whole in an instant. He leaned into the wild vortex of wind, his hair and clothes whipping against him, and focused his control, struggling to bend his magic to his command without surrendering its wild power as the fire inched closer.

Then, like a fae from an auld story, Barrett appeared at his shoulder, both hands raised and pouring his fire at the demon. The heat nearly took Kyran's breath away. The three magics mixed into a deadly, whirling column, forcing him to turn his face away.

The demon's teeth clicked shut, its spout of flame extinguishing, and Barrett bore down on it, but the beast simply turned and fled into the dark.

Barrett dropped his hands, his fire fading. "Are you okay?" he asked, not taking his eyes from the darkness where the demon had disappeared.

"Aye." Kyran panted, gritting his teeth against the ache in his side as he brought his magic to heel. "How did you find me?"

"I followed your magic."

"How?"

"I—"

"Hunter," the demon hissed from somewhere in the shadows.

Barrett's hands went up, instantly wreathed in black and crimson flame. Kyran raised his knife, fighting his magic as it struggled to free itself and lash out at the beast.

"How kind of you to find me another treat," it said.

"Shut up!" Barrett spat.

"I do so love the taste of mages," the demon continued, its voice coming from a different place, somewhere off to Kyran's right.

Barrett's fire flared, crackling as the flames grew larger. "I'll give you a taste of somethin'! Why don't you show yourself?"

"You don't remember me?"

Its face loomed from the dark, barely more than a silhouette, before its skin flared with lines of molten light again, exposing it. But instead of attacking, Barrett stood frozen, his gaze fixed on the beast, eyes wide.

"I killed you," the hunter whispered.

The demon grinned its lipless smile, its thin tongue lolling over its teeth. "You tried," it purred, looking to Kyran. The moment its black sockets met his gaze, *something* seemed to reach out of the darkness between them with a vicious slap that nearly bent him in half.

Kyran staggered, a little chirp of surprise clogging his throat, as the foreign power bore down on him.

His control slipped. Magic boiled out of his blood, bright and cold, and the weight against him seemed to lessen.

"Let him go!" Barrett snarled.

"Or what, hunter? You'll kill me?" It let out another hissing laugh. Fire rippled up its throat and licked past its teeth in hungry little tongues before it vanished into the dark again, its final words lingering behind it: "Like last time?"

The air around Barrett practically ignited as he let out a sound Kyran had never heard issue from a human's throat. Barrett chased after the demon and was swallowed in darkness.

The pressure of the demon's magic lifted as suddenly as it had appeared. Kyran nearly buckled in sheer relief, but he forced his legs to move, to carry him after Barrett.

But the air seemed to thicken as he went, dragging at him. He fought a growing sense of claustrophobia as it pressed against him once again, cutting off his senses. He cursed the foul place. He could neither hear nor see Barrett and the demon, but he kept running, certain he would have to find them eventually.

Weeping broke the heavy silence, and Kyran spun in place, his magic ready. It sounded like a *wean*. Cautious, he followed the sound. The cries grew louder until his blood illuminated a lad scarcely over four crouched against the ground, hugging his knees and sobbing.

"Dear stars above," Kyran whispered. How had a *wean* gotten here?

The lad's head snapped up, and he screamed, making as if to run. Kyran caught him around the middle and scooped him up in his arms, pressing him to his chest. "It's alright," he soothed him. "I have you. I'm goin' ta get you out of here."

"Are you now?" A toothsome grin leered out of the dark, flickering with unnatural fire.

Oh, by all the Graces in the Isles, no.

"I forgive you your claws, pet," it said, stalking towards him. Kyran struggled to keep his grip as the lad shrieked, thrashing in his arms. "I haven't tamed you yet, but I will."

Kyran locked an arm around the lad's chest and arms, pinning them to him, and threw his other hand at the demon, sending his magic lashing out at it. It spat a mouthful of flame, just enough to engulf his attack, and kept walking.

"Where's Barrett?" he demanded, throwing another burst of magic at the beast.

"Gone," the demon hissed, spitting out another mouthful of fire.

"I dinnae believe you!" Kyran snarled, his blood burning bright as he threw its fury at the beast, grinning fiercely when the demon recoiled.

"Mageling!" it roared, and the crushing weight of its power slammed into him again. He staggered back, lifting his hand as if to ward off the demon's assault.

Someone called his name again.

Barrett.

He turned towards the voice, the weight of the lad throwing off his balance, and staggered into an awkward run. "I'm here!"

Chapter Nine

BARRETT HURLED FIRE after the demon as he chased it, his hate burning hotter and higher as the thing somehow evaded him each time, its outline growing dimmer as it outstripped him on all four legs.

"No!" he roared, willing himself to go faster. But too soon it disappeared into the blackness. With a wordless roar of rage, he threw his hands forward. Fire poured out of him, but the flames simply dissipated, striking nothing. "Coward!" he shouted.

It was the same one—the same demon that had killed Raleigh and nearly killed the last living member of his family. It had to be, but he *knew* he had killed it. He had plunged the dagger in himself and watched its body turn to ash. How was it here?

There was a throb of power from someplace around him. He threw another gout of fire after it, but it still struck nothing.

You foolish human, his own demon said, its voice a low grating in his ear that made his neck prickle. *It lured you here, away from your mage.*

The fire in Barrett's hands flickered out as his fury turned to sudden, icy horror. "Oh, Graces."

What had he done? How could he have been so stupid? He had let the demon rile him talking about Raleigh and lead him away into the dark so Kyran would be left unprotected. Again. *Stupid, stupid, stupid!*

He turned and started back the way he'd come, searching for magic to guide him through the featureless dark, but he sensed nothing. Panic, bright and sharp, shot through his chest. He couldn't be too late yet, could he?

Go deeper, his demon commanded him. *It took him farther out.*

Barrett fumbled blindly for the sensation of shifting he had felt before and pulled himself through the black. It was harder this time, the air physically straining against him like deep water, and he panted at the effort as he stumbled out into the new depth of the Inbetween. The air was thicker here, harder to breathe and move in, muffling everything. But he could feel them, Kyran and the demon, feel their magic close by. Summoning his fire again, he chased after the sensation.

Light appeared in the darkness, a bright, wintery blue-white—and he all but screamed the mage's name, praying he would hear. The light grew larger, brighter, until Barrett could make out Kyran's form. He almost did not recognize him. The mage was running towards him, flying through the dark, his body burning with light so cold and intense that it blurred the edges of his outline. He looked utterly inhuman, like something out of an old story, an aelf or an Isleish faerie. Despite the direness of the situation, Barrett's breath caught in his throat.

A furious, deep, reptilian hiss bellowed from behind Kyran, and crimson-edged flames burst into life, licking at the mage's heels as he ran. Barrett roared back in challenge, racing to meet Kyran. He clenched his fists as he ran, calling every bit of fire he could control into them.

Another crimson and black sheet of fire exploded behind Kyran, and he saw the mage stumble, his arms curled awkwardly to his chest. The flames bowed around him like a hungry maw before Kyran found his feet and kept running.

"Don't stop!" Barrett shouted, desperate to make it in time, when he finally caught a glimpse of why the mage's arms were not swinging with his stride. Held tightly against his chest was a child. *One of the missing children!* He was alive!

The distance between them closed, and as Kyran flew by in a wake of aching cold, Barrett swung as if he intended to put his fist through the side of a mountain, letting go of the magic he had stored in it. His fist struck nothing, but his fire carved through the incoming flames, and for a split second he saw the utter ruin Kyran's magic had wrought on the demon's flesh before his fire splashed across its hideously humanoid face.

The toothy beast shrieked with pain, its head and chest engulfed in flame, its momentum carrying it forward into Barrett's next swing. But at the last possible moment, the demon reared back. Barrett's swing missed, the fire going awry into the dark, and before he could recover his balance, the demon clamped its too-many teeth down on his forearm.

He did not have time to scream. It whipped its head. His shoulder wrenched in agony as the demon threw him bodily through the air, the pain redoubling untold as he hit the ground several feet away. He did scream then.

Fire kindled scarlet in the darkness, and he tried to call his own fire to guard himself, but the pain made it impossible to concentrate. His magic flared impotently, nowhere near strong enough to protect him, and he suddenly dreaded that he was watching his death come for him.

There was a torturous shriek of air being ripped apart, and a wintry blast of magic slammed into the demon with a crackling sizzle. The fire bursting from its maw splashed harmlessly across the ground.

"Mageling!" the demon hissed, its teeth clicking and scraping as it rounded on the Isleman, spitting fire at the mage that fizzled to nothing in the wake of his magic. Kyran stood his ground, bright as starlight, one hand raised as he poured his cold out against the demon, the child still clutched to him in his other arm.

With another deafening yowl, the demon lunged forward, claws raking out. Kyran twisted away just in time to avoid a gutting, slashing at the demon's face with his free hand. The beast jerked back, a red-hot line appearing across its dark skin, and Barrett saw the glow of hot metal in Kyran's hand—his knife.

The demon spat another globe of fire, and Barrett heard Kyran's harsh gasp echo his as the fire almost caught him full in the face before dissipating, blinding him for a split second—all the demon needed to catch the mage with the back of its hand. The hit sent Kyran spinning to the ground, and Barrett paled as Kyran's light faltered. The vivid image of Raleigh's fading runelines haunted in his mind.

"No!" Barrett struggled to get to his feet, clenching his teeth as his shoulder and arm throbbed in protest.

The demon crawled towards Kyran on all fours, flames licking between its teeth as it opened its mouth wide.

"NO!" Barrett screamed. Something within him snapped. For a fraction of a second, he was burning alive from the inside, his body overfull to bursting. Then he heard his own demon snarl from within him. Fire erupted from every inch of his skin in a single, violent burst. It ripped the demon from its feet and threw it into the dark.

Panting, Barrett slumped to the ground, exhausted to his core. He felt hollow, empty. All he wanted was to lie there in the dark and let himself pass into the sweet oblivion of sleep.

But sudden desperation stirred him to get up. He had not seen how Kyran had survived the blast. "Kyran?" he croaked, turning until he spied the mage's light.

Barrett's heart caught in his throat. He was on the ground, much farther away than he had been before, his light faint compared to its former radiating starlight. Had he...?

Barrett staggered forward, clutching his wounded arm, and crumpled to his knees at the mage's side. Kyran had curled around the child on the ground, who stared, glassy-eyed, at nothing, lips blue and body wracked by violent shivers as he clutched at Kyran's shirt. He must have protected the boy from the blast with his body and magic.

The mage hissed softly in pain and lifted a hand, groping at something on his hip. He was alive, but Kyran's light was waning before their eyes.

"Kyran?" Barrett asked again, terrified he had done something terrible. If he....No, he couldn't live with himself if that were true.

There was a brush of cold, and Kyran's eyes fluttered, his mouth relaxing from the grimace of pain. His light brightened again. His hand left his hip, and he let out an exhausted sigh. But the sound was lost beneath a shrill scream of rage that ripped through the Inbetween behind them. The demon. It lived.

Barrett's body ached, and the emptiness inside of him seemed to throb in time with his shoulder. They could not do this. If they stayed and faced the demon like this, they would die.

The admission hurt more than his wounds. This demon, more than any other, deserved to die, and he owed it that death a thousand times over. But it would have to wait. He couldn't risk Kyran and the child.

"We have to go." Barrett got to his feet.

"What about the demon?" the mage grunted, pulling the boy up into his arms as he stood, apparently unharmed.

"It's too strong. We have to get out of here now. Get to a hearth, some kind of light." He reached for Kyran's shoulder to bring him through the Inbetween, back to the human world, but the mage shied under his hand, moving several steps away so it never touched him.

He shot Barrett a wide-eyed look of warning, his mien stiff.

"I'm not going to hurt you," Barrett insisted, all too aware of the demon still prowling the dark. He turned his hand over, holding it out to Kyran. "I'm goin' to get us out of here. Hold onto me, and don't let go of the boy."

Even with the threat of a furious demon rushing from the dark, Kyran still hesitated before he set his cold hand in Barrett's. Barrett clamped his fingers around the mage's and, drawing power from depths he had not known he possessed, reached with his magic into the very space around them, and pulled.

The darkness slid past them, an oily, tangible current as he towed them out of the Inbetween, towards the light and life of their world. It was harder moving this way, like wading upstream. He did not know if it was because he was moving away from the demon realm or because he was bringing Kyran with him.

His body wavered, his legs burning as they began to totter, threatening to buckle beneath him as he slogged forward. But he kept going. He had to keep moving. If he did not keep moving, they would be trapped here, and the demon would only have to come find them to finish what it had almost accomplished.

And then it let go. As suddenly as that, he could breathe. Warm, humid air flooded his lungs and brushed across his skin, and the clogged feeling in his ears vanished.

He cracked his eyes open to find they were not in the inn room he had entered through, but a cellar, surrounded by drying herbs, crates of wine, and baskets of potatoes and onions. Sunlight was pouring in through an open door at the top of a short set of wooden stairs.

"How...?" They had been in the Inbetween maybe a quarter of an hour if he had to put a guess on it, and yet out here, the entire night had passed. Whatever mechanism had caused it, he was not sorry to see it. They were safe.

"Come on." Barrett slogged towards the stairs, pushing through the throbbing ache in his shoulder and arm.

There was a tug on his hand. Kyran, stood solidly rooted in place, his eyes wide and mouth tight.

"What?" Barrett asked. "It can't follow us into the—"

"Let go."

He looked down. He was still gripping Kyran's hand tight, and quickly let go. The mage retracted his hand and wiped it on his kilt before settling it around the boy he held.

"Sorry," Barrett mumbled, more confused than ever, but determined to stand outside in the full sunshine before he worried over anything else.

The stairs seemed to go on forever, and Barrett was never so glad as when he stepped through the trapdoor into the bright sun and slammed it shut behind them. By the look on Kyran's face, the mage felt the same way.

But it wasn't over. The demon was still alive, and it had made its goal clear. It wanted Kyran, and it was going to come back, possibly tonight. No place was safe. It had taken Kyran right from the tavern, and Raleigh....

Barrett swallowed against the pain the name alone sent through his chest. Graces, it had already been nearly two years. But how? It was dead. He had watched it die.

And yet it wasn't.

He needed answers. But first, he needed help. The guild outpost was full of scholars, couriers, and people whose only job was to placate the people of Oareford with just enough information about the guild's goings-on in their city to curb their curiosity and soothe their fears. None of them were trained hunters. The guildhall proper was at least a week's journey away in the capital—a week of nights the beast would be stalking them.

A curse fell off Barrett's tongue as the answer occurred to him, hating it even as he knew it was right.

"Come on," he said at last, gingerly cradling his arm as he turned, squinting through the sun to see where they had wound up. "I know someplace we can go. Let's get our things."

Chapter Ten

KYRAN MUTELY FOLLOWED Barrett back to the Drunken Wind, blinking in the morning sun shining over the rooftops. If it were not for the *wean* clinging fiercely to his hand, and the hunter just before him, he would have thought the entire thing a dream—or a vivid nightmare. It simply felt so unreal now that he was standing in the sun, alive, the fear and desperation only a cold memory.

"You go ahead upstairs," Barrett told him as they drew near the tavern. People thronged in the street outside, and they began to stir at their approach. Barrett took the lad's other hand, drawing him from Kyran's side. "Pack your things and be ready to leave. I'll be up after I speak with them. They'll want to know what happened, and one of them might know the boy's parents."

Kyran nodded, shrinking back as the crowd began to move towards them, clamouring for Barrett's attention. His presence did not go unnoticed though, and several calls of "Oye! Isleman!" were aimed his direction as he quickly escaped into the tavern.

It was strange inside, the fire extinguished, every candle unlit. The air was empty of the laughter and conversation of just a few hours' past, leaving the room in a gloomy twilight. He did not linger, and hurried up the stairs, careful not to touch the door without his kerchief as he pushed it open.

There he hesitated. It was even darker up here, and the only light came from the ambient glow of the sunlight peeking in around the shutters, but it was still enough to see the destruction. The room was a wreck, tables and chairs overturned, their belongings scattered carelessly, the beds moved.

A cold stone settled in the depths of his stomach, sharpening the ache in his side as the events of the night struck him with their full weight. He had been in the Pit, the place of demons and monsters farthest from the Light, dragged there by one of their kind that had intended to kill him.

And it nearly had. Stars, it had been strong—nothing like the first creature he had faced. And the way its power could touch him....

The skin at the back of his neck and along his arms prickled despite the warm air. He reached into his purse, withdrawing a small, carved sun charm, pressing it between his fingers. He went to the window, throwing open the shutters with his kerchief-shielded hand so he could stand in the sun while he said a quick prayer of thanks that he had not been lost in that place. The prayer did not lighten his heart, though. Clutching the charm in his palm, he touched the dangling amulets at his hip, grateful for the first time in his life that he had sussed out how to make such things. If it were not for that extra power he had stored....

His hand drifted to his throat, remembering too vividly the sensation of ashen skin against his, of his utter helplessness as the demon had tried to choke the life out of him.

Shuddering, he pulled his hand from his neck, the rays of his charm biting into his palm as he squeezed it even more tightly. He hated feeling helpless, hated it more than anything else. He wasn't weak. He was a mage. He had power—*magic*—and yet he had always been utterly impotent, unable to protect himself and always having to rely on others.

But Barrett didn't. Barrett could fight demons with his power, and people didn't fear him, but respected him for it. It was everything Kyran had ever wanted and more, and maybe, just maybe, he would have it, if the guild would take him.

Kyran clung to that thought as he looked at the room again, past the creeping shadows to the tasks that needed doing. Bemoaning his situation had never changed it before. His blood was still cursed, no matter how many times he'd wished it otherwise. But there were other productive things he could be doing.

He started with the tables, turning them upright and sliding them out of the way before moving the beds back to their places. Then he began collecting the papers and other items scattered across the floor, neatly stacking them on the table for Barrett to sort later. It felt good to have something to do, even if the bending and stooping made his body throb and ache in protest. He silently thanked his ma's wisdom about the ills of idleness.

He had most of the room organized when he heard Barrett's startled shout from below in the tavern: "Kyran?"

"Aye," Kyran answered, though it came out rough, his voice scratching his throat. He cleared it, wincing at the raw ache, and called again, a bit more loudly, "Aye."

Footsteps pounded up the stairs, and Barrett appeared at the doorway, mouth agape in horror. "What are you doing?"

Kyran balked at the man's harsh tone, setting the papers in his hand down. "I was—"

"After what just happened?" Barrett hurried to the nearest lantern, nearly throwing the tin cover away as he yanked it off. Fire sparked between his fingers, igniting the wick in an instant, suffusing the room in warm, golden light. "Are you mad?"

"No, but you might be," Kyran bit at the man, rising to his feet as Barrett went to the next lantern. The friendly warmth he'd felt towards Barrett froze over like a shallow pond in winter. "You mind telling me just what has gotten inta ye?" His accent, already thick, deepened with ire.

"That demon is still out there, and you're in here in the dark without a single bloody lantern lit."

"And just what has that got ta do with anythin'?"

"What has—" Barrett looked up from the lantern, his brow furrowed as if he could not believe what he was hearing. "Are you pullin' my leg?"

Kyran gave him a flat look.

"Graces, you really don't know anything."

"I'm na a *bairn*," Kyran snapped back, cinching his control down as his blood bucked against him in anger. "Ye keep telling me about how I dinnae ken anythin' about demons, yet ye havena told me a bloody thing about them when I tol' ye there are na any demons in the Isles! "

The hunter's teeth clicked audibly shut, his jaw flexing. "Well, while we're accusing each other of keeping secrets, why don't you actually try telling me the truth about somethin' for once?"

"Come again?"

Barrett folded his arms over his chest. "I may not be that observant, but I'm not stupid. You aren't here in Tennebrum just to travel about."

Kyran stiffened at the accusation, his lips drawing back along his teeth. "This isna about my business," he argued, his tone flat and cold. "This is about demons and why this entire bloody country is so keen on the dark."

The hunter scoffed, pinching the bridge of his nose as if he could not believe what he was hearing, and Kyran's temper ratcheted a notch higher.

"That's how demons get through," Barrett said. "Why else?"

"Is that so?" Kyran replied, his syllables tightly clipped.

Barrett paused at Kyran's reply, tilting his head. "Yes," he said after a moment, more calmly. He dropped his hand and glanced at the open window and the bright sunshine streaming through. "Look, I...I didn't mean to be an ass, but we need to go. There are things I want to do before the sun goes down—"

"No."

The hunter actually balked at Kyran's short reply. "No?"

"No," Kyran repeated, his temper piqued at Barrett's accusation. "I want ta know what ye are na tellin' me."

"What are you—?"

"About demons. Or should I say tha' one in particular, cause you dinnae get inta such a twist after the first?"

Barrett's face clouded. "That one was different."

"So I ken. My ears work plenty fine, even in the Pit."

"The what?"

"The Pit," Kyran repeated tersely. "Tha' bloody dark place we crawled out of."

"That wasn't the Pit. That was only the Inbetween."

Kyran gave him an arch look. Barrett scratched at his beard before continuing.

"It's...like a bridge between our world and the place the demons live. It can only form where it is dark—I mean, truly dark."

The mage's frown deepened as he strung the vague pieces of information together. "Ye mean ta say *any* place that is dark enough, demons can come through?"

Barrett let go of his face, wobbling his hand left and right. "Normally, no. Normally, it is only in very dark places that demons cross through—caves, unlit cellars, that sort of place. But if the demon is strong enough and something attracts its attention, they can come through in any place so long as it is not in direct light. Hence the lanterns."

"The lanterns were lit last night," Kyran pointed out.

"The demon we faced is old and very powerful. And it will be comin' back."

"Why?"

"I don't know!" Barrett snapped. "I don't know why it's done anything it's done. All I know is it will be back. If I knew it would keep you safe, I would tell you to pack your things and leave—get as far away from me as you can. But I can't risk it. It's seen you and knows you've worked with me, and I can't...." Barrett's voice broke with a rough sound, and he had to clear his throat. "I don't want you to have to suffer that same fate."

Like last time.

"Whose fate?" Kyran asked, recalling the demon's taunt.

"It doesn't matter. I just—"

"Whose fate?" Kyran demanded. "Ye canna let my business be, but ye are na truthful yerself."

The hunter's face reddened with anger, and he looked fit to burst until he took a long, slow breath. "The last mage that worked with me," he said, his words tight and clipped. "He died at the hands of the demon we met last night. I thought I had killed it, but...." He shook his head, running a hand over his face again. "I don't know. I don't know how it's still free."

He was scared. The anger, the outburst—it suddenly made sense. Barrett was scared. For Kyran. The mage shifted uneasily. He had seen how much power Barrett wielded. And how even their combined efforts had been utterly surpassed by this one demon.

Kyran strangled the bitter sound that threatened to escape his throat. It had taken every inch of his power and then some to even withstand the beast. Stars above, but if that thing caught him alone someplace, there was no way he would escape it. It had been so terribly strong.

He shut his eyes, pressing his fingers into his eyelids as if he could block out the mental image of its dark, eyeless sockets. The sensation of a hot, immovable weight pressing him down into the ground. The indescribably intimate pain of the demon's sheer presence bearing down on his mind, crushing him into nothing even within himself.

If I were not toying with you, I would be feasting on you already.

Spitting a curse, Kyran pushed his fingers through his hair. That helplessness—that stomach-sickening fear he'd felt in that long moment as his magic drained and he had been trapped beneath that thing—was something he never wanted to feel again. The monster had toyed with him. Taunted him. Lauded the idea of keeping him in a cage until it was ready to... what? What had it wanted? Nothing it had said had made any sense.

"Are you alright?"

Kyran let his hand drop back to his side, his thumb passing over his charm again. "Aye," he said dryly.

Barrett took another harsh breath, cradling his arm to his chest again. "Look, I....I'll figure something out. You and I still need to talk, and I promise to tell you everythin' you need to know, but I'd prefer it next to a roaring fireplace, with a drink in hand."

"Aye," Kyran relented with a heavy sigh. "I could use one."

"Maybe two," Barrett agreed heartily. "Maybe more."

Chapter Eleven

Their destination lay on almost the opposite side of the city, across the River Oare. Unlike the seedy quarter the Drunken Wind lay in, the streets here were paved with cobbles, the buildings constructed of handsome stone and wood, and instead of the overcrowded tenement housing, there were actual homes, built in neat rows.

They finally stopped at one of the larger homes. Tenderly letting go of his injured arm, Barrett produced an iron key from his pocket. It turned in the lock with a heavy *thunk* that sent his nerves rattling.

The door opened to a small entry hall, bare but for a lantern hung from a metal arm high on the wall, its wick turned low, the doors on either side both closed.

"If you'll just pull the door to behind you," Barrett instructed, opening the door to their left.

Kyran did as he was asked without remark, ducking beneath the mantle to follow Barrett into the main living space. Another lantern stood, unlit, on a small table in the center of the room. The walls were whitewashed, lending a sense of brightness even in the dim light. A large fireplace lined with large, smooth river stones took up most of the right wall, but the fire, normally left to burn low when no one was home to tend it, leapt in the grate. So they were not alone. A single wooden rocking chair sat before it, its back to the large bookcase set against the opposite wall, filled with books, papers, and other bric-a-brac. Every door was closed.

"It's big in here," Kyran remarked as Barrett slung his pack down next to the fireplace, hissing as his shoulder gave a hot burn of pain.

"That's exactly what I said when I first saw it. I thought Kat had gone mad pickin' it."

"Who is Kat?"

"Oh, ah." Barrett glanced towards the back of the house out of habit, half expecting her to be standing there. She must have been in the kitchen, he guessed. "Katherine. My sister. She's older than me. Our father trained her to be a hunter before me."

"Is she a mage as well?"

"Ah...." Barrett pulled his arm up against his chest, stalling as he chose his words. "No, but she is dangerous with a sword."

Kyran's brows rose in interest. "A sword, aye?"

"Don't tell me you can use one too."

"No. I cleave more ta knives."

Barrett's eyes flickered down to the top of the Isleman's boot, where the bone hilt of that little knife of his peeked out. "So I gathered." He shifted his grip on his arm, wincing again at the deep ache. The pain in his forearm, where the demon had bitten him, had lessened dramatically during their walk, but his shoulder had only gotten worse.

"I need to get some things from the larder for my arm. Do you...." He stopped, mortified as he realized his neglect. "Are you hurt anywhere?"

But the mage only shook his head.

"Alright, then." Barrett sighed in relief. Graces, the long night was really beginning to tell. "Make yourself comfortable. I'll see about some food and drink for us."

He let himself through one of the doors at the back of the room, stepping out into the sunlight. A well-tended garden took up every available inch of soil behind the house, walled off by a waist-high fence from the neighboring houses. An uneven path of stones—the siblings of the fireplace's river rock—led to a wooden outbuilding that took up the rest of the tiny space.

The door had been left propped open, and the smell of the cooking fire and stored spices drifted out into the summer air as he neared. He could hear the creak of the table inside as someone worked dough on its surface, the same creak it made when he kneaded bread for dinner.

"Kat?" Barrett called, hesitating on the path.

"You can hear I'm busy," she said from inside the kitchen, her tone short. "Come here so I don't have to yell."

He swallowed, the dread that had been building in his gut swelling even further. He followed the path to the kitchen, pausing just inside the threshold, waiting for his eyes to adjust to the dimness.

Everything in the kitchen was as he remembered. The large stone hearth was built of more river stone, its fire banked to preserve the coals. Overheard, strings of herbs, vegetables, and flowers hung from the rafters, drying, and barrels of meal and flour sat in their respective places. To his left, rows of shelves held pots, pans, jars of preserves, and baskets of fresh produce and bread.

His sister stood at the heavy table in the center of the room, its benches pushed beneath it, out of the way, as she worked a lump of dough. She glanced up as he stepped inside, and he noticed for the first time that her hair, the same golden blonde as his, was trained back in a heavy braid that reached past her waist.

She hadn't worn it completely back around him since the attack. But now he got his first real look at her in almost two years. The features of one side of her face, the same strong jaw and high, flat cheekbone as Barrett, showed the creep of age in the deep creases around her eyes and finer lines around her mouth. The other half was marked by scars from demon fire—ripples and discolorations that swirled over her skin like the surface of a brook. There was more of it beneath her clothes and on both her hands. He had seen those before, once the bandages came off.

She set the dough aside with a loud thump as her gaze quickly found his arm and the ruined sleeve he cradled against his chest. "You're hurt," she said simply, dusting her floury hands off on her apron. "Bring me the basket. Tell me what happened."

He fetched the supplies from their place on the far end of the shelf, then waited while Kat pulled the bench out from under the table and took a seat. He sat next to her, placing the basket between them, and held out his arm when she gestured to see it, trying his best not to stare at her face. His gut churned guiltily. Kat would tell him again that it hadn't been his fault, but it had. She and Raleigh had both been hurt because of him. Because he hadn't been fast enough or smart enough.

Kat gingerly peeled his sleeve up, and he cringed in anticipation of actually seeing the wound. He had avoided looking at it since escaping the cellar, keeping his arm tucked close so anyone they encountered would not be frightened. But when the fabric came away from where it had stuck to his arm, the blood drained from his face as he saw what the demon had done to him. Beneath the grime and dried blood were ragged rows of dark, bruised marks where he had expected punctures. The skin was closed.

"No," he whispered, running his fingers over the marks. They were tender and hot to the touch. He scratched at one with his nails, ignoring the throb it sent through his arm, but the coloration did not budge.

"That's not dirt," Kat said calmly.

Barrett yanked his arm away. "No. No, it can't be." Getting up from the bench, he found a wash rag folded next to the basin of water by the hearth and dunked it in, scrubbing at his arm. The marks did not change.

"That isn't going to work," Kat insisted. "Sit down so I can finish looking your arm over."

"How could this happen?" he asked her. "How do I get rid of it?"

"It happened because you were injured and your demon knit you up. And it either goes away, or it doesn't. There's nothing you can do about it other than keep it hidden."

He swore fluently and yanked his sleeve back down, wincing as his shoulder's complained at the rough treatment.

"Language," his sister reminded him tartly. She patted the bench with the palm of her hand, but he ignored her.

Barrett had seen the marks on other hunters more than enough to know what it was. He'd been witch-marked. The demon nesting within him had used its own power and flesh to mend his injuries. Kat had never borne one of the marks, but their father had confessed to bearing one along his back, though Barrett had never seen it. The man had always been careful to keep it hidden, as it would give away the guild's secret far too easily.

Now he had to do the same. If Kyran or anyone outside of the house saw the mark, they would know what he was, and he would have more to fear than the guild's reprimand. There was only one way people treated witches.

"Kris," Kat said, her tone dry. "Sit down. You're a hunter. These things happen."

"But—"

"Sit. Take off your tunic, and tell me what happened."

He did as she asked, pulling his tunic off over his head using only his good arm. But as he tried to pick up the thread of his story—his reason for coming—the words wouldn't come.

"Kris," Kat said again, prodding at his shoulder, "what happened?"

"It....It came back," he said slowly, the horror of last night washing over him again in cold waves. He had nearly died. Kyran had nearly died.

"What did?"

Barrett swallowed, running the back of his hand over his mouth. "The demon. The one that attacked the house. It came back."

Kat's hands stilled against him. "That's impossible."

"I know. But I saw it. I fought it. It remembers me."

She pulled her hands from him, yanking a cloth from the basket and folding it with stiff, jerky motions. "How?"

"I don't know, but it's after me. Me and Kyran."

"Who's Kyran?"

"A mage I met the other night."

She slapped her hands down on the bench, making Barrett jump. "Blessed Lumen!"

"Kat!"

"Put your tunic on," she barked, keeping her head ducked as he clumsily pulled it back on. "Where is he now?"

"In the house."

Her eyes widened—not in shock, but anger. "You brought him *here*?"

"Where else was I supposed to bring him?" Barrett finally snapped back.

"It would be safer for us all if he were at the guildhall." She grabbed his wrist, set his injured hand on his opposite shoulder, and picked up the folded fabric, sliding the cloth under his elbow. "Talk to the couriers at the guild post. Send a letter ahead to the guild to notify them of what's going on, and let one of them escort him to the guildhall."

Barrett could not believe what was coming out of his sister's mouth. "The demon would overtake them long before he reached the capital. Graces above, it could come back for us tonight."

"And you want it to appear here?" She tied the fabric behind his neck, jerking the knot harder than necessary. "After what happened last time?"

"No," Barrett said. "No, I don't want it to come back at all."

"But it will. You know that."

"I know." He sighed, grinding his teeth. "But I don't know what to do. I was hopin'...." He lifted his eyes, looking at his sister, at the scars she'd gotten trying to save Raleigh. "I was hopin' you would."

A muscle along her jaw twitched, and her shoulders tensed beneath her blouse. "I told you what you should do. Send him to the guildhall. They can help him."

"He'll never make it," Barrett repeated, searching Kat's face for an answer to her indifference, but she wouldn't look at him, her gaze fixed on her lap. "Kat, I can't just let it kill him."

"And what about you?" she demanded, her voice quiet and even. "The demon nearly killed you last time, too."

And her.

"I know," he admitted, hissing as he tried to move his injured arm to push his filthy hair from his face. "But I can't leave him. I got him into this."

"Then go to the guild together. But by the Graces, why would you bring him here?"

"I only came here to see if you knew anything that could help. Apparently I was mistaken."

She let out a tired sigh that was nothing like the sister he knew. "I'm old, Kris. Old, and retired. I can't help you fight it. I told you the smart way to deal with this demon."

"I am not abandoning Kyran," Barrett snarled. He surged to his feet, the scent of woodsmoke curling across his nose.

"He's not your responsibility."

"He—"

"He's not Raleigh, Kris!"

His fists burst into dark flame, crackling up his arms. Kat leaned away, her scars standing out, livid, as her face went deathly pale.

"You...." he started, but his words failed as he noticed her hands clenched in her apron. The flames flickered and died along his skin. "I shouldn't have come back," he muttered, his anger twisting into something else. Something he was nauseatingly familiar with. He turned to leave.

"Wait—" Kat started.

"I don't know what I was thinkin'."

He crossed the garden in long strides and shoved the back door open. Kyran glanced up from the fire, still standing where Barrett had left him. For a brief moment, Barrett's ire faded as a strange feeling stole through him, as if he were seeing a reflection rippling over the surface of the scene. It almost felt familiar, and yet....

"Are you alright?"

The illusion broke, and Barrett shook himself from his stupor. "We're leavin'," he said shortly, kicking the door closed behind him. "Grab your things."

"Where are we going?"

"Back to the Drunken Wind," he answered, "where we can get a drink and plan what to do next. Most importantly, a drink."

Chapter Twelve

The late afternoon sun was in its last golden hours by the time they made it back to the Drunken Wind. Kyran was not eager to set foot in the tavern again, but despite his initial hesitation, he offered no resistance when the hunter suggested Kyran go ahead upstairs while Barrett got them drinks.

Kyran skirted through the least full tables, hurrying up when he heard calls of "Isleman" echo through the crowd of patrons who had returned to their watering hole.

As soon as he shut the door, he went to the shutters and withdrew his charm. Pressing the smooth, worn sun to his lips, he whispered a prayer to Lumen, thanking the god for the gifts of light—first the stars, then the moon and sun, to light the chaos of the dark for humankind. He asked the Graces to carry his words and keep watch over him.

His shoulders eased as he finished the prayer, comforted. He slipped the charm back into his purse and withdrew his kerchief from his belt, using it to close the shutters and latch them firmly. He sat on the side of his bed, intending to wait for Barrett, but as he sank into the straw mattress, his body sagged with exhaustion. Every inch of him ached with fatigue. His eyes heavier than the highest *ben*.

"Just for a nip," he told himself, stretching out on top of the quilt.

But the moment he closed his eyes, he began to dream—of dark eyeless sockets and teeth he could never outrun.

He jerked awake with a gasp, his eyes searching frantically until they landed on the nearest lantern. Only a dream. He sighed, relenting back down into the mattress.

"You alright?"

He lifted his head again at the slurred voice, pushing his hair from his face to find Barrett watching him over a steaming mug from his own bed across the room. He was slumped against the headboard, the side of his face blackened by a bruise and a bit swollen. His drink rested on his chest, balanced by his left hand. His right arm was bandaged where the demon had bitten him while he'd defended Kyran and the lad in that Inbetween.

It smarted to see the hunter's injuries so plainly, the full weight of the events that had occurred in that dark place still sinking in. Kyran had almost died. It was no exaggeration to say as much. He only breathed still because of Barrett's help. The demon they'd faced this time had been nothing like the first. Nothing at all.

"Aye. Bonny and bright as the sunrise," he said at last, dragging himself upright. He glanced at the shutters, but no sun peeked through them. He had gotten some sleep then, even if he didn't feel like he had.

Barrett snorted loudly. "Left you a drink." He jerked his chin towards the table.

"Thank y—" But Kyran's stomach interrupted him with a long, low growl. His cheeks prickled, blushing.

"And some dinner," Barrett added, snickering into his drink.

"Thank you," Kyran repeated a bit more tartly, plucking his kerchief from his purse as he got to his feet and crossed the room. He reached for the drink first, wiping the heavy tankard's handle and lip.

"You don't like bein' touched by much of anythin', eh?"

Kyran stiffened at the remark, the back of his neck and arms breaking out in gooseflesh.

"Don't like people?" Barrett asked.

"Tha' isna your business," Kyran said tersely, focusing his attention on the texture of the kerchief against his fingertips as he continued to wipe the tankard.

"I don't mean anythin' by it. I just—"

Kyran shot him a pointed look over his shoulder, and Barrett's teeth clicked shut. "It isna your business," he repeated, waiting until Barrett ducked his head to his drink before he turned away again. He nudged the chair out from the table with his boot and sat, taking up his drink with his kerchief. Ale, and it was as good as it had been the first time. He savoured it, enjoying the warmth it kindled in his empty belly.

"You're right," Barrett said, breaking the quiet of the room. "Your business is your own. I suppose if anyone owes any answers, it's me." He shifted against the bed, the frame creaking noisily as he sat more upright. "I promised to tell you more about demons."

"Aye," Kyran agreed crisply, taking another draw of his drink.

"I wanted to apologize for earlier," Barrett said after a long moment. "I said some things I know were...."

"Rude?" Kyran finished.

The hunter winced. "Yes," he admitted, taking another sip of his steaming drink. "I just....When I ran up here and saw you alone with none of the lanterns lit, I got angry. We had only just barely escaped that demon, and there you were, invitin' it to come after you again."

"I dinnae ken that," Kyran reminded him stiffly.

Barrett inclined his head. "I know, and that's my fault too. You told me you didn't know anythin'." He tipped his mug, peering into it. "I guess I didn't realize how little 'nothing' meant."

Kyran eyed Barrett, but he could already feel his ire ebbing.

Barrett shifted on the bed again, hunching over and cupping his drink with both hands. "I suppose the first thing to say is that they aren't all like the one from last night," he said, plunging right into the topic. "That one is old and clever. Powerful."

Almost human, Kyran added silently, drumming a finger against the tankard. Compared to that beast, the first demon they had faced had been little more than an animal. "Do they all speak?"

"No. There aren't many that can. Only the oldest ones. Did it say anythin' before I got there?"

"Aye, though I dinnae ken what any of it meant."

"What did it say?"

Kyran stared into his drink, watching the ripples along the ale's surface as the click of his nail grew louder. "It called me half-blooded. Said it wanted ta eat me ta gain my power. That I was one of the Auld One's." It made him uneasy to say the words out loud, as if they didn't belong out in the sun. "If I thought beasts like that could be mad...."

"Oh, it is completely mad," Barrett agreed with a dry laugh that trailed unnaturally into quiet. "That's what it did to my last partner, y'know," he continued, but his amusement was gone now, his voice ringing hollow. "He was a mage like you, and it pulled this same trick. It lured me away, and while I was gone, it attacked him and it....It ate him, just like it meant to do with you last night."

Kyran was silent. He didn't know what to say at such a revelation. Eaten. Alive, if he had any measure of the beast's nature. He suppressed a shudder at the thought. The hunter's frantic anger made a terrible new sense. "I am... sorry for your loss," he offered quietly.

"Yeah. So am I. He didn't deserve what happened. He wasn't...." Barrett swallowed, his tone rising in pitch. "He wasn't a fighter. He did it for me." His breath gave an ugly hitch, and he tipped his cup up, draining it.

Kyran's ear caught on the hunter's choice of words. The idea seemed daft, but it sounded like Barrett and his last partner might have been...closer than simply hunting partners. But Kyran had seen the way he looked at the barmaids. Had he been wrong then, or was he wrong about the partner?

Barrett dropped his empty cup back to his knee and continued, interrupting the trail of Kyran's thoughts. "I won't let what happened to him happen to you," he declared, a rough edge clinging to his voice. But his words were even. "I don't care what it takes. That bastard *will* die this time."

Except they had both already stood before this demon, and even together, they had come up woefully short.

"Why is it doin' this?" Kyran demanded, expecting no answer. His fingers tightened around the tankard as he struggled not to touch his throat. His blood pressed against his control, his frustration mounting. "Why is it hunting mages? Dinnae we have enough trouble without one of them hunting us like *connies*?"

"*Connies*?"

Kyran groped for the Common word. "*Connies*," he repeated uselessly, then crooked two fingers, bouncing his hand like a small, hopping animal.

"Rabbits?"

Kyran nodded, relieved to be understood.

"I wouldn't call us rabbits. We hunt their kind, too. If we face it on our territory next time, it won't stand a chance." Barrett leaned forward, looping his left arm around his knees. "To answer your other question, though, it's the magic that attracts them. They seek it out because it's how they get stronger—by eatin' other demons and mages."

That simply didn't track. Kyran could excuse the strange logic of demons eating other demons for power, uncanny beasts that they were, but mages? "Why would eating mages give them power?"

"It's in the bloodline."

"Come again?"

"The bloodline," Barrett repeated, as if what he had said had been obvious. "The thing that made you a mage."

"I dinnae ken what you're on about," Kyran replied slowly, an uneasy feeling slipping into his gut. Barrett couldn't mean....He was a mage too. He wouldn't believe *that*.

The hunter raised his brows. "Well, I don't know about the Isles, but here in Tennebrum, the stories say that a long time ago, a demon and a woman had a child, the first mage, and it is from that child that all mages—"

"That isna true!" Kyran spat, the tankard squeaking against the table as he barely resisted throwing its contents at the hunter. "I am sick ta death of hearin' that lie. There isna a wit of it true."

Barrett's mouth hung open in shock, but the mage pressed on. "If this is yer idea of a joke, I dinnae find it funny. This," he held up his hand, letting control slip just enough to set the lines beneath his skin aglow, "is no demon-blooded curse. But it is a curse, sure as anything."

"A curse?" Barrett sputtered. "You're not cursed—"

"Oh, aye? But I'm supposed to be some demon-blooded cur?"

"It's *not* a curse!" Barrett argued, his voice rising. "Your magic is a gift. You can help people."

"If it's a gift, then the Light that gave it can take it back."

"You don't mean that. Your magic is so stron—"

"Ta the Pit with ye!" Kyran snarled, lips peeling back to show his teeth. "What do ye ken about me or what I've been through? Ye've lived your life here in the guild, where people praise ye, *thank* ye, for what you're doin'. Ye dinnae ken the first thing about me, so dinnae stand there and try ta tell me what ta think!"

His words rang in the air between them. Barrett looked caught halfway between startled and furious, his mouth and throat working, his fingers clenched against his knees. Kyran cinched his control around his magic again, the glow of it vanishing from his skin, and pushed his drink away. He wasn't certain he could stomach it now.

"No," Barrett said at last, his voice tight but even. "I don't know you or what you've been through. I didn't mean it to come out that way. Just...." He pressed his lips together, taking a breath through his nose. "You don't have to believe anythin' I've told you except this: demons *are* attracted to mages. All of them, not simply this one. Just remember that while you're in Tennebrum. Not that you'll struggle much with the beasts," he added with a strained chuckle. "I meant what I said about your magic bein' strong. We wouldn't be here talkin' if you hadn't had your magic."

"Aye," Kyran agreed bitterly, winding his kerchief around his fingers. "There's truth ta that."

The room fell silent between them again, and Kyran felt an impetus to leave. Leave and return to what he was doing before, subsisting by doing the odd job here and there for grateful farmers. It was simpler and much quieter. But the promise of the guild, of the title of hunter, stayed his decision.

He reached into his purse, fingers brushing over the carved sun nestled at the bottom, and uttered a silent prayer that Barrett's promise would not evaporate like a will-o-wisp.

"I'm sorry for insulting you," Barrett murmured at last, breaking the quiet again. "I didn't mean to. I just....I'm no good at explainin' things. That's why Raleigh always did the talking." He sighed, tapping his cup against his shin, then slid out of the bed. "I'm going to drink in the tavern for a while. You're welcome to join me if you want, or you can stay up here."

He paused, as if waiting to hear Kyran's answer, but the mage remained silent, watching Barrett from the corner of his eye. The hunter made as if to say more, then apparently thought better of it, and let himself out without another word.

    Kyran listened to his noisy boots on the stairs. Slumping in his seat, he turned his hand over, releasing just enough of his power to cool him and light his blood beneath his skin. His cursed blood. How was it that he and Barrett were treated so very differently, with the same wretched lie upon them? How were the mages here in Tennebrum praised for their service in the guild when people believed them to be the sons of the very beasts they hunted?

    He flexed his fingers, watching the light glimmer beneath his skin. But Barrett's power had never shone this way. He had fought beside the hunter twice now but never seen any lines on the man's skin. Did he control it somehow, or was he simply blessed to be without them? Or, a dark little corner of his mind suggested, was he wrong about Barrett's power? But if Barrett wasn't a mage, what could he be?

    Kyran had, of course, heard the tales of the hunters—that they fought with gifts given to them by Lumen—but he had somehow thought they had meant blessed weapons, like the dagger Barrett had impaled the demons with before they turned to ash. Had it really meant magic? But if Barrett's power came from Lumen, why was Kyran's from the taint of a demon?

    Kyran's stomach gave another plaintive growl, and he surrendered with a sigh. Perhaps he would finish his drink after all, before he made another go at sleep.

Chapter Thirteen

For a day and night, Barrett stayed in the tavern drinking until the wee hours of the morning, wishing more than anything that he could fall into his drink and disappear. It was the only way he would protect anyone from any more of his screw-ups. Raleigh, Kat, and even Kyran had all paid a price for his utter failure to do anything right. Some steeper than others.

He missed Raleigh. Up until the last few months, he had managed to push the pain down beneath drink and his work for the guild, but seeing this demon—and hearing his own sister's harsh words—brought the pain doubling back until it sat in his chest like a naked blade, cutting into him with every breath.

Raleigh. His sweet Raleigh. He hadn't deserved what had happened to him. If Barrett had only been faster, better, he would be alive. They would be together.

It was thoughts of Raleigh that drove Barrett to finally slosh his way back to the room. Drunk as he was, he had not forgotten the danger lurking in the night outside. He had sensed nothing, and the bells hadn't rung, but the beast had come for Kyran directly before, taken him straight from the room. And if it wanted to try again, Barrett would be there.

He woke briefly at dawn, opening one eye just long enough to see Kyran at the window in the sun, murmuring his prayers, before he fell back asleep. It wasn't until late afternoon that hunger that drove him out of bed to find dinner. Then, begrudgingly, he dragged himself to the outpost and crafted a letter to the guild describing his encounter with the demon and imploring them to send aid. It hurt his pride to write it, but he was out of ideas, and he had no intention of screwing up again.

After sending his letter on with one of the couriers, he wandered the market until he found something he had not realized he was looking for.

He was patting the parcel under his arm, pleased with his purchase and eager to get back to the Drunken Wind to see what Kyran thought of it, when he noticed a faint pull at his attention, something tickling at his thoughts. It seemed familiar....

He sucked in a sharp breath as his ale-soaked thoughts finally started working. Magic. There was a demon.

Spitting a curse, he bolted down the road, clutching his injured arm to his chest as his shoulder screamed in protest from beneath the drink and herbs meant to dull it. He made for the tavern, the thread of magic strengthening against his senses. Graces above, it was at the tavern again, in broad daylight this time. If the Light would grant him any ounce of mercy, he prayed he'd get there in time.

He pounded up the stairs of the tavern, two at a time, and the bottom fell out of his gut when the pull of the magic vanished.

"Graces, no!" He threw the door open, sending the wicks of the lanterns aflutter, only to find Kyran sitting cross-legged against the far wall beneath the window. Spirals of frost curled out along the floor and up the wall around the mage, and his copper hair sparkled almost white with ice. His always-straight back was hunched over, his hands curled around something.

"Kyran?" Barrett's breath fogged in the chill air.

"Aye?" the mage answered without looking up, sounding irritated, but hale.

"Are you alright?" Barrett asked after another moment, forcing himself to take a deep breath and trying to slow his racing heart as he closed the door behind him. "You weren't...?"

"There wasna any trouble," Kyran assured him.

"That....That's good, but what are you—Graces above, is that blood?" The mage's fingers, cupped in his lap, were stained dark.

"Aye," Kyran answered more slowly this time, drawing his hands farther into his lap.

"What in the world are you doin'?"

The mage didn't reply right away, his expression hidden, but Barrett could see the line of tension in Kyran's shoulders draw even tighter. "I am working on my amulet," Kyran said at last, lifting his cupped palms as if that explained everything.

Barrett frowned, moving closer to try to get a better look at what Kyran was holding and shivering in the cool air. "What d'you mean? What sort of amulet requires blood like that?" The only amulets he knew of were the ones the hunters used, like the one around his neck, and they were made by the guild wizard. He had never heard of mages being able to make any, but then again, there was hardly anything anyone knew about mages. There were so very few of them, and almost every one ever found had proven to be vastly different from the others, in strength and abilities.

With a defeated shrug, Kyran uncurled his fingers, revealing a smooth, round stone with a perfect circle worn through the center, smeared liberally in blood. Blood stained his palms and fingers almost black. "I figured out how ta make these when I was still a *wean*," he explained. "My magic comes from my blood, so I use my blood ta make something capable of holding my power. It gives me another well I can tap inta when I need it."

Barrett's brows rose in surprise. That was an interesting concept. Unlike mages, his own magic was seemingly bottomless. The only thing that prevented him from simply drawing it endlessly was the toll it took on his body. It was normally just fatiguing, but it could bring him to the point of collapse if he drew too heavily. He'd learned that the hard way.

"How long does it take to make one of those?"

"Days, if I spend most of my time working on them. A week or more if I am preoccupied."

"Sorry to interrupt," Barrett said, going to the washbasin and picking up one of the clean rags hanging from the stand.

"It's fine," the mage said coolly, fingers curling around the stone again. "I wasna expecting ta finish today."

"Well, in that case." Barrett flinched as his fingers touched the frigid water, but he dipped the rag in the basin. Squeezing the cloth out, he padded over to the mage and offered it to him, carefully holding it only by the very corner. "I brought you somethin'."

Kyran looked pointedly at the rag. "I can see that."

"Not the rag." Barrett scowled playfully, shaking it. "Wipe your hands so I can give it to you."

Gingerly laying the stone on his knee, Kyran accepted the rag with just the tips of his fingers. Barrett waited while Kyran mopped at the blood on his hands, then held out the parcel he had purchased. Clumsily, Kyran shook his kerchief out from his purse to cover his palm, and accepted the bundle, setting it in his lap. It looked like nothing more than a large leather pouch tied shut by a leather thong.

Barrett watched, arms crossed, as Kyran picked at the thong until the knot came undone, and unrolled the pouch across his lap. It opened up to four knives, neatly tied in place by more strips of leather. The blades were slightly curved, and the grips were simple leather wraps.

"They're small. Good to tuck away for when you need a quick weapon," Barrett remarked as Kyran ran a hand over the blades. They were good craftsmanship, even by Barrett's untrained eye. "They're balanced, too," he added, "if you've any talent for throwin' blades. Or so the merchant assured me."

"It was a way ta pass the time on the *ben*," Kyran admitted almost shyly.

Barrett let out a surprised chuckle. "Well, now. You'll have to teach me sometime."

Kyran flicked an eye up at him. "I can try."

"Oh, *aye*?" Barrett snickered, enjoying the way Kyran's mouth turned at the tease, his cheeks flushing faintly.

"Thank you for the gift," Kyran said after a moment, looking up from the knives, his expression openly pleased, and Barrett smiled warmly in return.

"I hope they are of use to you. Happy birthday."

Kyran ducked his head, picking at the leather thong on the pouch and fiddling with his stone to hide his smile, but Barrett didn't miss it. He had hit his mark squarely.

"You dinnae have ta," Kyran insisted quietly.

Barrett's smile broadened. "I wanted to," he maintained, reaching to tug at the leather tie in his hair. "But I have to ask....What in the world is a *ben*?"

Kyran's eyes flickered back and forth; he evidently had to search for the Common word. "A mountain."

"So you lived on a mountain?"

"Cairngorm, aye."

"And where's that?" The knot to his tie slipped free at last, and his hair fell down his shoulders, his scalp tingling in relief.

Kyran gave the man an odd look. "You havena heard of Cairngorm?"

Barrett shook his head, scratching at his head with one hand. "No, but I was never as learned as....Well, I was never much learned. Tell me about it."

Kyran scoffed at the hunter. "It is a sacred mountain in the Isles, a place where the snow never stops falling. Its name is in many of the Isles' old tales."

The hunter's brows rose. "You lived on a sacred mountain?"

Kyran nodded.

"Did it really never stop snowing?"

Kyran tilted his head. "It was lighter in the summer, but it was always falling."

The hunter gave an exaggerated shiver. "Weren't you and your family cold?"

Kyran laid his stone on his knee, then picked up the wet rag and patted at his fingertips again. "My family dinnae live with me there."

"You were alone? For how long?"

"Since I was seven."

Barrett's hand dropped. "Seven?" He couldn't imagine any reason why a seven-year-old boy would be forced to live alone on the side of some mountain, mage or not.

Although...he was beginning to piece together an image of what Kyran's life had been like in the Isles with what he had observed, and what answers Kyran would not give. It showed in the little ways. The way the mage was always careful to wear long sleeves in the summer heat, to check that the cuffs were all the way down. The way he'd carefully avoided looking at the other people in the tavern. The way he'd referred to his magic as a curse.

Living alone was likely the smallest price he'd paid in his life.

"Why?"

Kyran shifted where he sat, rubbing at his fingers with the rag for several seconds. "It was safer," he said quietly.

"For you, or for them?" Barrett asked, his tone sharper than he'd meant, but he simply couldn't wrap his head around what he was hearing. "Graces, it's no wonder you don't like people."

Kyran's hand stilled. "Come again?"

"I haven't known you long, but you always eat in our room, and you don't let anyone...." Barrett's gaze drifted to the mage's shoulder. "Well, you don't even shake hands."

"It isna—" Kyran started before he bit his explanation off, clenching his teeth.

"It isn't what?" Barrett prompted gently, anxious to hear the mage's explanation, though aware that he was likely skirting dangerous territory.

"It isna...that I dinnae like people," Kyran said, picking his words slowly as he gathered his stone and knives and got to his feet. "It is...hard ta be around them after living alone so long."

But that wasn't all. Barrett could hear the gap in the mage's words, the answer he didn't give. It only strengthened his suspicions, feeding the righteous anger that was slowly building in him. Graces forgive him if he ever got confirmation of that.

"You mentioned family, though," Barrett said, changing tactics, hoping the mage would indulge him. There was just so much about Kyran that was an utter mystery. Not that they'd spent much time talking these past couple of days. That was Barrett's fault. But he wanted to know more. "You have any siblings?"

"Aye." Kyran set the knives on his bed, dropping his stone into the purse on his hip before heading to the washbasin. "Three brothers and a wee sister."

"Are you the eldest?"

"No. Duncan and Murray are elder. Isobel and Tavish are younger."

Barrett nodded, sitting heavily on the side of his bed. "Kat's about fifteen years older than me. She used to tell me ma wanted more kids, but pa wasn't home much." He scratched his face. His facial hair had grown out into thick, golden curls over the last week; he could almost call it a beard now. "How much older—"

A low growling rumble interrupted his question, and Barrett stifled a laugh. "You haven't been down to eat today, have you?

Kyran's face colored faintly, and he kept his eyes fixed on his hands as he dried them on a clean rag at the basin. "No."

"Well, if you'll give me a moment, I'll get us somethin'," Barrett offered, kneading his injured shoulder tenderly. "You want anything particular?"

Kyran lifted a should in a half-shrug, dropping the rag back on the side of the basin. "I dinnae care."

Barrett chuffed and shook his head in disbelief. "Kyran," he called softly, pleased when the mage spared him a quick, neutral glance. "Come on. I know there's gotta be something you're partial to. Stew? Porridge? Bread and butter? Tell me."

Kyran pressed his lips together, watching his finger begin to ooze a few drops of blood again. "I wouldna say no ta a pot of honey with the bread," he admitted after a moment before setting his finger to his lips.

Barrett felt his brows rise in surprise at the request, but he nodded. So, Kyran had a sweet tooth. "Alright. Some honey it is." He waited a beat longer in case the mage had any other requests, but his silence was answer enough. "I'll be back shortly."

He worked hard to keep from smiling at his success until he pulled the door shut behind him, grinning into the hall. Finally. It was satisfying to have finally learned something about Kyran.

It wasn't like him to be so nosy, but Barrett couldn't help it. Since he had met the Isleman, he had wanted to know more about him, to unravel the intriguing mystery surrounding his circumstances in Tennebrum. Not simply out of curiosity, but almost compulsion, an itch he couldn't quite scratch—and one Kyran did not make easy to satisfy.

The mage was hiding something. He was absolutely certain of that, now more than ever. Something had driven Kyran here, something Barrett suspected more and more the truth of, and Graces help the soul or souls responsible if he ever caught hold of them.

Chapter Fourteen

"WHAT IS THAT?"

"Yours." Barrett nudged his unbandaged hand towards Kyran, mouth curling in an amused little smirk when Kyran leaned back from him. "Don't look so suspicious. It isn't a frog. It's your part of the pay from the guild."

Kyran glowered up at the man, but produced his kerchief and covered his palm, holding it out for him. Barrett snickered, the scent of mead thick on his breath, and dropped a neatly folded bundle of crown notes into his hand. Kyran stared at the notes. It had to be a mistake. Stars above, but that was more money than he had ever seen, let alone held at once. "You're sotted," he accused, offering the notes back to Barrett, but the man waved his hand away.

"Maybe," Barrett relented, running a hand over his jaw, the thick growth of his beard scratching against his hand. "But you risked your life. You deserve your part."

Kyran didn't know what to say. "Thank you," he finally settled on, carefully tucking the notes away in his purse.

"You're welcome. You eaten yet?"

"Aye," Kyran lied, folding his kerchief to put it away.

Barrett seemed surprised, but he smiled, bobbing his head. "Well, you know where to find me."

In the tavern, drinking, as he had every day since they had returned to the Drunken Wind—and had come staggering into the room too sotted to walk straight more than once. He'd never acted untoward, but Kyran endeavored nonetheless not to sleep while Barrett was in the room.

"Oh." The hunter paused at the door, looking over his shoulder. "Are you going to be working on your amulet today?"

"No," Kyran replied, touching the leather thongs at his hip. Barrett had started asking after the first time when he had apparently mistaken Kyran's power for that of a demon. Kyran still did not quite understand how Barrett's gifts allowed him to sense magic, but he hoped it might be something he could learn with the guild.

"Alright then." Barrett offered another nod and let himself from the room, the heavy shuffle of his step fading down the stairs. But the mage's disquiet did not lessen without the hunter there. He would be back, sotted with drink. Every evening previous, he had simply come up and fallen into bed, but it would only take one time for the man to decide elsewise.

Kyran idled in the room another hour, counting the notes he had been given and going over what he had on his person. It was scant. The money, however, was not, and he quickly compiled a list of what he could use from the market if it could be had. He did not plan to leave the hunter's company, but if he decided to, he wanted to be prepared.

He slipped from the room, locking it behind him with the spare key Barrett had gotten him from the innkeep. He didn't have to take care to be quiet on the stairs. The noise of the patrons more than drowned out the subtle tap of his boots. The place had not remained empty for long after the incident with the demon. Normally the crowd would be more than enough to keep him upstairs, but for once, he was glad for it. It meant he stood a fair chance of slipping out unnoticed by Barrett, especially if the man was deep in his cups.

Steeling his nerves, Kyran ducked his head and made for the door. He looped as far to the left as he could to keep as many people as possible between himself and Barrett's favoured table, ignoring the looks he always garnered on his rare appearances, and pretending not to hear them calling him.

He raised his head as soon as he was beyond the doorway, gulping down a breath of sunlit air in sheer relief as the pressing closeness of the bodies inside released him from its grip. But he did not slow. Stretching his long legs, he put them to use, hurrying down the street until the tavern was long out of sight.

There were plenty of places to buy in the town, but the main market seemed the best choice. Barrett had pointed it out when they'd first arrived. It occupied the open center of the city, hemmed in by an easterly bend in the river, the city's house of worship, and the unusually tall buildings that crowded around the soaring belltower that rang out whenever a demon was discovered. Kyran mused that must be the location of the guild post Barrett frequented.

The market was thronged with people hawking, haggling, and simply talking with one another. There were stalls that seemed to have been built as permanent additions to the square, while some people were selling out of the backs of wagons they had rolled up that morning. Clothing was sold next to food sold next to a pen of young pigs and a stall for jewelry in a dizzying labyrinth of snaking avenues through the crowded square. It was more than a little off-putting, but Kyran grit his teeth around the urge to retreat back to the tavern. He needed these supplies.

Height working to his advantage as he peered over the other people at the vendors' wares, he waded into the crowd, searching for what he needed. But he was not spared the feeling of being surrounded, the mass of bodies closing in around him in a suffocating crush. He felt the stares he was gathering as he moved through the stalls, and heard snatches of conversation about "the Isleman."

At last, he found what he was looking for. Sharing a single stall, a pair of older women eyed him with interest as he approached. "If you're looking for a dress, I don't think we have any in your size, Isleman," one of the women laughed as the other turned to deal with another customer.

Kyran gave her a sour look. "I need thread." He pointed at several spools set out next to a stack of fabric bolts. "How much?"

The woman threw out a price. It sounded like a lot, but Kyran fished in his purse and handed her the closest amount he could to her figure. She took the money without hesitation, examining it before stuffing it into a purse lying on the table behind their goods. "Unusual to see your folk this far south," she said conversationally, slowly counting out his change.

"So I ken," Kyran responded neutrally.

"Are you with the guild, then?"

"Aye," he said, though it was more a half-lie. He was working with Barrett at the moment, who'd allegedly written a recommendation for him. But if all went well, he could very well be a member soon.

"Are there many of you working for them?"

"Come again?"

"Isleish." She prodded the coins in her palm with one thick finger, counting them again. "Heard there was a few more of you a town over in Woodhearth. I thought maybe if you were here on guild business, maybe they were, too."

A pit yawned in the bottom of Kyran's stomach, draining everything but a cold, sick dread from his belly. It couldn't be....It made no sense. They weren't supposed to follow him here. It had to be a coincidence.

"You alright, boy?" the woman asked, holding his change out to him. If it weren't for his dire need, he would have told her to keep it, but it was uncertain where his next bit of coin might come from, so he shook out his kerchief and held it out to her.

Her lips curled in anger, and she retracted the money. "You have a problem with my money? Think I'm dirty?" she accused.

"No, I...." But he had no ready explanation for why he needed the bit of fabric. Why he couldn't stand the feeling of other people's touch, even what was left behind on the things they came into contact with. How it left a palpable mark on his skin.

"You?" she prompted.

"It's just my way," he assured her. "I mean no offense."

She sniffed indignantly, but dropped the coin into his palm. "Brat."

"Thank you," Kyran replied through his teeth, sliding the coins from his kerchief into his purse.

"These Isleish you heard about," he prompted, using the cloth to pick up the spool he had paid for. "You wouldna happen ta have heard what they look like?"

"They're Isleish," she huffed.

"Aye, but what were their colors? Of their cloth?" He pinched the edge of his kilt, lifting it so the woman might catch his meaning, but she only shrugged, her scowl deepening.

"How should I know? I didn't lay eyes on them. If that's all you're buying, why don't you bother somebody else this morning and let the paying customers through?"

She shooed him with one hand, and Kyran obliged her, falling back into the current of bodies moving between the stalls.

But his thoughts remained with her, pinned by her words. The Islemen.... It had to be *them*. In all his weeks in Tennebrum, he had seen only one or two Islemen after he left the port, and none in the last week before he'd arrived in Oareford. It was far too much of a coincidence that a number of his kinsmen should be in the neighboring town now, of all places, and he wasn't in the habit of believing in coincidences.

But how? No, that didn't matter. He should run, keep moving ahead of them until they gave up. They would have to give up eventually. They couldn't chase him forever.

But the demon. The guild.

He swallowed a curse that threatened to fly off his tongue. He would give it another week, stay out of sight. If there was no demon by then, nor word from the guild, he would take his chances on the road again. Perhaps when things were safer, he could make his way to the capital and visit the guild himself to see if Barrett's claims that they would take him were true. For now, the best he could do was stay vigilant and pray against his curse for a change in his luck.

Chapter Fifteen

BARRETT STARED DOWN into his empty cup, frowning. Had it truly been a week? He pushed the cup away, sour with himself. He'd started drinking again to quiet his mind, but it hadn't helped. He couldn't keep from thinking about his sister. She hadn't reached out to him again since he'd gone to her for help, and he was strangely discomfited by that. They had never truly gotten on even halfway to well, but they had always tried, especially after their father had passed.

But things had been different the last few years, after Raleigh had died. Everything had gotten complicated and messy. They lived in the same city, but barely saw one another. But she was all he had left of his family. Maybe he should try to make amends.

"Letter for you."

He blinked from his sleepy stupor, surprised to find a courier at his elbow. It was not Alex, but a young man.

"Thank you," he said absently, taking the letter and turning it over. His spine straightened; the guild seal was stamped into the wax. This could be it. The letter he had been waiting for about Kyran. "It's about bloody time."

He stuck his thumb under the flap of the envelope, peeling the wax up, the glove he had taken to wearing on his right hand making it more difficult. Tugging the letter free, Barrett shook it out and angled it towards the nearest lantern for better light. But as he began to read, the giddiness that had been building at the prospect of telling Kyran he had been accepted fell flat.

Kyran Roche...wanted for crimes in the Northern Isles...ensure the mage does not leave...sending a guild captain with a small company to arrest and escort...to ensure proper relations are secured between countries....

Barrett read over the letter twice more, but the words didn't change. What, by all the Graces, was this?

"Everything alright?" the courier asked.

Barrett snapped his head up, feigning a smile. "Of course," he replied, folding the letter and stuffing it back into the envelope. "Was there any more correspondence?"

The man shook his head. "No, but if anything else arrives, I can send someone your way."

"That's alright," Barrett assured the man, already moving towards the door. "I'll come back by tomorrow morning."

"As you wish."

He read the letter again, but the words made no more sense than the first time. If it was true, this had to be the reason Kyran was in Tennebrum. The real reason. Barrett had suspected Kyran wasn't telling him something, but this....Kyran had to be accused of something serious for the guild to get involved like this, and there were few crimes he could think of that fit the circumstances.

But it didn't make any sense, not for the mage he knew. Why would he...?

He thought of the way Kyran avoided touch, the way he had shoved his bed to the furthest side of the room. How he never seemed to sleep anymore when Barrett was around. Maybe there was another reason.

Barrett's stomach lurched. No. Graces, no, it couldn't be that. The guild would never be involved in something that hideous. Not if it knew.

If.

What was he supposed to do now? It felt like a betrayal to pretend everything was normal until a captain arrived to apprehend Kyran after Barrett had promised to protect him. But to do anything else crossed the guild, which was as good as treason to the Crown. He could lie, tell Kyran to run and explain to whatever captain showed up that the mage had given him the slip and he could not pursue out of obligation to his duties in the town. But there was still the matter of that bloody demon. If Kyran ran, he would be an easy target for that beast. There was no simple answer.

Barrett stuffed the letter in his pocket and ordered a plate of breakfast for the mage before trudging up the stairs with a bowl of porridge and cup of water. He paused outside the door, stalling, listening to the room within. Sometimes, if he was quiet, he could catch Kyran humming or singing in Isleish while he was alone, though it had been quite a few days since he had caught the mage at it. There was no music today, only a soft scratching noise he took to be the mage's whittling.

Balancing the bowl and cup in one hand, he eased the door open. Kyran was seated at the table, his chair turned out, bent over his knees with his knife out and scratching at something in his palm—the whistle, if Barrett were to guess. The mage glanced up as Barrett entered, but otherwise kept at his work.

"I brought you some food," Barrett offered, pushing the door shut behind him with his foot.

"Thank you," Kyran said, blowing on the piece he was working, bits of wood flying out.

Barrett set the food on the table and took the other chair. "Did you sleep alright?"

"Aye, well enough."

"That's good to hear."

Kyran slid his knife back into his boot, tucking the whistle into his purse and drawing his handkerchief out to take his plate. Normally, Barrett didn't mind that Kyran was quiet-natured, but it was almost maddening today. It left Barrett with nothing but his thoughts sounding loudly in the room's silence.

He already knew what he was going to say. He'd known even as he questioned the wisdom of it downstairs. He couldn't abandon Kyran. Hang the consequences. He had already screwed up every other part of his life. If he could do even one thing right to help someone, he would not regret it. The Guild and Crown could fall into the Pit. He wasn't blindly handing Kyran over to whatever power had chased him all the way from the Isles to see him punished for his "crimes." He only hoped Kyran would hear him out.

"Kyran, I got a reply from the guild," he started, reaching into his pocket. He hated how Kyran's face softened as he looked up from his meal in anticipation, hated knowing how that expression was doomed to change in just a few words. "The letter wasn't what I expected. There's...." He faltered, dreading the words even after having made up his mind to speak them. He drew in a deep breath. "There's been a warrant issued for your arrest. The guild is sendin' a captain to collect you."

Kyran's spoon dropped into his porridge, his expression flickering between confusion and something else, something Barrett had not seen on the mage's face even when facing down a demon in the Inbetween. "I have na crossed the guild, that I ken," he said quietly, folding his hands in his lap as he sat up straight in his chair.

"Not the guild," Barrett corrected him gently. "This was sent from the Isles."

His words struck home. Every drop of color drained from Kyran's face, his breath catching audibly for a heartbeat. "I dinnae ken yer meaning," he said a little too quickly, standing abruptly from the table and pacing to his bed on the opposite side of the room.

"I think you do," Barrett pressed, trying to keep his voice gentle.

Kyran did not respond—merely gathered a few small items he'd left on his mattress and put them into his purse, never quite turning his back fully to Barrett.

"I shouldn't be doin' this," Barrett murmured, withdrawing the letter from its envelope and holding it out to Kyran.

"What is that?" Kyran asked, not moving to take the letter.

"The reply to your membership recommendation. You can read it if you want." He set the paper on the table where Kyran could get it.

A faint glow traced beneath the mage's skin. "What does it say?"

"Just that you're wanted for crimes in the Northern Isles. They'll be sending a captain, who will probably brief me more on the situation. I'm not supposed to be tellin' you 'bout this. I'm supposed to be keepin' an eye on you, but I...."

"But ye...?" Kyran prompted him.

"But I don't feel right doin' somethin' like that without knowin' anythin' 'bout what you're accused of. I've only known you a short while, but you don't seem like a criminal to me. Just someone runnin' from some....*thing*. Someone. I thought I would try to talk to you first."

"About what?" Kyran finally looked at Barrett, patterns of light limning his eyes as he met Barrett's gaze squarely. Barrett noticed for the first time just how startlingly green the mage's eyes were. "What is the guild plannin' ta do?"

"I'm not sure," Barrett admitted. "If I had to guess, apprehend and send you back to the Isles."

The faint anger vanished from Kyran's expression, replaced by a naked, sickly fear. "I canna go back," he said, his voice barely audible. "Ye canna make me go back. They'll kill me. Whatever they said is a lie."

"I haven't been told anythin'," Barrett assured him, slowly rising with his hands up. "Look, I can't help you if I don't know what's going on. Maybe I can talk to the guild."

"They willna listen," Kyran insisted, backing away from Barrett until his back nearly touched the wall, the glow of his blood brightening. "They dinnae care what really happened. All they'll see is this bloody curse."

"Kyran, listen to me, please. They're not even here yet." He lowered his hands, watching how Kyran's eyes jumped right to them, then back up at his face. He was terrified, more frightened of whatever was pursuing him from the Isles than he had ever been facing down demons. That alone was proof enough for Barrett that something was not right. "I'm not goin' to do anythin' to you. And I won't make you do anythin'."

"And the guild? Ye said they're sending a captain. That they mean ta arrest me." He lifted his chin, glaring defiantly down at Barrett. "I'll na go with them."

"We'll talk to them. The guild isn't unfair. They will hear your side of things."

"That willna matter if they take me back to the Isles. Stars above, I'd rather face that demon again."

"Kyran, be reasonable," Barrett chided, frustrated and terrified. This wasn't going anything like he'd hoped. He was losing him. He was going to bolt. "It won't matter if you're innocent or not if you won't tell anyone your side of things. I just need somethin'. Anythin' I can use to defend you. You can trust me."

Kyran's eyes hardened, his fear closing behind a mask of stone. "No."

Barrett hadn't known a single word could hurt as much as it did then, but he pushed through the sting, frantic to make the mage hear him. "Kyran, please. You can't run. The guild will send people after you, and there's the demon—"

"I dinnae care, and ye had best na try ta stop me." Kyran lifted a hand, the air chilling noticeably as his blood grew brighter still. "Stay where ye are."

"Kyran, you can't," Barrett pleaded, watching helplessly as Kyran circled him as if he were a mad dog. "It will kill you."

"Then why hasna it come back?" He was almost to the door, groping behind him with his kerchief.

"I don't know. I swear on the Graces, I don't know, but it will come back. Please, don't go." Kyran's hand found the latch, and he pulled the door open, stepping backwards through it. "Kyran!" The door slammed shut between them, the mage's boots breaking into a run over the boards in the hall.

"Graces above," Barrett swore. He only wanted to protect the mage, and now everything was quickly spiraling out of control.

He hesitated to act, caught between decisions. He could chase the mage down and force him to wait for the guild captain, but if Kyran did not want to stay, Barrett wasn't confident he could make him. Not easily. If it came down to a fight between them, it would take everything Barrett had to subdue him, and he couldn't promise it would not hurt the mage. But he couldn't just let him run, either. Not for fear of the guild, but the demon. It was still out there. There was only one thing he could do.

Lurching into motion, he yanked the door open and sprinted after the mage. "Please, let him listen for once," Barrett prayed, flying down the stairs.

Chapter Sixteen

Kyran fled down the street, breaking intermittently into a run as he tried to navigate the winding streets towards the south gate. This had been a mistake. He never should have stayed here, clinging to the delusion that he could become a hunter, that he could be more than just a blood-cursed mage. He shouldn't have believed he could outrun his curse and the laird's unabating wrath.

The street he followed dead-ended. With a curse, Kyran doubled back. He had not seen much of the town, spending his days in the room at the Drunken Wind, keeping his head down, but he knew there was a southern gate opposite the one he had entered Oareford from. He could get there from the center of the town. It would be easier to go back the way he'd come, but that was the direction of the town the other Islemen were rumored to be, and he was not about to tempt his ill luck.

He took a few wrong turns, always doubling back to where he had gone astray, before he could finally make out the River Oare at the center of the town, the market and House just ahead. He should be able to simply follow the river out and—

The lilt of Isleish struck his ear, and Kyran snapped out of his thoughts with a start. He scanned the crowd and quickly found them. There were five, readily distinguishable from the throng around them by their kilts. Two were chatting with a friendly merchant, and another pair held their own conversation in Isleish, but the last—a broad-shouldered man with dark, curly hair—was looking straight at him.

Kyran's heart lodged in his throat, blood pounding in his veins. They did not have to be the laird's men, he reasoned, even as the curly-haired man said something that drew the others' attention, then pointed right at Kyran.

Kyran paled, his gaze fixed on the men's kilts. They could have simply been some of the rare kinsmen that travelled Tennebrum, but he could see their cloth now—they wore Roche colors. They were the laird's lads.

And they had found him.

He fled down the main street, winding through the milling throngs. His mind raced. How had they found him? He was supposed to be safe in Tennebrum. It made no sense to follow him across the Isleish Sea. He was supposed to stay here, beyond their reach, until Dunbar and Connal forgot him, until his da told him it was safe to come home. So why were they here? How had they found him so quickly?

Unless he found someplace to hide, they would chase him out of the city. They had come this far; they were not like to stop just because he had fled the gates. If they captured him, he was as good as dead. They would either kill him on the spot or drag him back to the Isles so the laird or Connal could do it. He had to get away. But where?

Skidding in the muddy road, Kyran took a sharp turn and nearly went down. But he caught himself on one hand and took off again through a narrow throughway, praying he would not hit another dead end. The men were shouting behind him, the sound of their boots pounding in his ears.

The throughway dumped him onto a narrower side street so clogged with people that it nearly brought him to a halt.

"Move!" he shouted, grinding his teeth and shoving through them, the touches scraping like nails across his bones until he was positively writhing in his skin. "Get out of the way!"

"Kyran!"

Kyran shot a glance over his shoulder. The first of the Islemen had exited the throughway behind him, slinging a bow from his shoulder.

"Get on your knees, mage," the man commanded in Isleish, nocking an arrow and aiming straight for Kyran's throat, "or I will help you to."

The people in the crowd screamed, panicking as they tried to get away, but there was nowhere to go in the narrow street. They shoved each other, slipping in the mud, several knocking into Kyran.

But he pushed his way forward, head ducked, nearly toppling into another throughway on the opposite side of the road. He darted around filthy puddles and waste pooling in the deep shadow between the buildings, taking another swift turn as the Islemen entered the throughway behind him.

The back of a building loomed ahead of him. It was a dead end.

Kyran spat a curse, raking his eyes over the buildings, searching for another way. There—a door. If he could force it....

He rammed his shoulder into the door, but it was surprisingly solid. It did not budge. He swore and smashed into it again, kicking it, but to no avail.

"Stop!" The first of the laird's men raced into view.

Kyran whirled around, praying there was another door, but one leg buckled under him in a burst of white-hot pain. He went down with a strangled shout, falling on his belly. He rolled onto his back, clutching his leg. Blood ran over his fingers. The shaft of an arrow protruded from both sides of his calf.

"Stay where you are!" the man barked, slowing and setting another arrow to his bow. The others fell in behind him, several with their blades drawn. They meant to have him, one way or another.

Kyran bared his teeth at the man. He had only two weapons on him, and his little knife wouldn't do him much good against a bow. But his magic....

All his life he had fought for control, struggled to contain his magic so he would not hurt the people around him. He'd sworn to himself that he would never use his magic against people, that it was dangerous—monstrous. Even when he should have, when he needed to protect himself, he'd tried to stay in control, and they had hurt him. Hunted him.

But if he didn't use it now, they would take him back to the Isles, back to Dunbar, and his blood would stain the great hall.

Prying the fingers of one hand from his calf, Kyran let his control loosen. His blood flared bright in the shadows and, with an abrupt crackle, began to freeze on his skin, the pain dimming.

He fixed his sneer on the man with the bow. "Touch me, and you will regret it."

They cursed him, several shrinking back, but the man holding the bow did not recoil. "We were ordered to deliver you alive, but consider this your final warning, mage. Come quietly, or this arrow goes through your heart."

Kyran's sneer turned to a feral snarl, and he let his control slip. The summer-wet air flashed to flakes of white ice. "You can try!"

There was a *twang* of bow string, and a cutting breeze brushed by his cheek before Kyran could even flinch. With a clatter, the arrow skittered across the ground behind him. The man drew another from his hip and nocked it, but his fingers were trembling.

"Dunbar only wants me alive so he can kill me himself," Kyran growled, peeling his hand free of the ice on his leg. Grinding his teeth against the hot stabs of pain in his calf, he rolled to his knees and forced himself up on his good leg.

The man stood his ground. "After what you did to his son? I'd want to kill you too."

Kyran's eyes widened with livid rage. "What *I* did!?" he hissed. "What did they tell you? What lies did they tell you?"

"Stay back," the man warned him again.

Kyran limped a pace towards the cringing men. "Did they tell you what Connal did?" he all but screamed at them. "What he did to me?"

"Just kill him," one of the other men jeered, his mouth twisted in an ugly smirk. "Like his ma shoulda done when he was born."

The air screamed and flashed opalescent white as Kyran's magic ripped from its restraints, his skin burning with light. The archer's arrow slipped from its nock, going wild as he flinched. The others' eyes went round and white, their mouths trembling.

He had never wanted to use his power so badly before. It would be so easy. He had fought demons with it. People were nothing next to those monsters. But he would only prove he was the monster they believed he was, that his ma and da had fought to prove he wasn't.

Again, he spat a curse at the men. Frost spiraled out from his feet in sharp, jagged lines, and they shrank farther back. "Out of my way, dogs," Kyran sneered. They would not touch him.

Kyran took another limping step forward, but the men's eyes moved past him.

A horribly familiar heat rolled across his back, and the sun seemed to blink out of existence. In a single, terrible moment, Kyran knew what loomed behind him.

He whirled, his magic lashing out blindly, and found himself face to face with a demon's eyeless sockets. It hissed with laughter, its breath fogging in the torturous cold of Kyran's magic before its body lit with a bloody red light.

Raw power slammed into Kyran's senses, hammering against him like physical blows. His skull felt like it would shatter, his scream of pain strangled to a whimper as he buckled beneath it.

"All of my planning and hunting," the demon simpered as it reached down and caught his waist with frightening delicacy, drawing him to his feet, "and I never thought you would simply run into my arms."

"Let...go," Kyran panted. He could barely speak; it took all of his focus simply to keep breathing under the weight of the thing's gaze. It was stronger. Oh, stars, it was so much stronger, and it had been hunting him. All this time, it had been waiting. Barrett had been right.

"After all my hard work?" The demon let go of his wrist and traced its long fingers along his cheek, its skin hot and rough with ash. "Never." Its eyes bored deeper into him, the darkness pressing into his lungs, suffocating him.

The mage gaped, straining to pull in a breath, his back arching. "Stop...." he mouthed, his fingers twitching at his sides.

But the demon caressed Kyran's parted lips. "If I had more time...."

It seemed to sigh wistfully when he flinched. Then it lifted him as easily as a child, its other hand catching him beneath his knees. It cradled him against its hot chest, its deep sockets never leaving his eyes.

"There is so much potential," it purred as it leaned down, its needle-filled mouth pressed close to his ear. "I will take good care of you until you ripen."

"No," he choked out as they lurched into motion.

By all the mercy in the Isles, he could not let it take him wherever it was going. It meant to put him in a cage, to keep him there until it decided to eat him. He would sooner die. "Let go of me!"

Kyran writhed beneath the demon's power, draining his magic as he struggled against it. The beast hummed pleasurably to itself, and with almost no effort, it pushed back with its own magic, crushing Kyran's down until his thin gasps were throttled again and his consciousness wavered on a knife's edge.

He could not move, could not think. Every fibre of him strained against the demon's magic. But he wasn't strong enough. He never had been.

Chapter Seventeen

"What in the name of all the Graces?" Barrett swore, racing down the street. This power he felt....It wasn't Kyran. He had been following the mage by tracking his magic, which had proven more difficult than he'd thought. Kyran was fast, and he had gone in anything but a straight line through the town. But this....This felt like more. It felt like a demon.

But that made no sense. It was daytime. The sun was shining bright overhead. The chances one of the beasts had come through even in the dark of a cellar were as likely as the mage was to be someplace like that. Unless it was another hunter. Had the captain made it to town without Barrett being notified yet and run into the mage?

The sensation faded, and the street ahead of him began to churn with excitement, screams and shouts reverberating as people fled from the street over. He dove into the crowd, shoving his way through the pressing bodies. It had to be there. Whatever he had sensed had to be that way. He could only pray he was not too late.

Then, ahead, he saw a flash of cloth: the familiar green, red, and blue striping standing out amongst the dull colors of the common Tennebrumians.

Islemen. They were escaping a narrow throughway between two businesses, their faces white in terror. But what were they doing here? Unless....Were they bounty hunters come ahead of the warrant? Then the magic he'd felt might have been Kyran, after all. Which could mean—

"Please don't let me be too late. Not again," Barrett pleaded, turning down the throughway. It was narrow and dark, barely more than a gap between the buildings. It turned sharply to follow behind the buildings.

Barrett's skin crawled as the hysterics of the departing crowd faded, leaving him with only the sound of his own panicked breaths. It was too quiet. "Kyran!"

Ahead, the backside of a building loomed, blocking the way forward. A dead end. And it was empty.

"No." It could not be. Not again. "Kyran! Please!" he called out desperately, staring into the corners of the throughway, at the doors. Maybe he'd gone through one of them. He could be hiding. "Kyran! You can come out! It's me!"

His eye caught on something—a black stain on the dirt. His stomach lurched as he knelt and touched it. It looked like blood, but it was hard and cold. Frozen.

"Oh, Graces," he swore, clutching his stomach as it threatened to upend itself. Kyran had been here. That had to be his magic. Barrett turned in place, searching for clues as to what had happened, and spotted a faint glint by the nearest wall. His heart sank as he held it up.

Kyran's boot knife. The mage never would have left such a thing behind, and if he wasn't behind those doors, then there was only one place he could be now.

The hunter shut his eyes, trying to recall the pulling sensation his demon showed him that would send him into the Inbetween, but it was much more difficult than he remembered. It must have been the sun, he reasoned, barely keeping from screaming in frustration. If the demon could do it, and dragging Kyran, he could too.

Do not be foolish. His demon's voice thrummed in his awareness without warning, and his skin prickled in alarm. *He will not be there by now.*

"He's somewhere," Barrett snapped back before he could stop himself. Years. His demon had remained dormant for years, and now it had spoken twice. Why?

He shook his unease away. He didn't have time for this. But when he reached for the power, it simply was not there for him to take. His demon was refusing him access.

If it did not eat him outright, the demon will have taken him to our realm.

Barrett faltered.

Raleigh. His limbs chewed off. His handsome face smeared with his own blood and tears. He mouthed at Barrett to run even as the demon set its teeth to his insides. The image had haunted him ever since.

Barrett's stomach heaved again, and he had to clamp a hand over his mouth to keep from losing its contents all over the ground.

He had promised. He had *sworn* he would not let this happen again. Guilt mounted upon guilt until it threatened to drown him. He couldn't do this again. He had lost Raleigh. He could not lose Kyran too, even if it meant going into the demon realm.

No hunter had ever crossed into that realm—or lived to tell about it, if they had. There were no records in the guildhall of such a thing, and no telling what would happen if he were to cross over, if he even could. But if Kyran had been taken there, it was the only way. Even if it meant entrenching himself in his demon's debt even further.

"How do I get there?" Barrett demanded.

The demon was quiet a moment, but Barrett could feel its mixture of amusement and disapproval as well as any words could have communicated. *Even if I pulled you through, he would not be there. The demon will have moved him, and the places our realms touch are ever-changing.*

So he *could* cross over. "Then I will look for him. Take me there. Now."

It is not that simple, the demon disagreed, its patient tone grating at Barrett's nerves. *Our realm is vast and full of other demons. While I am strong, I am not eternally powerful. It would be a fool's errand to search the entirety of our realm for wherever this demon you are looking for nests.*

"Then what do you suggest?" Barrett snarled, his knuckles popping as he clenched his fists. "I am not goin' to just abandon Kyran."

He had a strong sense that his demon was annoyed before it answered again. *Find a demon that knows this one's nest. Your mage will likely be kept for a while, fattened before the feast. You can use the demon to guide you to him. If he is alive, that is.*

"He is!" Barrett hissed.

But rather than responding, the dull pressure of his demon's close presence simply vanished.

"He is," Barrett repeated, staring into the gloom around him. He felt sick at the idea of what he was about to undertake, of what he was racing to prevent. Again. How had he let this happen again?

No. It was too late for that. There was no time to waste on self-pity and -loathing. He would get Kyran back and, so help him, kill the monster that had done this.

He forced himself to turn, to stagger back out of the throughway, as the bells began to ring over the city.

Chapter Eighteen

THE FIRST THING Kyran noticed when he woke was the dark. He blinked consciously, trying to make out more as he slowly returned to awareness. He was lying on his back on something hard, his left leg aching fiercely, and, but for the sound of his own heartbeat and the whisper of his breathing, it was utterly silent.

He lifted a hand to touch his face, trying to discern if his eyes were covered, or even open. They were open; there was simply not a trace of light about him. He let his hand fall onto his stomach, swallowing the frustrated sigh that welled in his chest. He was alive, but where? The last thing he remembered was running from the laird's men when the demon had appeared....

The demon.

His blood turned to ice in his veins. Had the demon brought him here? He loosed his magic, his blood glowing beneath his skin as his hurts eased—the cuts and bruises and, most potently, his calf, becoming distant things—then sat up and took stock of his surroundings. He could not see more than the ground beneath him, a floor of bricks laid precisely in an alternating pattern. The rest was wreathed in darkness. Was this the cage the demon had threatened him with?

He stretched his leg out to examine the wound. To his surprise, his calf had been tended to. The arrow was gone, his boot laid to one side, and it was bandaged, the fabric partly soaked in dried blood. It had to have been the demon's doing. There would have been no one and nothing else to do it.

Kyran shuddered. The notion was more than mildly disturbing. This strange tenderness contrasted sharply against the vicious horror of the beast that had nearly killed him, and which talked so gleefully of eating him.

Wherever *here* was, he had to find a way out. He was not about to wait for the demon to come back. With difficulty, he managed to get to his feet and, using the glow of his blood as his guide, limped forward until he met a wall. It was built of the same strange, ashen stone as the floor, and seemed to bend away into the darkness. Laying one hand against it, he followed the curve. The brick was rough beneath his fingers, neither warm nor cool. He found no doors, no windows, no ladders. No feature of any kind, save for the individual stones. After a while, he determined he must have walked in a circle, but it was impossible to tell. He further loosened his grip on his magic.

The fae light of his blood just barely touched the far wall. The bricks of the floor formed a concentric pattern; he could just make out the flat bottom of a cylinder at least thirty feet in diameter. He strained up into the darkness, at whatever roof formed the top of his cage, but he could see nothing but walls rising upward.

He reasoned he could try to climb out, if it turned out not to have a roof at all. But for his wounded leg, he was a good climber, having spent his childhood living on a *ben*. Even then, it would be no mean feat. The hand- and footholds were small, just mortared cracks between the stone blocks, and he would be essentially climbing blind. One slip, and he would be dead. But it was climb free or wait for the demon to return and eat him.

Kyran quickly removed his other boot and, fitting his fingers into a crevice, began to climb. He made it as far as it took for him to try to use his injured leg. It buckled the moment he tried to put weight on it, his toes slipping, and he landed on his backside with a jarring *thump*. He grit his teeth, hauled himself upright, and tried again, this time without using his bad leg at all, simply tucking it close to the wall.

He did not make it much farther. Without the use of one leg, he was forced to either haul himself up by his arms or make an ungainly hop upward and blindly find the small gaps with his toes. He slipped after only a few feet, his teeth clacking together as he dropped to the floor. Stubbornly, he gave it another go, but this time, he landed on his injured leg.

Kyran clenched his teeth around a scream, clutching his calf as the bandage grew wet again and then hardened with flat crystals of ice as his magic numbed away the throbbing pain.

Glaring at the wall, he cursed in frustration. As much as it galled him, he needed both of his legs as hale as they could be to climb this. He would have to wait and bide his time until his leg was strong enough to climb free. If he was here because of the demon, he did not think it had any intention of killing him just yet, or it would have done so already.

So he hoped, anyway.

But with his mind made up, that left the most difficult task—waiting.

He tried to stay busy, to occupy his thoughts by mapping his escape and exercising his leg, ignoring his growing hunger as the silent hours slowly slipped by. He had no way to mark the passing time in the quiet darkness. He tried climbing the wall again, but his leg would still take no weight, and he could managed no great height. Eventually, he had nothing but his own mind for company.

    Guilt was his first companion in that dark silence. He should have dealt with the Islemen better. He should not have gone pelting off. If he had not been so stubborn about not using his magic, he could have dealt with them easily. They were just men. He should have been able to handle them on his own. If he'd just killed them, the demon would not have been able to reach him. They were going to do the same to him anyway, either then or when they took him back to Laird Dunbar. And there was only one punishment for the accusations Connal was likely making, if men had come all the way to southern Tennebrum to hunt him down.

    "What am I thinking?" he muttered aloud. Kill them? Stars, he was going out of his head. He didn't want to kill anyone. He just wanted to be left alone. To live in peace, like anybody else. Why could he not have that? Why did he have to be born under this curse?

    A muscle along his jaw fluttered in anger. While he was asking questions, why had Connal done any of this? Why was he so obsessed with Kyran that he'd sent people this far to hunt him down?

    And what of this demon? Why did it want him so badly? Kyran felt like a *connie* with hounds at his heels, chasing him into the fox's jaws. Why did he always have to be so weak?

    He tried to resist, but eventually he gave into the mounting exhaustion and slept. It was far from restful, haunted by eyeless sockets and grasping, choking hands, and he woke slumped onto his side, clutching his arms. After resting a while longer, he made himself get up again, testing his leg gingerly. It would hold no weight; he was reduced to hopping slowly on his one good leg along the wall. But anything was better than simply sitting and waiting

    Pacing his prison, Kyran examined the walls again by the light of his lines, tracing his fingers down the ridges and lines of the bricks, deciding where it might be best to try to climb up when he was ready. The walls were mostly uniform, but there were a few irregularities—places where the bricks didn't quite meet right, cracks, and missing grout—places he might be able to make use of.

    When he grew too tired to keep hobbling along, he leaned back against the wall and sat. He touched his hip, searching for his purse, but it was gone, along with his kerchief and amulets. So he folded his hands, tracing the lines of the sun into his palm with his thumb before he whispered a prayer into the dark, asking the Light to guide him out of this place.

    He let his hands drop into his lap, intending to simply rest a while again, but he quickly nodded off. It was no more restful than his first attempt, and again he jolted awake from eyeless nightmares only to face the same silent darkness that made up every waking moment. There was no wind, no animal sounds—nothing but the pulse of his own heart in his ears.

Getting up, he paced the prison again, letting the pain of his wounded leg distract him until he had to sit down. Still, he waited. A nameless, restless anxiety began to creep through him. What if the demon intended to leave him here to waste? It didn't make any sense after everything it had said, and after it had proven so powerful, but he could not help but consider it. It was possible the demon could have been killed after bringing him here, too, by another demon or a hunter. Maybe even Barrett. What then? Would he just die down here? Starve to death? Or this could be his eternal punishment—imprisonment alone in his own special place in the Pit, with a lame leg to keep him from escaping.

Kyran tried to consider if that was better or worse than being eaten alive, and simply found himself growing angry. He did not want to die down here or spend his death trapped eternally here. After everything he had ever been through, this was wrong. He did not deserve to be here, trapped in some dark hole, waiting to either starve or be eaten—along with the prospect of being dragged back to his country and killed for the crime of defending himself should he manage to escape.

It wasn't fair. Not that life had ever been fair to him. This was just one more cruelty in the string of bitter circumstances that collected together to form the tale of his life. Where was the justice in that?

Of course, he of all people should have known there was no justice in the world for him. His curse saw to that.

There was a soft scrabbling noise from far above—claws on stone.

Kyran pressed his back into the wall, straining to see, his heart pounding. At last something was happening. It sounded too large to be some manner of vermin, if there were any in this realm. It had to be a demon.

But was it the same demon, or a different one? If it were a different one, perhaps he could subdue it and make it take him back to the human realm. Clenching his control tightly around his magic, he dimmed his lines as much as he could without his injured leg throbbing. He touched his hip out of habit, but the comforting leather thongs of his amulets were gone.

The scratching grew closer as whatever it was climbed down the walls of his prison towards him, and he bit back a swear. The noise halted several yards from the floor. Then something landed with a soft *thud* on the far end of the circle. A sour, meaty smell wafted to him, and his stomach growled hungrily despite himself. Cautiously, he loosened his magic, letting his blood brighten until he could make out the familiar silhouette crossing the prison in long, elegant strides.

His captor.

Kyran pressed his back more firmly into the stones, his breath coming faster. It was finally here. But what did it want?

Lines of bloody scarlet brightened beneath the demon's ashen skin, illuminating its eerily almost-human form while drawing Kyran's eye to the too-long, spidery-thin limbs, and its eyeless, human face split by a mouth far too large and crammed with black, needle-like teeth. It carried between its clawed hands a lump of flesh the size of a melon, which sizzled audibly. Juices dripped between its fingers as heat shimmered from its palms.

"Hungry, pet?" It stalked closer, pinching into the meat and pulling off a piece. It tossed it towards its prisoner, making an amused noise. The steaming bit landed near Kyran's boot.

He eyed the lump of meat, his stomach growling with hunger, but did not reach for it. He was starving, but there was no telling what the demon had brought him, and he was not keen on accepting a meal from a beast that meant to eat him.

"Humans require sustenance more often than demons, yes?" the demon curmurred, untroubled by his silence. "Sometimes two or three times a day. Hungry beasts." Its lipless gash of a mouth spread even wider, baring its teeth in a hideous smile. "It has been longer than one of your human days. Surely you are ready to eat."

Looking away from the piece of meat, Kyran instead fixed his glare on the beast's empty sockets, his chin lifting in silent defiance. He would not be mocked, either.

"Such pride," it simpered, coming closer.

The heat of its body washed over him. The demon shifted the large chunk of meat to one hand and stopped just a few yards away, extending like some grotesque gift.

Even this close, Kyran could not tell what sort of animal the meat had come from, strengthening his suspicion. It was difficult to make out the proper color of the meat in the contrasting lights of his and the demon's magic, but it looked dark, and it smelled off, as if it had been allowed to spoil slightly before being roasted.

"What is it?" he asked.

The demon leaned forward, its offering inching towards him, but he turned his head away.

"Stubborn mageling," the demon scolded, amused. "It is demon flesh, to make you stronger. And I will *make* you eat if you will not on your own."

Kyran's lip curled in a sneer, and he told the demon in Isleish exactly what it could do with the meat. He would not touch demon flesh.

The creature's mouth twitched. Without warning, it snatched his shirt and belt and shoved him down onto his back. He kicked at the beast, his magic biting at its flesh, but its skin only glowed more brightly, resisting his cold as it crouched over him. The air turned to suffocating heat.

"Excellent idea," it replied, to Kyran's surprise, in slow, husky Isleish. It knelt over the mage and grabbed his jaw tight. Jerking his head, the demon squeezed painfully until his mouth was forced open, utterly unconcerned by his clawing at its fingers. It clenched the meat in its other hand and pulverized it, turning it to mush. "I will feed you like the stubborn child you are."

He tried to catch its hand, but it shoved right through his grip and crammed a handful of meat into his mouth. It had a strange texture, at once both softer and stringier than any meat he had ever eaten. Its taste was just as hard to describe, something like pork, but with a disturbing bitterness to it, as if laced with something poisonous.

Before he could cough or spit it out, the demon's hand closed over his face, covering his mouth and nose. His chest pitched with an unrealized gasp, and he twisted in the thing's grasp, trying to free himself to draw a breath. One of its thumbs stroked his bare throat, and, horrified, he felt his throat move in a reflexive swallow.

"Good," it purred, finally letting him go and running a moist finger over his cheek as he coughed, sucking down air. "Not so bad, is it, pet?"

Kyran glared up at the beast. The demon gripped his jaw again and held the remaining wad of meat near his mouth.

"Do not fight me again, or this time I will not be so gentle in forcing it down your throat."

But he would not be so docile as to let it do what it wanted with him. It might have taken him against his will and imprisoned him here, but it would not make him eat demon flesh.

Spitting an Isleish curse at the beast, Kyran grabbed the demon's wrist and yanked it from his chin. Turning his face defiantly away, he jammed his fingers down his throat. His stomach heaved, and he vomited, gagging as the meat came back up and splattered wetly across the bricks in a sour mess.

"You ungrateful half-breed!" the demon roared.

Kyran sneered up at it and spat a mouthful of bile in its face. It drew back a hand and cracked him across his cheek. Fire shot through his skull as his head snapped to one side. The demon seized him and wrenched his mouth open again.

"I find the most palatable breed of demon, and this is how you repay me?" It shoved more of the meat between his teeth, but this time, it jammed its fingers into his mouth and forced the food roughly past his tongue and down his throat. He gagged violently, but it simply shoved more down, over and over, giving him no room to breathe, no time to vomit, until every scrap of flesh was gone.

Finally, it released him and watched him roll onto his side, clutching his throat and gasping for air. He squeezed his eyes shut, his throat burning, his head pounding—and immediately stuffed his own fingers down his throat and vomited again, bringing up every scrap of meat he could from his stomach. He did not stop until he was dry heaving and there was nothing left to come up.

Kyran wiped his mouth and sat up, cradling his aching head, squinting into the dark. But the demon was no longer there. He managed to get to his feet and hobble slowly away from the foul-smelling mess.

His belly ached, and his throat was painfully raw from the vomit and the demon's rough treatment. But he had done it. He had resisted the beast. It was not much of a victory, but it brought a fierce grin to his face nonetheless. He would rather starve than allow himself to eat demon flesh, and he had proven that the creature could not make him. If it wanted him to live, it would bring him other food, or he would starve.

Once he was far enough away that he could not smell the mess as strongly, he collapsed against the ground, curling into himself, and quickly passed into an exhausted, restless slumber.

Chapter Nineteen

No demons. Not even a rumor of demons in the entire city for three days now. Any other time, Barrett would bless his luck for such an uncommon occurrence, but now....Of course it would only happen when he was looking to find a demon—any demon capable of understanding threats. The land outside the city offered him little in the way of improving his odds. The surrounding countryside had been flat farmland for generations now, with only the spare tree here and there. He would find no deep copse to bury himself in to hunt for them. He could only continue what he had been doing: searching cellars and sealed attics every night and even past dawn for any trace of the beasts and drawing on his power to attract their attention, should any be lurking Inbetween.

And he would still be looking now if it weren't for the necessity of food. Fortunately, with food came drink, and with enough drink came forgetting—at least for a little while. Dragging his heavy feet, he summoned up a small feeling of gratitude at the sight of the heavy steins lined up behind the bar of the Drunken Wind, already imagining the smooth taste of mead.

"Hunter Barrett."

Barrett let his eyes fall shut at the calm, familiar voice. Here? Now? He must have truly angered the Divine Light.

Opening his eyes again, a man he recognized was sitting at his accustomed table.

He looked the other man up and down. The man's black hair had been swept back from his face, drawing the eye to the flat plane of his cheeks and dark, almond-shaped eyes. His skin was pale, though not in the same way Kyran's skin was naturally pale. His looked a bit more sickly, as if he had spent far too much time indoors, away from the sunlight, an image not helped by the lean frame beneath his well-tailored but practical clothing.

"Since when have you been a captain?" Barrett demanded wearily.

"Quite recently," the man replied, getting to his feet and offering him a hand. He came only up to Barrett's chin.

Barrett traded grips out of forced politeness. The man's dry skin scratched against Barrett's glove, and the sensation of the captain's demon pressing faintly against Barrett's awareness.

"Does that make you Captain...?"

"Griswold," the man replied as their hands parted, "yes."

Barrett inclined his head with just enough deference to pass for curt politeness. He had known the man during his time at the guildhall, more by reputation than in person. Griswold was well known for his extensive knowledge of the guild and Crown laws, to the point that even the guildmaster had consulted him more than once. He had also been Katherine's partner in the field when she had possessed the family amulet.

"You're who they sent for Kyran?" Barrett accused as the captain took his seat again.

"Along with a number of Crown guardsmen who are currently enjoying the fruits of another establishment," Captain Griswold replied, folding his hands neatly in his lap. "So, to address matters at hand, where may I locate the mage you contacted the guild about?"

Barrett's nails dug into his palms, his leather glove creaking. Of course that was all they cared about. "I couldn't tell you."

If he was surprised, the captain didn't show it. "What do you mean?"

"I mean," Barrett said, his voice breaking as he choked down a near-hysterical laugh, "if I knew where to go to get him back, I would have gone and done it already instead of scroungin' through other people's musty cellars all day and night lookin' for one of the bloody beasts to guide me."

The man leaned forward, setting his forearms on the table as he said in a perfectly neutral tone, "I am afraid I do not follow."

"I'm not surprised," Barrett scoffed, ploughing a hand through his mess of unkempt hair. "It's insane, I know, but I don't have a better idea right now."

"I will need you to explain," Captain Griswold insisted, gesturing to a chair across from him. "Please, sit."

"Only if you let me buy my drink first," Barrett demanded. "And you might as well buy your own. You'll need it by the end."

"I will pass."

Barrett shrugged. He didn't much care one way or the other if the captain drank. It wasn't for him. "Suit yourself."

He went to the counter, signaled for one of the barmaids, and ordered a cup of mead. The sweet drink had always been his preference. It was just a coincidence that it also happened to get him drunk quicker. Sipping at the mead, he slowly made his way back to the table. The idea of lying to the captain occurred to him for a brief moment before he dismissed it. There was no point. The story was so ludicrous, he wasn't even certain the captain would believe him anyway.

Taking his seat again, Barrett started his tale without preamble, beginning in the village where he had met Kyran and concluding with the chase through the city and his plan to find another demon. He reclined in his seat, watching as the captain processed the information. But if Captain Griswold felt anything at all at Barrett's story, he did not betray it, his head ducked in the same position he had assumed to listen to Barrett.

"It's the same thing it did before," Barrett pointed out, signaling for the barmaid to fetch him another cup. "I'm sure it's the same demon."

The captain nodded, finally lifting his head, a faint crease forming between his brows. "And you are certain about these other Islemen? That they pursued Kyran here in the city?"

"I saw them with my own eyes comin' out of that alley, and everyone I asked said they had seen Kyran running from 'em." He paused as the barmaid returned with his drink, and swallowed a mouthful. "They had their weapons drawn. That sort of thing tends to stick with folks."

"Do you think you could describe them?"

Barrett shook his head. "I wasn't exactly looking for them when I crossed them. They were wearing the same sort of garb Kyran wears, but so do any other Isleish, I imagine. They were bigger men, most of them." He shrugged, his memory failing to produce anything else that might be even remotely useful.

The captain nodded again, tapping a finger against the back of his other hand. "I believe that will be all I need from you at the moment," he said at last, rising from his seat. "See that you do not attempt to leave town. Wherever this mage has gone, you are now the last known person holding guild authority to have contact with a known fugitive. If I cannot prove that your story is true, you will be held responsible for his escape. Additionally," he continued over Barrett's protest, "if your story does prove true, I will need to make arrangements with the guild to find someone to temporarily take your position here so you may return with me to the guildhall to make an official statement for the Crown regarding the loss of said fugitive."

"And what about the demon?"

"I can have a description of it drafted and sent to the guild library. The scholars may be able to enlighten us on other instances this demon has been spotted. They can also have a general warning sent out to the other hunters to keep a wary eye out for it."

"But what about my idea?"

"It is foolishly reckless." The captain's voice dropped, and Barrett felt an unnatural press against his ears, as if someone had clapped their hands over them. "No hunter has crossed into their realm, or, if one has, he did not return. Our numbers are shrinking as it is. We cannot afford such a risk."

"Of losin' me, or this?" Barrett sneered, grabbing the amulet beneath his shirt.

"Both, of course."

"Of course," he scoffed. He didn't know what else he'd expected. Of course the guild wouldn't care about Kyran outside of what they needed to fulfill orders. They did not even care about Barrett, so long as they didn't lose the ability to inflict this miserable life upon someone else. As long as the amulet and dagger were passed on to someone else to carry on killing demons for them, they did not care who carried it.

"Should I require more information, I will find you. But be prepared to leave as soon as two weeks from now to travel to the capital." Griswold paused, as if expecting Barrett to object, but he had nothing to say to the captain. As if the man would listen. "May your lanterns stay lit, then," Griswold said in parting, waiting another beat for Barrett to complete the other half of the blessing before he took his leave. The pressure against Barrett's ears disappeared as the captain passed him.

Barrett stared into his cup. Two weeks. He had two weeks before the captain dragged him to the capital. He could run, of course, but where would he go? How would he escape? Captain Griswold would be able to sense him, and even if he managed to get far enough away to escape him, all the guild would have to do was put out a warrant, and they would come for him. He wasn't even safe outside of Tennebrum, as the guild's power extended to every known country where demons could be found. Except the Isles, apparently.

No, he couldn't run. But that was fine. All it meant was that he had two weeks to find this demon by himself. If they wouldn't help him, then he would just keep searching on his own. And he would find the demon. Even if he had to claw his way into the Pit itself.

Chapter Twenty

Kyran was unsure how long the demon stayed away. He felt as if he were coming to after a night of far too much ale. His throat was raw, his mouth dry, and his head pounded. When he tried to limp his way across the space, his steps were uneven, faltering as he attempted to cross the vast emptiness in the middle of the circle. He ignored it all, stretching his injured calf as he circled his pen again, trying to build a mental map of where the irregularities in the wall were, counting his limping steps, then counting the bricks. Anything to distract his mind until he felt tired again and lay down to sleep.

This time, he was woken by his stomach cramping hungrily. His head felt as if someone were taking a hammer to the inside of his skull. He curled in tight, hugging his belly as it growled and gurgled, willing it to stop its noisome complaining. He only had to hold out long enough to escape. He had gone without food for extended periods of time before.

But as time passed, Kyran began to realize that without food or, more importantly, water, he was rapidly growing too weak to escape. It became an effort to sit up, to even hold his head upright, and after a while, he simply lay curled on the ground, his head pillowed against his arms as it pounded, his throat parched, the floor seeming to tilt and wobble beneath him. Still the demon did not return. Apparently it intended to let Kyran keep his promise, and he knew, someplace in his thoughts, that he would not survive much longer like this.

That was fine, Kyran decided at last. He would starve. He would starve before he submitted to that beast's will like some broken pet. Lumen would understand.

He declined rapidly after that, his mind made up. He simply waited, drifting in and out of consciousness, too weak to do more than lay on the ground and stare into the dark, listening to his own pulse and hoarsely whispered prayers.

Kyran wondered faintly what Barrett was doing. Had he worked out what had happened, or assumed Kyran had left? If he'd even tried to find him.

He began to imagine the hunter appearing from the dark, having fought his way down to this realm to find him, dagger in one hand, the other extended to Kyran to pull him up the wall. Sometimes it was his da, finally come to tell him he could go home.

But after each imagining, when he opened his eyes to the same bleak, grey stone, he knew help was not coming. He would not see Barrett again, or his family. Not outside what his imagination could dream up while he lay waiting to fall into a sleep he would not wake from.

The muffled wailing of a *bairn* drew him from his dreaming. He cracked his eyes open, baffled, and started when he found the demon standing before him, cradling a wee lass against its body. She was dressed in tattered, filthy rags, her dark hair matted to her head, and her skin caked with dirt and other, unmentionable things. The demon had one clawed hand clamped over her mouth, clutching her to its chest, but he could still hear her desperate, frightened whimpers. Her dark, canted eyes ran with tears. In its other hand, the demon held a fresh chunk of meat.

The beast tossed the lump of sizzling meat to him. It rolled to a stop just in front of his face, the pungent, sour smell of it wafting thickly to him, drawing a painfully nauseous growl out of his stomach.

"Eat," the demon commanded.

"What are you doing with that lass?" Kyran croaked in alarm, his voice barely a whisper through his dry, raw throat. His head pounded as he sat up, pressing his back to the wall.

The demon ran a long, black tongue over the lass's face, chuckling through its thicket of teeth in Kyran's direction. "You have a fondness for children, do you not? I saw how you protected the last you stole from me."

Wrapping its free arm around her middle, the demon grabbed the lass's hair and pulled, exposing her frail neck. It opened its parody of a mouth and sank its teeth into her shoulder.

"No!" Kyran shouted. Stars, no—it was going to kill her! He staggered to his feet, stumbling forward as the lass jerked and screamed until the demon pulled its teeth free and backed away from Kyran, its dark sockets fixed on the mage all the while.

"Eat," it repeated. "Or I will eat her."

The lass sobbed, blubbering in pain and fear, and the sound of it ate at him. Anything. He could withstand anything else the demon could do to him but this. He could not stand to see *weans* hurt.

Kyran let his wavering balance take him to his knees. His wounded leg spasmed painfully. "No." His voice was broken. "Dinnae hurt her."

"All you have to do is eat," the demon replied evenly, its black tongue lapping at the lass's shoulder. "If you behave, maybe I'll even let you keep her for a while."

Kyran looked from the demon to the hunk of flesh. He'd sworn he would starve before he ate demon flesh willingly. He looked up again—not at the demon, but at the frightened lass, her filthy face scrunched up in pain and streaked with tears.

Slowly, grinding his pride beneath reason, he reached for the greasy meat. Picking it up, he pinched a strip off, placed it in his mouth, and swallowed without chewing. It was savoury and bitter. His empty stomach clenched painfully around it.

The demon brushed its teeth against the lass's wounded shoulder, drawing a shrill sob out of her. "All of it," it hissed.

He pulled off another piece, put it in his mouth, and swallowed. Then another, his eyes never leaving the demon. His heart hardened with hate as he peered into its empty, sneering sockets. It knew it had won a victory over him and forced him to do something he resented with every fibre of his being. But if this was what it took to save the lass, then fine. He would do it. He would eat whatever that beast brought him. But he would spend every waking second trying to escape and kill it.

The demon watched him take every bite until the meat was gone. His stomach ached from the sudden burden, but he kept it down, waiting for the beast to let the lass go.

"Good, pet," the demon whispered, wrapping a hand around the lass's throat. She let out a panicky wheeze, her tiny hands flying up to clutch at its fingers.

Kyran's eyes went wide. "Stop!" He lurched back to his feet, clutching his stomach as it cramped around the greasy, sour meat, his magic flaring brightly. "Put her down!"

"Do you want her that badly?" it purred, its fingers flexing around her throat. "Let me hear you beg for her."

He could not believe what he was hearing. "What?"

"I will not repeat myself."

The lass continued to gasp, struggling more and more as it craned her head back.

"If you do not want her, I will have my fill. Her owner did not satisfy my hunger."

Kyran's lips peeled back from his teeth. *Beg.* His already wounded pride ached, but he had no choice. He would do this, or the demon would kill her. Fine. It would only make its death sweeter when he escaped.

"Please." The word was bitter on his tongue, but it was spoken.

"*Beg.*"

His eyes narrowed at the beast, the air around him shocked with cold. "I beg you," Kyran said carefully, a muscle fluttering just beneath his eye, "let her go."

"Again." It tilted its head, hand unmoving, and the lass began to still, the fight leaving her limbs. "On your knees, pet."

There was a loud pop, and a crack appeared in the bricks under Kyran's feet, sharp white crystals of ice spearing up from them. It was mocking him with a lass's life in its hands. His pulse throbbed in his veins as he wished every hateful thing he could on the beast. He was not going to just kill it. When he got free, he was going to hunt this demon down and tear it apart.

Slowly, he dropped to his knees again, no longer able to feel his injured leg, one hand over his aching stomach. "Please," he said again, grinding the words out through his teeth, "I beg you. Let her go."

Finally the demon released its grip on the lass. She dropped to the ground at its feet, landing in a heap with a hoarse gasp.

"If you spit out any food or refuse to eat again, I will kill her," the demon threatened.

Kyran watched it go in frigid silence, following its glowing red lines as it climbed up the walls. For the first time, he caught a glimpse of the top of his prison. There was no roof, only a wide aperture far, far above, showing only more darkness beyond.

A wave of exhaustion swept down on him, and he slumped onto his backside, catching himself on his hands. His stomach was cramping in earnest now, but, wary of the demon's warning and unconvinced it had left entirely, he endured.

The lass had gone when he looked to her again. He could hear her, the scuffle of her movements and her quiet, coughing whimpers in the dark, startlingly loud after however many days or hours of utter silence he had endured thus far.

"Lass!" he called into the dark, voice cracking. She did not call back or reappear. He supposed he could not blame her after what had happened, but he needed to find her. She was hurt, and while there was not much he could do to help her, he could at least bandage the wound. He limped forward, searching, until he nearly stumbled over her.

She was curled against the wall, her back pressed to the ashen bricks, the tattered remains of her filthy dress tucked over her legs. Her skin was so stained with dirt and filth that she was almost indistinguishable from the bricks. She had dark, almost black eyes canted in a delicate almond shape on her small, round face. They were stretched wide in obvious fear, their whites shot with red as she stared up at him through her stringy, overgrown bangs. The rest of her long black hair was matted in soiled snarls around her head.

"It's alright," he called in rasping Isleish. "I won't hurt you."

She said nothing in return, only stared up at him. He took a limping step closer, and she let out a low, terrified whimper. He stopped where he was, whispering more lilting Isleish as if soothing a spooked horse.

How long had she been here, in this realm, with these creatures? It was loathsome enough for him. He could not imagine what it would be like for a *wean*, stolen from her home by one of these monsters, kept like some unwholesome pet. Or cattle.

He choked down his anger, not wanting to scare the lass. He would get out of here. He would get them both out of here, and that creature would pay dearly for what it had done.

"I willna hurt you," he tried to reassure her, switching back to Common. He was not certain if she understood him, but he hoped she might understand at least his tone. She did not look like anyone he'd ever met, either in the Isles or in Tennebrum. She must have been stolen from some other distant country that did not speak Common.

As she picked her head up to look at him, her eyes brimmed with tears. She made the same, low whine, but did not move as he laboriously knelt by her. Pulling the hem of his shirt free, he grasped at his calf out of habit, but found no knife waiting there. The blade was gone—lost—and the sudden reminder it was not there was a blow to his gut. His da had given it to him when Kyran had left home to live on the mountain. The handle was carved from the antler of a stag Kyran had killed as a lad. He'd treasured it. And now it was gone—one more thing stolen from him.

He clenched his jaw, pushed his finger through a place his shirt had worn thin, and yanked, tearing the hem. Tightening his control on his magic, he leaned towards the lass. It was harder to see with his lines so dim, but he did not want to risk hurting her.

She cringed at his touch, but he was able to see her wounds well enough this close. One of her small hands was pressed against her shoulder, half-hiding the ugly, uneven punctures from the demon's bite and the red, blistering skin between where it had burned her. She did not appear to be bleeding from the bite, which seemed unusual, but it would still need bandaging. Kyran had nothing to clean the wounds with, though, and it seemed likely they might putrefy. His jaw clenched again. She did not deserve this. She was just a *wean*. Innocent. The beast would pay for this.

Gently, he pulled her hand away from the shoulder and laid the makeshift bandage over her wound, trying not to hear the frightened whimpers as they became soft, pained cries while he wound the cloth around her shoulder and arm. He murmured a prayer softly in Isleish, trying to soothe her before he finally tied the cloth off and let her go. She clutched her shoulder again, sniffling softly, and scampered off into the dark.

Shifting from his knees to sit against the wall, he let her go, expecting her to run off into the dark again. She was scared, but at least she was alive.

"I'm sorry, lass," Kyran offered, though he was not certain she could hear him. "I willna do it again." He let his head fall back, eyes closing as exhaustion began to grip him again. It was unfair that he should still get tired in this place, or hungry, when he could not even tell how long he had been awake.

He drifted in and out of consciousness, not quite awake but not quite asleep, until something pressed against his side. He jerked fully awake, lifting his arm to find the lass huddled against him, her tiny form trembling, her breath coming in short sniffles, though he could not tell if it was from fear or the cold of his magic.

"I dinnae ken if I would stay there, lassie," he murmured, uncertain what to do. "My magic is like ta freeze you."

But the girl did not move away, instead curling closer. It reminded him of the way his wee brother Tavish had reacted when he had come home for the first time after going away to Cairngorm. He could hardly do anything without the lad clinging to his side.

Kyran lifted his hand and awkwardly set it atop the lass's head, trying to comfort her. Her dirty hair was oily to the touch. She wriggled against him, as if to get closer, and a tiny hand reached up and grabbed his, gripping it with surprising strength. His fingers curled around hers, and he tightened his control over his magic until his blood hardly glowed at all. The ache in his leg instantly began to throb, but he endured it.

It was not long before the lass fell slack against him, her breaths slowed to a gentle rhythm. A glance revealed her eyes shut, tears still wet on her cheeks. He brushed them away with his thumb, and she did not stir a hair. A smile crept across his features, and his resolve strengthened. He would get out of here, if for no other reason than to ensure she was free of this place.

Chapter Twenty-One

Barrett watched with bitter disappointment as the creature beneath him dissolved into ash. Nothing. He had finally caught one of the beasts after days of searching, and it had given him nothing, no more intelligent than some wild animal.

Jamming his dagger back into its sheath, he stood and hurried towards the fires burning in the House's gardens. The captain was there, his attention focused on controlling the flames closest to the House's walls, but the fire had spread everywhere within the low stone walls. Under the crackle of flames and steady ringing of the guild's bell, a buzzing drone filled the air as bees, disturbed by the fire that had destroyed their food and boxes, swarmed furiously above their ruined hives. An older man in Lightbringer's robes and two other figures dressed in acolytes' garb frantically ran to and from the back door, carrying buckets of water to douse the flames.

"Are there more?" Barrett asked the man, pointing at the bucket.

"Yes! Yes, here!" The older man thrust the bucket into Barrett's hands. "Hurry—before we lose them all!"

It didn't take long to put the fires out with all of them working together. Even then, over half of the House's bee boxes had burned, and many of the planting beds, but the House itself was only minimally scarred by the flames.

"Thank you," the old Lightbringer exclaimed, clutching the guild members' hands in turn, giving Barrett a chance to finally look the man over. He was small, standing only as high as Barrett's chest, and balding, dressed in the traditional orange frock. A yellow teacher's stole with the single flame stitched on the bottom hung over his shoulders. "Thank you for your help."

"If there's nothing more we can do, I must be going." Captain Griswold said.

"Oh, but you must stay!" the man insisted, looking between them both. "I was just about to put supper on, and we could always use the company."

"I must be off," the captain insisted, "but I thank you for the offer."

"If you must," the Lightbringer surrendered graciously. "You have done this House a great service, both of you."

"It is our duty, Lightbringer." Griswold bowed his head, then, addressing Barrett, continued, "I will make the necessary reports at the post. You need not attend."

Barrett nodded, offering no other reply as the man excused himself one last time and left the garden. Barrett had nothing to say to the man who continued to hang around Oareford, but made no discernible effort to help him hunt down the demon that had taken Kyran, spending his days in the guild post writing letters and doing who knew what else.

"And what about you?" the Lightbringer asked Barrett.

The hunter smiled politely, not wanting to hurt the man's feelings, but wasn't certain he could in good faith accept the offer. He needed to keep looking, and, after all he had done, he was fairly certain he shouldn't be welcomed in any House of Light.

But when he started to make his excuses, the man interrupted. "Please, you must let me thank you," he implored. "It is rare for me to have the opportunity to break a meal with anyone other than my acolytes."

"I can't," Barrett said, looking up at the House's high roof. It was the largest building in the town, for certain, with elegant, high-arched windows blazing with lantern light, built to catch the morning and evening sun. But it paled in comparison to the Houses in the capital.

"Well, if you are not hungry, perhaps you would like a nip of my special medicine, hm? I've a batch ready in the kitchen as we speak. You can be in and out in a moment, if you choose. It will keep you warm while you hunt. Please. It would warm this old man's heart if you'd let him."

The man's smile was infectious, and as much as he didn't want to, Barrett surrendered with a good-natured sigh. There was no point in hurting the man's feelings. If another demon did rise in town, he would sense it before the bell tolled anyway.

"I cannot stay long," he relented.

The old man's smile broadened. "Ah, thank you. Come. Follow me. There's a much more wholesome fire inside we can warm ourselves at."

He led Barrett around the corner of the House to where a door stood ajar, letting firelight out into the garden to mingle with the lanterns' glow. Warm air smelling of dried herbs and baking bread rolled over Barrett as the man tugged it open, and he had to stop and take a deep breath. Nostalgia for his childhood—and the future he had once imagined—settled, warm and comfortable, in his thoughts.

"Nothing like it, hm?"

Barrett opened his eyes. The Lightbringer was pulling a fresh loaf from the fire, setting it on the table to cool.

"I have always enjoyed the kitchen," the old man said. "There is something satisfying about making something with your own two hands and then being able to enjoy it with others."

"There is," Barrett agreed, stepping in and pulling the door to behind him. It was a small kitchen, made even smaller by the wooden table in its center, providing additional space to prepare food. Every square inch of the place was spotlessly scrubbed and stacked high with neatly organized supplies. A rack of drying herbs and mushrooms was suspended from the peaked beams above, and there were a few plates and bowls tucked away there to make more space.

"Oh, how rude of me," the man muttered to himself, wiping his hands on his robes before thrusting one at Barrett.

It was gnarled with age, the earth-toned skin stained with ink and small scars that covered the fingers and palm like ripples in his skin. Barrett knew the type well: old burn scars. His grip was firm against Barrett's leather glove, his crooked fingers surprisingly strong.

"I am Lightbringer Horn, though you are more than welcome to simply call me Myles. I find formalities this far from the capital a bit stiff."

Barrett ducked his chin sheepishly. "My apologies, Myles. It has been a while since I've used my manners. I'm Kristopher Barrett."

The Lightbringer only chuckled. "I understand that far too well myself. It is good to meet you, Kristopher."

Kristopher. That took him by surprise. It was strange to hear his full first name. He had largely gone by "Barrett" for years to avoid being called by the same name as his father, bastard that he was. Only his sister called him Kris.

"But you aren't here to listen to an old man ramble. I do like to hear myself talk." The Lightbringer chuckled, plucking a wooden cup from the table. "Please, sit wherever you like."

Despite his earlier protests, Barrett accepted the offer, settling on a stool with a long groan.

"That sounded refreshing," Myles laughed, bending in front of a barrel by the fire and pouring a drink from it.

"Oh, it was," Barrett agreed, setting his hands on his knees. He had not realized how tired he was, but now the days of nonstop hunting were catching up with him like a sudden, heavy weight across his shoulders.

"You definitely need my medicine, then." Myles straightened with a stiff grunt and set the cup in front of Barrett, winking as he grabbed another. "I think old Myles could use a nip, too. These old bones aren't used to all this excitement."

The door on the opposite side of the kitchen opened abruptly, admitting a young man in blue acolyte's robes. He was not tall, standing just below

Barrett's shoulder, with thick, kinky hair that had been clubbed at the base of his neck.

"The rest of the House is safe," he told Myles, his voice soft and even, though his eyes kept stealing quick glances at Barrett. The hunter quickly checked his sleeve to be certain no marks were showing. "All of the lanterns stand."

"Blessed is the Light," Myles murmured, filling his cup. "And you and Helen? You both are alright?"

A smile flickered across the young man's face as he darted another furtive glance towards Barrett. "Y-yes."

"Good." The Lightbringer straightened again and took the young man's hand, setting the drink in his palm. "Take this to Helen for me."

"But she is—"

"I am certain she has already gone back to the candles, but trust an old man when he says he knows what he is talking about. Take her the drink and return to your work with her."

The young man looked unconvinced, but he took the cup, bobbing his head to them both before taking his leave.

Myles laughed once the door swung shut, taking up another cup. "Young people."

"Let me," Barrett insisted, getting up and reaching for another cup.

"Oh, alright," the Lightbringer relented easily and shuffled back to the table. "I learned a long time ago it's better to let my pride ache so my back doesn't later."

Barrett snorted with amusement.

Myles cocked his head at him, no less amused. "You'll find out how right I am when you're as old as me."

If he made it that far. Hunters weren't revered for their long lifespans, and Barrett's family line hadn't proven to be long-lived so far. He crouched in front of the barrel and turned the stopcock, admiring the golden drink as it splashed out and hoping it tasted as good as it smelled.

"What is troubling you, Kristopher?" Myles asked when the hunter set the mead in front of him. "And don't say 'nothing.' I've been at this for too long not to recognize when someone is carrying more than their shadow around with them."

Barrett let out a bitter huff of laughter and slumped onto his stool again. "Where do I even start?"

"The beginning, traditionally," Myles suggested, grinning as Barrett shot him a look. "But speak on or of whatever moves you, if at all. You don't have to indulge all my silly whims."

"You wouldn't want to hear this story," Barrett assured the man, finally tasting the drink. It was sweet and gloriously smooth, so much better than the contraband mead the Drunken Wind had been selling to get around buying it from the Houses.

"Oh?" Myles challenged him. "You don't have to tell me, but you might be surprised at what I've seen in my lifetime. Being old just means I've outlived my mistakes, not that I haven't made any."

Barrett frowned. He'd never heard anything like that, especially from a Lightbringer. "I doubt anyone has screwed up as badly as I have."

"You'd be surprised," Myles repeated, but Barrett seriously doubted that. How many people could boast the sins that dogged him through waking and sleep? Of having killed the man he loved and another he had vowed to protect from the same fate? Of failing at every turn to repair his ailing relationship with the last member of his family he still knew to be alive?

"Were you raised in the guild?" Myles asked.

Barrett shook himself from his misery at the strange question, caught off guard. "No," he said. "I was raised mostly by my mum. My sister was the one my father trained as his apprentice. I was apprenticed to be a baker, before...everythin' else."

"Did you enjoy it?"

Barrett had to think. It had been so long ago now, and at the time, he had been jealous that his sister was the one chosen to inherit their family's prestigious legacy, not him. That it was her, not him, that their father had spent every free moment with. But now that he was older, he could admit that he'd loved what he'd learned from his mother—loved the simple labor of it, and the way it made others happy simply to taste his work.

"Yes," he answered.

"Is it something you would like to do again if you ever chose to give up the title of hunter?"

The question gave Barrett pause—not only because there were so few people outside of the guild that knew hunters could retire, but because he'd never considered what might come after for him. He had never looked farther than tomorrow. Especially now, when every day that passed made it less and less likely that he was attempting a rescue so much as vengeance.

"Maybe," he said after a long moment.

"You should think about it." The Lightbringer folded his hands around his cup. "You only grow old once. It is good to grow towards something, or even someone." He tilted his head. "Is there someone?"

"No." The word was bitter on Barrett's tongue, stinging even as he said it. "Not anymore."

Myles bowed his head. "I am sorry for your loss."

"Me too," Barrett huffed bitterly, taking another sip of his drink. "It was my fault it happened to h—" He caught himself. He could not say "him" in front of this stranger—a Lightbringer, no less. "To them," he corrected. "And now the same thing is happenin' again."

"Did you kill these people?"

Barrett balked at the blatant accusation, spoken so calmly. "What?"

"Did you take your knife and kill them?" the Lightbringer repeated, just as calmly and steadily as before.

"No."

"Did you pay someone else to kill them?"

Barrett smacked the cup of mead on the table. "No! What are you—"

"Broke their hearts or ruined their families?"

"No!" Barrett's stool toppled backwards. He leaned over the table, looming over the Lightbringer's serene face. "Just what are you trying to insinuate?"

"Well, if you didn't do any of these things, then what happened could not have been your fault."

Barrett stared hard at the old man, seething. "You don't know what you're talking about."

"Don't I?" The Lightbringer lifted his cup to his lips. "I've lost people too. I know what you are going through."

"No, you don't," Barrett snarled, fire flaring lightly along his hands. "You can't possibly—"

"It was my wife," Myles interrupted again, "and my little girl. She was barely six when a demon took them both from me."

The black flames covering Barrett's gloves flickered out, his anger dying beneath a cold wash of horror at his own callowness. "I...." He groped for the right thing to say. "I'm sorry. I didn't know."

"I know," Myles said, the first strains of weariness coloring his words. "I wouldn't expect you to; we've only just met. I'm telling you now, though, so that when I say that I understand what you are feeling, you do not think I am offering empty comfort. I am not that kind of Lightbringer, and I am not that kind of man. Not anymore."

The Lightbringer gestured to Barrett's cup. "Please, sit and drink with me. You don't have to tell me your troubles, but I would have you know that you are welcome here, and that if you ever need an ear, or even just some more medicine, I would be happy to supply both. We've plenty of room should you need a safe place to rest, though you might find my definition of safe a bit dubious after having to stop a demon from burning my hives to the ground."

Barrett offered a weak chuckle. "No place is truly safe from them."

"An unfortunate truth," Myles agreed. "Times are dark, and growing darker still, but that only makes it that much more important for the Lightbringers and the Houses to be there to light the way."

Barrett didn't know what to make of the man. He had never met a

Lightbringer like him—Graces, he had never met *anyone* like him. He wished he had met Myles when he was younger, when he still believed in things like faith. Maybe things would have gone differently.

After finishing his mead with the Lightbringer's companionable silence, Barrett got up from his stool. "Thank you for the drink, Lightbringer, but I really should go."

"Myles," the man corrected, getting stiffly up from his stool as well and hobbling over to offer Barrett his hand again. "And no need to thank me. I hope I haven't put you off from visiting again with my rambling. It was a pleasure to have you."

Barrett took the man's hand, smiling despite himself again. "Far from it," he assured him. "You've spoiled me for drink anywhere else."

"Well, beg pardon if I don't offer my apologies for that." Myles chuckled as their hands parted. "But go on; I'm certain you have important work to get to. Don't let me hold you up from it."

"May your lanterns stay lit."

"And may the Light guide and keep you."

Chapter Twenty-Two

Kyran peered up at the walls of his prison, silently cursing them. His leg was still too weak to bear his weight, let alone the lass's, and he'd already had to tighten his belt. If he meant to get to the top while carrying her, he would need the use of his leg and, in all likelihood, to gain strength in his arms. Even as malnourished as she was, she would still be extra weight. It would make it even harder to escape, but he would not leave her here. Not with that thing.

"Have you got a name, lassie?" he asked between panting breaths as he leaned against the wall. His dry throat and mouth warped the words. He needed water, but was not about to wait around for it. He had to keep climbing and getting stronger.

The lass looked up, watching him attentively, but made no attempt to respond. It only strengthened his belief that she did not know Common. Despite that, she had made no attempt to hide from him in the dark again, clinging close to his side.

"Dinnae worry yourself about it," he continued regardless, more for his own benefit than hers. It was strange to talk after sitting in mute silence for however long he had been down here. "You can tell me when you like."

She cocked her head to one side like a small, attentive bird—then bolted into the dark. A moment later, the stone above creaked and clicked. The demon was coming. Kyran stood up straight, squaring his shoulders, and pressed his back to the wall, facing the darkness.

He heard its weight settle on the ground, and only then did its bloody lines illuminate it. It held a fresh slab of raw flesh in one clawed hand and a bowl of some kind balanced delicately in the other. The meat instantly began to steam and sizzle, and the perverted odor of cooking demon flesh filled their cage.

There was a shadow of movement on the ground before the beast, and Kyran watched with confusion and unmasked horror as the lass crawled on hands and knees up to the beast and bowed her head to the floor in apparent supplication.

The demon laughed, throwing its head back. "I see someone trained you well," it sneered. Tearing a small chunk of the flesh off with its teeth, it spat it on the floor in front of her. Without any hesitation, the lass dove onto the meat and bit in, ripping little pieces off with her teeth. In mere seconds, there was nothing left. Kyran pressed the back of his hand to his mouth, fighting his stomach's threat to disgorge itself.

"You look ill, mageling," the demon rumbled, stepping past the lass. "But fear not. I will take care of you."

Kyran narrowed his eyes at the beast, and it hissed with laughter. It stopped just out of arm's reach, and Kyran was finally able to make out the contents of the bowl.

The bowl was bone, that much he could tell at a glance, but the longer he stared, the more he decided it looked like the rounded top of a human skull that had been sawn off and turned upside down, the zigzag of suture lines still visible along its curves. It was filled nearly to the brim with a steaming, black liquid that smelled much like the meat sitting next to him.

Kyran wrinkled his nose in disgust. "That is blood."

"Demon's blood, yes," the demon purred. "To wet your throat. I had all but forgotten how thirsty you creatures are. It is lucky I remembered."

Kyran's lip curled in disgust. Blood? Was this what the beast expected him to survive off of?

It held the bowl forward in both hands, head tipping to one side. "Do you need me to feed you again, mageling?"

As revolting as the idea was, he knew that if he wanted to placate the beast and regain his strength, he would have to drink it. But he could not help but ask. "Why blood?"

The demon's grin widened, and it rocked forward, holding the bowl almost under his nose. "To make you stronger, pet. Now, drink."

Grudgingly, Kyran took the bowl, revolted by the greasy texture of the bone against his bare skin. He sorely missed his kerchief. His hands trembled with the effort as he lifted the bowl to his lips, trying not to look at the dark contents or smell them. It was not thick, like he had been expecting, but rather watery, as if he were swallowing hot ink. He tried to drink as quickly as he could, but he had to keep stopping as he choked on the liquid, his dry throat making him cough. Finally, he got it all down. It had a salty taste, with an undercurrent of the same bitterness that marked the flesh, that lingered after his last swallow.

He held the bowl out to the demon. It took it back, nails grating against the bone, and held the meat out in return, making a pleased noise when Kyran took it without complaint.

The meat dripped with juices, its color paler than the last piece the demon had brought. Kyran looked up at the demon's expectant expression and made sure it saw him tear the first piece off and place it in his mouth. The texture was as different as the color. It felt less like eating meat than some sort of fungus. It was spongy, though still laced with stringy fibers, almost impossible to chew, and possessed an intensely bitter aftertaste that almost made him gag just to put in his mouth.

But Kyran swallowed each and every bite, his eyes never leaving the demon's face. He needed to eat this so he could stay alive. So the lass would not be hurt. So they could escape and kill this thing.

He finished and wiped his hands on his kilt, forcing himself not to react to the painful cramp stirring in his stomach.

"Good pets," it praised them, turning its eyes to the little girl as she crawled back to Kyran's side, pressing against his leg. "The hunting has been good. I will return with more food soon."

Kyran held his tongue, watching the beast with his head high as it climbed from the prison. As soon as it disappeared over the rim far above, the lass left his side and groped around in the wan light Kyran provided, scratching at the stones like a hound searching for scraps.

He saw again how shockingly thin her limbs were, just barely more than skin and bones. There was no telling how long it had been since she'd had a proper meal. She paused at one spot, her scratching getting more insistent, and raised her fingers to her mouth, swallowing whatever bit of grit she had found. She started on another spot, picking at the drippings where the meat's juices had soaked into the stone.

The unwholesome food in Kyran's belly squirmed, and he clutched at his stomach, squeezing his eyes shut as a wave of nausea passed through him, trailed by heavy guilt that he had not thought to try to give her some of the horrid meat the demon had brought. Next time, he would be sure to ensure she got a fair portion. Still, he was certain the demon would disapprove of wasting its precious meat on the *wean*. As if she could eat much of it.

The corner of his mouth twitched, and he let out a short, rasping laugh. "The beast can hang," he muttered, tightening his arms over his middle.

He managed some rest, and his belly had ceased most of its complaints when he woke again, the lass tucked against his side. He felt better than before, though still far from good. He hated to admit that the blood the demon had brought had done him good, but there was no denying it.

Getting to his feet, Kyran began his pacing along the wall. The lass followed closely, as she had before, silent but for the scuff and patter of her bare feet. He made approximately one circuit before he stopped, gazing up the wall to pick a place to begin again.

Fitting his thin fingers into the grooves between the bricks, he started to climb. He did not go higher than a foot or two from the ground, his arms shaking with just the effort of clinging to the wall, his fingers quickly growing tired until they could take no more, and their grip slipped. He dropped onto his backside, breathing hard, his skin damp with sweat, and his throat burning with thirst. Mercy, but he had a long way to go.

He lifted one trembling hand and tried to run it through his hair, but its tangled snarls caught his fingers before they got far; he must have looked a mess. Laying back on the ground, he wished he could just taste clean water again.

As promised, the demon returned in what felt like a much shorter time than before. Kyran was dozing on the ground when he heard it coming and got to his feet, unwilling to be on his back when the beast reached them. It growled as the lass approached it from somewhere else in the dark, making her pause in her tracks.

Its sockets found him, the air shimmering around it as it began to cook the meat in the claws of its right hand, the bone bowl balanced in its other hand. It strode over to Kyran, crouched in front of him, and held the bowl out first.

Steeling himself against his disgust, Kyran silently took the bowl and quickly drank the bitter contents, handing it back to trade for the piece of meat. His eyes moved past the demon, catching sight of the lass as she shifted in the dim light, and he remembered watching her dig at the stones for greasy spots. He tore a chunk from the meat the size of his palm, intending to give it to her when the beast left.

"What is that?" the demon asked, pointing at the piece as he began to eat the rest of the meat.

"I'm giving it ta the lass," he said firmly, between bites. "She has ta eat."

The molten veins in its face glowed, and it hissed at him in displeasure. "You will not get more."

"Fine," he bit back, setting another piece of the revolting flesh in his mouth and swallowing.

"I will not hunt for more than your share."

Kyran's lips drew back from his teeth in a feral, not-quite-smile. "Aye. As you please."

"Arrogant child," it sneered. "You are rather bold with your new pet."

"She is not a pet."

"She certainly begs like one." The demon tilted its head to watch the lass edging closer on her hands and knees. It simpered something at her in a sharp, bird-like language Kyran had never heard, and she bowed abruptly to Kyran, head on the ground and hands palm up.

Kyran's eyes narrowed at the demon, his heart sick to see the lass begging him for the foul scrap of flesh. "You dinnae hafta do that," he told her quietly, setting the spare bit of meat in her fingers.

She picked up her head and quickly devoured the meat, cramming it in her mouth. She made as if to hold out her hands again, but the demon caught her by the wrist and dragged her away from Kyran. "Enough!"

Kyran dropped the meat still in his hands, reaching after the lass as she cried out in pain. "Dinnae hurt her!"

The demon yanked hard, drawing a shriek out of the lass as it slung her around and let go, sending her tumbling into the dark. Kyran started after her, but the demon caught him by his throat and jerked him up, his toes barely reaching the ground.

Its will slammed into him. Kyran shuddered at the force of the blow. But he did not break—not this time—and the air between them shrieked with bitter, cutting cold as the demon's weighty presence faltered.

With a snarl, Kyran let his grip on his magic loose and grabbed the beast's hand at his throat as his magic ripped through its flesh.

"There it is!" the demon hissed, its own magic burning bright and bloody beneath its skin. But Kyran felt none of it. The monster's fire could not touch him through his wintery aura. "There is the Old One's blood you will give me!"

"Let me go!" he choked around its crushing grip, spittle crackling at the corners of his mouth as his magic froze it. As he clutched at the demon's arm, the ruddy lines of its magic dimmed as its flesh began to steam.

The demon grinned, rearing its other hand back, and slugged him across his face. Pain exploded through his skull, and his vision skittered, the taste of blood blossoming across his tongue. Another fist caught him high on the cheek, and he heard the lass scream something before a third hit close to his temple. His thoughts scattered like only so many pieces of hay. He slumped, insensate, in the beast's grip as its power shoved past his conscious will and burrowed down inside his skull, past his every defense down into the center of him.

Things came drifting out of the black of his mind, memories he had done his best to bury—those that still hurt to recall, those that he had yet to reconcile—all replaying at once, a terrible cacophonous jumble of overlapping voices and emotions.

No more. I canna do this anymore. I dinnae want ta see you again. Stop shouting. We both know you like it. I'm sorry, Kyran. You bastard! You demon-blooded bastard! I'll kill you! No! No! Stop! Don'! What if I meant it? What a shame to kill you like this, so weak and frail.

And beneath them, beneath the avalanche of voices, were the scents of blood, stale spirits, vomit, and dry hay, and the distant sound of a scream that grew louder and louder.

It was in his head. It was in his head, and he could not even make himself scream, his body simply not responding. He was trapped in his own skin, unable to do anything but watch as the demon raked through his mind. It dug at his thoughts, pawed through his memories, tasting them, savoring his remembered pains, his most intimate and private moments plucked from his mind. Everything. It saw everything, and he could not stop it.

Eventually, he dimly became aware that he was curled on his side, clutching himself so hard that his nails were biting into his skin. He shuddered violently as the pressure inside his skull gave a final ebb and retreated. He lay there, trying to order his mind, but the memories would not go peaceably. They seemed to scream inside his skull, fighting and tangling with one another until they were almost inseparable, clawing at the curves of his bones as if looking for a place to escape.

A prayer stuttered off of his tongue, and he curled into himself more tightly, only to meet resistance. Something warm and small was pressed against his belly. He peeled his eyes open, blinking away the phantoms that flickered in front of his vision until he recognized the wee lass curled against his middle. Hearing the scratch of claws on stone, he jerked his head to see the demon climbing up the wall. He had no memory of it even letting him go. He watched it climb until it was gone, then let his head fall back, unconscious before it even hit the stone.

Chapter Twenty-Three

Kyran shivered beneath his blankets, the woven wool scratching across his skin. His body ached with fever, his skin damp from the vicious rise and fall of his illness. He cracked his eyes open, but he could not see anything beyond his little cot. The room was dark; his da had quenched the hearth when he'd complained the light hurt his eyes too much. He could hear the distant sound of horse hooves where his da must have been working out in the yard.

"Ma," he croaked weakly, throat parched. "Ma."

"I'm here, Kyran." A hot, dry hand touched his forehead, brushing back his sticky curls. A figure leaned over him and resolved itself into his ma's sweet features, her auburn hair hanging in a thick plait over her shoulder. "Just lie still," she soothed him, leaning away into the dark, reaching for something.

There was a squeak of a cork being drawn, and she reappeared at the limits of his vision—only it was not her any longer. Her hair had drawn shorter, its color softening to the pale yellow of freshly churned cream, and her eyes were no longer a sun-baked brown, but the color of summer skies.

"I've got you," Barrett said in his soft tenor, pressing the lip of a flask to Kyran's mouth. Warm water trickled past his parched tongue, and he near moaned in relief. He swallowed clumsily, feeling his throat stick, and had started to swallow again when a sour sense of familiarity clenched around his ribs.

Had he not woken to this very nightmare before? He was not home, in the Isles. He was not seven years old, trapped in vicious fever. That was not Barrett.

"No," he wheezed, pushing the flask clumsily away. "Get away from me!"

"Kyran?" The illusion reached for him, and Kyran cringed in anticipation before its hand brushed across his cheek, fever-warm, and he flinched from it. "What's wrong?"

Kyran's eyes shot wide as the man's voice shifted, regaining the lilt of an

Isleish accent. The illusion's hair turned lank and black, its mouth twisting into a leering grin. "I thought you liked it like this?" The thick scent of whiskey and dry hay clung to Kyran's nostrils, and he tried to push the thing away, but his arms would not move. None of him would move.

"Stop!" he wanted to shout, but his voice was as frozen as the rest of him. He fought to make some part of him obey him. Pain chewed at his bones, flaring hot and bright, but he couldn't move an inch. He was pinned down. Helpless.

"Da was right," the man chuckled, leaning over him until he could feel the heat of his body pressing down against him. "You're nothing more than a demon-blooded animal."

"Kyran!"

He jolted awake, his heart stopping in his chest. Barrett gazed back at him, his rugged, unshaven face illuminated by the cold light of Kyran's blood.

"Barrett?" Kyran tried to say, but it came out an ugly, weak croak from his dry throat.

"You need to drink," the hunter whispered, his voice familiar and comforting, but warped by the strange surroundings. Kyran started to protest as Barrett lifted a bowl to his lips, confused and hardly believing what he was seeing. Barrett had found him.

"Drink," the hunter urged, tipping the bowl so water trickled past Kyran's parted lips.

The water was warmer than he would have liked, with a strange saltiness. But as it rolled over his tongue and down his throat, Kyran was suddenly aware of how incredibly thirsty he was, to the exclusion of almost everything else. He swallowed eagerly, coughing as his parched throat tried to remember how to work. Barrett tipped the bowl away, waiting patiently for his coughing to stop before giving him more. He drank as fast as he could, choking as much as drinking, but Barrett patiently nursed him until the shallow bowl was empty.

Then Barrett set the wooden bowl aside and helped Kyran lie down beside it on the ground. "I will fetch more for you. It has been too long since you were fed, pet."

Pet.

Fear, cold as the winters on the *ben*, iced through Kyran veins, and he paled as he stared up at the perfect mimic looking back at him through Barrett's summer-blue eyes.

"You...are na Barrett."

As if in response to his sudden clarity, there was an ungentle stirring of foreign, malicious glee inside his mind, and Kyran screamed as the truth came to him in its full and terrible weight.

"No!" He clamped his hands over his ears, his fingernails digging into his scalp, and squeezed his eyes shut as hard as he could, blocking out the mirage. "No! What have ye done ta me?"

It was in his mind. It was in his mind, and he was seeing things. Barrett was not there. He had not been found. He was still trapped in this dark, stone prison, alone.

The demon let out a low, shuddering moan in Barrett's voice. "Oh, and I was right: you *were* still holding out hope that your hunter would come and save you. Did you like seeing him again?"

Kyran jerked his hands from his face and shoved himself upright, his magic lashing out at the demon. Frost snapped against the stones and bit at his face. "Shut up!" he snarled, his voice cracking painfully.

The demon's own lines brightened beneath Barrett's skin, and Kyran could hear the rush of wind as the heat of its magic warmed the air around them. "Yes, I think you did," it chuckled, but it was in its own, rasping tones now.

It leaned down over him, smiling through Barrett's face, though it was an expression Kyran had never seen the hunter wear before. It was smug and cruel, his mouth twisted in an unkind smile. "You let me hold you. And feed you. I wonder what else you would let me do if I looked like him?"

Kyran's lips peeled back from his teeth, the air whistling around them as his magic boiled out of his blood. "Dinnae dare touch me, beast!" he spat.

The demon's lines turned bright, molten red, and the presence inside his mind squirmed against his thoughts, pulling an image out of his mind of a man, his black hair lank and greasy, the stink of ale strong on his breath. Kyran flinched as coarse fingers pressed against the back of his neck, and he heard the demon laugh again before something brushed his face. He flinched again, and the face was suddenly replaced by the demon's, its empty sockets leering from above its thicket of needle-like teeth.

"Little mageling, if I truly wanted anything from you, I could just take it. You would not be strong enough to resist me." It leaned back, straightening to its full height above him, the lines of its magic bright and bloody. "Now be a good pet and wait right here. I brought you dinner."

It turned away, scooping up the bowl it had laid aside as it went to the nearest wall and began to climb it almost effortlessly. Kyran stared after it, his mind struck dumb by the sheer power over him the beast had shown. How could he escape something like that?

Not minutes later, it returned with another full bowl of what could only be more demon's blood and a fresh piece of roasted meat. It held the familiar bowl out, and he took it, ignoring the itch under his skin. Without a word, he drained the bowl and handed it back, accepting the piece of meat.

The demon left as he started to eat, its chest rumbling in a pleased sound as it climbed up into the dark. He stopped eating as soon as he could no longer hear the click of its nails on stone, letting his hands fall into his lap. He stared at the ugly meat, his stomach twisting sickeningly with more than hunger. He felt powerless. He had never been in control of his own fate, always too weak to protect himself from those that meant him harm, and never was that more evident than now, here.

There was a soft sound in the dark, and his eyes found the tiny figure of the lass at the edge of his light, shivering in the cold as she peered up at him with wide, frightened eyes. She must have hidden when the beast came down. Her lips parted in an anxious whine, and she crawled towards him, her gaze darting up at the wall every few steps. He tightened his control over his magic, his light dimming, and she crawled up to his side, pressing against him, her body quivering. He looked down at the meat in his hands, ripped a chunk off, and handed it to her. She gulped it down, licking her fingers clean, and he tore off another hunk for her, which she ate just as fast.

The bitter hopelessness faded as he watched her, the steel of his anger hardening again. He did not have time to sink into self-loathing and pity. He had to escape. If he was too weak to kill the demon here, they'd simply have to escape while it was away hunting. He could kill it another day, when he was stronger—and he would kill it, he promised himself that.

He tore off another piece of the meat to hand the lass, but she pushed his hand back towards him, shaking her head. He glanced at her, and she mimicked eating with her other hand, pushing the meat towards him again. He sighed, smiling despite himself. "I suppose you are right, lass. I willna get any better if I dinnae eat."

She smiled back, patting his arm as he placed the bite into his mouth. He grimaced again at the bitterness mixed inextricably with the meat. He was not certain he would ever be able to touch roast again after this.

It was difficult to chew, his jaw still swollen and sore from where the demon had struck him, but he got the meat down, wiping distractedly at his nose as it began to warm. Blood trickled down his lip. He looked up at the grey walls of his prison with a resigned sigh. There was no better time than the present. Kyran got to his feet, looking for a place to start climbing. He would go as high as he could today without falling. Then, when he climbed next, he would do the same, and again, until he could reach the top. He had to push himself harder. If he did not get out of this place soon....

He suppressed a shudder as the tangle of fragmented memories tried to resurface, and quickly turned his attention to finding his first handhold.

Chapter Twenty-Four

Barrett sank against the stone support of the bridge, peering up through the rain and gloam at the ringing bell. There was no demon; he was sure of that. It was merely the House tolling the end of service, its doors expelling the Grace-guided and the Light-worshipping back to their barstools and market stalls. How anyone could believe there was a merciful Light when beasts like demons roamed the streets at night and haunted their cellars and stole their children was beyond him. What was the point of praying to a god as deaf and merciless as the sun he'd once created? They might as well beseech the stones of the House for help.

And yet here he was, waiting in the pouring rain for mass to empty so he might find his own mercy. It wasn't Lumen he sought, though.

Once the trickle of stragglers had fallen off, Barrett pushed off the foot of the bridge, keeping his head ducked against the rain as he crossed the square, headed for the garden gate on the river side of the House. He let himself in, following the path that wound through the House's hives, repaired since the demon's attack.

Rounding the back corner of the House, he approached the kitchen door where he had entered last, and knocked. He waited, too tired to wipe the rainwater from his eyes, fighting the doubt stealing in through his misery. Why was he here? He didn't follow Lumen. He didn't even pray.

The door swung open, and a robust young woman with mousy brown hair peered out at him, her expression quizzical. "Yes?" she asked, her voice much sweeter than Barrett had anticipated.

"May I come in?"

The woman blinked, as if caught off guard by the question, before she stepped from the doorway, holding the door open for him. "Of course. Any soul is welcome in our House."

He smiled thinly, trudging through the door into the blanketing heat of the kitchen. There was a cauldron over the fire and the table was a mess of scattered vegetables and tubers, with two cloth-covered lumps at the center that he guessed might be rising dough. Voices in conversation echoed beyond the open inner door—likely some worshipper speaking with Myles.

"Is there something you needed?" the woman asked as he shuffled towards the fire, leaving a trail of puddles behind. "Shall I fetch the Lightbringer?"

"Please," he told her, crouching in front of the fireplace, sighing comfortably as the heat began to soak into his face and the front of his drenched clothes. But it couldn't even begin to warm the hollows inside him.

It was a moment before the Lightbringer came. "Ah, Kristopher."

Barrett twisted to look over his shoulder as Myles moved stiffly through the doorway.

"It is good to see you again. Pardon if I don't join you down there, but I don't think these old joints could handle it today."

"Are you alright?" Barrett asked, getting to his feet, suddenly wary he had come at a bad time.

"Oh, as well as I can be," the man grumbled good-naturedly, sitting heavily on a stool by the fire. "My joints decided many years ago they don't like the rain." The Lightbringer stretched out his hands to the fire. His knuckles were swollen, twisting his already gnarled hands. "It's nothing I haven't learned to live with, but it can be troublesome when there's dinner to be made."

"I can help," Barrett volunteered without hesitation, eager for something—anything—to distract him. "Just tell me what I can do."

"That's very kind of you. I've left some dough rising that could use some work, if you would like," Myles offered, gesturing to a bowl on the table with a cloth draped over it. "I can get started adding to the pot."

"Of course." Barrett said, looking about until Myles pointed to a barrel in the corner where the flour was kept. Cracking open the lid, Barrett took a cupful of flour and sprinkled some of it over the table before turning the dough out onto it. He was about to start when he realized his gloves were still on. He glanced back at Myles, but the man was busy warming his hands still. What would he think if he saw Barrett's witch marks? What would any Lightbringer think if he saw witch marks?

Pinching the tips of the gloves, he carefully peeled them off and set them aside, leaving his sleeves down to hide the marks. He glanced at the Lightbringer, but Myles still had his back to him, oblivious to the monster behind him. Rubbing his hands with flour, Barrett began to work the dough.

His mind soon fell into a comfortable blankness as he simply focused on the rhythm of his work. It had been some time since he had done baker's work, but he was surprised to find how naturally it came back to him, how much he truly did enjoy the simple honesty of it. This could have been his profession, in a different life. He could have stayed a simple baker in Willowvale, met some simple farmer's girl, and lived a simple, happy life.

Instead, he had let his jealousy drive him to the life of a hunter—one he was only just beginning to recognize as a life no one should choose. There was nothing but tragedy and unrecognized sacrifice as its rewards. He had thought becoming a hunter would make him powerful. Instead, he was only given the means to discover how truly powerless he was, at the price of everything dear to him.

He slapped the dough back into its bowl and covered it with a cloth, his eyes stinging. Why? Why had Raleigh and Kyran had to pay the price for his stupidity? What had he ever done that was so terrible that they deserved to suffer? Why would this happen?

"Are you going to tell me what is wrong, or shall I guess?"

Barrett's head snapped up at Myles' question. The man still had his back to him, but had begun chopping up vegetables.

"Something had to bring you through the rain to my doorstep, and I doubt it is my company. You do not attend service, so it is not the guidance of Lumen you seek. I was hoping, perhaps, you might have come back to talk to someone you might consider a friend. If not now, maybe one day."

"You wouldn't want to be friends with me," Barrett assured the man bitterly.

"And why not?"

Barrett scoffed, his eyes wandering back to the fireplace. "Bad things always happen to people close to me. And besides," he added, leaning on the worktable, "you're a Lightbringer, and I'm a hunter."

"And?"

"And we can't be friends," he said firmly, the bitter truth hurting despite his efforts to resist it. "If you knew what I was, you'd never want to see my face again."

"That isn't true," Myles insisted gently, and Barrett couldn't help a dry chuff of a laugh.

"You only say that because you don't know."

"That hunters are witches?"

Barrett was stunned. His mouth gaped, opening and closing like a fish as he struggled to grasp what he had just heard. "Y-you....You know?"

Myles nodded sagely, still bent to his task of chopping vegetables. "I worked quite closely with the guild when I was younger."

"You know and you still...?"

"Of course. 'Light the path for all.' Is that not what Lumen commands of the Lightbringers? Not *some*, but *all*."

"But...." Barrett just couldn't wrap his mind around it. "I'm a witch. Doesn't that scare you?"

"People have always feared that which they could not understand. It is why our god took pity on us and gave us light. Many forget that some of the Graces they call upon were once borne most brightly by hunters." He set his knife down and plucked another carrot from the basket. "There are even some who would call them living bearers of Grace—the divine amongst the mortal, bearing the heavy sword of light against the threatening dark."

The divine? He had never heard anyone, especially a Lightbringer, speak of hunters in such a way. What kind of House had he wandered into? Barrett had lived at the guild, had known his family, and he knew himself. There was nothing about them that suggested the divine or the Graces worked in him, or any other hunter.

"I think you mean rather the opposite," he said.

"I don't believe I do," the Lightbinger said mildly, taking up his chopping again.

"We make deals with demons," Barrett pointed out.

"In order to destroy the ones that would do us harm," Myles retorted.

"Maybe, but there are other reasons, selfish ones, that people become hunters. The money, power, status—"

"Are we talking about other people now, or about yourself?"

Barrett's head shot up, his stomach twisting. "What?"

Myles scooped the cut vegetables into an empty bowl. "Is that what is bothering you enough to bring you here? You think you are selfish?"

"Aren't I?" Barrett asked, his voice cracking.

"I wouldn't know. You haven't told me anything about yourself. But I have faith."

Faith. Barrett scoffed again. "I haven't put much hold in faith since I was a child." *And too ignorant to know better.*

"You are not the first to tell me he feels that way, and you will be far from the last," Myles sighed, picking up the bowl and hobbling towards the fireplace. "Know that it is against the Lumen to say as much, but I know there are not many hunters who hold faith in the Graces and keep the Light in their hearts. Given the hardships and sacrifices their lives demand of them, it is more surprising that they can keep forging ahead without faith to hold them and guide them. They are better men than me."

He said it so mildly, as if he had spoken common knowledge. Barrett found himself almost gaping at the man.

"Times are dark, and growing darker still," Myles continued, picking up an iron crook from beside the fireplace and using it to swing the cooking arm out from over the flames. "But that only makes it that much more important for the Lightbringers and the Houses to be there to light the way."

Barrett didn't know what to say. He had never encountered such a strange Lightbringer. But as hopeful as Myles' words were, Barrett couldn't help but feel they weren't meant for him. He had done too much. Failed too many people. If he was deserving of anything, it was to turn in his amulet to the guild and walk into the lake at the center of Willowvale, never to walk out again. It was the only way to ensure no one ever got hurt because of him again, and it was only his promise to Raleigh that kept him from it.

"Kristopher."

Barrett raised his head at the Lightbringer's gentle voice, his smile striking him like a physical blow.

"I may look like a foolish old man, but I understand better than you might think what it is like to live with regrets and sorrows. I wasn't always a Lightbringer."

"You can't have messed up as badly as I have," Barrett disagreed, pressing the heel of his hand to the ache in his chest as it swelled again, threatening to collapse his ribs. "I've hurt people."

The Lightbringer's smile softened a degree with something like sadness. "So have I," he said, taking up the crook and pushing the arm back into the fire.

"Not like I have," Barrett said. The ache in his chest sharpened, cutting at him from the inside.

"You might be surprised." The Lightbringer's voice was unexpectedly heavy with grief. He hobbled back to the table. "How much do you know about the riots in the capital during King Edrick's short reign?"

The name was vaguely familiar. He had attended school at the guild for a few years, but it had mainly been to learn how to control his magic, and, since he had been raised to be a baker, he had not studied history as extensively as his sister, under his father's strict tutelage.

He knew the riots had to do with hunters and a demon outbreak and the faith, but all the details were hazy. It would have happened when his father was young. "Not much," he finally admitted. "I believe it is credited as the cause of the tension between the guild and the Lumen."

The Lightbringer twirled one of his fingers. "Not quite. It was more the other way around. The riots broke out because of the tension between the Lumen and the guild, fostered in part by King Edrick, and in part by the Cult of the Guiding Light—rather uncharitably called the Cult of King Edrick by some now."

He handed his knife and a potato to Barrett. "All that violence and fear churning day and night of course lured demons to the streets of the capital. They were very dark days." He shook his head, reaching up to rub at a thin patch of his short, white hair before fishing out another potato and handing it to Barrett. "King Kaiden is a much more temperate man than his uncle, and he has helped guide Tennebrum to peace and prosperity since assuming the throne."

Barrett nodded, turning the potato over in his hand before setting the knife to it and beginning to peel it. "But what does that have to do with anything?"

"I am getting to that," Myles replied, picking up another knife and joining Barrett. Chewing at his lower lip, Myles peeled away at a potato. His shoulders sagged. "Ah, forgive me. I set out to give you an honest explanation, and I have only been giving it to you in parts. I suppose I am not so proud of my younger years as I was when I was living them. I was a member of the Cult of the Guiding Light." His mouth twitched up into a grin at Barrett's wide-eyed stare. "Not such an unassuming old man now, am I?"

"It is...not what I expected you to say," Barrett admitted haltingly, shocked. "So, when you asked about the riots...."

"It is because I was directly involved in them, yes. But that was an age ago now. Life is long, Kristopher, and the wise learn to grow with it." He chuckled softly, almost to himself. "Not to say that I am wise, but I have learned a thing or two in my years." He held up a finger. "The first was the ability to admit when I am wrong. And the second," he held up another finger, "was learning to forgive myself."

Barrett winced at Myles' words. They cut right to the heart of how he had wound up here in the first place, and the truth stung.

"They were not easy lessons, but they were important," Myles continued, his gaze drifting to the fire crackling up around the new log. "Terrible things happen to good people all the time. You must know this."

"But Kyran and Raleigh...." The knife clattered loudly on the table as the dam around Barrett's heart finally burst. "They're dead," he sobbed, the words tearing themselves from his throat as hot tears spattered the tabletop. "They died because I wasn't strong enough to protect them."

"From what?"

"A demon. The *same* demon. The one that's been takin' the children." He was certain of that now. Not a single child had gone missing since the demon had taken Kyran.

"Oh, Kristopher." There was a gentle touch at his hand. "I am sorry."

"If I had stayed a baker, none of this would have happened."

"Can you say that for certain? Do you know for sure that this demon would not have found these people on its own without you?"

The touch slipped away, and Barrett glanced up through his wet lashes.

The Lightbringer hobbled towards the fireplace. "When I lost my wife and daughter, I tore myself apart with guilt. But you know what? No amount of pain I inflicted on myself brought them back."

It wouldn't. Barrett's heart ached with guilt, even as he knew someplace in him that Myles was not wrong. Except... "But I might be able to save one of them still."

"You believe one of them is still alive?"

"Yes," Barrett whispered without hesitation. He had to believe it. He had to believe there was still time. "If the demon was going to kill him immediately, it would have done it there, in the street where it caught him, not taken him."

"How are you planning to find him?" Myles asked, taking a cup from the top of the barrel next to the hearth.

"I have to find another demon—one that can speak and knows where the demon that took him nests in their realm." Which was easier said than done. He had only faced two speaking demons in his years as a hunter, one of which was the very one that had taken Raleigh from him and stolen Kyran.

He heard the Lightbringer inhale sharply, his hand twitching through the sign against evil. "Graces guide us; light protect us," Myles murmured in prayer before he easing himself down into a crouch. "You are planning to try to go to their realm?"

"I have to," Barrett said, his guilt lessening beneath a surge of determination. "I swore I would not let this demon do to him what it did to Raleigh."

"He must be a very good friend for you to risk so much for him," Myles said, leaning on the barrel as he opened the spigot and poured out a measure of mead. "I will pray to the Graces to protect you both."

A smile came to Barrett's face as he tried to envision the mage's reaction to being called a friend, and remembered the whistle Kyran had been carving. "Yes," he answered more quietly, then frowned to himself. "Actually, I don't really know him. We've been workin' together for almost a month, and I barely know anythin' about him. He doesn't talk much, especially about himself."

"But you are still willing to risk your life for his."

Barrett shifted on his stool, scratching at his unshaven face. "Yes. He didn't deserve what happened to him."

"I would argue that nobody deserves to meet their fate at the hands of a demon," Myles remarked, setting the cup back on top of the barrel and slowly levering to his feet again. "But you would not go into that place for just anybody."

"No," Barrett agreed, uncertain where the Lightbringer's line of inquiry was going.

Myles shrugged, giving him an odd smile as he straightened and returned to the table with the drink. "There are not many who would do the same for their loved ones. But for a man you know so little about, you would face down death and worse. I think he at least deserves the title of your friendship, don't you?"

Barrett's face suddenly felt too warm. "Yes. He does."

The Lightbringer chuckled and set the mead before Barrett. The cup was nearly overflowing. "If only we all had friends like you, Kristopher."

"I don't think everyone would like that," Barrett remarked drily, taking the drink with a grateful nod.

"Oh? And why not?" Myles asked. "I think we should all like to have friends that would go to the ends of the earth and beyond for us, no matter the circumstances." He leaned over the table and patted Barrett's hand again. "By the Graces that guide us, you will find him. Have faith, Kristopher, if not in Lumen and his Graces, then in yourself."

Barrett blinked against the sudden surge of emotion that threatened to fill his eyes again. He had needed to hear that—to hear someone believe in him, believe that Kyran was still alive. It spun his spider's thread of desperation into hope instead of madness.

"Thank you," he said with more meaning than he could express, taking Myles' crooked grip.

"Of course. I only hope you will come back and introduce this man to me when you find him. He must be quite the person to have earned a friendship like yours."

"I will," Barrett said, staring at the ground as he struggled to control the tide inside of him. He had to be focused and deliberate. There wasn't much time left before Captain Griswold's deadline. He had to find Kyran before it was too late.

Chapter Twenty-Five

CRACK!

Kyran jolted from his sleep, eyes snapping open to find one of his nightmares had come to life. His blood was burning bright as landed starlight, setting alight the opalescent frost tracing over everything around him. He had not lost control like this since he had been a *wean*. He cinched his control down on the power, but instead of retreating, his magic surged through his blood even more viciously, pushing every last vestige of warmth from the prison as if it were a living, hungry thing.

He closed his eyes, concentrating, focusing on the mental dams he visualized stopping the magic inside his blood. The air crackled as its temperature plummeted even further. He growled, setting his teeth, and strained harder, but it was like trying to stop a river from flowing. So he did as men had done before him to stop rivers—he diverted it.

Setting his palm to the wall behind him, he focused on the stones. The bricks, warm from the natural, lingering heat of the demon realm, squealed in protest as his arctic-cold magic flushed the heat from them in an instant. A deafening boom echoed through the walls. Dust and frost rained down on Kyran's head as several bricks cracked and shattered under the strain.

His magic ran wild, and he focused just enough to keep most of it pouring into the wall while he slowly gathered his control, cinching down until, with a last wrench, he brought it to heel.

Breathing a sigh of relief, he did not let his concentration waver as his magic bucked against him. That...That had been difficult. He lifted one hand, staring at the lines of his blood. They were dimmer than a moment before— much so—but were still far from the faint glow they usually subsided to when he exerted this much effort in controlling it. What was wrong with him?

Kyran heard cloth slide across stone and the soft smack of a body hitting the floor, and his heart seemed to stop. The lass. Oh, stars, had he hurt her? Had he....

"Lass?" he called. He looked across the circle of stone, but it was too dark for him to see the other side. "Are you alright?"

She made no noise in reply, and his magic seemed to press against him with a fearsome will as his chest squeezed in fear. Why was she so quiet? What had he done? He got to his feet, still straining to rein in his magic. The bricks beneath him had split in a long, jagged line from the stress of the temperature change. He held his breath, trying to hear her. A whimper. A cry. Anything.

Something moved at the edge of his light, and he started towards it, anxious to see she was unhurt, and terrified he might find different.

The frost scrawled across the stones in a white mosaic beneath his feet as he crossed the room, and more of it chafed from his skin and clothing in sparkling dust. His eyes raked through the dark, fearing more and more what he might find, until his light illuminated her small form. She had curled up against the far wall, her hands wrapped over her arms, shivering violently. The frost had made it even this far, curling over her filthy dress and coating her thin arms and matted hair.

"Lassie?" he called again, and she gasped. He stopped, afraid he had frightened her, or worse. She shifted on the ground, lifting her head to peer at him from beneath her arm. He saw no sign that his magic had actually hurt her. "I'm sorry, lass. I dinnae mean ta frighten you."

The *wean* watched him from beneath her hand, then pushed herself upright, still shielding her eyes as her head tilted curiously.

"*Rass?*" she parroted, the word so butchered by her chattering teeth that he almost did not catch it. She had spoken.

Kyran blinked in surprise. In all his time down here with her, she had only ever hummed or made small animal noises. The pronunciation was off, but he understood her well enough.

She rocked forward, stretching as far as she could, and touched his arm, tracing a finger along his glowing lines. He watched her, uncertain what had made her suddenly talkative, and astonished at the thrill of hearing a voice that was not his or the demon's or some ungodly hallucination crafted by the beast. He turned his hand over, wiggling his fingers. She giggled softly and pressed her hand against his.

"*Rass*," she repeated.

He let his fingers curl over hers' and squeezed. "Ah, aye. A lass is...." He struggled to remember how to properly pronounce the Common word, even though he knew she could not understand him. It felt more normal to hold a conversation anyway. "A *girl*, like you."

She grinned up at him, her chin trembling as it struggled not to chatter, and he was about to tell her she should probably sit away from him for now when his magic pressed against his control again.

"Sorry again, lass," he murmured, taking a deep breath as he slipped his hand from hers. He closed his eyes and fixed the dams and stops in his mind as firmly as he could, his jaw clenching at the effort. "Cursed blood, settle," he hissed.

It bucked again, and the lass scrambled up, her feet softly pattering across the stones. Fresh white frost coated the ground around him. The lass backed away along the wall to the edge of his light, shivering.

By all the Grace in the Isles, he could not let it stay like this. He had to control it.

Turning away from the lass, he set both palms to the ground, loosened his dams, and let his magic pour into the warm stone again. Another boom rocked through the prison as deep cracks carved through the bricks. Still he let it pour out of him until, at last, he was able to close his will around it with ease.

He let out a pant, the mental task of having to focus on and manipulate his power so consciously more taxing than he remembered it being in ages. Something was happening. Something was wrong.

Touching his face, he recalled the bloodied nose he had gotten after each time the demon had invaded his mind for its perverse amusement. After appearing as Barrett, it rarely wore its own guise, but always came in the guise of someone else—his da. His brothers. Connal. Even Ben.

But Barrett was its favorite.

It should have been easy to know it was not real, to remember he was trapped in the demon realm with a beast that could pluck things from his mind, that none of the people it pretended to be would ever find him down there. But his mind was unraveling, the demon's hideous presence twisting his thoughts. Every day spent down there made it harder and harder to tell what was real and what was not. He could feel himself slipping into madness. When he was certain he was awake, he sometimes found himself sitting in silence for hours, eyes fixed upwards, straining to hear the click of the demon's claws on stone. And when he slept, he dreamed so vividly that his nightmares felt more real than waking to the empty darkness of the prison.

Could the demon have left some sort of lingering damage? Was his mind broken in such a way that he was losing control of his magic? The implications of that were horrific. He remembered acutely what it had been like when he was young, waking from a virulent fever to magic he had no control over at all. It had been terrifying. And even after gaining his initial control, he was always having to relearn as his power grew not in a steady increase, but in sudden, violent leaps forward. But it had not done that in a long while, at least three or four years.

But what if...?

He looked at the floor and wall, coated in glittering frost. What if that was exactly what had happened? What if his magic had taken one of its terrific leaps and gotten stronger, so strong that he was struggling to keep it under control? Or....

He caught his fingers tapping against his thigh as his mind ran ahead of him. The demon had mentioned endlessly how the meat and blood it brought him would make him stronger. He had presumed it simply meant feeding him to preserve him until he reached a certain age. But he could not resist the idea that it had a different intention.

Demon-blooded cur.

"It isna true," he whispered to himself. "It's a lie." It was something else. It had to be. He was not a monster.

But as he looked at the field of white around him and saw the lass's shivering breaths clouding before her across the prison, the tangled voices at the edge of his thoughts shouted their disagreement, reminding him of frost-burned skin and flesh turned hard and white, or worse—shrunken, dead-black from the touch of his power. A power that was almost alive, that wanted to be used, that fought against his control. He was helpless against this ancient demon, but amongst other humans, one slip of his control could kill them. To them—the humans that knew what only his strength of will restrained in his blood—he was anathema, the demon-blooded mage.

Was he truly the monster Connal had thought him?

"*Rass?*"

Kyran looked up at the young, innocent face and gave her a hollow smile.

"Do you have a name?" he asked, determined not to answer the question his mind had proposed, or to see the terrible truth lurking behind his thoughts. He only had to hold out a little longer, only had to keep his mind together just long enough to set her free.

He pressed a hand to his chest, as he would to explain to a very young child. "Kyran," he said, carefully enunciating, then gestured to her, making his expression one of plain questioning.

She made a noise and mimicked his gesture, pointing to him.

"Kyran," he repeated, touching his chest, then pointed to her.

Her lips quivered as she pointed at him. "*Kee—*" she whispered, the syllable almost sounding like a timid kitten.

It brought a smile to Kyran's face. "That's right," he said. "Kyran."

She took a sharp breath, still looking a little nervous. "*Kee—*" she tried again, voice even softer. "*Kee-rin.*"

"Aye, that's about the sound of it," he encouraged her, the strain of his smile easing. He gestured to himself, repeating his name again, and then to her.

She looked at his hand and simply made another little animal noise.

"I dinnae ken if I can pronounce that," he said in gentle teasing. "But I canna keep calling you lass," he told her, and she tipped her head again, recognizing the word. "It doesna seem right."

But simply giving her a name when she had her own did not seem fair either. "I'll give you a nickname, something ta call you by until you can tell me your real name. You ken?"

"*Kee-rin*," she repeated, scooting closer, and he smiled. It was hard not to smile at her. She was a bonnie *wean*, and sweet.

It did not take long before he thought of a name. "What do you think of Effie?"

The lass stared up at him.

He chuckled before gesturing to himself again. "Kyran." And, extending his hand to her, "Effie."

She poked her chest. "*Ef-ee?*"

He nodded. "That's right."

She grinned up at him. "*Kee-rin. Ef-ee.*"

"Aye. I think you ken it now."

"*Ef-ee.*"

Turning to look up at the walls, he clutched that small enjoyment close as he considered his task for the day. Another round of practice. Always grueling, always exhausting. But every attempt brought him closer to escape.

He could scale up almost to what he judged to be the midway point now even with the lass on his back, secured in place with the knotted excess fabric of his kilt. It was hard. Her weight made a world of difference, but he pushed himself, climbing higher and higher with each attempt, always careful of his footing so he would not fall, always mindful to be back on the ground before the demon could catch them.

But why stop there? His calf was finally healed. He had recently removed the makeshift bandage, getting his first look at the two sunken scars on either side of his leg. Why not try for the top?

"What do you think, Effie?" Kyran asked, studying the wall. "Ready ta be out of this black hole in the ground?"

The lass clung to his leg, following his gaze upwards, and he made his decision.

No more practice climbs. No more lying in the dark. No more choking down demon flesh and blood. No more squirming things in his head. He was leaving, and no matter what happened, he would not see the inside of this cage again. He would make certain of that.

"Come on," he murmured quietly, holding his hand out. "Let's get started."

He led Effie to his memorized starting place. After crawling over much of the walls, he had found they were not as perfectly uniform as he had first assumed. This area had proven to have the most deformities, the most places to slip his fingers and toes into.

Kneeling, he let the lass clamber onto his back, as they had practiced. When her legs and arms were securely wrapped around him, he took the loose parts of his kilt he normally kept tucked out of the way, and wrapped the fabric around her, tugging it tight and knotting it on his chest. There was plenty to spare. He had tightened his belt as far as it would go, and still the thing was almost too loose.

Fitting his fingers into the cracks, he started his climb.

It was hard, even with the use of both of his legs. Sweat dripped down his face into his eyes, making them burn, and his muscles ached and burned. He was over halfway, farther than he had ever gone before. He had to be close. His arms began to shake, his limbs slowly turning to lead as he climbed higher. Still the wall stretched upwards, on and on, until....

He saw it. The ledge. It was just above him. He pulled himself higher, trying not to rush. If he took one misstep here, he and the lass were dead. Reaching as far as he could, he laid a hand on it—on his freedom. He stretched farther, feeling about until he found the edge of a brick, and locked his nails in the groove. With a grunt, he hauled himself up, setting his toes into another hold, and reached with his other hand, feeling for another handhold.

The nails on his right hand broke.

"*Nngh*—no! No!"

He caught the lip of the ledge, clamping his fingers on it as hard as he could, and pushed off the wall with his feet, leaping upwards. He managed to get his arms over the lip, and locked his elbows against the stone, clawing at the bricks for a better hold. But his nails scraped over the stone, finding no purchase as his body slowly slid back over the edge, his toes scrabbling at the wall in panic. They were going to fall.

"Effie! Lass, climb up! You have ta climb up!"

Except, she did not understand Common.

Reaching over his shoulder, he grabbed her by her dress and yanked, his feet skidding down the wall. The lass squealed with fright and wriggled against his back, struggling to get free of his kilt. Kicking her way loose, she clambered over his shoulders onto the ledge, but instead of running away, she grabbed his hand, gripping it fiercely, and pulled hard.

He kicked at the wall, his toes just catching the edge of a narrow crack, and lurched upwards. Digging his elbow into the stone, he wriggled forward as Effie strained to keep him from sliding back. Kicking and fighting, he finally got his hips up over the ledge. He nearly collapsed just there, but he made himself crawl the extra few feet until none of him was hanging over the precipitous pit before lying flat against the stones, breathing hard.

"Thank you, lassie," he panted, setting a tired hand on Effie's head. "I dinnae think we would make it for a moment."

She smiled and made a soft *hummh* before tugging his arm, as if to encourage him to get up.

"Aye," he said between breaths. "I ken we dinnae have much time." He forced himself up. His legs were jelly, but he made them hold him as he tried to get his bearings. The light of his magic spilled farther out here, as if the air up here were more willing to hold its light than that in his prison.

What he saw was as breathtaking as it was terrifying. The deep prison appeared to be the centerpiece of the decaying remains of a giant, ancient architecture carved of the same ashen stone. It was built on a cyclopean scale, monstrous and towering, but with a surprisingly elegant design. There were arches high on the walls where long-missing windows had long ago stood that matched the once-precise geometry of buttresses and a soaring, crumbled, peaked roof.

What had built this place?

He might have described the building as a strange sort of house of worship if his light had not revealed a more gruesome detail. Carpeting the ancient structure were bones—a sea of ivory, ebony, and sickly grey, all jumbled together in careless heaps. Kyran recognized the vacant grin of a human skull perched upon a pile of bones that might have belonged to demons. The sheer amount was staggering. There must have been hundreds of skeletons to account for that many bones.

Gazing upon them, Kyran soon became keenly aware of the horrible silence here. No small animals stirred amongst the remains. No scavengers prowled looking for what might be left behind. There was only a waiting, pregnant silence that filled every dark crevice.

The skin along the back of his neck tightened, and with a quickly whispered prayer, he hurried towards the entrance. Barefoot as he was, he had to pick his way around the bones, trying not to disturb them, lest they break the silence. He had no idea how close or far the demon was, but he would take no chances alerting it. Effie followed close behind, her tiny feet adeptly tracing his path.

He didn't let out his breath until they had stepped out of that perverted House, but what he saw made no sense. Above him was a sky, night-dark and starless, but it still had the depth of a proper sky. It was not the night sky he had grown up looking into, either, though; as he stared up into the vast darkness, he could just barely make out solid shapes.

Floating clusters of rock, varying in size from small boulders to vast swathes of land that could have housed his family's entire farm with room to spare—islands littering the sky.

They seemed to have exited into a courtyard of sorts, the ground changing from the strange House's smooth, bone-strewn stone to familiar grey bricks, hedged by a low, broken wall. At its center, a monolith stood watch. It was badly worn, but as Kyran swore he could make out the faint features of a statue.

Past the monolith, Kyran spied a narrow road leading away from the House, a void dropping off on either side. But where did it go? Where was he? He had been so focused on simply overcoming the monstrous challenge of getting out of his prison that he had given no thought at all to his next step. If he was trapped down in the Pit, then how in the world was he going to get out of it? He struggled to remember what Barrett had tried to explain about the realms and the Inbetween. The Inbetween was supposed to be a place between the two worlds, a place demons used to cross over in the dark. Kyran had no idea how to do such a thing. But demons did.

He fastened onto that idea. A demon could cross over. He needed to find a demon.

At least...after he got farther away from here and the beast that had captured him.

Mind made up, he crossed the courtyard to the road, Effie in tow.

He hesitated only a moment as they stepped onto the narrow path, all too aware that he and the lass were impossibly suspended over a vast nothingness. He made a point not to look down again.

Chapter Twenty-Six

On and on, Kyran and Effie went, farther and farther from the perverted House, down roads and across other courtyards, through the crumbling ruins of other cyclopean wrecks. Always alone. Always in silence. It was unnerving how empty the realm seemed to be. With as many of the beasts plagued the waking world as there were, Kyran would have thought he'd have seen dozens of demons by now. At least, if he had guessed his location correctly.

Perhaps he should not have cursed his luck yet.

As if precipitating from his thoughts, he heard the soft scrape of claw against stone, and a chill ran down his spine.

He and Effie had just entered what might once have been a ruined city before some disaster and time had rendered the landscape down to its foundations. Broken stone and rubble were heaped into a mountainous pile at the center like some strange offering. Even more bones were littered about, these almost exclusively the pale ivory of what he had come to presume were human remains. It was as if he had strayed into a bear's den, a mistake he had made only once in his youth.

He looked for the next exit, but the closest arch was partially collapsed, its entrance clogged with stone. They would have to cross a section of the city and scramble over the arch to get to the road beyond. There was another soft scrape, and he heard stone shifting out in the leveled city. They hurried towards the arch.

A sleek form darted from behind the foundation of a building ahead of them. Kyran slashed his hand out, letting his control over his magic slip, and frigid cold lashed across the beast. It let out a shrill yowl, its form illuminated as his blood flashed bright.

It was grey, almost the same grey as the ashen stones. It only faintly resembled a hound with its sleek, almost graceful body, four claw-tipped paws, and lashing tail. Running down its back, though, were heavy, rigid plates, like armor. Several small, beady eyes rolled in pain along the sides of its face, and its snout split not horizontally, but vertically down its center to reveal black, rotten flesh jammed full of sharpened teeth. Shaking its head, it turned and leapt away behind a broken wall.

A cacophony of howls answered from behind Kyran. He shot a look over his shoulder, and his eyes went wide. A whole pack of demons had emerged from the ruins, fanning out behind them. No two were alike, varying in size from that of a hound to a draft horse, with varying numbers of limbs and tails.

He dragged Effie up into his arms and sprinted for the arch. The lass let out a low, trembling whine, clutching to him.

"Hold on," Kyran panted. The arch was not much farther.

The hunting pack at their backs let out another howl, and he heard an answer somewhere ahead of him to his left and right. They were flanking him, attempting to cut him off and surround him. He pushed his legs harder, his muscles screaming in protest after the hard climb, but he made them work, flying over the stone.

He caught a glimpse of movement from the corner of his eye and flung his hand out. The air screamed with cold. Another demon, this one more reptilian than the last, bucked midair from its leap and hit the ground, skidding across the stone with a horrid shriek. Kyran did not stop to see if it stayed down, his attention already shifting to his other flank and another charging creature. This one was about the size of a bull, its shoulders heavy with muscle under a shaggy pelt of greasy fur.

Kyran slashed at the demon with his magic. Its flesh froze fast across its shoulders and beetle-like face, enormous white blisters pocking its skin beneath its grey and black fur. But it let out a brassy bray and kept charging until Kyran had to all but throw himself out of the way. The stones shook as it thundered past.

He twisted as he fell to protect Effie and landed hard on his side, elbow first. Pain shot up his arm before his magic quenched it, but any shout he made was lost in sheer noise of the beast's passing. Shoving the lass with his other arm, he pushed her to her feet.

"Keep running!" he shouted, rolling to his knees as the beast came around for another charge. He could hear the others getting closer. The arch was barely a dozen yards behind them, but it might as well have been a lifetime away. The shaggy demon let out a higher-pitched bray and lowered its head, racing at him.

Kyran released his magic on the demon.

The beast's hide opened across its chest as its flesh flash-froze and then ripped open from the momentum of its own charge. Black blood spurted from the wound and froze in sharp crystals that bit at its skin, tearing it further. The demon's forelegs crumpled, its bray turning to a wail of agony as it slid along the stone. Kyran whirled and pelted after Effie, who had taken off towards the arch. She was fast for such a wee lass, but Kyran had his long legs to his advantage and quickly caught up.

He heard another beast and whirled to see a small demon, no bigger than a goat, dart after Effie. The lass shrieked as its maw caught her tattered garb, dragging her from her feet. Kyran snatched the back of her dress and yanked her up, twisting to shield her as the demon snapped at them, raking its teeth down his forearm.

"Son of a whore!" he snarled and slapped the beast with his free hand. It dropped to the ground, squealing and pawing at the hand-shaped welt of blisters Kyran left across its flesh.

Scooping Effie back into his arms, Kyran took off running again. The bite stung like fire, dripping effervescent drops of blood. The demons behind them were howling again, and the pounding of their claws and feet was getting louder. They had his scent.

Effie sobbed in earnest, clinging to Kyran, but he pulled her free as they finally closed in on the collapsed arch. He almost flung her at the stones out of desperation, but stopped himself and instead set her on the pile of rock as high as he could reach, urging her up the precipitous climb as he turned to face their pursuers. If she was going to make it to the other side of that mound, he would have to buy them more time.

The first three demons barreled at him, including the small beast that had attacked Effie, its toothsome face swollen and misshapen. Kyran bared his teeth at them. His control slipped further. Frost snapped over the stones around him as his blood flared bright and cold under his skin. He pushed sharply out, directing his magic to devour the heat from everything in front of him.

In an instant, swirls of white hoarfrost engulfed the demons, and the beasts let out muted sounds of pain as they stumbled and crashed into the ground, writhing in fitful spurts against the stones.

Kyran clenched his control about his magic again, not willing to waste such a precious resource when there were more demons to cull. But when he searched for the others, he found their shadowy figures prowling just outside the circle of his brightest light, no longer rushing blindly towards him.

His mouth curled in a feral smile, thrilled at his power. Finally, he was no longer just simple prey. He backed towards the mound of stones, stepping up onto it. The stones shifted and rolled underfoot, biting into the bare soles of his feet and making the climb more treacherous, but he dared not turn his back to the beasts. They slunk forward, maintaining a wary distance, their malicious attentions fixed on him. Then something else made them whip their heads around towards the city.

Before Kyran could begin to wonder what they'd sensed, he felt it himself—an almost subsonic rumble that quickly grew until the ground trembled beneath his feet. With a boom, the wall of the closest ruined foundation collapsed, sending rubble scattering in every direction as another demon blundered its way up from beneath the building. It was at least twice the size of a draft horse, and all the more enormous for how close it stood. Its pale hide was thick and pebbly, and while it walked on two legs, its arms hung low, with near-boulders for knuckles. It lifted its head, sniffing the air, before turning to look at Kyran. It had flat, blocky teeth and a grotesque protuberance of a nose, but no lips or eyes. The rest of its face was simply pitted, pale skin, but he had no doubt it knew he was there.

The other demons scattered as the enormous beast let out a deep-chested, gleeful bay that threatened to burst Kyran's ears.

He raised his hand, sending magic whipping out at the beast, and it recoiled as if in shock, raking its fingers at the frost where it sprung along its skin. Kyran poured his magic out, willing the beast to flee, to die, to do what he wanted. Instead, with one flailing arm, it swatted up at him, missing entirely as it connected with the stones below Kyran.

He felt the pile shift a moment before the rocks beneath his feet gave way.

His back smashed into the rocks, and his skin tore. His bones bashed against stone as he careened down the pile of rubble, but the pain of it simply vanished beneath his magic. He hit the hard ground and rolled to his knees. Frozen crystals of his own blood were smeared across his arms, hands, and legs, the flesh underneath glowing where his blood pooled beneath his skin in what would later be deep bruises.

But he forced his legs to move, to propel him into a sprint as the beast made another gleeful sound and gave chase on all fours, running on the knuckles of its forearms.

And it was fast. It galloped after him, sending shocks through the ground that made Kyran's teeth rattle. He had to dive to one side as it bulled through the space he would have been, braying and snorting. Snatching up a rock the size of his fist as the demon skidded to a halt and came around, Kyran hurled it right at the beast's oversized nose.

The demon jerked back in surprise. It let out another keening bay, sliding up in pitch until it was ear-gratingly shrill, before plunging headlong after him. Kyran had to clamp his hands over his ears to keep his skull from splitting at the pain of the wail.

The memory of the first demon he'd faced down bubbled to the top of his mind. Only there would be no Barrett flying in on his horse to fight beside him this time. Kyran was alone.

But he stood his ground, waiting, knees soft and ready, recalling his distant youth on his da's farm, wrangling horses. He pivoted out from in front of the creature, his magic raking along its flank. It brayed in pain, blundered to a stop, and began to shake like a dog shedding water, but the frost clung, unmoving, to its side. The massive beast came around again, howling, and Kyran kept his stance loose, ready.

He waited until the last possible moment, then repeated the maneuver, leaving a wake of agonizing cold behind him. But rather than continuing to charge past him, the demon slid to a stop and turned sharply, mouth snatching at the mage. Its teeth missed, but before he could get out of the way, the demon lunged. Its head drove into Kyran, flinging him down. He landed on his hip. Luckily, his head came down on his arm, or he would have split his skull. Stars sparkled in front of his eyes, and he tasted blood, but he had no time to languish: the demon's enormous maw suddenly gaped over him.

Kyran slapped the thing across its nose, his magic biting into the large, sensitive protuberance. It yelped and smacked an enormous hand down on him, crushing every breath from his lungs in a single, painful *whoosh*. The demon leaned down, jaw gaping wide, intent on devouring him. With almost mindless drive, Kyran thrust his hands into the beast's mouth, shoving his magic down its wet, glistening throat.

It jerked back, mucus pouring from its nose and freezing in disgusting icicles as it thrashed its head back and forth with a rasping bellow of pain. Kyran rolled to his hands and knees, sucking down air in aching, ragged breaths until the pain vanished, and got to his feet. But he did not run, instead circling the demon to its injured flank, minding its thrashing head. Kyran poured his magic through its already chill-rent flesh.

The demon lurched away, slamming its fists down on the ground with another shrill shriek, and broke through the stone. Kyran's skin stung as shards of stone caught his exposed legs and arms, drawing lines of blood that seemed to frenzy the beast even more. It bucked frantically, head thrusting blindly after Kyran. The mage obliged its gaping maw with another swallow of arctic air and scrambled back before it could make another swipe at him.

There was a flicker of motion, the only warning before something slammed into the beast with a concussion like boulders colliding. Kyran threw his arm up to shield his face as a bright white light suddenly burst over the broken city. The air turned to choking heat.

The demon began to bellow and squeal in pain, but above it, an all-too-familiar voice snarled, "*Mine!*"

Kyran blinked against the light, almost not wanting to believe his eyes as he peered over his arm, his breaths turning to shallow, frightened gasps. It was the other demon, the one that had dragged him here, its body not its usual simmering smolder of shadow, but burning a pure white, molten light radiating so hotly that the lesser demon was cooking alive beneath it with a sickening sizzle.

"It is mine!" his captor snarled, its talons carving out huge chunks of burnt flesh.

Kyran bolted towards the collapsed arch. He did not see Effie at the top any longer; she must have made it over. He flung himself onto the rocks and climbed as fast as he could, heedless of the sharp edges that sliced his bare feet and hands open.

The demon's screams abruptly cut off behind him, and Kyran forced his legs to keep moving, keep climbing. He was almost there. The top was just a few more feet ahead.

Heat blossomed against his back, and white light flashed across the stones. A clawed hand caught his arm, yanking him around to face the demon and its eyeless sockets.

"I underestimated your climbing prowess," it growled, slapping his hands away. It pressed its claw down into his chest, pinning his back to the stones with a weight greater than its slender body should have possessed. "I will not do it again."

Its other hand closed on Kyran's ankle.

"No! No, not that!" he begged, panic shooting through him. If it broke his leg, he would never outrun it. He kicked at the beast with his other foot, dragging himself backwards against its grip. His magic lashed out of his blood, but the demon did not even seem to feel it.

"Let go!" he cried.

The demon released Kyran's chest. He twisted at the waist, clawing at the broken stones, his breath coming in frightened gasps as it slid its hand up his thigh, unperturbed by his resistance. Its body glowed more and more hotly until its touch seared against his thigh and ankle, burning him even through his magic.

Then he felt the first grazing touch of its teeth against his skin.

"No!"

Long needles of teeth sank into the flesh just above his knee—slowly. Kyran went rigid, the pain shocking him into utter stillness. A whimper rose in his throat, high with genuine fear and pain. It was not just going to break his leg. "Please...."

It peered up at him with those bottomless black sockets and, with a soft growl that he felt through its teeth, said, "No."

Then it began to eat.

In neat little jerks of its head, it tore the skin and flesh from his joint, fire licking out from its jaws as it fed. He screamed until his voice broke.

Then he screamed in silence, his mouth stretched wide as his body fought with mindless purpose against the demon, against the agony. He kicked and clawed and fought until the demon clenched his knee in its teeth, reached up, and bored its eyes into him, its thunderous will slamming into his mind. He fought that too, resisting out of sheer panicked determination.

And it worked—for a moment. But the demon had only to bear down again before his body slumped bonelessly onto the stones, his breaths coming in rasping, choking pants.

He wished he would simply die, or at least slip into the merciful oblivion of unconsciousness, but he was horribly aware, trapped awake as the beast kept stripping the flesh from his leg until he saw the white gleam of his own bone beneath the bright, glowing blood and the hideous black that had been his flesh.

*Stop. Stop. Stop. Stopstopstop....*His mouth formed the word over and over as he watched the demon's claws close over his calf. He could not feel it— not through the fiery agony ripping through his thigh and shooting up his hips and through his middle. The stench of his own burnt flesh choked his nostrils with each breath. His stomach heaved, and he retched, bringing up bitter bile.

The demon let out a low, furious growl, and it jerked its hand sharply up at his face. There was an ugly, splintering crack, like a thick branch that had broken under stress, and Kyran's world turned utterly, blindingly white.

"No," the demon's voice echoed in that painless nothingness. "You will not hide there. You will watch."

The white disintegrated as pain burned its way back into his consciousness, and his eyes were wrenched open to meet the demon's black stare. In its clawed hands, it held a long, slender limb, pale beneath a thick coat of grime and blood. Kyran's stomach clenched again as he recognized with a sickening, jolting suddenness that it was his leg. Looking at it that way had an alien wrongness about it, one his mind could not seem to grasp properly. Even as he knew it was his leg, his mind revolted at the very idea, insisting that it must be someone else's, *something* else's.

"Watch," the demon hissed, crouching next to him until it filled his vision—it, and the end of the limb it held. Then it began to eat again. He tried to close his eyes, to look away, but he could not, his eyes trapped by the black gaze that never left his, forcing him to watch as the demon peeled the meat off of his own limb, his blood running down its chin. And after it had taken the muscle and skin and fat, it crunched and suckled on his long bones with delighted slowness, mewling and moaning until it had swallowed every last bite.

"Ah, mageling," it purred, its clawed hand tracing down its throat and belly.

"You...." It shuddered violently with evident pleasure, the red lines under its skin glowing. "You are truly the Old One's blood. I have not had a treat so decadent in so very, very long."

The demon leaned forward, its body almost pressing to his. Its heat scoured across Kyran's skin, but he barely registered it. He simply stared up into the demon's vacant sockets, wishing again he would die to escape the pain, and knowing with a horrible surety he would not. The demon gently caressed his cheek, its fingertips blistering with heat, and hissed with laughter when he still flinched.

"Now, mageling," it purred, its clawed thumb wiping under his eye, smearing something wet along his skin. "I want you to scream prettily for me again."

Kyran did not have time to open his mouth before the demon's will slid into his thoughts with a terrifying familiarity and began to simply tear him apart from the inside until he could do nothing but scream. He had thought nothing could hurt worse than his own leg being chewed off. He quickly found he was wrong. There were limits to how far the body could be wounded, but in his mind, there was no bottom to the depths that could be reached. And, unlike flesh, which, once wounded, needed proper time to heal before wounding again, the mind could be flayed over, and over, and over again.

Chapter Twenty-Seven

BARRETT SUMMONED HIS fire again, holding the flames aloft in his palms, but he didn't need to see. It was a mad idea, sitting in the dark and using his power in the hopes of attracting a demon, but it was the only thing he could think of to move things along faster. There wasn't time to simply wait and hope the right demon would happen to cross into Oareford.

He pulled more magic into his hands, feeding the flames as he reclined against the damp cellar wall. He had been lucky to find this place beneath a house nearly toppled from neglect, just outside the city wall. There had only been a few squatters calling the place home, and they had quickly vacated once he'd told them his plan. Fighting down here was going to be a challenge. It was tiny, not even large enough for him to stand. But it also meant there was less room for the demon to get away.

For hours, he sat in the dark, waiting, exhausted to the brink of collapse, but too anxious to even think of sleep. In truth, Barrett was at his wits' end, sitting night after night in the dark, dangling himself like a lure and whiling the agonizing hours away alone. He couldn't take much more, knowing every minute he waited was another ticking against Kyran. If this didn't work—and soon—he was going to cross into the demon realm and start his hunting there whether or not his own demon was cooperative.

Then, at last....His head came up from the spot he was staring into the floor as he felt it—the furtive stirrings of power in the room. He tried not to move. His pulse raced through his veins and rattled against his ribs as the sensation built. Something was coming through.

The air swelled with power, washing over Barrett's senses, but he bowed his head against it, concentrating, searching, until he felt it.

Right there.

He surged to his feet, lunging across the room, hands wreathed in fire as he connected with something in the dark. The creature let out a shrill squeal, writhing in his grip as he slammed it into the ground, snatched his dagger from his hip, and pressed it to its bony chest.

"Give me the answers I want, or I will drag you into the sunlight until you burn, then put my dagger through you. Do you understand what that means?"

"Yes," it squealed. "Yes! Ask, hunter!"

It *spoke*. Barrett's hands shook around his dagger. It spoke. Finally, after weeks of searching, he had a demon that spoke, and he was not going to let it get away.

"Good." Barrett shifted his weight atop the demon, settling his knee more firmly into its middle. His free hand slid up until he found its throat and gripped it tightly. The other pressed the tip of his dagger into the demon's breast. "I am looking for an old demon," he told it, his voice quavering with feverish excitement, threatening to break. "It has black skin, its body is shaped like a human's, and it wields fire."

"There is a whole realm of us, hunter, if you did not kno—*AH!*" The demon squealed in pain as Barrett summoned his fire in a brief, hot flash, searing the creature's throat.

"I need more details," it rasped between shrieks. "Describe it! Describe it more!"

"My height. Big mouth full of long teeth. Long, scrawny limbs that glow like molten metal when it calls on its fire. It has a taste for mages."

"That one! Yes, I know him! Guards his territory well. He is a mad one. He has an appetite to put the gluttons to shame."

A thrill went through Barrett. At last. At last he had an answer. He sucked down a breath, forcing himself to focus, to keep his grip from loosening on the demon's throat. "You had better not be lying," he threatened, "for your sake."

"Not lying," it whined, squirming against his grip until he tightened his fingers.

"Good. Then you can answer another question." Barrett wet his lips, but caught himself wavering at the last moment, uncertain if he really wanted the answer he might hear. But he had to know. "Has it been in possession of a young mage? He would have used ice magic."

The demon went dead still beneath him. "Ice?" it hissed.

"Yes," Barrett answered carefully, confused by the creature's reaction.

"Did he steal it from the islands in the north?"

Barrett's concern deepened. "Why?"

"Is it from there?"

His fingers flexed against its throat in warning. "Yes."

The demon shuddered with a sound like a low mewl of pleasure. "It is one of the Old One's spawn," it purred throatily. "Such a treat. He *would* be one to catch such a thing—" Its voice broke with another shrill squeal as Barrett's fire flared along with his anger.

"He is not a treat!" he snarled, digging his nails into the demon's sizzling flesh. "He is not food! He is not a *thing* for demons to have!"

He let the beast burn for several long seconds before wrestling his magic back under his control. He could not kill this demon. It was the first—and only—link to Kyran he had found. He could not lose his temper and ruin what was likely his only chance of finding the mage and his captor. "Now answer my question. Does the demon have a mage?"

"I do not know!" Its voice rasped in its burnt throat. "I do not make the mistake of wandering into his territory. It is part of why I still live."

So Barrett would not know if Kyran was still alive until he hunted down the ancient demon and made it show him. His heart sank before he seized onto his determination again.

Fine. He had planned on killing the beast anyway. "You will lead me through the Inbetween into your world, to this demon." He pressed his dagger into the demon's flesh, just enough to pain it, making sure the beast was looking at the blade when he continued. "You know what this is. If you try to double-cross me or lead me astray, I will not hesitate to put this through you. Do you understand me?"

It nodded emphatically.

"Good." He unwound his fingers from the demon's throat and got up from its back, stooping to protect his head. He called more fire into his palm, using its half-light to watch the demon crawl to its feet. It barely came to his chest standing upright. Its skin was pale and marked with ugly, puckered scars, its body mostly humanoid but for its long, knife-like claws and overlarge eyes, which gave it an almost childlike appearance that turned Barrett's stomach.

He clamped his other hand on the beast's shoulder, anchoring it to him as he felt it call its magic. The shadows around them began to shift and thicken, and he dropped his flame as he was pulled into the heavy dark of the Inbetween.

"Lead on," he ordered the demon sharply, squeezing its shoulder, and the beast ambled forward, towing him deeper into the thick murk. Unlike before, when he had felt a sensation like slipping down a slope when treading deeper into the Inbetween, it felt much more like when he'd tried to leave it—the air itself fighting him as they went, like wading against a gale or a rising tide.

"Stay close, hunter," the demon murmured, its voice taking on an oddly muted quality. "Have you been to our realm before?"

"No. Now shut up."

It is not like crossing into the Inbetween. If it were so easy, more demons would make the journey.

Barrett scowled into the dark, angrily pushing aside his unease at the voice in his head. "Finally decided to talk again, hm?"

His demon chuckled politely, stirring in his awareness like a cat rousing from sleep. *You finally found one of us to take you to your mageling. Well done.*

Barrett sniffed in reciprocation, surprised it actually sounded pleased with him instead of patronizing. He was of a mind to ignore it, but its initial remark seemed to hint at an obstacle he had not considered. "What did you mean about the crossing not being the same?"

His demon did not reply at first, and he got the impression it was searching for the words to answer his question.

Stepping into the Inbetween is like walking to the bottom of a lake. Crossing between the realms is much more. The very space around you will resist you, trying to keep you from entering our realm, just as your realm resists us. We are not meant to exist beyond that barrier, and yet those that are strong enough are able to break that fundament.

"Fundament?"

The fundamental truths that govern this existence.

"What does that mean?"

He could almost hear it sigh.

It means, hunter, that there are some things you will never understand outside of knowing that it is simply the way things are meant to be. The way they were created.

Barrett rubbed at his forehead. "That doesn't make any sense."

Not to you, no.

He resisted scowling at the demon; it would not do any good. Instead, he focused on the increasing difficulty of simply moving his legs forward. Even breathing gradually became an exercise of will, and still they waded deeper until, at last, they reached the precipice.

"We are here," the small demon announced, its voice so muted that it was barely audible.

I will try to shield you, his demon murmured. *But I do not know how much I can do.*

"Fine. Let's just keep going," Barrett snapped, dragging down a lungful of air.

The demon under his hand stepped forward, and Barrett had to bite down a scream as he met the wall between the realms. It was not a solid thing, but made of flaying knives, as if something were tearing the flesh off his bones layer by layer, starting with his skin. He made himself move towards the pain, but every step was a new agony, the sting chewing deeper into his flesh until it reached his bones, burrowing into his very marrow. His teeth wrenched open, and a ragged scream boiled out of his throat, but still the demon pulled him forward. He was going to die. He could feel his body coming apart, raw and bloody and awash in more pain than he had ever known. He could not keep going like this. He—

"Oh, Graces," he gasped as, with a jarring suddenness, the pain vanished. His legs buckled beneath him, and he collapsed in a heap, utterly uncaring. Not only was the pain gone; everything was. He was numb, and it had never felt so good. He lay on the ground, enjoying the bliss of not feeling. Still, he had to get up. He had to keep moving.

But when he tried to move to get up, his limbs would not respond. He tried to move again, and felt his arm shift. Fire blossomed in his palm, illuminating the darkness around him. But it was not his doing. His other arm came into view as it snatched—apparently of its own volition—at the pale demon skittering away from him. Shocking blotches of black spread over his pale skin like an infection, his skin's suppleness becoming taut and dry. Like a demon. Like *his* demon.

He was becoming an abomination. He had played right into his demon's hands after all. *Stop!* he screamed silently: his mouth would not form the words. *Don't do this to me!*

"You are too weak to protect us here," his own voice rasped, its tone foreign. "If I do not assume control, we will die."

Barrett tried to argue, but a sharp, splitting pain ripped through his back, breaking his words into an agonized scream. *Oh, Graces! What's happening?*

His arm dragged the pale demon towards him, and his lips grinned fiercely as his body slowly stood. His veins glowed through his blackened skin like a mage's, and heat rolled through his back before the pain faded to a blissful numbness. Barrett's eyes flicked around him, and in the reddish light cast by his veins, he saw what looked like the crumbled ruins of a wall. It towered over him, built of enormous blocks of stone the same color as the bricked pathway that stretched ahead of him into the dark.

"Lead," his voice commanded the other demon.

"Yes. Yes," the creature whimpered, not quite looking at him any longer. "This way." It scurried ahead, and Barrett was only able to watch as his body moved to follow.

Barrett struggled in vain to push to the surface, to take control of his body again. He was not strong enough. The demon had snatched his body from him as easily as if he'd posed no resistance to it at all, and now he was a passenger in his own body. Well, what had been his body. The demon had changed it, transformed him into a true monster. An abomination.

"Do not bemoan your situation so direly, hunter," his demon murmured through his mouth. "I have no intention of remaining this way. I only stepped forward to ensure we both live to return to your realm. Perhaps you might use this time to learn something of how to wield my power."

The light of his veins brightened, illuminating the landscape around them even more brightly, and the angry retort on Barrett's tongue died in awe. It was not simply a wall. The pale demon was leading them down a wide, stone-bricked road through the midst of the broken ruins of buildings and carved columns of a size unlike anything he had ever seen. He had expected the demon realm to be an empty, dark wasteland.

What is this place?

"This is our birthplace," his demon answered.

Did the demons build these?

"No."

Then where did it come from?

"Where did demons come from, hunter?"

Barrett paused, confused by the question. *Here?*

His chest rumbled with laughter. "Yes, but what gave birth to us in this place?"

According to the Book of Lumen, it was humans' fear of the dark and unknown that gave birth to the demons.

"Your book is closer to the truth than most of your kind imagine it to be."

That was not the answer Barrett had expected. *What do you mean?*

"We are not creatures born of flesh and blood like you. You should speak with your scholars at the Guild. Your father and sister found the information gathered there quite informative."

The reminder of how much less trained Barrett was than his sister stung. He had never been meant to take up this life, and that was becoming more and more apparent as he was forced to confront the gaps in his knowledge. If he made it through this, he swore he would do everything he could to become stronger. If he had been a better hunter, none of this would have happened.

"It is better you focus your attention on the here and now," his demon chastised, apparently reading his thoughts as if he had spoken aloud. If Barrett could glare, his eyes would have cut into the beast.

And how will my focusing affect anything? You stole my body. You are in control.

"Yes, but your speaking is distracting. This realm is a dangerous place, and you are not hunting a weakling like this paltry beast." His attention sharpened on the pale demon leading them, and it shrank under his gaze, hurrying forward. "You want to kill the demon that killed your two mages. We must both be on guard while we are here so we are not taken by surprise. Do you understand?"

It was unreasonable that his demon—the creature that had taken possession of his body against his will—should sound so sensible. But it made a painful amount of sense. He either refused to cooperate with the demon and potentially distracted it at a crucial moment, ending them both then and there, or he could accept that there was nothing he could do but trust it to keep its word. Given that only one of those two scenarios ended with the demon he was looking for dying, there was no true decision to be made. He could not abandon his mission this close to its climax.

His silence was all the confirmation his demon needed.

No longer fixated on the abject horror of his circumstances, Barrett was able to observe their surroundings, a process his demon facilitated without comment by letting his eyes roam over the landscape as it unfolded around them. There was more to it than even Barrett's heightening expectations could keep up with.

At the edge of the ruined city—as Barrett had decided the collection of buildings must be—they stepped out onto a road built entirely of a crumbling, ashen stone that seemed to make up all the local structures. It was suspended by no conceivable support over a vast abyss of darkness. It was not an entirely empty abyss, though: floating islands with precariously arching bridges stretched between them. He tried to capture more details, drinking in the strange landscape before the demon pulled his eyes away, focusing on the one leading them again.

Despite his lack of control, a pulse of excitement lit through Barrett as he felt his magic swelling. With each beat of his heart, his veins brightened, setting more and more of the strange landscape aglow. He would be more than a match for the demon when they found it.

The pale demon led them for quite some time, threading through the ruins of broken cities and long stretches of empty, ashen roads that connected the fragmented landscape. Barrett could see why his demon had advised against pursuing Kyran into the realm without a guide. It was a veritable maze of pathways, and if the connection between this realm and the human one was ever changing, there was no telling where they might have entered.

For all their walking, though, they never encountered another demon, and he did not sense any other than the one leading them—and even then only faintly, compared to the sensation of its magic in the cellar. Barrett wondered if it was because the realm was so much vaster than he could countenance, or if the sheer power thrumming through his veins was to blame. What beast would not find some other place to be rather than face the towering might of his demon, nurtured through generations of his family?

The demon leading them finally paused at the edge of one of the many islands, cringing low in front of him. "This is the farthest edge of his sacred territory," the demon hissed. "If he has your mongrel beastie, it will be someplace within here."

Barrett's demon eyed the precipice, and he could almost feel it considering the pale demon's fate. "If you have led me astray," his demon growled at last, pinning the small beast with its gaze, "I will track you down and feed you alive to one of the other mindless beasts residing here."

Not waiting for a response, Barrett's demon moved to the very edge of the ground and peered below. There was another floating landscape there, much farther than Barrett would ever dream of dropping without killing himself. He heard the other demon scrabbling across the stone as it fled before his own body pitched forward into empty space.

There was an awful moment of sheer panic as he watched his death hurtle towards him before he realized what the pain in his back when his demon had seized control of his body had been: wings. He could not see them, but he could feel them as they arched behind him, catching the warm air in an effortless glide down to the lower island.

Barrett had never experienced anything like it, and it was as terrifying as it was exciting.

I didn't know there were demons that could fly!

"Any demon may, if it wishes. Our forms are mutable, though it takes a considerable amount of power to form wings large enough to be useful."

His feet touched down lightly on the island. They felt a thrum of power.

The demon, Barrett gasped with a thrill of frenzied rage.

"No." His demon chuckled and briskly walked towards a thready path of ground surrounded by boulders. "That is your mage's power."

The rage evaporated in an instant. *Kyran? He is alive!*

"Do not rejoice so soon," the demon warned. "He may be alive, but you do not know what state this demon may have left him in."

As if in response to its statement, the power waned drastically.

Oh, Graces, what's happening?

The demon did not respond, and Barrett could have screamed when it did not break into a run. Something was happening. They had to hurry! He tried to gather his will again to force his body to move faster, and his demon's powerful will overwhelmed his.

"Stop," it commanded, coming to a halt. "We will get to your mage."

But he could be dying! He could—

"He has been down here almost a month of your time, and even longer by this realm's accounting," his demon replied calmly. "If he has survived that long down here, dying is the least of his concerns. Rushing blindly forward will only make it that much more likely we race into a trap. You will cease your squirming, or I will crush you down where you cannot see or speak or hear until I carry us back into your realm."

Fear, bitter and palpable, lodged in Barrett's throat. He was already a passenger in his own body. To become even less than that, to cease to have any meaningful existence at all, threatened true terror. *No. Please, don't.*

"Then remain quiet and observant while we walk in the enemy's territory."

Barrett let his mute silence be his answer again as he considered once more what he had done by coming here. How had he never even grasped just how powerful his demon was? How had he never acknowledged that it was only the whim of this powerful beast, and a few transparent words, that prevented it from simply crushing him out of existence? Anytime his demon so chose, it could kill him and keep his body. It could remain here forever, or return to the human realm. It could choose at any moment to not rescue Kyran, to leave, to do anything else, and there was nothing he could do about it.

Every instance in his life he'd thought he had been powerless was suddenly trivial in the wake of that revelation. Never before—not when he could only watch his sister's career as a hunter spiral to a close, not when he'd lost Raleigh, not when he'd failed to save Kyran, and not during the weeks of searching for him—never, during any of those events, was he actually truly powerless. Not like this. Now he was truly at his demon's mercy.

Chapter Twenty-Eight

They walked for what could have been minutes, hours, or even days. There was no sun or stars or any other way to tell time, and Barrett's demon was tireless. It simply kept walking, on and on, its pace steady, brisk, constant. Twice more Barrett felt the strong pulse of Kyran's magic, and each time it disappeared, he thought his heart might burst. They were so close. As they got closer, he also began to notice another presence that came and went, fluctuating with proximity.

"That is the demon," his own demon said at one point, "patrolling and hunting his territory. He is quite sated, or he would have noticed us by now."

You and the other demon keep callin' it a "he." Why?

"Why not 'it'? The weak....They are simply animals. They are no more than hungering beasts. But the oldest of us are more than that. This demon we hunt is no weak animal, and to call him such is an insult to my own intellect."

The demon paused along the length of suspended road they were following, staring up at the crumbled ruins of a building looming ahead. It was not the first building they had passed in the demon's territory—which had proven to be much vaster than Barrett had imagined—but it was definitely the largest. It towered over the landscape. The remains of elegant arches, high pinnacles, and delicately formed windows gave the overall impression of a once beautiful and grand House, but on a scale that would have dwarfed even the capital's place of worship, and even the palace. The blocks of stone that made up its walls alone were the size of some farmers' houses. Again Barrett wondered who or what had once lived here.

Movement caught his eye, and the demon's attention jerked downward just in time to catch something pale and small flit through the yawning entrance of the building. With a derisive snort, the demon kept walking. Whatever it was, it was not even powerful enough to be sensed.

The road ended at yet another archway which led into a rectangular courtyard boxed in by decaying stone walls. The building's entrance towered opposite them, more than twice Barrett's height. It had no door, only darkness shielding its interior.

It was only then that Barrett felt something else's magic press against his awareness. It did not feel like the other demon or like the strong pulses his demon had identified as Kyran. It was small and feeble, like the last flickers of a candle wick before it went out. It grew no stronger as they crossed the courtyard, but it did seem to draw closer. Whatever it was, if Barrett had to guess, it seemed to be coming from below him.

His demon hesitated at the threshold of the entrance and summoned power into his veins, casting ruddy light into the dark space. It was vast—an empty space so large that the demon's light could not reach the far walls or the ceiling except in the dimmest shades. But the floor it illuminated more than enough to show the endless sea of bones carpeting it. Black, grey, and white, in heaps and strewn haphazardly, some whole and others broken and crushed. Barrett had never seen anything like it.

"What a waste," his demon rumbled to itself, scanning over the refuse. "But I believe we have found your demon's nest."

There was a soft clatter off to one side in the dark, but the demon paid it no heed, starting forward across the bones.

What was that? Barrett prompted anxiously, straining to see from the corners of the demon's vision.

"A scavenger. It will not bother to waste my time or irritate me if it wishes to live."

As they continued forward, Barrett became aware of another light glowing dimly farther in the building. It was difficult to make out, especially through the red glare of his demon's magic, but it seemed to be emanating from a place on the floor. It was not until they drew closer that he became certain of what he was seeing, and his heart began to throb painfully. It had to be him. *Please let it be him.*

The faint light was emanating from a deep hole built into the floor of the building. The bones parted around it, leaving a gap of smooth, naked stone before the floor transitioned into grey bricks. His demon stopped at the edge of the hole, leaning over to peer down inside. Cold rolled up and over the edge like water lapping out of a well, and far below, Barrett could see a figure carved of fey starlight curled up against the wall.

Oh, Graces. Kyran.

He was alive. They had found him. If he'd had control of his body, Barrett would have wept with relief.

"Quiet," his demon warned him, crouching on the rim as it spread its wings behind him and stepped off into the hole, descending in a controlled spiral to land opposite the mage. Swirling white patterns of frost covered the floor and walls, glittering in a kaleidoscope of blue and red light, and Barrett's breath clouded thickly in the air.

As they approached, Barrett began to worry in earnest. Kyran, while obviously alive, judging by his glowing runelines, was not moving. It wasn't until the demon crouched at the mage's side that he could see past the pale light what had been done to the mage.

Kyran lay on his side, his back pressed to the wall, his legs tucked under the tattered remains of his kilt, and his hands curled limply before him. His normally vibrant hair was an oily, knotted mess, stained with a black crust, and every inch of his skin was smeared with grime and blood. His shirt, or what was left of it, was almost black with it, and hung off his frame like a scarecrow. The lower half of his face was drenched in blood, both dried and fresh, some still trickling from his nostrils down his cheek as he panted for breath. His eyes were sunken, hollow, their lids strained wide, and he stared, unseeing, out of pupils stretched so far that the emerald in them was only a thin ring at the edges.

But he was alive. Barrett had found him in time. Whatever was wrong with him could be fixed after they got him out.

"Hunter," the demon murmured to Barrett. "It would be more of a kindness, as you would call it, to put the mage out of his misery. He is too damaged to be of use."

To the Pit with you, Barrett growled, wishing with every fiber of his consciousness that he could push through the demon's control and kneel at Kyran's side. *Pick him up, and let's get out of here.*

"You do not want to slay the demon? The boy's mind is ruined. A few hours longer will not do him any more harm."

Pick him up. We'll come back. Or lure the demon to us. It will want Kyran back. But we have to get him out. Now.

The demon growled, but knelt and gathered the mage into Barrett's blackened arms.

But something was wrong.

What the...? One of Kyran's legs was gone, only a short stump left under the mage's kilt. *'Oh, Graces, it...it was already starting to....*

"To eat him," his demon finished, its own pang of hunger making Barrett's mouth salivate sickeningly. "Yes, and if he is what the demon you found named him, then he truly is a rare delicacy."

Do not even think about hurting him, Barrett snapped at the beast, loathing that he could feel its intent. It made him sick.

"I can hardly not consider it, hunter. But I am wiser than to evoke the Old One's wrath. He is a jealous father, and he guards his rare offspring with zeal." His demon inhaled, long and slow. "Even still, you cannot begin to imagine the potential locked in this flesh, hunter, even after you felt his power through me before." It slurped noisily, saliva pooling hungrily on his tongue. "I can smell it in his blood."

I don't care what you smell. Get us out of here. Now. He needs a healer.

A low chuckle rumbled through his chest. "As you say."

The demon rose, easily lifting Kyran. He was shockingly light. He had always been frail-looking, but he was near gaunt now, his ribs pressing into Barrett's bicep, his hips sharp angles against the hunter's stomach. Tucked against Barrett's chest, the mage's limbs looked as fragile as spun glass.

A throb of power pulsed through the air, and Barrett's demon snapped his head up, nostrils flaring. It let out another low laugh. "We have been noted."

The other demon. It knew they were there. It would be coming. *Hurry! Can't we cross over here?*

"Not if we want to exit in Tennebrum."

Curse it, Barrett swore. *We have to go all the way back the way we came?*

"No. I told you our worlds are ever-shifting. We must leave in a different place."

And you know where that is, right?

His demon stared up the high wall of the prison and let out an impatient sigh. "I will find it. First, we must hasten out of this demon's territory if you still wish to avoid confronting it, though I still consider that a foolish decision."

I don't care, Barrett insisted.

"Very well." With little regard for delicacy, his demon draped the mage over his shoulder. It was an inelegant solution, but there was little else to be done. Barrett's fingertips began to burn, and he watched with a measure of horrified fascination as his black-stained nails began to stretch and grow, thickening into long, hooked claws. The same burning began his toes, and, shifting from one foot to the other, the demon kicked off his boots as his toenails grew to match his fingers.

Reaching up the wall, the demon dug his nails into the grooves between the bricks and slowly began to climb. It was maddening. The prison had not seemed so deep when they'd descended, but climbing out again seemed to take an age. Every second they took getting free, the other demon was drawing nearer, its power an angry thrum. Barrett had never felt so clearly how powerful the beast was.

At last they crested the top. The blue and red light of his and Kyran's magic, casting weird shadows across the heaps of bones, illuminated a tiny figure crouched nearby.

Oh my Graces, Barrett breathed. *That's a child.*

Never had he imagined seeing such a thing here. He knew, of course, that demons preyed on children, but it had never occurred to him that the demons might bring them back here, or that some might escape their captors.

"Interesting." The demon dismissed him and stalked forward, quickly carrying them towards the exit.

Wait, Barrett protested, straining to look back as he heard the child hurrying over the bones behind them. *We can't just leave her here!*

"If we want to escape before that demon finds us, we will. It will only slow us down."

We are not leavin' a child in this realm.

His demon growled, pivoting to face the child. "Then the consequences are on you," it spat, staring the child down.

It was a girl. She was as filthy as Kyran, her dark hair matted beyond repair, her body stunted and thin beneath her rags, but just the sight of her sent a keen pang of regret through Barrett.

She crouched under the demon's gaze, tucking her limbs in close as if to make herself smaller. But it was not Barrett's face she peered up at, but Kyran's.

"*Kee-rin,*" she cried plaintively, and Barrett's heart twisted.

Kyran. She had said his name. The mage must have helped her somehow. It was the only thing that made sense.

We are not leaving her, Barrett repeated.

"As you say." Without further delay, his demon reached out and plucked the girl from the ground by her arm. She let out a high, frightened shriek before her voice broke into breathless little whimpers as the demon settled her against Barrett's chest before picking up a brisk pace again.

Thank you, Barrett said after a moment, relieved. He had Kyran—alive. He had done it. It had not all been for nothing.

There was another, yet more powerful surge of magic. Only this time, it did not fade, but pressed against Barrett's awareness like a clamoring bell.

"Do not thank me yet," his demon replied grimly, stopping at the edge of the courtyard beneath the arch.

What are you doing? We have to keep going!

"I am freeing my hands," it replied, lowering the girl first, then shifting Kyran from its shoulder. "Your prey is here."

Chapter Twenty-Nine

THE SOUND OF nails scratching against stone reached Barrett's ear a moment before a molten, white-hot figure climbed up over the lip of the suspended road ahead of them. He could not see it well through the light, but he knew which beast it was. It could be no other.

It crouched in the center of the road on all fours, limbs spread like some great, fiery spider.

"Poacher!" it hissed. A wave of scorching heat washed over them.

His demon did not lift his head, its attention focused on setting the mage down with uncommon tenderness, cradling him gently as it lay him against the wall just inside the archway of the courtyard. The girl huddled next to him, pressing as tightly into the mage's belly as she could.

"Return my pet, and I will kill you quickly," the other demon snarled, sending off another boiling surge of heat.

Pet?

A hot, bitter rage seethed through Barrett, and his demon rumbled with dark amusement as it straightened, finally turning its full attention to the other demon. "It is not poaching if I am reclaiming what is mine, thief."

The other demon let out a low, reptilian hiss Barrett recognized as its perverted laughter. Tongues of black flame licked between its long teeth. Sinuously slow, it stretched to its full height, its lipless mouth open to show its thicket of needle-like teeth. The air shimmered with heat between them as its empty sockets bored into his eyes, and Barrett distantly felt his demon's magic flare in response, the heat thickening.

"You have gotten stronger since I last tested you," his demon chuckled, the sound low and rumbling as stone shifting against stone.

The needle-toothed demon's sockets widened visibly. "You...." it hissed. "You are the beast yoked to the hunter. Tell me, what is it like to be another's pet?"

"It serves me quite well. I am nothing if not infinitely patient."

"You must be, to serve such an incompetent master."

"Even untrained, he is strong enough to weather most trials without my hand directing him."

"Except protecting his mages," the toothy demon sneered. "I must thank him for finding me such a treasure, which you will return to me." It cocked its head. "What would you, a hunter's pet, want with a half-breed, anyway?"

Barrett felt his knees bend almost imperceptibly, the wings at his back shifting close to his body in readiness, and his hands heated as magic gathered there, ready for use. "To take it away from you."

They stared one another down, neither moving or speaking, each gathering their power as they waited for the other to act.

The needle-toothed demon moved first. It dropped to all fours, belching black fire. The heat swept over Barrett, threatening to sear his eyes, but his demon did not blink or flinch. Instead, it reared a fist back and swung, slamming into the side of the toothy demon's face as it lunged through the flames.

Its teeth snapped shut, and it dropped to the ground with a snarl, sweeping a clawed hand for Barrett's ankles, its thick talons more than capable of slicing through flesh and bone. But instead of retreating out of reach, Barrett's demon merely lifted his leg and smashed his heel into the other demon's face. Barrett heard his sole sizzle at the contact, but there was no spike of pain.

The beast reeled at the blow, skittering backwards, but Barrett's demon followed it in long, heavy-footed strides as the amulet on his chest began to burn. Power surged through him, more potent than he had ever been able to call upon himself, and Barrett reveled in it. He felt strong, as if he could effortlessly crush this toothy demon beneath him, as it deserved for everything it had ever done, for everyone it had ever hurt.

Before he could close on the other demon, though, it charged again on all fours, its body radiating light so bright it burned Barrett's eyes. His demon lunged for the beast when the light seemed to burst. His hands closed on something hot enough to blister his skin, but his demon only gripped harder. Fire poured from his palms into whatever part of the needle-toothed beast he held. It shrieked, clawing and fighting against his hold, but his demon did not flinch, only pouring out more fire.

Then Barrett heard something over the roar of flames—a child's terrified scream.

The girl!

His demon whipped his head around, squinting through the haze the bright light had burned into his eyes. A mirror image of the toothy demon was fleeing towards the titanic House.

What, by the god of Light and Life...? It has Kyran! Clutched in the demon's arms was the mage's limp form.

"See what power you could have if you were not yoked to your worthless hunter? The beast they had caught laughed.

Barrett's demon growled. Planting his feet, he twisted and flung the beast, yowling, over the side of the road and into the empty darkness beyond. But Barrett's demon did not wait to watch it fall, racing towards the House again.

It's getting away! Barrett shouted frantically. Kyran was going to disappear right before his eyes.

"Be silent!" his demon roared, unfurling its wings and stretching them forward like a swimmer's first stroke. It was the first glimpse Barrett had of them. They were massive, shaped like a bird's, but instead of feathers, they were covered by skin, their bones standing tautly out beneath. Disturbing in design, but crudely effective. They cupped the air as Barrett's demon leapt, pulling them back in a powerful stroke that propelled them forward over the ground, Barrett's bare feet skimmed the stone as they made the long vault.

It repeated the motion, letting out a burst of fire behind them. The hot air swelled its wings and thrust them forward. They plunged into the dark building, sending bones scattering from their path as they closed on the other demon.

It tried to twist out of the way at the last moment, but was too slow; they slammed into it from behind, knocking Kyran from its arms. Bones went clattering in every direction. With a savage snarl, Barrett's demon sank his teeth into the other demon's shoulder and ripped out a mouthful of flesh hot enough to blister Barrett's mouth. The needle-toothed demon screamed, and even through his own agony, Barrett felt a righteous gratification in hearing its pain after all the suffering it had caused him.

"It has been a long, *long* time since I have tasted the raw flesh of my kin," his demon mocked its prey, swallowing the mouthful of meat.

"No!" the beast shrieked, thrashing against his hold, but Barrett's demon only tightened his grasp on its throat. Its body arched, black flames licking between its teeth as its head lolled against the ground. It spat a stream of fire across the stones. Where Kyran lay.

No!

Barrett's demon rolled, grappling with the beast, and Barrett could only scream at the crash of bones being flung everywhere, unable to see what was happening. The toothy demon let out a hissing laugh, and Barrett's fear tempered into a bottomless rage. Gathering everything he had, every scrap of hate, every searing drop of anger, he shoved against his demon's control.

With a jarring sense of half-waking from a nightmare, Barrett could feel his limbs again—not simply in the distant way he did when his demon was in control. He could move them, could feel his muscles clenching to hold the beast in his arms. He grinned and let go of it with one arm, reaching for his hip.

The toothy demon bucked furiously, wresting itself from his grip, but it was too late. He yanked his dagger from its sheath and thrust it up into the beast's chest. It froze, staring down at the hilt of the dagger protruding from its ribcage. Barrett laughed, even as his own demon dragged him back under the surface of his mind.

"Hunter," his demon snarled, its anger palpable. "If you attempt that again, you will find my patience does have an end."

It's dead, Barrett announced, watching with satisfaction as the demon's thin body crumbled into ash, his dagger bouncing on the stone between his legs.

"This weak fragment is dead," his demon replied tersely, picking up the dagger. It turned the blade over in his hands, examining it. "I have no doubt the other still lives, despite its little tumble."

Barrett's amusement withered. Graces, how had he forgotten? He started to ask his demon as it got to its feet, replacing the dagger in its sheath at his hip, when he caught a glimpse of dim, blue-white light.

Kyran!

His demon paced over to where the mage lay sprawled, his limbs contorted in odd positions from the fall. But his blood was still glowing. He was still alive. The fire must have missed him.

Barrett ached to reach out to the mage, to gather him up and simply hold him, when his demon began to walk away.

Hey—stop! Where are you going?

"The other demon will come hunting for him again. It knows you will keep him alive. It was likely relying on that fact when it split. It is best we hunt it down and kill it now so it cannot surprise us later."

But Kyran—

"Will be easy prey, and the demon will not give up on this mage. It will keep coming unless we take care of it now."

Barrett wanted to disagree; he wanted to take Kyran now, take him somewhere safe, somewhere he could get help. But all he had to picture was the mage lying in a sickbed while he stepped out for just a moment to get food, only to come back to an empty bed.

Alright, he conceded, though it made his heart sick to simply leave Kyran on the ground, alone and unguarded, after searching so hard to find him.

"There are not likely to be any demons nearby foolish enough to challenge this nest," his demon reassured him. "He will be safe enough while we hunt."

He'd better be.

Chapter Thirty

BUT THEY DID not find the demon.

Below the road, they had discovered another island floating almost beyond sight in the dark, giving credence to the demon's presumption that their prey had survived and fled. But despite their search, they could find no trace of the beast, nor sense its presence, and were forced to conclude it must have fled fast and far, if it was alive.

Reluctantly, his demon surrendered the search, returning to where they'd left Kyran.

Only he was not alone. Crouched next to him was the ragged little girl. She whimpered at the sight of them, hunching lower over Kyran, but she did not run away when Barrett's demon approached, nor when he knelt by the prone mage.

"Move, girl," his demon growled, shooing the child, and she shuffled to one side, still hovering close. Leaning over Kyran, Barrett's demon gathered the mage's limp form into his arms before looking at the girl again.

"Come," it said in simple command, and began to walk without looking back. Without any hesitation, light footsteps fell in behind him, following closely.

As the demon shifted Kyran in its grip to a more secure position, Barrett could see more fresh blood trickling from the mage's nose. The mage's eyes were twitching in their sockets, as if struggling to tear away from some vast horror he was locked within.

I'll fix this, Barrett murmured, wishing he could move, could take Kyran's hand or wipe away the blood on his face—anything to comfort the mage. *I promise, Kyran.*

After an interminable length of time, his demon halted, looking around them. They had turned away from their original path through the realm long ago and now stood amidst the ruins of another truly immense building. The little girl was standing at Barrett's side, her eyes flicking nervously around them. How she'd kept up with the demon was beyond Barrett's understanding, but he was relieved she had.

"Here," his demon announced. "This is the closest point I can find to where we crossed over."

I'm ready, Barrett replied.

"Good." His demon reached down, clamped a hand on the little girl's shoulder, and, with a swell of power, pulled them into the Inbetween. It carried them steadily forward through the coagulating blackness until its resistance turned once more to pain raking across Barrett's senses, setting his skin ablaze. He wished with every step that it would end, but it went on and on until the skein of darkness broke.

Barrett stumbled as he was thrust unexpectedly to the forefront of his mind and body, out into the dim, grey world. He stared dumbly around him, trying to comprehend how there was so much light before recognizing that he was standing in a field. The walls of Oareford were visible in the distance, even through the rain.

His knees buckled, and he let them, collapsing in sheer relief. Frigid water soaked through his trousers, and he let his head fall back so the rain washed over his face, welcoming the vivid sensation. He was in control again. He had survived.

Shaking his head, he sent droplets flying, then fixed his gaze down at the mage in his arms, almost laughing as the truth struck him again: he had saved Kyran. Trembling, Barrett touched the mage's face to assure himself it was real, and froze when he saw his hand. It was normal again. No claws, no ashen skin. He'd never been so relieved to see his own fingers.

Tracing the tips of them across the mage's forehead, Barrett brushed the dirty strands of hair from his eyes. He felt the texture of dirt and grime, of the tangled knots of hair, and the subtle cold of the mage's magic. He felt real. He really had found him.

Barrett's gaze drifted down to the mage's kilt, then to the empty space where his leg used to be, and his mouth set in a grim line. This was not over yet. Kyran needed a chirurgeon, and fast. But where could he take him while he went to find one?

The answer came to him a moment later. Of course. It was perfect.

"*Kee-rin.*"

Barrett started at the soft voice, his gaze snapping to the tiny girl crouched by him. She was shivering, her matted hair and dirty rags clinging to her emaciated body. Her dark eyes were fixed on Kyran. He had completely forgotten about her. He tried to speak, to say something soothing, but all that came out was a croak that broke into a dry cough.

"Hey," he tried again, managing a soft wheeze. "It will be alright now. We're going to find help for you both." Her eyes darted up at him, then away.

He looked at the mage again, already feeling the tired ache in his arms just from holding him. He did not think he could carry the girl too. "You'll have to follow me," he told her. "I promise not to walk too fast."

She did not reply, did not even look away from the mage, but he had to trust she understood. With a heavy grunt, he hauled himself back up to his feet, adjusting his grip on Kyran until he had the mage curled more comfortably against his chest.

"Just hold on, Kyran," he murmured. "You'll be safe soon."

Chapter Thirty-One

"Myles!" Barrett bellowed, kicking at the door, unable to knock with Kyran in his arms. "Myles, I need help!"

After mere moments, he heard footsteps inside, and the door swung open. A young man in blue acolyte's robes stared at him, wide-eyed. "Mr. Barrett!" he exclaimed. "You—"

"I found him!" Barrett interrupted, pushing through the door, the girl close on his heels. "I found him, and he's alive!"

"Who....What happened?" the young man asked, scrambling to close the door.

Barrett knelt by the fire, laying Kyran on the dirty bricks. The girl huddled by the mage's hip, clutching his filthy kilt with both fists.

"I need to find a chirurgeon," Barrett continued, hauling himself back to his feet, his body aching, and nearly toppled sideways as the room lurched and spun. He caught himself on the hearth, shaking his head to clear the dark fog gathering at the corners of his vision. "I just need you to watch him while I get help."

"This is....What?"

"Just watch him," Barrett snapped, staggering back towards the door. "I'll be right back."

"Wait! Hunter Barrett—"

"Chester, what is this....Kristopher!"

Barrett spun to see the Lightbringer and the second acolyte, Helen, at his side. "Chester, help Helen get a cot and bring it here," Myles commanded, gaze never leaving Kyran, and hobbled into the kitchen as the acolytes hurried to obey. "Is this him?" he asked as he drew near the hearth. With a gasp, he noticed the girl. "Oh, and who is this little one?"

"I don't know," Barrett answered. "She was in the demon realm with Kyran."

Myles sucked down a breath, paling. "So you did make it there?"

"Yes. Look, I promise to answer any questions you have, but Kyran needs help. I need to get a chirurgeon to look at his"—the word would not come until Barrett forced it past his tongue—"leg."

"Blessed is Lumen, god of Light and Life," the Lightbringer murmured, touching his brow as the acolytes returned, carrying a wood and canvas cot between them. "By the fire," Myles instructed, and Barrett knelt by Kyran, gathering him into his arms again.

It felt strange, handling the mage so freely, when Kyran would not even allow Barrett to set a hand to his shoulder while conscious. It only served to stress how ill the mage was.

"Chester," Myles continued as Barrett gently set Kyran on the cot. He was too tall for the frame; his bare foot hung over the end. "Please fetch the chirurgeon. Helen, go inform the guild post what has happened."

"No!" Barrett shouted, startling Chester almost out of his skin and making the girl cringe at the foot of the cot. "Not the guild. I don't want them involved."

"Kristopher," Myles said, his joints creaking as he came to Barrett's side. He set a gnarled hand to his shoulder. "You are a member of their guild, and Kyran is a mage. If you are here, they already know."

He was right. Captain Griswold would have been able to sense Barrett's demon the moment he'd set foot in the city. "Don't tell them about Kyran yet."

"They will have better access to medicine for your friend than any small-town healer," Myles pointed out.

But Barrett waved him off. "They sent a captain and Crown soldiers for him, not one of which helped me find him." He looked down at Kyran. His anger dissolved into the bitter, heavy guilt that had hung from his shoulders since the day he'd come back to the tavern with that bloody letter. "I can't just let them take him. You didn't see his face. You didn't see the look he gave me when I told him the guild was goin' to take him back to the Isles."

Four loud knocks reverberated through the House from the front door, and Myles let out a long sigh. "There are not many that knock on the door of a House," he said, his tone unexpectedly solemn. "Chester, please see our guests in."

Myles offered Barrett a small smile. "I expect that will be your captain or someone else from the post. Let them come and see you both, then I will send them for the chirurgeon, and we will see what can be done for your friend, alright?"

It wasn't alright, but it was too late to do anything differently.

The echo of boots on the stone floor grew closer and louder until Captain Griswold's familiar face appeared at the doorway. "Barrett," he said by way of greeting, stepping through the doorway. "So it was you I...." His words trailed as he caught his first glimpse of Kyran lying on the cot. "You found him."

"I did. No thanks to you."

"So it appears," Captain Griswold replied neutrally, sending Barrett's pulse skyrocketing in frustration.

"Captain," Myles interceded, "the young man needs a chirurgeon urgently."

"Of course," Captain Griswold said with a short nod. "Has one been sent for?"

"Not yet."

"Then I will fetch one and return. May your lanterns stay lit."

"And may the Light guide and keep you."

The captain hurried from the room, breaking into a run for the House's door the moment he was free of the kitchen, and Barrett found himself taken aback by the man's apparent earnestness in finding help.

Or in summoning the guards, he cautioned the faint flicker of hope.

Myles muttered another prayer. "It will still be some time before the chirurgeon can reach us. We had best do what we can to help before then. May I take a look?" he asked Barrett, and the hunter nodded.

Pinching the tattered edge of Kyran's kilt, Myles peeled the sodden fabric back, wincing as it stuck to the mage's thigh. Barrett reached past the Lightbringer and pushed heat from his fingertips into the fabric, melting the white crystals that had already begun to form in the folds of the kilt without the constant contact of Barrett's magic. Myles nodded his thanks and pulled the fabric up to reveal the grisly stump.

It was all Barrett could do not to turn his head and vomit at the sight. It was evident it had not been the work of a saw, but the demon's teeth or claws. He could only pray Kyran had not been awake for it, not like Raleigh. But even as he did, he knew it was an empty hope.

Myles laid the kilt back down, covering it, but Barrett was certain the sight was not something he would forget for a long, long time.

"Helen, will you see about the girl while Kristopher and I tend to this young man? Fetch the basin and put it in the sleeping common. I think it would be best to wash the girl up there," Myles said, hobbling stiffly to the fire.

The acolyte swiftly nodded and excused herself from the room.

"And Chester, will you go see if you can find some old rags to make clean bandages?"

"Yes, teacher," the young man replied crisply from the hall, robes flapping as he scrambled to start his search.

Barrett watched the flurry of activity with the sense that events were spiraling out of his control. He had sacrificed everything to save Kyran, and now it was over. All he could do was watch as things played out in front of him.

"Kristopher?" Myles said gently.

He lifted his head, staring wearily up at the Lightbringer, who smiled down at him.

"You did it. You saved your friend. I knew you could."

"I found him, but—"

"No buts," Myles said, cutting him off. "You brought him here. No one else has done what you did. Whatever else comes, you have done something truly amazing, and I am glad to have borne witness to it. I will do everything I can to help you both."

The words touched something in Barrett, something beneath the hollow dread and ugly guilt. Something like gratitude. "Thank you," he told the old man, voice cracking with sincerity.

"No need," Myles assured him, clasping his shoulder again before nodding towards the fire and the iron hook hanging over it. "Now, help me fill this kettle so we can get some hot water on for the chirurgeon, hm? I'm sure you noticed the rain outside, because these bones sure did."

Barrett nodded, not trusting his voice to work, and got to his feet, swaying momentarily before taking the iron hook and swinging the arm out of the fireplace so he could reach the kettle. "Just tell me what you need me to do."

Chapter Thirty-Two

THE LIGHTBRINGER KEPT Barrett busy while they waited, preparing hot water in pots and the kettle, both over the fire and, after Barrett suggested it, using his magic. It sped up the process dramatically, and Helen was able to use some of the water to fill the washbasin for the girl, who had climbed up onto the cot in the commotion. She lay curled up against Kyran's side, her fingers clenched in his shirt, shivering against him. She looked even smaller than before compared to Kyran's height.

Setting aside the bucket she had been using to haul the water between rooms, Helen approached the cot and bent to scoop the girl into her arms. But the moment the acolyte touched the girl, she jolted awake with a piercing scream. Barrett started at the sound, knocking over the pan of water he had been heating and sending hot water spraying across the kitchen floor.

"It's alright," Helen soothed her, gently trying to pry the girl from the cot. "It's alright, little one." But the girl only kept screaming, kicking at Helen and holding onto Kyran's shirt as if her life depended on it.

"Girl," Barrett called, reaching to try and soothe her, and caught a tiny heel in the back of his hand. "Girl. We aren't goin' to hurt you, girl."

An idea lit in his mind. "Lass!"

She flinched at the Isleish word, but her screams tapered off to sharp little whimpers, and she stopped kicking. Barrett's mouth twitched into a smile. If he had any remaining doubts that she had known Kyran, they were gone now.

"Lass," he said again, reaching forward to run a hand gently over her matted hair. She cringed at the touch, nestling deeper into Kyran's side, but one of her dark eyes still peered back at him. "It's alright, lass. We aren't going to hurt you."

"Lass?" Helen asked, brows high in question.

"Isleish," he answered, "for girl. I've heard Kyran use it before."

Her eyes flicked to Kyran's kilt, connecting the statements before she nodded once. "Clever." She put her arms around the girl again, murmuring softly. He caught the word lass a few times. Slowly, the girl let go of her tight grip on Kyran, still whimpering, but no longer screaming. Helen scooped her up into her arms and carried her from the room.

"Poor child," Myles sighed heavily. "I admit, I was not prepared for the idea that there are children taken alive by the demons to their other world. It puts a chill in my heart to think what she must have gone through."

"Me neither," Barrett agreed stiffly, bending to pick up the pot he'd knocked over. How many? How many others like her were there? Like Kyran? The other children he had been looking for....Had this been their fate? And had this same demon been taking them, too? No others had gone missing since Kyran was taken.

He carried the pot to the barrel of water they had been filling them from when, at long last, there came another four knocks at the House's door.

"That will be the chirurgeon," Myles assured him and slid off his stool. Taking an armful of the rags he'd cut from old robes the acolytes had donated, he dumped them into an empty pot. "Kristopher, could you pour the kettle into this pot for the bandages? I'm afraid my hands are starting to give me trouble."

"Of course." Leaving the pot he had been filling, Barrett grabbed the thick cloth from where Helen had left it near the fire, lifted the kettle from its arm, and carried it to the table, pouring it over the blue and yellow strips.

"Thank you," Myles said, rubbing his swollen fingers. "I am blessed to have lived this long, but it does not come without its drawbacks."

"It's no problem," Barrett assured him, refilling the kettle and hanging it back over the fire as the quick steps of several someones hurrying through the worship space echoed through the House.

"Right this way," came Chester's voice.

Another man came through the doorway. He was on the shorter side and well groomed, with a neatly kept beard beneath his small brown eyes. Scanning the room, he bowed his head when he saw Myles.

"Lightbringer," he said gruffly and nodded towards the fireplace. "This the young man in need of my attention?"

"It is," Myles confirmed.

"Good. Are you able to assist me?"

"Anything you may have need of," the Lightbringer said.

"Good. Everyone else out."

"Wait," Barrett protested, a sudden panic seizing him at the idea of leaving Kyran. What if something happened? What if the demon came back? "I can help."

The chirurgeon looked sternly at him. "Is this your friend?"

"Yes, he is."

"Then you will not want to watch me cutting on him," the man insisted, setting his bag on the table. "Please, leave."

Barrett cringed at the man's choice of words, shutting out vivid images of him taking a knife to Kyran.

"Kristopher," said the Lightbringer, "go on and wait in the sanctuary. If anything happens, on my honor, I will come and get you."

"Better start undressing him," the chirurgeon said, opening his bag. "I'll need to see his wounds to address them."

Barrett froze. Undress the mage? Somewhere in his sluggish, sleep-starved mind, he knew that they would have to take the filthy garments off, but actually considering doing such a thing felt utterly...wrong. Even though they'd shared a room, Kyran had always maintained a careful privacy. He'd never changed in front of Barrett and always excused himself from the room when Barrett changed.

"Go on," Myles said again, dragging Barrett's attention back to him. "I'll take care of him."

With a jerky nod, Barrett set the kettle on the table and let himself from the room, pulling the door to behind him. It was hard to walk away from that door—from Kyran. After all Barrett's days and weeks of hunting for him, Kyran was in other hands now. Barrett could only wait and trust.

Chapter Thirty-Three

Following the faint sound of voices down the hall, Barrett came to a set of shallow steps that, upon ascent, he found led to just behind the altar from which Myles led the Sun Service. A lit brazier of hammered copper stood upon the altar, surrounded by a congregation of candles in the colors of each of the Graces lit upon their own carved wood and copper pillars.

Chester was seated on one of the rows of benches in the sanctuary, speaking in low tones with an older woman. The roof was vaulted, giving him an impression of loftiness. The walls were filled with tall, leaded windows that would let in the light when the sun was high, but now they were dark from the rain's gloomy twilight. It would have awed Barrett when he was young. Now it only reminded him of the perverted House the demon called its nest.

Barrett found the bench farthest from any of the odd number of people seated within the House, their heads bent in penitence, and watched the brazier's fire as it danced and flickered on the altar, the symbol of Lumen's first gift to the peoples of the world. He wished it meant something to him, like it did when he was young. When he believed without a doubt that there was someone listening to his prayers. What he would not give for the naive surety of his youth, before he'd learned better, when he'd still said his prayers by dawn and dusk.

Ducking his head, he turned his hands over in his lap. They were bare, as were his feet, and his clothes were in tatters from his time in the demon realm. He imagined he looked half mad to any bystander. And maybe he was half mad. All he had done, every choice he had ever made, had led him down a path that had destroyed everything he had ever held dear, and this—dragging Kyran out of the clutches of a demon intent on eating him alive—was the only mark against that path.

It was only a faint mark, though, since it had been his carelessness that had allowed it to happen in the first place. He was a walking disaster, a storm that cut a swath through every life around him. And maybe it was time he let the wind take him someplace else, somewhere far away from the people he cared about. Somewhere he could harm no one but himself.

He remained in his seat, head bent, listening to the comings and goings of the worshippers. The sounds of their devotions grated on him. How? How could they keep such an empty, thankless faith to their deaf god? When had Lumen or the servant Graces ever granted them what they prayed so fervently for?

The House's door opened behind him, and the touch of power brought Barrett's head around as Captain Griswold entered. He was soaked from head to toe, his black hair plastered to his head. He glanced around the sanctuary briefly, then, finding Barrett, quietly made his way over.

"Any news?" he asked, keeping his voice low.

Barrett shook his head. "Is it supposed to take this long?"

"I wouldn't know. I imagine it will take as long as it takes." The captain took a seat on the bench in front of Barrett, facing him, and folded his hands in his lap. "Have you given thought to what comes next?"

"You mean the part where you tell me you're draggin' Kyran back to the Isles?" Barrett sneered, cutting his eyes at the captain.

Griswold turned his hands over in his lap. "You know as well as I do that the Guild, and therefore you and I, cannot defy a Crown warrant."

"Kyran might be dyin' in there, and all you can think of is the bloody Crown?" Barrett snarled, clenching his fingers in what remained of his trousers so he wouldn't give into the temptation to strangle the man.

"It is my job to consider such things," Captain Griswold replied. "But before you accuse me of acting without feeling, know that I have taken into consideration the mage's health. As soon as the chirurgeon is finished with his work, I want you and the mage prepared to travel tomorrow under Crown escort to the guildhall, where—"

"Me?" Barrett interrupted, incredulous.

"You," Captain Griswold repeated with no uncertainty. "You are to go with them as part of the guild-sanctioned escort so that you may deliver your first-person account of the events that occurred between your first encounter with the mage and your arrival at the guildhall."

Of course there had to be an official reason behind it all.

"But can't I just give you my report to take?"

"In any other circumstance, perhaps. But this involves the Crown, and Guildmaster Selah has asked me to take extra measures to ensure everything is documented thoroughly. What's more, if I am to understand correctly, you said the mage had been taken by a demon to their realm—and yet, he is here." He leaned forward, locking eyes with Barrett before adding, "If that is not reason enough for the scholars to want to speak with you, I will know you were lying all along."

Barrett balked at the accusation. "I didn't lie," he hissed. "Why would you even think that?"

"I assumed you did so to facilitate the mage's escape," the captain said plainly, straightening again. "If you did accomplish what you have claimed, though, it is not inconsiderable. Well done."

Any other time, Barrett would have been dumbfounded by the compliment, especially coming from one of the guild's captains. But his accomplishment didn't feel so grand when he considered all the misery that had led to it—and that was sure to follow. Even if Kyran woke and never saw that demon ever again, he had lost a leg. That kind of injury....That changed a man's life. Or what might be left of it, if the guild had its way. Unless....

Barrett's hopes buoyed as a desperate idea occurred to him. If he was there, maybe, just maybe, he could find a way to at least make Kyran's voice heard at the guild. No one else knew him. No one else had seen how desperately frightened the mage had been at the very idea of returning to the Isles. No one else would stand up for him. And no one would miss him here if he left.

"Right," he agreed. "I'll get my things soon as I know Kyran is alright."

"Good. I will draw up an official notice for you to carry to the guild. It will state that I will be temporarily replacing you here in Oareford and that you will have all the powers of an acting captain while escorting the mage until such time—"

Barrett stood up, cutting the captain off, as he noticed Myles coming around the altar. He stepped over Captain Griswold's knees, nearly breaking into a run. "How is he?" he asked before even reaching the Lightbringer's side.

"Sleeping," Myles said wearily. "Our chirurgeon John administered ether before he began his work."

"Can I...?"

"Of course."

Pressing past the Lightbringer, Barrett fought to keep himself to a brisk walk until he reached the kitchen door. The smell of blood and spirits near knocked him off his feet. A bundle of soiled rags lay in a heap in the center of the floor. There was no mistaking what stained them.

"Kyran," he whispered, dropping to his knees at the side of the cot. The mage's eyes were closed, his breathing much more even and regular, and he was covered by a blanket, but he otherwise seemed almost unchanged. He was still filthy and painfully thin, and the empty place next to his hale leg was only all the more evident with the blanket's attempt at hiding it.

"I've done what I can," the chirurgeon said from across the kitchen, his back to Barrett as he washed up. "It was a messy injury. I recommend keeping a close eye on it for any rot that may try to settle in."

"Thank you," Barrett said earnestly.

"You are welcome."

There came a sleepy whimper from the hall, and Barrett glanced back as Helen carried the girl back into the room. The acolyte had worked quite the miracle on the girl. Her hair now hung in a flat-edged bob that reached no farther than her chin. Her skin, no longer thickly coated in grime, was a pretty ivory with warm, yellow undertones complimented by the blue dress Helen had apparently cobbled together for her from the scraps of an old acolyte's robe. She wore matching slippers from the same fabric.

The girl let out another sleepy whine and squirmed, legs kicking, until Helen let her down. Without hesitation, she went to the side of the cot. Clutching the wooden frame, she reached up and patted gently at Kyran's cheek.

"*Kee-rin....*" she babbled, her lower lip trembling. "*Kee-rin.*"

"He'll be fine," Barrett murmured, touching the girl's back. She flinched, her head snapping around with wide, frightened eyes, but then her attention drifted back to Kyran again. It hurt, but Barrett tried to remember not to take it personally. The girl had only just been rescued from the demon realm.

"You should look after yourself now," Myles remarked as he joined them in the kitchen. "A hot bath, some clean clothes, and some supper ought to keep you from collapsing."

That did sound nice. But there was something else he had to do first, though he was not quite certain how to accomplish it without leaving the mage unattended.

"Actually, I need to prepare for tomorrow," he said, eyeing Captain Griswold as the man stepped out from behind the Lightbringer. "The captain has informed me that I am to go with Kyran to the capital in the mornin'."

"The morning?" The Lightbringer turned to the captain. "That doesn't leave much time."

"The guild is anxious to resolve this matter as soon as possible," Captain Griswold explained, approaching the cot and peering down at Kyran. "It will also put the mage into the hands of our chirurgeons that much sooner, should anything else go awry with his recovery."

"His name is Kyran," Barrett corrected him tersely. "He has a name."

The captain nodded. "You are correct. And you are also correct in that you should go prepare. I will stay here with Kyran until you return."

"And, if it isn't too much trouble, do bring some clothes for the young man," Myles added. "I fear nothing here will be tall enough for him, and I will admit, I haven't the faintest how to get that garment of his folded back again."

"His kilt?" Barrett hazarded a guess.

Myles nodded sheepishly. "Just so."

Barrett nodded, letting his eyes drift over Kyran one last time before he made himself get to his feet again. The sooner he left, the sooner he could return, and the sooner they could leave.

"I'll be right back," he assured them as he let himself out into the garden and the pouring rain.

But he could not quite make his thoughts leave that room as he walked barefoot back to the tavern. He had avoided going back to the guildhall for so long after Raleigh, but there was nothing for him here at Oareford anymore. In one fell swoop, he had managed to destroy everything he might have cherished.

But at least there he still had a chance to do some good.

"Just hold on, Kyran," he murmured into the rain, raising his head. The cold droplets ran over his filthy face. "Demon or guild, I won't let anyone take you again."

Chapter Thirty-Four

It took less time than Barrett had thought to clear his room at the Drunken Wind. It had been his home for two years, but everything he owned and kept in that room fit in his travelling pack. As he looked around the messy room one last time, his heart hung heavy. Despite everything, he would miss it. It had been his, or as close to his as anything had ever been, paid for with money he had earned.

He would likely be back. Oareford was his assigned territory. But somehow it still felt like goodbye.

After locking the door, he returned the key to the tavern owner with an apology for the missing spare. The woman assured him it was just fine, only asking if there would be another hunter in town while he was gone.

"Yes. One of the captains is fillin' in for me. I have to go to the capital for a while. Guild business."

"Oh. Well, I'll miss seeing you about the place. Hurry back," she said with a smile.

Barrett ducked his head and muttered a goodbye, hastening outside before the woman could see the emotion on his face. Graces, he was a mess.

He started back for the House, but when he reached the garden, there was someone waiting for him.

She had her hair down this time, its honey blond hanging in a limp curtain against her back as she sheltered beneath the protective eaves.

"What are you doin' here?" Barrett asked, stepping under the eaves next to her.

"Hammond told me you were back," Kat said.

It took Barrett a moment to recall Captain Griswold's first name. He scoffed. "I'm sure he did. Everyone seems to like talkin' 'bout me behind my back. Did Alex ever return?"

"You disappeared for four days—"

"Four days?"

"—and left a mark so strong that Hammond was able to track down exactly where you'd disappeared. We thought you were dead."

Barrett held out his arms, flinging water against the stone wall. "Well, I'm not. Not this time. Sorry to continue to be a disap—"

"Don't be an ass," she cut him off, folding her arms over her chest.

"Sorry," he said automatically. Letting his hands fall back to his sides, he glanced at the door.

"You're not coming back, are you?" She gazed out into the rain, her expression hidden by the curtain of hair.

Barrett followed her gaze, but he only saw the wet earth and grey buildings of the place he had lived for two years without really living. "The guild might make me."

"But you want to stay with him."

"He has no one. There is no one here or at the guild that he knows or that knows the first thing about him."

"He's a criminal."

"Kyran's not a criminal." He rounded on her, his voice rising. "You'd only have to spend ten minutes with him to see that. He was terrified of going back to the Isles."

"If he isn't guilty, why is he scared?"

Barrett clenched his fists, stepping out into the rain so he could face her, look her in the eye. "Is this why you came here? Because you don't want me to help him? How can you hate mages when you were a hunter?"

Her hands tightened into fists at her sides. "I don't hate mages."

"Don't you?"

"No. But they're dangerous."

"Dangerous?" He lowered his voice, stepping closer so only she could hear him over the rain. "Like we aren't? Like I'm not?" He touched the amulet under his shirt, lifting it so he was certain she saw. "And we chose this life. They—Kyran and Raleigh—didn't."

"It doesn't change what they are," she said quietly, lowering her arms. "Let the guild handle it."

"I *am* the guild, or a member of it. I am handling it." He stepped back, disgusted to even be having this conversation, and with his sister, no less. "If this is all you wanted to say, you wasted your time. Go home. I'm gettin' out of the rain."

"I'm coming with you."

"What?" That couldn't be—

"I'm rejoining the guild."

His fingers tightened around his amulet. "You can't—The amulet—"

"Not as a hunter," she corrected him. "More like what pa was doing after I first joined."

"You mean the thing that got him killed?"

"I'm more careful than him."

"That's what they all say," Barrett scoffed.

"Except you." She cocked her head, looking past him and into the rain again. "I still have things to get ready. I'm giving my house to the neighbor's daughter. She's getting married this autumn."

"Good for her," Barrett growled.

"I'll see you in the morning, Kris." She paused, as if waiting for him to say something in return. But when he didn't have anything to say, she left him, walking out into the rain, and he wasn't certain if it was relief or disappointment he felt when she disappeared from view.

Chapter Thirty-Five

Captain Griswold had a horse and cart waiting at dawn, accompanied by the five Crown guardsmen that had been sent with him to deliver Kyran. They looked to be around Katherine's age, maybe a bit younger. It was difficult to tell with their hair so close-cropped. All wore red quilted surcoats sporting the Crown's eagle, with heavy broadswords at their hip.

Katherine was there as well, waiting astride a horse with Sweetheart's reins in hand. The palomino looked aggrieved to be standing in the rain. His sister said nothing, watching the proceedings with exhausted indifference.

It had not ceased raining, though it had at least lessened to little more than a light drizzle. Fortunately, Myles produced a tarpaulin from among the varied supplies in the House's cellar which served both to keep the rain off Kyran and hide his scent from the horse as Barrett carefully carried him to the wagon.

With his eyes closed in apparent sleep, it almost looked like Kyran was simply resting, or maybe even passed out from drink. But the limply hanging fabric of his borrowed left pant leg and the rapid flickering of his eyes beneath their lids broke the illusion.

The moment Kyran was settled in the cart, the girl appeared, clambered up the back of the wagon, and settled down in the hay next to Kyran, her arms wrapped around her knees. Her attachment had precluded any discussion of leaving her at the House. Barrett and Captain Griswold had discussed it briefly last night and come to the conclusion that the ward at the guild would be able to offer her better help.

Then, all at once, it was time to go.

"Thank you for your assistance, Lightbringer," Captain Griswold said to Myles in farewell, offering his hand.

"It was my pleasure, Captain," Myles said, taking it. Then, "Kristopher." He bowed his patchy head to Barrett. "I only pray it is enough."

"You have done more than enough," Barrett assured him. "More than anyone."

Myles laughed. "Don't count yourself out."

Barrett's face colored, and the man broke into another chuckle. "I hope your friend will be alright. You will have to bring him to visit when he is feeling well again. I should like to meet the young man you went through all this trouble over."

The color in Barrett's cheeks darkened, but he couldn't help but to smile in the face of the Lightbringer's infectious optimism. "I will."

"Good. I wish you all a safe journey. May His Graces keep your lantern lit and brighten your path."

"And yours as well," Barrett and the captain answered in kind.

The party departed immediately—all but the captain—but travelling was slow. The weather refused to relent, turning the roads into rutted, muddy messes, and the horse, despite being one of Mihai's well-trained geldings, did not gladly suffer having to be near Kyran. It took a firm hand from the guardsman to keep it from bolting even when things were calm. But it was evident barely an hour after they set out that Kyran's injuries lay deeper than just the cruelty inflicted upon his body.

Barrett felt the press of magic just before the carthorse let out a bray of fear. The guardsman sitting as coachman fought with the reins as the horse threw its head, bucking and plunging in its tresses as the back of the wagon began to glow with blue-white light. Frigid air rolled up and over the wooden sides like water overflowing a bowl.

Acting before the horse could take off, Barrett leapt from his saddle and clambered into the back of the cart, scrambling over the wet hay to Kyran's side. "Kyran?" he shouted over the horse and guardsmen, but the mage's eyes were shut, his expression taut in a grimace of pain or fear. "Kyran!"

But the mage did not respond.

Barrett reached for Kyran's shoulder to shake him, but stopped just shy, unable to bring himself to touch him while he lay unconscious.

"Curse it!" He retracted his hand, his attention switching to the tiny, shivering form near his knee nestled halfway into Kyran's lap despite the ice forming in her damp hair. He summoned his magic to warm her and was thrown onto his back when the horse let out another shriek and plunged down the road.

It took the guardsman several minutes before he could wrestle the horse to a stop and Barrett felt like he could let go of the sideboard. He rushed to examine Kyran and the girl after the violent ride, but both seemed unharmed. Kyran's runelines were fading, his expression melting back into a semblance of sleep. Cautious of startling the horse again, Barrett called the barest measure of his power into his palm and smoothed it over the girl's hair, melting the ice from it. She didn't seem to notice, her eyes scrunched closed and tiny fists clenched in the tarp. He wanted to reassure her somehow, but he had no idea what he should do or say. He'd never been around children.

"What in the black Pit was that?" one of the guardsmen demanded.

Barrett started to reply with a sharp word, but a glance at the man's weapon stopped him. "I don't know," he admitted instead. "It must be because of his injury."

The man swore fluently. "This is just perfect. We'll be lucky not to break our necks even if it doesn't draw every demon in the province."

Black flames crackled over Barrett's fists. "He is not an *it*," he snarled, leaning down over the man. "His name is Kyran, and I will handle any demons that dare show themselves."

The guard's face twitched, his eyes flickering between Barrett's hands and his face, and Barrett recalled the letter resting in his pocket. He was acting captain for the guild right now. "Do I make myself clear?" he demanded, enjoying the way the man's face paled a degree.

"Yes, sir," the guardsman bit out, squaring his shoulders.

The corner of Barrett's mouth tugged upwards. "Good."

He didn't have any more trouble with the guardsmen after that, or at least not in front of him. They camped outside of any towns they encountered, unwilling to risk drawing any demons there with the presence of a mage. Barrett would volunteer to stay with the horses and cart while the guardsmen went into town for supplies. They didn't often come straight back. Katherine usually stayed with him, though she kept to herself.

It suited Barrett just fine; he used the time alone to care for Kyran's wounds and dry his clothes. But despite doing all he could to keep the mage warm, dry, and with clean bandages, he noticed after the first day that Kyran's naturally cool skin was slowly getting hotter, and the skin above his ruined leg had turned colors. The wound was rotting. He was getting worse. He was getting sick.

It was not soon enough when he finally saw the lit walls of the capital rising before him across the cleared countryside. The night watchman at the gate let them through without hesitation, bowing his head to the guardsmen.

The streets within were cobbled and lit brightly by evenly spaced lampposts on both sides of the road. Barrett marveled as he had since his first visit, in his youth, at the ability of the city to keep so many lights burning throughout every night. But with so many people living in a single place, and the guild's headquarters located at its very heart, the risk was too great to take any less precaution against demons. It was a risk that had already been proven before, and the city had burned to the ground for it—twice.

Unlike the smaller towns, people still moved about on the streets here at night, especially since the rain had finally broken the night before. The pubs in particular were filled to the rafters with light and laughter as they drove past, and he envied the people and their carefree night while he raced to the city's center.

The guildhall was even larger than Barrett remembered, sprawling across the heart of the capital. It had been a long while since he had been back, but he was certain there were parts grown up over its wall that were new.

He did not have to present his amulet to the guild member at the gate. He could feel the thrum of power in the other man from his demon just as he knew the watchman could feel it in him.

"Please help," he said without any preamble, not recognizing the older man. "I have a mage with me. He's badly wounded. He needs a healer as soon as possible."

The man nodded and set his fingers to his lips, letting out two sharp, piercing whistles. Even as exhausted as the horse was, it jerked in surprise, starting forward several steps before the guardsmen wrestled it to a stop. "Your horse won't go any farther," the man told him, reaching to grab its bridle. It made another sharp snort, trying to pull away, but he held it fast. "They'll be here in a moment for your mage."

"'They'?"

"My men." The man turned a critical eye up at Barrett, scanning him briefly, and Barrett eyed him in turn. His hair had gone silver with age, but his shoulders and jaw, defined by their strong Sanmetzki features, were squared, and he did not hobble like a feeble old man beneath his thick leather armor.

"What's your name?" the watchman asked.

"Barrett."

"Barrett," the man repeated with a measure of familiarity. "I remember the name."

"You would," Kat remarked, dismounting and joining the two of them.

A man grinned, his teeth glinting white the lantern light. "Katherine. It's been some time. You decide to take me up on my offer?"

"Yes, actually."

The man's brows shot up. "Really? That's great. The apprentices need someone else to hate when they're sore every evening."

There was a commotion across the open courtyard, and a moment later, several men came through the large archway, lanterns hanging at their hips and a stretcher carried between them. The first man nodded to the watchman as they approached, then at the wagon.

"In the back," the man answered. "It's a mage, so be careful. You know how they can get."

"What is that supposed to mean?" Barrett demanded.

"Hm?" The watchman cocked his head at Barrett without looking away from the other men.

"*You know how they can get?*" Barrett repeated, not backing down. "What is that supposed to mean?"

The man's eyes flicked briefly towards Barrett, then Kat, and back to the wagon. "Have you ever been around any of the mages at this guild when they have been injured or sick? They are dangerous. They are not like you or me or any of the other hunters. If they're not fully in control of themselves at all times, their magic goes wild. We almost lost an entire wing of the guildhall to one of them. Near burned the whole thing to the ground."

Barrett's face warmed. "There are plenty of young hunters that can claim the same."

"Not as many as you would think, and they usually manage themselves after a year or two. Mages are like that their entire lives, short as those usually are, the poor bastards."

Barrett's mouth drew into a tight snarl. "You—"

A shrill cry interrupted him, and he whipped around to see the girl hunched over Kyran, her head ducked fearfully, as two of the men that had come with the stretcher tried to get to the mage to pick him up.

"Lass," Barrett called to her, but she didn't look up. "Lass, come here." When she still did not move, he climbed over the wheel into the back of the wagon. "Lass," he repeated, but it was no use. He looked helplessly from the girl to the waiting men, unsure what to do. She would resist if he tried to move her against her will, but she wasn't listening, and Kyran needed to get to the chirurgeon as soon as possible.

So, steeling himself against whatever came next, he bent and scooped her up in his arms. She let out a deafening shriek, kicking and squirming in his grip until he had to tighten his arms around her. The men worked quickly, lifting the mage and handing him down off the wagon to the waiting stretcher. As soon as they had Kyran secured, Barrett let the girl go.

Her ear-piercing wails cut off the moment her feet touched the wagon, and she scrambled after the stretcher as the men carried it into the guildhall.

"I'll talk to the ward about her," Kat offered.

"And I'll get someone to take care of your horse if you will follow them," the watchman said when Barrett climbed out of the wagon. "Tacita will want to hear what happened to him. You guardsmen can head inside. There's hot food and dry clothes if you ask."

Barrett only offered Kat and the man both a crisp nod before falling in behind the others carrying the stretcher, one man to each corner. They moved briskly but smoothly, making an obvious effort not to jostle Kyran between them. As they passed under the stone archway, its ornate carvings stood out in the stark lantern light flooding the area. Among the uniquely organic and geometric shapes were depictions of previous leaders of the guild who stared down solemnly from above the guild's coat of arms—a shield depicting a pair of crossed arrows above a field of stars, held by the forelimbs of a stag and a hound while the king's eagle perched above. Heavy, iron-banded doors stood open on either side of the archway, ready to be drawn shut and barred in times of need.

Beyond the archway was the sprawling labyrinth that was the guildhall. Rebuilt, refurbished, and expanded over and over through the decades, it had become a confusing mesh of styles and histories. Barrett had never been good at navigating it, and had been rescued more than a few times by Raleigh when he had gotten lost on his way to one of his lessons.

His heart ached at the memory of Raleigh's breathless laugh when the mage had found him wandering down the same hall for the third time in a row, at the faint echo of his soft, cool hand in his as he lead him not to class, but to another secluded corner for an entirely different sort of lesson. Barrett ducked his head and pried himself out of the memory. He didn't have time to let himself sink into the past. He was needed here—now. He could let himself fall apart when he was certain Kyran was going to be alright.

The men followed the outside of the main building, passing several entrances until they got to an older section of the guildhall, one still made of the original clay bricks. Someone was waiting for them, holding open one of the heavy doors as they marched up the short stairs, still mindful of their charge. The sterile scent of linen and strong spirits laced with ash and the iron tang of blood met Barrett's nostrils, and he wrinkled his nose in distaste. He hated the smell of the hospital. He had not spent much time in it, but even the few times he had were more than he cared for.

They carried Kyran up a flight of stairs just as a woman came sweeping from one of the open doors. She was dressed in grey woolen leggings, short boots, and the practical canvas coat of a chirurgeon. She was of average height, and somewhere just beyond her middle years, her dark skin creased deeply around her steel grey eyes and wide, soft mouth, though what he could see of her body where it pressed against the fabric was all hard, working muscle. Her hair was cut close to her skull, silver and white showing in calico patches with the black.

"In there," she commanded them when she got close, her voice crisp and deep for a woman. She watched the men carry Kyran past, then fixed her attention on Barrett, offering him a hand.

"Barrett," she said in greeting. Her grip was firm, her hands calloused from work, but he did not sense the touch of magic from a practicing hunter. He never had from her.

"Tacita," he replied in kind.

"Been a while." Their hands broke, and she set her fist to her hip. "Tell me what happened."

"He....He was captured by a demon. It was feeding on him. I don't know if his"—he gestured vaguely towards his own leg—"leg was something that happened right after it took him or shortly before I found him. He hasn't woken up since I've had him, but his magic keeps...." He struggled for a word to describe the sudden bursts of frigid cold.

"What sort of magic does he have?"

"Ah, ice?" That was not really the best way to describe what Kyran did. "He can chill the air, and freeze things without touching them. His control is normally incredibly strong."

The chirurgeon's brows knit, her lips pursing. "Ice? I have not heard of that one before. Does it respond to fire?"

"Yes. It's how I have been managing it while we've been traveling."

"Good." She nodded, deep in thought. "It's best I get started," she said, offering Barrett a soft smile. "It will likely take some time to help him. If you would wait downstairs....One of the captains will be looking for you."

He nodded dumbly, and she stepped into the room, pulling the doors shut behind her with a firm clap that reverberated through the sterile air.

It was out of his hands again. All he could do was wait. A more religious man might have prayed; Graces knew he needed a miracle right now. Kyran needed one.

"He'll be alright," he mumbled to himself as the guilt that had been plaguing him rose thickly at the back of his throat again. "He'll wake up."

Part Two

Chapter Thirty-Six

It took far longer for the scholars to finish with Barrett than he had initially anticipated. Every time he thought he was done, they would reappear, prying every little detail about his crossing into the demon realm. He was not sure how much of what he told them was useful; words had never been his strong point, and he found himself groping for vocabulary he did not have to describe what he had seen. But he tried his best.

At last, though, the scribes only came to talk to him once every few days for clarification on whichever point they were mulling over. Before he was finally left to his own devices, though, Captain Griswold had given him a new task.

"I want you to try to find any information in our records about the 'Old One' the demon you were pursuing mentioned."

"Can't the librarians or the scribes do that?" Barrett argued. That was their job, after all.

"They are too busy right now to take on another task," the captain explained. "But I am confident this is not the first time this Old One has been mentioned in a report, which suggests some truth to what the demons told you."

"And?" Barrett prompted. He was not an idiot. He knew why the captain was asking him to do this. This was just busy work, a way to keep him out of the way. Barrett wanted to see Kyran. He had only been able to see the man a couple times, when he'd managed to get free of his obligations and visit him in the hospital wing.

Kyran never woke. Sometimes his head would start to roll, and he would moan softly between heavy pants, his eyes dancing beneath his eyelids, but they never opened. In fact, the only change in the mage's condition was that he was getting worse. The last time he had visited, Tacita had told him Kyran's magic was getting more difficult to control, and the cold from the magic was playing havoc with his fever. More and more, it seemed like Barrett had saved the mage from the demon realm only to watch him succumb to infection and whatever the demon had done to his mind. And if that happened, he wanted to be there. He didn't want to hear about it while he was off doing some busy work. He wanted to be there for Kyran, whether he died or finally woke up.

"And," Captain Griswold continued, "if there is a demon out there that even a seasoned hunter's demon will not cross, the guild needs to know about it, especially if there is a link between it and Kyran, as the demons claim. Have you considered what may happen if what your demon said is true, and this Old One decides we are a threat to Kyran's life and appears here?"

The thought had not crossed his mind. But now he could only imagine the horror of the scene as it unfolded in his imagination, the kind of raw power the beast must have had to be shown the sort of deference his demon—a hunter's demon, fed power for generations by his family—had given it. He imagined this Old One climbing through the Inbetween into the guildhall, unstoppably wreaking its vengeance on every member of the guild it could get its claws into.

Barrett frowned. "But why would a demon be interested in what happens to Kyran? I've never heard of a demon defending a mage before."

"In your reports, you mentioned that your demon referred to Kyran as the child of this Old One. Perhaps this demon has taken an interest in preserving him because it feels some connection to him through his bloodline?"

Barrett considered the idea. He knew the story behind the origin of mages—that a demon and a woman gave birth to the first of them, and that all of their bloodlines stemmed from that first mage. The reason there were so few mages was because the bloodlines did not run true, often skipping many generations before reappearing, and those born a mage were not able to produce children of their own. Could it be possible that this originator—the demon that spawned the mages—was still alive somewhere and actively working to protect, or at least avenge, the descendants of its progeny? But if that were the case, what about Raleigh? Why was Kyran different?

Did he steal it from the islands in the north?

He had not given much thought to the toothy demon's reply at the time, but he realized now it had guessed Kyran's heritage simply by his type of magic. But what did Kyran being Isleish have anything to do with his magic, or the Old One in particular? And if the Old One *was* the demon that gave birth to all mages, why did the demons seem concerned almost exclusively about Kyran evoking its wrath, not any other mages? Why had none of them been concerned about Raleigh?

There was a gentle cough, and Barrett realized he had been standing there silently, engrossed in his thoughts. "Alright," he agreed peevishly. He still would have rather been with Kyran, but the captain's arguments had a point. There was nothing he could do for Kyran at his sickbed, but he could find out why this had happened, and possibly prevent it from happening again.

"I'll see what I can find."

The library was enormous. Taking up a full fourth of the guildhall's land, the structure stood separate from the others—a precaution against fire. Within its towering arches were hundreds of manuscripts, meticulously ordered and stored by the guild's scribes and librarians—histories of the guild, Tennebrum, other countries, and the world as it was known; notes; tomes of accumulated knowledge on a multitude of subjects; reports—anything and everything. It could all be found there.

The woman busily working at the tiny desk at the front greeted him as he stepped into the library. She had plain but pleasant features, with warm brown skin. She introduced herself as Ilham, one of the many librarians employed under the guild, and offered her help in finding anything he needed in the archives. When Barrett told her what he was looking for, she hesitated for only a moment before bustling off to find a good collection of reports for him to begin with.

What proceeded was day after day after week of pouring through manuscripts. The name was mentioned more than Barrett expected in vastly different hunters' reports, from as far back as the establishment of the guild and earlier. But that was all it ever was—mentioned. No one seemed to have any more information on what exactly the Old One was or its motivations, only that it was the name of an ancient demon other demons seemed to hold in reverent awe; at least the intelligent ones did.

There were a few pieces written by guild scholars proposing, as Barrett had guessed, that this Old One was the first demon, which would make it the progenitor of the mage bloodline. But there was no other mention of mages in conjunction with the name, leaving Barrett still to wonder what was so unique about Kyran.

Barrett closed the book he had been staring at for the past several hours and leaned back. He was tired of chasing his tail. There was nothing to find.

"Still nothing?"

Barrett shook his head. "Nothin' yet."

Ilham approached with another tome in her arms.

"I don't think there is anythin'," Barrett sighed.

"Well, we will not know unless we keep looking," she encouraged him, her low voice warm and hopeful.

"I don't think I can." He ran his hand over his face and the rough scratch of his stubble. His head throbbed. He had plenty of questions, and looking only seemed to be making more. "Not today, anyway. I'm not sure how y'all do it."

"Oh, I love it." She set the tome down on the table. "I love reading the books here, especially since all the people in them and the things that happened to them and what they did are real. It makes it so much more interesting."

"Well, I'm glad someone thinks so."

Ilham giggled, tapping the side of her spectacles. "I can keep looking for you, if you like."

"No, I don't want to be any trouble."

"It's no trouble at all. I said I liked looking, and so long as I complete my other duties first, the Head won't mind." She nudged his arm. "You look like you might go a little mad if you are stuck here with me any longer."

"No, you've been very helpful," Barrett assured her. "It's just....I was never one for books or studyin', and I've got a lot on my mind."

"I understand." Her expression sobered. "I'll keep looking, and I'll let you know when I find something, "

He almost disagreed and insisted he stay, but the thought of staring at those musty old pages for just five more minutes was enough to drive him to his feet. "Thank you. You have been more help than you know."

"It is my pleasure, Hunter Barrett. I hope I can find something of use to you."

Barrett was not so certain. Whatever the Old One was, it seemed like the other demons were reluctant to call its attention to themselves by revealing too much. Perhaps a hunt for a more talkative creature might prove more fruitful than digging through volumes of old notes. But it would not hurt to let her keep looking. If anything, she would be far more likely to find any information there than him.

"Thank you again," he said and saw himself out.

He wandered across the brick courtyard, his hands jammed in his pockets. The weather had grown cold since his arrival. The end of the year was drawing near, and Kyran still hadn't woken.

Barrett found his way to his room near the top of the dorms and collapsed onto his bed. As a visiting hunter, he had been granted a senior room for the duration of his stay, meaning he did not have bunkmates, but it did little to help him rest.

Sleep was hard to come by. As exhausted as he was, Barrett found himself staring at the unfamiliar ceiling, his mind turning in restless knots.

He sat on the edge of the bed, toying with the idea of leaving his boots on for just a few more minutes' chance at sleep, when, with a soft sputter, every lantern in the room went dark.

Instantly, Barrett was on his feet, conjuring fire to his palm and snatching the nearest lantern. Distant screams sounded out; the lanterns must have gone out elsewhere. He smacked the lantern back down and drew his knife with his free hand.

It must be a demon.

Kyran.

Throwing the door open, Barrett bolted down the stairs and out into the lamplit courtyard, pushing past anyone that got in his way when he felt power slam into his senses hard enough to make him stagger. It did not let up with that single blow, either, but pressed against him until he was forced a step back, then another. Others around him were on their knees, and those on their feet reeled backwards.

There was a crash of breaking glass. Frigid wind howled out of the building across the square from him, sweeping across the stones, so cold it made his skin ache. The sky began to darken, clouds building and churning with unearthly speed. But even the booming shocks of thunder could not entirely drown out the shrill screams from inside the hospital.

"Kyran!" he screamed into the wind, but he couldn't make his body move. He had never felt a demon's power this strongly before, this directly. It was almost a force of nature unto itself.

He forced his magic out against the monstrous will, conjuring enough fire to guard against the cold that seemed to be deepening by the second. Abruptly, the pressure lessened, and he was able to move forward again.

Inside the hospital, the air was not simply cold; it burned to even try to draw a breath. Ice crawled down the walls in familiar patterns, and the air drifted with fine mist. Barrett had to blink against the agony that bit at his eyes, face, and any other exposed flesh. There were people huddled near the walls, hospital staff with no magic themselves. Some cowered on the stairs, and it was only after a moment that he realized they were furtively tugging at their hands, stuck to the banisters by the sudden frost.

Another hunter staggered into the doorway behind him, and Barrett pointed to the people caught in the cold with no protection. "Help them!"

Only waiting just long enough to see the woman nod, Barrett pulled yet more deeply from his magic to guard himself against the dreadful cold and took the stairs two at a time. But his fire seemed fitful and weak in his palms, struggling to remain lit. If this was Kyran's magic, it was much, much more powerful than he had ever shown while he fought at Barrett's side.

By the time he reached the top of the stairs, he had started to shiver violently, his shoulders, back, and arms twitching jerkily to try and keep him warm. More screams echoed from the other rooms, and a door flew open as someone fled towards him, then down the stairs. The door to Kyran's room was open, and someone stood in the doorway, back to him. Swearing softly, Barrett tucked his face into the crook of his arm to protect his burning lungs.

He had started to say something to the person blocking the doorway when he caught a glimpse over their head of the bizarre tableau within the room.

A creature hunched over the mage's cot, so large it seemed to fill the room. It was not so terribly human-looking as the needle-toothed demon that had stolen the mage, but it stood poised midway between something humanoid and beast. Its body seemed to be carved from solid ice, slender to the point of fragility. Its attention was fixed on Kyran's limp form lying beneath it, its long, brittle fingers stroking through his hair as if caressing him.

"Get away from him!" Barrett tried to yell, but his voice only came out a harsh wheeze as the cold cut through his magic. He shoved past the person in the door to find others just inside the room cowering against the gale, eyes fixed on the enormous demon, when his own demon stirred within him.

No! it bellowed, grappling with his will until he could no longer move. *You cannot! He will kill you without even a mote of thought.*

"It's hurting Kyran!" Barrett coughed, choking on the air as it seemed to turn crystalline in his lungs. "I can't—not after everything—"

Do not be a fool. He would never harm one of his children.

Barrett's eyes shot wide before he had to close them tightly against the whipping wind again, his eyes burning as if he had set them aflame. "He...?"

The Old One.

The Old One. He was standing before a demon that inspired fear and awe in its—*his*—own kind when nothing else could. This was the oldest of demons, the father of mages, and his simple presence here in the guild was so powerful that none could go near it.

And Kyran was caught beneath it.

Barrett could feel his demon summoning its magic, shoving it through his body to ward off the Old One's bone-chilling aura. He tried to peel his eyes open, but one was stuck shut.

The Old One stood utterly still, as if he had become the ice he seemed to be made from, his empty sockets fixed down on Kyran as if mesmerized. Then he stroked Kyran's face in another gentle caress, passing down the mage's body all the way to his missing leg. A low, mournful wail, like a gale through treetops, emanated from the beast.

With a violent shudder, Kyran jerked into a taut bow against the cot, his mouth stretching open into a soundless scream. His runelines burst to life beneath his skin. The demon was hurting him.

"No," Barrett wheezed. "Stop—please!"

The demon lifted his head. His hollow sockets swept across the room, passing right over Barrett as if he were nothing. The Old One had an unexpected elegance, his countenance an uncanny blend of graceful, androgynous features and the elongated proportions of an elk, his face a bit too long and eye sockets set just a bit too far apart above the delicate arch of cheekbones to look human.

Withdrawing his hand, the demon backed away from the cot on all fours until he was pressed into the far corner, his gaze never leaving the mage. With another jolt, Kyran slumped against the cot again. Gradually, the demon's light dimmed until, with a last flicker, it went dark, and Barrett felt the beast slide between realms. The wind disappeared immediately, leaving only a crystalline cold.

Fire came boiling out of Barrett's skin, setting the air steaming and churning with shimmers of heat. His eyes watered as their lids unstuck from the ice that had formed at their edges. He took a deep breath, marveling at how good it felt to draw warm air in again. His demon's presence withdrew from his conscious awareness, and he staggered as his limbs unlocked. The other hunters began to move too, babbling and gasping and swearing. He could hear other people in the hall behind him calling to one another, and there were footsteps on the stairs, but all he could think of was Kyran.

"Please," he begged as he made his creaking legs carry him to the bedside, afraid he would find Kyran still and lifeless despite his glowing runelines. "Please...."

The ice coating his skin looked like something from a faerie story, set aglow by the lines that ran beneath it, shining cold and bright through Kyran's translucently pale skin. A dark red crystal beneath the mage's nose was the only blot of color to mar the image. The demon had hurt him somehow, hurt him where even Tacita could not help him.

"I'm sorry," Barrett whimpered, his voice lost in the fray of voices and scuffing boots as the other hunters poured into the room. "Graces, I am so sorry I couldn't protect you." He reached as if to touch Kyran's face, to melt away the ice from his cheeks and eyes, when the mage let out a tiny whisper of sound, barely audible over the confusion.

It couldn't be. Barrett thought his aching heart might just stop right there. He searched Kyran's face. He had to be hearing things.

Emerald green eyes, flushed with fey light, flicked up to Barrett, focusing as they hadn't in months, as he said again in the barest rasp of a whisper, "Barrett?"

Barrett couldn't breathe around the agony of relief. Kyran was awake. He was alive. Barrett could not hold the flood of tears back or stop the tremble in his jaw.

"It's me," he whispered back, afraid that if he spoke any louder, his voice would break. "I'm here."

The mage's brow pinched, and he opened his mouth to say something more when there was a sharp cry from the hall, followed by Tacita's gentle shushing.

"None of that," she chided, appearing in the doorway with the small girl Barrett had found with Kyran. The girl was squirming fiercely in her arms, and a familiar young woman followed them closely. The child's eyes went wide as she spied Kyran and let out another cry, kicking and writhing until she tumbled free of Tacita's arms. Scrabbling to her feet, she shot across the room, clambered up onto the cot, and burrowed into the mage's side, wrapping her arms around him.

Kyran blinked in surprise before his gaze moved down to the girl, the ice on his skin cracking at the movement. His lips moved again, forming a word Barrett did not recognize this time. The girl picked her head up, letting out a delighted squeal, and clung to him through the ice as if he might disappear if she let go.

"We were with another patient when it happened," Tacita said briskly, moving to the opposite side of the cot. "Lilyanna, please begin removing the ice while I examine him."

The younger woman nodded, expression composed and serene as she bent over the foot of the cot and, with an extraordinary measure of gentleness, began to carefully work the sheets of ice from Kyran's skin, her power only the barest flutter against Barrett's senses.

"Hunter Barrett," Tacita addressed him, "were you present for what happened here?"

Barrett nodded dumbly as she leaned forward and took Kyran's chin in her hands. She tipped his head up and inspected each of his eyes.

"There was a demon," he told her. "The Old One."

She looked up at him sharply. "Are you certain?"

"Yes. It is what my demon named him."

A hand fell on his shoulder, and Barrett whirled around.

Captain Griswold was at his side. "Is everything alright? What happened?"

"There was a demon," Barrett repeated, turning back to the cot. "It was here, bendin' over Kyran."

"Is he alright? What did it do?"

"It...." Barrett frowned, looking down at Kyran, who stared around him as if not comprehending anything he saw. "It didn't...do anythin'. It just touched him, and he convulsed. It didn't attack anyone." It—*he*—had barely even acknowledged Barrett had been there.

"It only touched him?" Tacita interjected. "Nothing else?"

Barrett shook his head helplessly, and her frown deepened, eyes shifting to the captain.

"I will clear the room," he said, "You handle the mage." Without a moment's hesitation, the man leapt into action. His soft-spoken demeanor vanished as he began to bark orders, his voice rising above the chaotic din.

He shooed people from the room and hall, sending for the other present captains and the guildmaster, and instructed others to begin relighting the lanterns. It was impressive to watch.

"Lilyanna," Tacita said quietly, drawing Barrett's attention back to the cot, "I need you to examine the mage's mind." Her eyes flickered to Barrett before adding, "as gently as you might."

The younger woman nodded and took Tacita's place by Kyran's head, her fingers delicately cradling his face.

"No matter what you see, Barrett, she is not harming him," Tacita warned, and Barrett felt a sudden surge of anxiety for the mage.

"He just woke up," he said, his voice rising in alarm. "What are you doin'?"

"Ensuring it is only Kyran with us," Tacita replied, her tone firmer.

There was a shiver of power much, much stronger than he had ever sensed from Lilyanna the few times he had been near enough to her to sense anything at all. She blinked several times until, with jarring suddenness, it was not *her* eyes peering from her face any longer. The whites had filled in, colouring black as night, her dark irises taking on a molten colour that resembled hot lead.

Kyran flinched in her grasp as she met and held his gaze. His mouth parted in a ragged gasp, and the ice on his limbs creaked as his runelines flashed so bright that even Tacita had to step away, breath fogging white in the air. The mage let out a short, high whimper, echoed by the tiny child pressed into his side. His eyes locked, unblinking, with Lilyanna's, and beyond the blue-white glow of Kyran's magic, Barrett could see his pupils stretch into wide, black pools.

Then, with measured slowness, Lilyanna closed her eyes, and Kyran shuddered, slumping against the cot, his face still caught in her hands. She leaned forward and pressed a kiss to his forehead before the child roughly pushed her away. The young girl crawled up the cot and crouched by Kyran's shoulder, glaring at Lilyanna as she withdrew, standing back with her head bowed and taking slow, even breaths.

Barrett managed a flicker of a smile at the child's protectiveness. "Well?" he prompted softly. "Is he okay?"

"No one hides in him," Lilyanna replied in her same soft manner. "It did touch him there, though." She raised her head, her eyes returned to normal, and she frowned faintly. "It...hurt him, but the hurt was...better than what had been."

"What do you mean?" Tacita asked.

The young woman's thin mouth worked into a deeper frown. "Like... breaking a bone to reset it, or...." Her eyes found the empty place in the sheet on the cot. "Or removing a limb to save the life."

"But why...?" Barrett's question trailed as an answer supplied itself. The Old One. He still didn't understand it, but it must have had something to do with the Old One's fascination with Kyran.

"It was more likely accidental," Tacita supplied. "A lucky chance that whatever it meant to do to the young man happened to help him." She inclined her head to Lilyanna. "Thank you. Please continue removing the ice. I will see to the other hunter."

The young woman nodded, returning to the foot of the cot, and began working at the ice under the watchful scowl of the young girl while Tacita knelt at the head of Kyran's cot. Barrett leaned over, realizing with a jolt that there was another person there, crumpled in a heap and covered in ice. He was not moving. Barrett swallowed thickly. That must have been the hunter assigned to guard Kyran when the Old One had come through.

"Guildmaster!"

Barrett looked over his shoulder at Captain Griswold's sharp announcement to see the captain holding the door open as a woman came sweeping into the room. She was older, maybe in her fifties, her hair the color of steel and pulled back into a knot at the base of her neck. In her wake followed Nowell, the watchman he had met coming into the guild and, as he had learned later, captain of the guard.

The guildmaster's golden-hazel eyes fixed on Barrett as she approached him, her mouth tight, brow drawn. Her face seemed to be cut from granite, all severe angles and jutting lines, at odds with the surprisingly feminine curves beneath her simple blue gown.

"Hunter," she greeted him crisply, back tall and straight. She barely reached his chest, but she emanated such an aura of absolute authority that Barrett rose to his feet without even thinking.

"Guildmaster Selah," he greeted her, bowing his head in deference.

She glanced past him at Kyran, then the two chirurgeons. "Tacita."

"Yes, guildmaster?" the older chirurgeon answered, rising from the floor.

"I want you to examine the mage. If he is fit, make whatever arrangements you deem necessary to have him moved."

"Yes, guildmaster."

Moved?

"Guildmaster?" Barrett asked.

Her attention switched to Nowell. "I leave you in charge. Alert me at once if there are any more problems. You will be the first to see the report of what happened."

"Yes, ma'am." Nowell clapped a hand to his chest in what Barrett recognized as an old military salute. "You." He gestured to Captain Griswold and began to give him orders as the guildmaster started for the door.

"Guildmaster," Barrett called again, but she didn't respond. He ground his teeth, looking back at Kyran again before he followed after her. "Guildmaster Selah!"

"Yes?" she replied without slowing a step.

"Where are you moving him?"

"Avonmouth is, I believe, the port Captain Griswold selected."

"Wha...?" The implication of her words finally dawned. "Wait, no! You can't be serious. He's only just woken up."

"I trust the opinion of my chirurgeon," the guildmaster insisted calmly, raising her voice only the slightest degree as she cut off his retort before he could even get the first word out. "He has been here three months, and in that time, we have received thrice the number of inquiries from the Crown on behalf of the laird who issued the warrant. If he is well enough to travel, we cannot subvert fulfilling this warrant any longer without provoking full legal action from the Crown. Were he a guild member, we might have some legal footing to stand upon, but as it is, refusing to comply is tantamount to treason, and I cannot justify it."

"But what's another week? Even another day?" Barrett pleaded.

She didn't reply right away as they stepped outside. The clouds that had gathered were thickening, threatening more rain. She let out a soft sigh, her mouth turning in a faint smile as Captain Griswold rushed up.

"Captain," she said.

"Guildmaster," he responded. Flicking a glance towards Barrett, he added, "Hunter."

The guildmaster wasted no time. "I expect full reports from everyone that was present by noon tomorrow, including the chirurgeon's assessment of this mage. If he is declared healthy enough, I believe it is in the guild's best interest to comply with the warrant as soon as possible."

"Yes, ma'am," the captain agreed, bowing his head. "I can have arrangements complete by the day after tomorrow."

"But...ma'am...." Barrett stammered. He could not believe this was happening—and only minutes after the mage had finally woken up. "There are demons hunting him, and—"

"Barrett," Captain Griswold barked. "Mind your tongue."

Barrett opened his mouth to snap at the captain, then closed it. This was not just the captain or his sister. This was the guildmaster he was trying to argue with, a woman who had more than enough power to revoke any help the guild was offering Kyran or even place Barrett under arrest.

The guildmaster waited, letting the silence after Barrett's outburst hang. "I understand you feel that my decision is harsh," she finally said, voice low, "but, as we saw, his being here attracts demons we are not prepared to repel while our numbers are thinned dealing with the matter in the west. We've been lucky until now, and I do not place my faith in luck."

She turned fully to him, her expression sombre. "You will, of course, be assisting as part of the guild escort to take the accused to the Isles. It is too dangerous to leave his guard to the Crown, and it is important to His Majesty that he ensures fulfillment of the warrant to maintain pleasant relations with the Isles' many peoples." She tilted her head, her mouth curving in apparent amusement. "I also believe it would be foolish to pretend you would not volunteer or at least force the issue, if given the opportunity."

She was, of course, right. He would not abandon Kyran now, not after everything. But the guildmaster's blatant address of his wishes came as a surprise, and his opinion of her lightened.

At a loss for words, he nodded.

"With that matter settled, then," Selah continued, "Captain Griswold, I leave the matter entirely in your hands. I trust your discretion and competence in dealing with this in a way that involves as few people as possible."

"Of course, Guildmaster," the captain replied mildly.

She nodded sharply to him, and Barrett thought he saw the woman's tight shoulders ease just a fraction. "Good. For what it is worth, Hunter Barrett, I am sorry for what has happened to your friend. It is never kind or just when these things happen." Her tone was still as hard and immovable as the granite she was made from, but it had lost some of the cold command in it.

"Thank you," Barrett replied stiffly, still reeling from all that had happened.

"I trust you both know what needs to be done."

The captain bowed his head. "May your lanterns stay lit," he offered.

"Graces willing, may yours as well," the woman murmured in blessing, then added, gesturing as Barrett had seen Myles and common folk do, "and the Light protect you both."

Captain Griswold turned to him as the Guildmaster continued on her way.

"You had best pack for travel and arrange your affairs. We will be off as soon as Tacita has cleared him."

Chapter Thirty-Seven

BARRETT HAD HIS things packed in scarcely an hour, intending on returning to the hospital, but a summons was delivered for him to go to the library to give his account of events. There he was met by Ilham, who conducted the interview at a table in a secluded corner of the library, dutifully taking down his words and asking pointed questions to help fill out the report further.

He had hoped he was near finished when Katherine appeared from around a bookcase. They hadn't seen much of each other since arriving; it was a large guildhall. She leaned against a shelf nearby, waiting until Ilham announced they were finished.

"Sorry to go so quickly, but I have to interview the others," Ilham said as she got up, her notes disappearing into a larger book she secured under her arm. "May your lanterns guide you safely on your journey."

"Thank you. May yours stay lit."

She scurried away into the shelves, and Barrett sank back in his chair, letting out an exhausted sigh. "You heard what happened?" he said without opening his eyes.

"Yes," Kat answered, her boots a soft thump on the wood floor as she joined him at the table. "I wanted to come say goodbye while I had the chance."

"Awful thoughtful of you."

"I have classes most of the day. I'm training apprentices in swordsmanship and teaching the fundamentals of hunting."

Barrett cracked an eye at her. He had known about the sword lessons, but not the classroom teaching. "Do you like it?"

A faint smile, the first he had seen in some time, appeared at the corner of her mouth. "I think it suits me better than baking."

"Good. I'm glad."

And he was. He and Kat might not have gotten along, but she was still his sister. He still wanted her to be happy, even if he also wanted to throttle her.

She nodded, and they sat quietly for some time before she spoke again. "You should get some sleep. You'll need to be well rested if you are going to keep your ward safe."

He grunted, already half asleep in his chair.

"Tacita and Nowell will make sure nothing happens to him before you leave," Kat said.

"Uh-huh," Barrett agreed, finally rising from his seat. "You take care."

"I always have. May your lanterns stay lit."

"And yours as well."

Despite his sister's words, Barrett tried to return to the hospital, only to be turned away by Nowell at the door.

"My people are watching him," the man assured him calmly, despite Barrett's sharp snarl. "Go on back to your room. I'll send a runner if he wakes up."

He tried to convince the man to change his mind, but after several unfruitful minutes, he was forced to return to his room and wait, catching what fitful sleep he could.

To his surprise, he was woken by knocking at his door at midday. Rubbing the sleep from his eyes, he received the runner—a small lad of barely eight years—who declared he had come to collect whatever items Barrett wished stowed for the journey, and that he had been asked to attend the hospital. Handing over his pack, Barrett made his way to the hospital with a growing knot in his belly. Less than a day. He would have been impressed at the guild's speed if not for what it meant.

A guild guardsman greeted him as he entered the wing. "Tacita is tending to another patient just now, but she will return in a moment. She told me to relay to you that Kyran is sedated, and you will be asked to accompany him to the wagon once word has been given."

"I understand." He climbed the stairs to Kyran's room, his stomach knotting at the sight of the mage unconscious again.

The little girl was not there. The hunter on watch informed him she had been taken back to the ward. It was probably for the best that she was away. He could not imagine trying to separate the two when he could not even explain to her what was going on.

He sank into the bedside chair to wait until, half an hour later, Tacita returned. "I administered more ether not long ago," she informed him, going to the opposite side of the bed. "He should sleep for most of the morning, and he may be disoriented when he begins to wake. But the reason I called you was to show you how to change his bandages. You will need to do this at least once a day—more, if the dressing gets soiled or wet. I will tell you what to look out for as well."

Barrett paled, his anger dissolving into horror. "I *what?*"

"You heard me." She gestured to Kyran. "You can show him how to do it once he is able, but for now, you will have to take care of him."

It was not an overly complicated process, though Barrett proved to have limited skill in it. After removing the bandages, Tacita showed him how to wash the blood and other fluids that had seeped through the stitches before demonstrating the proper way to reapply the bandages so they would put pressure on the leg's stump and remain in place. Then, she removed them and had him try several times until he managed to pass her approval. He likely would have gotten it sooner if he did not feel so awkward simply handling the mage like some over large doll, not to mention the sheer distraction of his nudity. That, in itself, just felt...wrong.

After a few of Barrett's clumsy attempts at bandaging Kyran while maintaining his dignity, Tacita pulled the linen sheet over the mage's lap, granting him a small measure of privacy. Barrett breathed a simple thanks before starting again on the bandage.

"I already sent down bandages and a jar of ointment to be packed with a note reminding you of their use," she informed him as she shimmied Kyran's trousers back up to his hips. They were the same ones Barrett had lent him, albeit clean again, as there were none that would fit the mage on hand at the guild. He still looked strange in the ill-fitted trousers and shirt instead of his Isleish garb.

A runner came in not long after, followed by several guards, to tell Barrett they were ready to bring Kyran down. Gathering the mage as gently as they could, the guards lay Kyran in a stretcher, and they and Barrett followed the runner down to the courtyard. Barrett cast a weary eye up at dark grey skies. Never before had he begrudged the Tennebrumian winter quite so much, but now the cold rain seemed like an excessive burden atop of everything else.

He hurried across the flagstones to the carriage the captain had procured for their journey. It was narrower than the farm wagon they had used to bring Kyran to the guild, but stretched across the arched wooden ribs over the bed was a canvas cover that had been oiled and waxed to resist the rain. The horses—one in the rig attached to the carriage, and others held nearby, ready to be ridden—shifted and danced nervously as Barrett approached, despite being bred for use by the hunters and kept on guild grounds.

"In the back," one of the hunters instructed, directing the guards to a small set of steps at the rear of the wagon. Barrett climbed in first. The horse moved uneasily as they approached.

Beneath the cover, their packs and supplies had been lashed to the sides of the wagon, and in the center, someone had laid out a thick pallet of blankets to lay Kyran on. With the guards' help, Barrett nestled the mage amongst the blankets as securely as he could, then climbed down again.

"Your mount," the captain said, handing him the reins of Sweetheart.

Barrett stroked the horse's golden neck, her ears flicking back to listen to him.

"Hello Sweetheart." He patted the mare's shoulder. "It's been a while."

The horse heaved a dramatic sigh.

"Oh, me too," Barrett agreed.

The captain had explained the plan briefly as they started on their journey. The two of them, along with two other hunters and a company of Crown guardsmen, were to take Kyran to Avonmouth, a northeastern port. From there, they would take a guild charter ship across the Isleish Sea, then up the eastern coast of the Isles to a port in the Highlands near Laird Dunbar's lands.

According to the captain, the Isles' lairds were not as unified as Tennebrum's nobility under their king, and simply traveling from one point to another in the country could be dangerous. But the captain was certain that by the time they reached the port, Laird Dunbar would have received the guild's letter from the Crown and would have men waiting to guide them safely to the laird's estate.

"Once we are at Avonmouth, only I will have to continue forward to fully represent the guild's presence in this matter," Captain Griswold explained to Barrett. "But I will not bother insulting you by asking if you will wish to continue as well."

"Good," Barrett replied. "Because I'm comin'."

Travel was slow in the rain, and they had barely made it an hour's ride north when a rider caught up to them from the guild. "A girl is missing," he relayed. "A child. Ijeichon. Favors the mage. No one has been able to find her. A Katherine Barrett recommended someone speak with you about it."

Barrett swore under his breath. He had a feeling he knew why his sister had sent the rider. He swung down from his mount, tossing the reins to the closest rider, and marched to the back of the carriage, climbing the steps. Inside, Kyran lay where Barrett had left him, still sleeping off the effects of the ether. He scanned the packs lashed to the sides, then grabbed a bedroll and pulled it out of the way. A tiny face blinked back at him from her hiding spot amidst the leather packs.

"She's here," Barrett called out to the others with a sigh. "I'm not certain how you snuck in here, but I can't blame you. I would've done the same."

"Bring her out; I'll take her back," the rider called.

Barrett held his hand out to the girl. She shrank from him, sinking deeper between the packs.

"Come on," Barrett murmured. "You have to go back. It is not safe for you to come with us."

She let out a soft whine and sank even farther into the packs.

"It isn't safe," he repeated to her, but she stayed where she was until he leaned forward and reached for her.

Shrieking, she ducked down into the packs, beyond his easy reach, crying, "*Kee-rin!*"

It struck Barrett right through his heart. He retracted his hand, and the girl quieted again, peering at him from between the bags. She was not going to come without a fight, and prying a little girl kicking and screaming away from the one person she was apparently fond of was about the last thing Barrett wanted to do. He knew what he was about to suggest was going to get him laughed at, but he steeled himself and stuck his head out of the back of the wagon.

"It's alright," he informed the rider. "Tell Katherine she's with me."

"What, you can't catch a little girl inside your wagon?" the man mocked.

"She is simply goin' to run away again," Barrett said sternly.

"Not if I am keeping a hold on her. Come now, bring the girl out so I can take her back."

"She's not goin' back," he said more firmly. "This is a diplomatic mission, or so Captain Griswold has told me a dozen or so times in the last day and a half, so it should be no trouble for her to travel with us. If she can survive however long she was in the demon realm, she can weather a diplomatic mission to the Isles."

The man snorted and glanced at the other hunters. "If you say so. What was your name again?"

"Kristopher Barrett," he replied, making certain to enunciate his last name clearly. "And I am certain my sister will understand the issue."

The man looked past the wagon at the captain, then, with a shrug, turned his horse and trotted off down the road.

Slowly, Barrett climbed out of the wagon, passing a glance back at the girl before stepping off into the muddy road. As he took his reins back, he waited for the captain to say something, for one of the men to berate him for the decision, but nothing came. Instead, Griswold was waiting patiently, his expression a mask of perfect calm.

"She is your responsibility," was all he said as Barrett settled in the saddle again.

Barrett nodded. "Yes, sir."

Chapter Thirty-Eight

THEY CONTINUED NORTH, staying inland of the coast to avoid the worst weather. The captain called a break midday at the shores of a swollen stream to let the horses drink and allow the men a moment of respite from the rain.

Barrett dismounted with a grateful groan. His horse riding generally only extended around the city of Oareford for short stints. He was going to be sore in unexpected places by the time they made it to Avonmouth.

"I'll take your horse, Hunter Barrett," Captain Griswold said suddenly, holding his hand out for Barrett's reins. "Go and check on Kyran and the girl."

Barrett handed his horse off without hesitation, then climbed back into the wagon. The girl had come out of the packs. She was kneeling on the edge of the pallet, her attention pinned on Kyran, as if she expected him to sit up at any minute.

Barrett's pulse thudded in his ears. "Kyran?"

The mage's eyelids fluttered, and Barrett's breath caught in his throat when two bright emeralds fixed on him. He was awake. Graces, he was alright.

"Kyran," Barrett called again. "Can you hear me?"

The mage's lips moved, but he had to lean closer to catch the hoarse whisper. "You are na real."

"No, I'm here. I'm real. I...." Barrett ran a hand over his face, taking a shaking breath as he remembered Tacita and Lilyanna's warnings about Kyran's mind, about the damage the demon had done to it. "Graces, I'm sorry it took me so long to find you."

Kyran shifted beneath the covers, his knee starting to bend as if he meant to sit up. Pain crossed his face, and his runelines brightened as frost snapped over the wood around him.

The horse in the rig whinnied abruptly. The wagon jerked beneath them, nearly pitching Barrett out, and knocking Kyran flat onto his back with a gasp of pain as the little girl fell into his lap. The air temperature plummeted, and the wagon lurched again as the horse gave a shrill, startled cry.

"Kyran!" Barrett called, clinging to the ribs of the wagon's covering. "Your magic! It's scarin' the horses!"

"Stay away from me!" Kyran snarled, dragging himself away from Barrett and the girl. The words twisted like a dagger through Barrett's chest. "I willna fall for it again."

"Fall for what?"

"This." The mage gestured angrily to the wagon, then to Barrett. "You!"

"Me?"

Did Kyran think he was still dreaming?

"This...*I'm* real," Barrett insisted. "You're awake. I found you—"

The men outside shouted as the other horses began to panic, the wagon still jolting forward.

"You always make him say that, even after I promised."

You? Him?

"What are you talking about?"

"I'll eat it! I promised I would, so just stop! Stop looking like h—" Kyran's voice broke into a ragged cough that made Barrett cringe.

But Graces, What was he saying? Did Kyran think he was still talking to the demon?

"It's me. It's really me. You're not in the demon realm any longer. I'm not forcin' you to do anything."

But the mage's expression of pain and distrust did not change, even when the girl whined and started to shiver at his feet. Kyran didn't even seem to notice her. Barrett let his gaze drop, uncertain what to do or say to help the mage.

Maybe time. Maybe he just needed a little while to wake up.

Barrett forced himself to take another breath, to keep his voice even. "Look...." He made himself meet Kyran's eyes again, face the suspicion and fear aimed directly at him. "You....You've been through a lot, but you're safe now. I won't...force anythin'." He paused, but the mage didn't say a word, didn't change his expression in the least. "I'll...leave. Just—I'll be just outside if you need anythin'. Alright?"

He backed towards the entrance, hesitating as his boot hit the first step. "You're safe," he added gently. "No one will hurt you."

But the mage said nothing, and it took a momentous effort for Barrett to leap down to the ground.

"Is he alright?"

He picked his head up to find the captain addressing him, no longer holding either horse. "He...is awake," Barrett answered slowly.

Captain Griswold glanced at the wagon as it rolled back and forth, the horse drawing it starting and pacing under its bit as the hunter in the driver's seat wrestled with its reins. "So we gathered."

"He thinks he is still in the demon realm. He thought I was the demon disguised to look...like me."

The captain's neutral expression pursed with a frown, drawing out the soft age lines around his mouth and eyes. "Perhaps with time," he offered.

"Perhaps." Barrett's heart ached for the mage. Tacita and Lilyanna had warned him of what might happen, but he had wanted Kyran to be glad to see him when he woke up. To be relieved. Not frightened. "Graces help him, I don't know what to do."

"You are doing what you can, Barrett," the captain reassured him. "That is all you can do."

But it didn't feel like enough.

They continued through the day, stopping only an hour before sunset to make camp at the side of the road. They could have stayed in an inn or tavern—there was a village close by—but Captain Griswold declared it was too dangerous for four hunters and a mage unable to control his magic to stay in town. They would sleep in shifts to tend the fire and make certain the horses did not bolt in the middle of the night. If there were any sign of a demon, it went almost without saying that the guard was to wake them all to take up arms.

Barrett volunteered to pull the packs from the wagon. Kyran was awake when he climbed in, and watched him the entire time, though he said not a word. The girl was sitting against his side, a blanket from the pallet wrapped around her.

One of the other hunters, Lainey, gathered wood and started the fire while Barrett, Hammond, and the last hunter set up their bedrolls with oilskins to keep the drizzle off. It had been a long while since Barrett had camped. He and Raleigh had done it a few times, always in the summer. It had made Barrett nervous, but Raleigh had loved it. He'd said he liked watching the stars while lying next to Barrett.

Barrett craned his head back, but there were no stars tonight. As the sun set, the wintery grey sky turned to a black velvet not even the moon's glow could pierce, and he remembered keenly why he had not slept outside again before this week. He'd had no one to keep watch for demons while he slept.

Dinner was a hot and surprisingly hearty stew cooked over the fire. No sooner had it been declared done than the little girl appeared from within the wagon. She approached them timidly, hiding behind Barrett's arm when she got close, and when it was his turn to ladle out some of the stew for himself, he handed the bowl to her.

"Careful," he warned her, setting a finger on the rim and tipping it down, away from her mouth when she went to gulp it. "It's hot." He fished in his pocket, drew out the spoon he had tucked away, and dropped it in the stew. "Here. Use this."

She grasped it, her face scrunching up in a pout behind her hair as the rain began to stick its black strands to her skin. But she stirred the stew with the utensil before scooping up a steaming mouthful and blowing on it. She gulped down almost half the hot stew, then held the bowl out for more.

"You haven't even finished what you have," Barrett chastised her, but she only thrust the bowl at him again. Taking the bowl, he ladled another helping into it and handed it back, expecting her to continue eating. Instead, she clutched the bowl and carefully made her way back to the wagon. Barrett stared after her. Was she taking it to Kyran?

"Well," Lainey chuckled, nudging the fire with one booted toe. "I suppose you'll be cleaning the pot, then."

Barrett summoned a dry chuckle for the woman as he reached to pull the pot from the fire. But honestly, he would clean up every night if it meant Kyran would get better.

He will get better, Barrett told himself silently, swirling the pot to help cool it down enough to eat. The chirurgeons had said Kyran needed time, but there was only so much time before they reached the Isles. All Barrett could do was hope it was enough.

Chapter Thirty-Nine

KYRAN STARED AT the canvas covering, trying to see past it, to make out the grey brick and darkness he knew were lurking behind the facade. For days now, he had floundered helplessly between nightmares and this quiet hallucination. Over and over, he had reminded himself that nothing he saw was real, that the people and sights and even the sensations he felt were all simply in his mind. But the delusion persisted, infinitely detailed, which only made it seem all the more genuine every time he "woke" from his nightmares into it. He was beginning to come to the conclusion that his mind had finally crumbled.

At least this delusion had the pretense of pleasantness. He had simply been riding in a covered wagon for several days while it rained, tended to by Effie and Barrett. The wee lass was always there when he was awake, either sitting nearby, watching him, or asleep, pressed against his side. She looked better in this illusion. Clean. Her dark hair was cut short and neat, and her skin had been cleansed of grime. Her cheeks looked rosy and plumper than before, and her unfamiliar woolen dress was unsoiled and green. He was happy to see her looking so well, even if it was only in his mind.

The rocking came to a halt, and he recognized the patterns of camp being broken. He dragged himself upright, running a hand over his lap as he loosened his magic enough to soothe the ache in his leg, disturbed as his fingers ran over both the backs of his thighs and the empty place where his left leg should have been. He stared at the flaccid place beneath the quilt, and could almost hear the ugly crunching and slurping of the demon eating it in front of him.

Watch.

"You're awake."

Kyran started at the voice, his head snapping up where a familiar figure stood at the open end of the wagon, illuminated by the glow of a lantern. His face was thick with unshaven scruff, and his hair looked as if he had done no more than pull it back in a tail for days. His clothes told the same rumpled story from beneath a heavy leather coat. And his eyes....Those summer-blue eyes were sunken and bruised from lack of sleep, heavy with what looked like pain as they stared at him.

A curl of steam rose from between the hunter's hands, and Kyran felt his stomach heave in disgust as he realized Barrett was holding a bowl. Not again.

You need to drink.

He shuddered at the disembodied memory of a voice, staring at the steaming bowl, at the truth seeping in through the cracks of this self-delusion. It was not Barrett, but that creature in its favorite guise, here to make him drink and eat again.

"How are you feelin'?" Barrett—*no, not Barrett; the demon*—asked, lowering itself to sit at the edge of the entrance. It sounded scared, uncertain, its tone scraping at the hollow of Kyran's chest. He wanted it to be real. It was a masterful touch.

It was a goading question, but Kyran answered it all the same to appease the beast, knowing that if he was right—that this was a delusion—that remaining silent only made things worse. The pain throbbing through what was left of his leg would be only the beginning of what that thing would do to him to make him speak.

"I am fine," he bit back crisply.

"I brought you dinner." It extended its arms, and Kyran leaned away, but the shift pressed his mutilated thigh down into the blankets—*the bricks*—and the pain in his leg turned to a hot stab radiating all the way up through his hips and back.

Frost flashed across the quilt as his magic flared in response, and he clutched at his leg, grinding his teeth to keep silent as he focused his magic into it. The sound of horses screaming erupted outside. He waited for the demon to laugh at him, to grab his throat in its claws and force him to eat, but it just watched him, its false face creasing with worry, its mouth falling open in a soft gasp.

"I'm not goin' to hurt you," it whispered, its hands knitting around the bowl in its lap and clenching until its knuckles turned white. "I know you don't think this is real, that I'm real." Its eyes didn't move from his, the pain in them so raw and vital that it looked utterly convincing. "I don't know what to say or do."

Kyran waited as the pain eased from his leg—waited for the illusion to fall away, for something awful to happen—but nothing did. The figure of Barrett simply sat there, watching him, eyes full of pain and fear not *of* him, but *for* him, all looking so very real.

But it wasn't. He had to remember that. The moment he started to forget was always when the pleasantness was stripped away.

"I'm so sorry that I couldn't find you sooner," the figure continued, choking on a smothered sob. "I didn't know how to get to you. I don't know where you think you are, but you're here. With me."

Guilt came up thickly in Kyran's throat. It wasn't real. He knew it was not, but it felt so genuine, he could not help imagining....

What if it *was* real? What if Barrett really had found him? How could he know? This wasn't the first time he had felt something while the demon toyed with his mind. Far from it. It seemed to take particular malicious pleasure in locking Kyran within the very worst of his memories until he was so wretched that he ceased even fighting them, simply letting the abuse happen, only for it to then take the pain away and offer him seductively a sweet peace that inevitably crumbled into agonies again.

Or it could be real. He could have actually been rescued by Barrett while his mind was too broken to perceive it. But that seemed unlikely, and there simply was no way for him to tell, no test to prove what was real, which alone indicated that he had gone out of his head.

His eyes widened as the realization finally came to him. "I've gone mad."

"You're not mad," the demon—*Barrett?*—said firmly. "You're scared and confused. I don't know what that...thing did to you, but you're here, with me, and I won't let it or any other demon take you again."

The comfort the words offered was hollow, their meaningfulness eroded by the simple fact that it might only be his own wishful thinking echoing off the vaults of his mind. But then, if he truly had gone mad, did it matter anymore? It felt real. If he wanted, he could simply let this become his world. He could stop fighting to find the truth and just allow this to be until it crumbled.

Barrett shook his head. "I'm sorry. I know you aren't well, but I can't wait any longer. There isn't much time left. Do you know where we are?"

Kyran shook his head. He still was not convinced he was not lying in the dark prison beneath the demon, screaming into the darkness, but that did not mean he had to go forward with this facade completely blind to what was coming.

"We're camped outside Avonmouth tonight. Tomorrow we're going to get on a ship headed for the Isles. Do you know what that means?"

The Isles. The blood drained from Kyran's face. "Oh, Stars," he moaned. "No. No, not that."

"I tried," Barrett pleaded. "I tried to tell them it was too soon, but the guildmaster said they couldn't put it off any longer. I'm coming with you, though. I'll be there."

The wagon seemed to sway beneath them, and Kyran had to press his palms into the floor to stay upright. So this was the blade lying hidden beneath this illusory world. Here, Connal had finally kept his promise. Even in an illusion, he knew what waited for him there. After everything Kyran had gone through, after everything he'd fought and survived, he was to be dragged back to the Isles to face the man. And not a soul would believe the word of a demon-blooded mage over the laird's son. They would kill him, and there was nothing he could do about it.

You willna get away with this! You hear me?

"No," he croaked. "No, I canna go back. I canna go back," Kyran repeated, his chest heaving and his blood roaring in his ears. His power bucked against his hold, and there was a loud crackle as his magic slipped through his grasp. Frost crawled over his skin.

Effie let out a startled squeak and scrambled from his side, the tips of her black hair frozen stiff as she stared up at him from between two crates.

Setting his teeth, Kyran fought against his magic's will, reeling it back under his control until his lines dimmed perceptibly. It was far from perfect, far from the discipline he had fought for and honed through the long years on Cairngorm, but his magic was different now than it had been then. It was willful and powerful beyond what it had been before he had been dragged into that dark realm, and the only theories why that he could think of were more than disturbing.

You're nothing more than a demon-blooded animal.

"If you take me back there, they will kill me."

"They won't. I won't let them hurt you."

It sounded so genuine, so reassuring. Kyran felt that familiar ache, craving for it to be real. By all the Grace in the Isles, why couldn't it be real? Why was it so impossible to believe Barrett really had found him? How could he know? All of the other nightmares had felt just as real. How did he know if this was not simply in his head too?

"I canna tell anymore," he whimpered. If this was of the demon's making, its design was uniquely tortuous in that it was only Kyran's uncertainty twisting at him now, like a dagger between his ribs, and all the demon needed to do to make it horrid was wait. Wait until Kyran settled in and began to accept this place, then take it all away from him. But there was no telling how long that might be. He could be locked in this illusion for relative years before it broke down. Though he doubted he could last that long.

"Kyran."

He lifted his head at the sound of his name, meeting the false Barrett's gaze. "I know it isn't fair to ask you this now, but we're runnin' out of time. Do you remember the warrant I told you about?"

How could he forget?

Maybe if you're quiet, I willna have ta tell anyone.

If he had just stayed quiet, that small, ugly voice of truth told him—if he had just let it happen, none of this would have happened. He would never have had to leave the Isles.

No. He clenched his jaw, teeth grinding together. No, he was not a thing. What had happened was wrong. He had no right to feel guilty about it. He should be angry. "I should have killed him," he spat, his lips curling back from his teeth.

Barrett sucked down a noisy breath. "Somethin' did happen."

"I thought you liked it like this?"

The stale scent of sweat and ale, mixed with the sweetness of dry hay wafted across Kyran's nose. His breath caught as a dark-haired man leered up at him.

"Stop," Kyran whispered, blinking, trying to clear away the too-real image before he could feel heavy hands against his skin again. He didn't want to go there, didn't want to relive that nightmare again. He wanted to stay in the wagon with Barrett. It might not have been real, but it was better than that.

There was another sharp bite of pain, separate from the memory, and he focused on it, worrying at it until, as suddenly as it had disappeared, the wagon came back into focus. He looked down at his lap, the source of the ache, and found he had scratched the back of his hand bloody. Dark crystals of ice were forming on his skin.

"Kyran?"

It was Barrett again, his voice soft with concern, and Kyran could have wept with relief. Real or not, he would rather be here than any of the other nightmares he'd experienced. He would rather dream of this than be awake in that dark prison.

He removed his nails from his other hand, clenching a fist as to stave off the inane need to keep scratching.

"Can you hear me?"

Kyran glared at the hunter. "He attacked me first." It was the truth, if not the entire, horrid whole of it.

"You were defendin' yourself," Barrett clarified, not a question in his tone.

"Aye, na that it will make any difference to them. What's the word of a mage worth?"

"No, that's—Captain Griswold said if you were innocent, he could speak on your behalf at the trial as a representative of the guild."

"There willna be a *trial*," Kyran spat, resisting the insane urge to laugh. "Laird Dunbar will drag me inta his hall, denounce what I have done ta wrong him, and remove my head."

"Wait, what?" Barrett's eyes went wide. "They can't do that! The captain will make them listen. He said all he needs is for you to tell him what happened, and he will have the guild's full authority to protect you."

"It willna matter," Kyran said quickly, shame coloring his anger. He did not want anyone to know about what happened, what Connal had done to him. How even after two and a half years, he could still feel those big, calloused hands on him. "They willna believe me. I am lucky my da did."

"I believe you." Barrett's quiet, even statement caught Kyran off guard more than any shouting might have. "I've only known you a little while, but you're a good person, Kyran. Better than me."

There was regret buried in his words, but stronger than that was his faith, utter and unceasing, that Kyran was telling the truth. It was oddly comforting, even if it ultimately meant nothing. It was not Barrett that had to believe him.

The hunter let out a harsh sigh and lifted his hands to scrub at his face. "We don't have to keep talkin' about this now. You should eat somethin', if you can manage."

Kyran stared at the bowl and its still faintly steaming contents. He tried to envision the warm, savory taste of stew and bread, but all he could think of was the demon's carved bowl of bitter, salty blood. He began to salivate, but his stomach lurched sickeningly, and he shook his head.

"You've got to try," Barrett replied. "You were so thin when I found you, and it's only worsened."

Eat.

Kyran knew he should just take it. If he resisted, the demon would only enjoy forcing him to eat, one way or another. But even the thought of putting one more bitter piece of flesh in his mouth, to strengthen his blood the demon planned to feast on, made him unbearably sick. Every bit of strength he gained, the demon would gain too as it slowly ate him, piece by piece, until there was nothing left, and by all the Grace in the Isles, he prayed that would be the end of it.

"Kyran!"

The mage blinked at Barrett's sudden cry, then winced at another bite of pain. Looking down at his lap, he realized he had been scratching at his bloodied hand again.

"I-if you don't want to eat, I won't make you," Barrett said quickly. "It can wait. I'll leave it here and bring you some water so you can get cleaned up a bit. Clean bandages. Tacita showed me, if you need help." He assumed a smile, but it looked unhinged, desperate. He didn't move immediately, watching Kyran as if waiting for something. "I will be nearby if you need anythin'," he said at last, then got up and left.

Kyran stared at the space Barrett had been, also waiting. Waiting to see the grey lines of brick he knew were lurking behind the facade.

"Mad," he whispered. "I've gone stark raving mad."

Chapter Forty

"How is he?"

Barrett wasn't certain if he wanted to laugh or shout at the captain. "What d'you think?"

"Has he worsened?"

"He's still wakin' up whenever I check on him, and he doesn't look like he has a fever, but I wouldn't say he's doin' well."

Captain Griswold made a thoughtful noise, ducking his chin. "Has he confided...?"

"No," Barrett replied curtly, finally rolling from the bedroll he had been lying awake on so he could put it away. The sun hadn't even risen yet. "And I haven't brought it up again."

"I need to hear his account," the captain repeated, as if Barrett were some idiotic child. "I cannot walk in there blindly and simply refute these accusations with 'he was defending himself.' Not with the guild and Crown's names tangled up in this matter. I need to *know* whether he is innocent."

"Why?" Barrett snapped, leaving his bedroll and taking to his feet. "Why is it always about the laird or the law? What about Kyran? He only just survived a living nightmare, and you want to drag him back to the people he's been running from so they can kill him!"

"That is not what I want, Barrett," Captain Griswold replied dryly.

"Isn't it?"

"No. If he is innocent, I want to ensure the laird does not wrongfully execute him."

Barrett scoffed. "That's what I'm talkin' 'bout, right there. You don't care—"

"Barrett." The captain's voice was still calm, but with an edge now. "I understand what you are trying to say, but you are not hearing what *I* have been saying."

"Oh, I have heard plenty of that—"

"No, you haven't, or we would not be having this discussion. You do not understand how serious this situation is." He patted his coat's breast. "This is not simply a warrant for a common thief. Have you read it yet?"

"No."

"The laird has listed some rather serious accusations." Captain Griswold pulled a trifolded piece of parchment from within his breast pocket and offered it to Barrett. "Assaulting a noble. Mutilation. Disfigurement."

"He was defending himself," Barrett refuted stubbornly, refusing to take the paper.

"Simply stating that as fact will not hold up in court," Captain Griswold said, tucking the paper away again. "This warrant was issued to the Crown by another recognized sovereign for a crime carried out against not just a noble, but his *son*. If the Crown—or we—refused to turn over Kyran, it would have major political ramifications should the laird take umbrage, which I well imagine he would."

"And you expect me to just give up on him for that? Because it *might* upset some noble in the Isles?"

"No. I expect you to want not to potentially sow the seeds for a war between our countries. And if you are thinking of trying to run with him, it will not be just me that tracks you both down, but the king's guard themselves."

Barrett took a step towards the captain. "Are you threatenin' me?"

"No. I am making you a promise. I will do everything within my power to help Kyran, but you and he must cooperate."

"And if the laird decides to simply kill him?"

"If Kyran has been tried and found rightfully guilty, then you and I will have no grounds on which to stand. But"—he held up a hand as Barrett made to interrupt—"if he is truly innocent, then I will intervene with the fullest extent of the power vested in me as the guild's representative."

Barrett's fists flexed at his sides, his teeth grinding, as he glared at the captain. "You bastard," he spat, his voice dripping with venom. "You utter bastard."

"Call me what you will, but I have said my piece," Captain Griswold replied, the hard edge in his voice gone, replaced by an eerie calm. "We will be breaking camp soon. Are you still intending to go into town before us?"

"Yes," Barrett ground out.

"You had best go soon. Our ship captain will not wait."

"Of course," Barrett sneered.

The captain offered no more reply than a measured stare before he turned to go. Barrett knelt, yanking the ties around his bedroll. Graces preserve him, but he could just strangle that man. It was obvious that talking about what had happened was the last thing Kyran wanted to do, and it wasn't right to try and force him, especially now. He wasn't well. But they were running out of time.

Barrett threw his long leather coat on, then carried his bedroll and pack to the foot of the wagon to be packed when the rest of camp broke with the dawn. There was a sound from within the wagon, of fabric shushing, and a soft slur of what sounded like Isleish. Barrett waited, wondering if Kyran was awake, but resisted peeking in. There would be time when he got back.

He had gotten the idea the day previous when trying to figure out how they were going to get Kyran on board the ship. Carrying him seemed the most logical, but for the mage's violent dislike of being touched, not to mention the affront to his pride. Captain Griswold had lauded the suggestion and was even able to provide Barrett with rough instructions on where he could go to find what he was looking for.

It was closer to the docks than he'd assumed, nestled into what looked like an extra space at a cooper's shop. Tying Sweetheart to a post, Barrett walked inside, smiling as he spotted a shelf of sweet little wooden dolls, with yarn hair and sewn dresses. Perhaps he would pick one for the little girl before he left, something she could have for her own. Various other knickknacks filled the tiny space—carved animals and ships, fishing rods, whistles, and a few miscellaneous tools. He found what he was after on the far side of the tiny store, next to a man he presumed was the owner, who sat whittling at a piece of wood. He lifted one thick hand in greeting as Barrett approached.

"Can I help you with anything?" he offered. "If you don't see it, I can likely make it."

"Ah, I was actually lookin' at these." Barrett touched the collection of walking sticks. They had been stacked in a couple barrels against the wall, and there was an enormous variety, from tall staves to short canes. Mixed in were a few of the kind he needed, ones that were meant to prop under an arm, with cushioned tops and a carved hand grip. "It's for a friend."

"Well," the man grunted, getting up from his stool. "Let's see what we can't find for him, hm?"

They sifted through the barrels as the shop owner described the different woods. This one was sturdier against the moisture. This one dealt well with elements. This one had a finer appearance. One in particular, though, caught Barrett's eye. It was a pale wood that he initially thought was birch until he noticed the silver streaks gleaming along the grain.

"Silverbark," the owner explained, "milled from a tree only found in the far north of the Isles and prized for its beauty and rarity. It's normally fashioned into much more elegant things, but I thought something like this might appeal to someone of higher taste."

Barrett turned the staff over in his hands. This was it. This was what he wanted to get for Kyran. It felt perfect. Even better, it was tall. Maybe too tall, but after a quick discussion, the owner admitted that he could file it down to a different height if it were paid for entirely. Barrett did not hesitate. He pulled out his coin purse and handed over silver coins for the staff and a doll with black hair and a green dress. He hoped the girl would like it.

Barrett met the wagon on the road in town, nearly to the quay. He nodded to Captain Griswold, who shared a mild smirk when his eyes landed on the stick Barrett had tucked into the crook of his arm and the doll clutched against his chest.

"Be quick," the captain instructed, taking Sweetheart's reins. "We will be boarding as soon as we get there."

Barrett nodded his understanding and climbed into the back of the wagon. Cool air brushed across his face as he lifted the canvas flap. Kyran was sitting up on the pallet with the little girl beside him.

It was comforting to see him awake and upright, and not curled on his side staring into nothing. He must have been awake for a while; he looked alert, and his hair had been neatly combed. A smile pulled at Barrett's lips at the way the mage's hair flowed smoothly around his face and down around his shoulders. It looked nice long, although the color looked duller. It didn't seem to have the same bright coppery fire to it he remembered. Yet another toll of Kyran's time in the demon realm, he reasoned.

"You're lookin' better," he said by way of greeting, easing into the wagon until he could sit and pulling the staff in over his knees. "I, um...got this for you. Thought you'd like to try to move around."

The mage's closed expression shifted subtly, coloring with interest as he took in the patterning on the wood. "Is that silverbark?"

Barrett could not contain his grin. He nodded, holding the stick out to him. "Yes, it is."

Unwrapping his arm from around the girl, Kyran pinched the edge of the quilt and accepted the stick with both hands, careful to keep the fabric between it and his skin, and lowered it across his lap. "Where did you find this?" he asked, turning the wood to examine it.

"Caught my eye in a woodshop. Owner said the tree was from the northern part of the Isles."

"It is," Kyran said, tracing a long streak of silver with his thumb through the quilt. "They only grow near the lakes and rivers high on the *bens*. There was a copse of them near where I lived on Cairngorm."

"I hoped it would be more to your likin'," Barrett admitted, his chest swelling at what he hoped was intrigue in Kyran's tone. "I thought you might prefer usin' it to..." He pursed his mouth, struggling to phrase his words delicately. "To relyin' on someone else."

Kyran's fingers twitched against the stick, mouth tightening as he nodded stiffly. Barrett had hoped for a bit more of a reaction, but he was pleased with how Kyran traced his long, slender fingers over the wood. A bold and colorful declaration wasn't something Kyran was prone to.

"Oh, I also got this"—Barrett plucked the doll from under his arm and leaned across the wagon to offer it to the girl, who peered curiously at it—"for the little lass. I never could get her name."

"I dinnae ken her real name," Kyran said, using the quilt again to gingerly pluck the doll from Barrett's hand and set it in her lap, "but I've taken ta calling her Effie."

"Effie," Barrett repeated, and her dark eyes flickered to him briefly. "That's a sweet name." He smiled as Effie fixated on the doll, turning it over before smoothing the hair and folding the legs so it could sit in her lap. "I'm glad I found her."

The wagon rocked to a stop. Barrett cocked an ear, listening as Captain Griswold called to someone.

"Ah, we must be there already," Barrett said. "We have to board, but take your time. Whatever you need to get up."

The mage rolled the walking stick in his hands. "I think I can manage."

Barrett let out a chuff of laughter at that. "Aye," he teased, receiving a familiar cold glare in return before climbing out himself.

They were farther down the quay than where he had gone to find the shop. Fishermen and sailors alike were already beginning their day, thronging along the planks and calling to one another. There were a few larger ships in dock, but, while Barrett did not know almost anything about ships, the one they had stopped in front of may have been smaller, but he could tell it was no less fine, proudly flying the guild crest between her sails.

An enormous Hassani man stood at the bottom of the gangplank. Not only was he taller than Barrett by at least a few inches—though he would not reach Kyran's height if he were standing—but solid with hard-packed muscle, thick through the neck, wrist, and ankle. His hands and forearms, crossed over his barrel chest, looked capable of tearing a man's head from its shoulders, though the heavy sword at his hip was more likely to be his favored method. His face bore the same heavy structure in all but his eyes, and was swathed in a thick, neatly trimmed beard of the same dark color as the stubble just starting to grow in on his scalp. His skin was the color of rich, freshly turned earth, marred by lines of scars up his thick forearms.

"I was starting to think we were only taking your word across the sea," he remarked. His accent lent an almost lyrical flow to his words. "Your missive made it sound urgent."

"My apologies," Captain Griswold replied. The captain was only an inch shorter than Barrett, but he was dwarfed next to the Hassani man. "The wagon and rain slowed us."

The Hassani man flicked his gaze past the captain and Barrett to the wagon. His feral smile set Barrett's teeth on edge. He turned and saw Kyran seated on the step of the wagon, clutching the canvas as he cautiously swung his leg over the side.

"So I see," the stranger said.

Barrett cut his eyes at him, but he paid the hunter no heed, merely gesturing up the gangplank. "If you would both like to board, I have a man waiting to show the mage to his accommodations while I see about getting us off in some semblance of time."

A sailor appeared beside them, taking the reins of Sweetheart and Griswold's mount and leading them off to one side to be boarded on their own time.

There was a loud *clack* from behind them, and Barrett turned again to see Kyran standing. He still clutched the canvas cover of the wagon with one hand, his walking stick clenched tightly in his other and set beneath his left arm. He held himself there, trembling with just the effort of standing, and Barrett had to clench his hands at his sides to keep from going to him.

Slowly, cautiously, Kyran let go of the wagon, his arm curling around his front to take hold of the stick. His emaciated arms shook with the effort, and his balance wobbled dangerously until he had to grab the side of the wagon again. He tried again, and when his balance only wavered slightly, he took a tentative shuffle forward on the crutch, leaning into it in a small hop before swinging it forward again, his balance threatening to give with every awkward step.

Barrett was equal parts gratified and anxious. Kyran was walking. He was awake, in the sunlight, and he was walking. But Barrett could feel his hands twitch at his side every time the mage wobbled, itching to reach out and catch him, to help him along.

Instead, he made himself turn away, gesturing for Captain Griswold to go before him. "After you."

The captain nodded, signaling for the guardsmen to wait to follow before he boarded the gangplank. The irregular thump of Kyran's walking stick and smack of his bare foot on the wooden planks drew near, a cold breeze rolling over Barrett's back before Kyran drew up to his side.

"I'll be behind you," Barrett told him.

Kyran said nothing, only lowered his head and started forward again, his mouth set in grim determination. Effie followed close behind, clutching her new doll to her chest. The mage seemed to figure out a pace that worked with the walking stick, but it was slow going, and by the time they got to the top of the gangplank, his limbs were shaking with fatigue and his breathing was becoming labored. Barrett started to offer to help him, then bit his tongue. He had to let Kyran do this. If he kept trying to interfere, he would only succeed in making the mage angry.

One of the sailors waved to them as they stepped up on deck, motioning for them to join him and Griswold. The crew was busily rushing around the deck, shouting back and forth as they made ready to weigh anchor. They were a motley bunch—mostly Hassani, with a few Sanmetzki, the arid country to the east of Tennebrum, and a single Ijeichon. There was one Tennebrumian man who seemed to be shouting most of the orders, and Barrett could feel a hum of power from him even across the deck.

A hunter.

"Morning, sirs," the sailor greeted them, drawing Barrett's attention back around. He was much smaller in frame than the captain, but still bound in heavy working muscle. A piece of carved ivory jutted from his left ear, and the marks of a tattoo showed against the dark skin of one arm. "The captain has graciously offered the use of the guest cabin for yourselves. You'll find it at the bow, where you will be free to remain throughout the journey, comfortable and safely tucked out of the way. As for the, ah, young man there," he gestured to Kyran without quite looking at him, "the captain has ordered that he remain in the brig below for the duration of the journey."

It took Barrett a moment to realize what the man had just said. Kyran—weak, injured, far from recovered—was to be held in the ship's holding cell. "No," he said sternly. "He will not be kept below deck like some prisoner."

The sailor cocked his head. "With all due respect, sir, but he *is*."

Barrett's knuckles creaked at his side, and he took in a slow breath. "He shouldn't be kept down there. He isn't well."

The man's expression set, becoming stubborn, when Captain Griswold spoke up. "Barrett, we should do as the captain asks. This is his ship."

"I will not leave him down there."

"We are not spoilt for choice."

"I can't," Barrett pleaded. "I can't leave him down there." He glanced at Kyran for support, but the mage was silent but for his laboured breaths, his gaze pointedly lowered at the deck. He was trembling so hard, clutching his walking stick like a lifeline until Barrett was not certain how he was still upright.

Captain Griswold took notice. Pressing his lips into a thin line, he addressed the sailor. "Is there any way we might convince the captain to allow this young man to reside in the cabin with us? He will remain under our watch while he is there, and we will be better able to manage his magic that way."

The sailor fidgeted in place at the mention of magic, but he shook his head. "Captain's orders, sirs."

"I don't care what the captain's orders are," Barrett snapped, fighting to keep his voice low. "This is ridiculous. He's stayin' with me."

"Is there a problem here?" came a deep baritone from behind them.

The voice sent a chill down Barrett's spine, and he slowly turned to find the man that had been standing at the bottom of the gangplank behind him. "Your men want to put Kyran in the brig," he replied, his tone moderated, though he was still furious. "He's in no condition to be kept locked away, *prisoner* or not."

"I do not care," the man replied evenly. "That is where he belongs on my ship."

"He's barely recovered," Barrett argued. "He needs a bed. He needs sunlight."

"He needs you to remember that I do not care what he is other than a prisoner your guild has paid me to transport to the Isles in my ship. If he did not want to be treated like a prisoner, then he should have taken care not to get caught." He crossed his arms over his chest, settling back comfortably. "If you are that worried about him, I have no issue with you joining him below."

Barrett clenched his jaw, glancing at Captain Griswold. The man said nothing more, and likely would not. If this was his only option, so be it.

"Fine," he replied, lifting his chin to look directly at the captain's face. It was dark and steadfast; there would be no further arguing with him. For now.

"Good." The man jerked his chin in a sharp nod. "You have your orders, Sibu."

"Sir, Captain." The sailor nodded, tugging at his earring. "This way."

Chapter Forty-One

Now, mageling, I want you to scream prettily for me again.

Kyran's eyes flew open, his body convulsing upright in a terrified spasm. He pressed his back into the brick behind him, his eyes raking over his surroundings, but he could not see the demon beyond the blue-white radiance of his light. Frost crawled along the floor and walls in thick, jagged swirls, and he heard the stone moan with pain, the air shrieking.

There it is! There is the Old One's blood you will give me!

A face appeared at the edge of his blood's light—Barrett's. Kyran's lips peeled back from his teeth. "Dinnae touch me, beast!" he snarled at the mockery of the hunter, pressing as close to the wall as he could.

"Get ahold of yourself!" the thing that looked like Barrett bellowed. "You're not *there*, Kyran!"

It sounded like Barrett. Stars, it *looked* like him, but it had before, too. He pressed against the brick harder, his fingernails biting into the soft stone. "Stop it!" he panted, squeezing his eyes shut. "This isna real!"

"You're right; it's not," the false Barrett pleaded. "Kyran, look at me! It's alright. You're not there!"

He heard hard boot soles striking wood, the sound disconcertingly out of place in that oppressive silence, and other voices were suddenly tangled up in Barrett's, arguing and overlapping with the shrill sound of distant screams. Kyran tried to cover his ears, to block out the confusing sounds, but his balance wobbled without at least one hand to hold him up.

"Kyran," Barrett called above the din. "Kyran, look at me. You're here. You're safe. You're not there anymore. Your magic—it's hurtin' the ship. You have to control it."

The ship.

As he sucked down a fiercely cold breath, Kyran's eyes snapped open again. A light—the natural, warm light of a flickering lantern—had appeared next to Barrett, casting him in the golden halo of summer. He looked frightened, his eyes wide and mouth parted as if in shock or awe, breathing curls of thick white fog that clung to his unshaven face.

Kyran's defiance dwindled as the same question that had plagued him every time he woke to this dream again occurred to him: what if this *was* real? How could he even begin to tell? Would it matter? *This*, the dream of having been found, of no longer being trapped and alone, was so much better than waking to that black cage again. But it would have to end eventually. Why couldn't he simply embrace it until that certain end? If that meant he had gone utterly mad, then so be it.

Fixing the image of Barrett's face in his mind, Kyran shut his eyes again in concentration as he silently struggled to order his mind, to pry it from the nightmare and into the dream, and force his magic back under control.

But it fought him, refusing to be restrained. He set his jaw. He was better than this. He was not an animal, or food. He was a mage and all that entailed, and not a slave to his power. He was in control. He had to be. Because if he did wake one day to see that monstrous beast leering down at him again, he would make it bleed before letting it try to hurt him again.

Slowly, inch by fraught inch, he brought his power to heel. It was not a perfect control—he could feel his magic bucking and fighting to be free—but he held it tightly. Opening his eyes, he saw not grey brick, but white-frosted wooden boards illuminated by the faint glow of his lines and the lanterns. The screams had quieted to sounds he recognized as frightened horses, hooves stomping and pacing. He was here, on a ship crossing the Isleish Sea, not in that miserable hole.

He let out an exhausted sigh, raising his head to find not only Barrett, but another man he did not recognize standing behind the hunter, half of his face and neck a mess of scars. Captain Griswold was there as well, and in his arms was Effie, ever watching.

"Kyran?" Barrett called out to him, his voice barely a whisper. "You've got to calm down. Look at me." He paused when Kyran lifted his head to him. "Do you know who I am? Where you are?"

"On a ship headed ta the Isles," Kyran answered, voice strained as he focused on restraining his power. "And I'm not so out of my head daft ta have forgotten your name, Barrett."

The hunter's expression softened to a grin. "It's good to have you back," he said quietly, then turned to the scarred man. "I told you it was a bad idea to force him down here. But he's alright, as you can plainly see."

The man scowled back, the heavy scarring on his face pulling at his mouth, only further twisting the expression. He was not a tall man—a full head and shoulders shorter than Barrett. But like the ship's captain, he was built stout. His skin had been tanned to leather, deep creases and lines worn into it from age. What was left of his hair was white and thin, and pulled back into a small tail at the nape of his neck. It was obvious he had suffered some great injury; the entire right side of his face and neck were a mass of melted, scarred skin, taking his ear and his eye. There were other scars plainly visible on his arms and chest, but they were covered by black ink, much like the captain and other sailors.

"And I told the captain letting a mage on board was just as bad an idea," the man slurred around a thick wad of tobacco in his cheek. "We've got enough problems without him sinking the ship underneath us."

"Well, you can go tell your captain he is under control."

Kyran's jaw twitched. *Under control?* Like some simple, unruly horse?

The man threw his hands out at the thick coating of ice over everything. "I wouldn't exactly call this under control," he retorted.

"I'll take care of it in a moment," Barrett snapped back.

"You had better take care of it for the rest of this voyage, or *I* will." The man spat on the floor, the brown wad crackling against the ice, then looked from Barrett to Kyran and back, as if daring them to contradict him.

Barrett drew to his full height, staring the other man down. The air around his fists shimmered with heat, and the leather of his gloves began to creak. "If you do *anythin'* to him, I'll—"

"Barrett." Captain Griswold did not shout, but the even flatness in his voice cut Barrett off more completely than anything Kyran had ever witnessed.

A tremor ran down both of Barrett's arms, and there was no mistaking the rage pouring from his seething expression, but slowly, he folded his arms across his chest and sank back on his heels, his hot glare fixed on the sailor.

The older man returned the look for a long second before pointedly breaking it and addressing the guild captain. "Keep them both in line, or it's the captain you'll be speaking to next, and you won't like looking at his face any better than mine."

"I understand," Captain Griswold replied solemnly. "I will have a word with them."

The man spat again and sniffed, wiping his mouth across the back of his hand. "See that you do." He shot another glare at Barrett, then down at Kyran before shaking his head and muttering to himself as he left them.

"He has a right to be concerned," Captain Griswold pointed out the moment they could no longer hear the man's heavy footsteps.

Barrett dropped his arms from his chest and began to swear. The shimmer of heat radiated not just from his hands, but every inch of his skin, melting the frost and ice to slick puddles.

"Kyran's magic could very easily split the hull of this ship and sink us all," the captain continued over Barrett's tirade, adjusting his arms around Effie.

"It won't happen again. I'll see that it doesn't."

"I trust you will."

The ship's boards groaned again as spikes of frost oozed up from the wood, and both men looked at Kyran.

He glared up at them. "I am na an unbroken stallion for ye ta tend," he bit, his words short and clipped. He cinched his control around his power, forcing it back to heel as more needle-thin barbs of ice grew from the floorboards.

The fury in Barrett's expression evaporated, replaced by utter dismay. "I didn't mean it like that," he said quickly.

"Of course ye dinnae."

"Kyran, I didn't—I'm sorry."

"Then dinnae talk about me like I canna hear ye. Like I'm some sick pet ye hafta care for."

Barrett flinched as if the mage had struck him. "You're not....It's not like that," he said softly, passing a hand over his face. "You aren't a pet, but you.... Your magic has changed. It's been lashin; out wildly. You've never lost control like this before."

Kyran's hard sneer turned bitter as he remembered waking in the dark hole to find his magic running wild, more powerful than it had ever been. It had been the first moment he had begun to realize the truth of his blood, and every reminder of that fact stung. "It willna happen again."

"You can't know that."

"*I* control my power," Kyran snapped, leaning forward to meet Barrett's gaze. "It isna the other way around. It willna happen again."

"Good."

Kyran and Barrett both looked over at the captain, both taken off guard by his declaration. Griswold looked pointedly at Barrett. "You should clean up the ice. It would be problematic if someone else came down here and saw it."

"I've *got it*," Barrett sighed, exasperated.

Apparently satisfied with his answer, the captain finally let Effie go and excused himself from the hold. The lass ran to the bars of Kyran's cell, latching onto them and peering through, her face screwed up in worry.

"Sorry, lass," Kyran murmured, leaning forward until he could reach through the bars to her, and she took his fingers, squeezing tightly. "I dinnae mean ta scare ye."

"How did you find that lil' one down there?" Barrett asked, heat shimmering around his hands as he began to circle the hold, running his gloved touch over the worst of the frost.

All you have to do is eat.

Kyran swallowed thickly as the bitter taste of demon flesh flooded his mouth, the stench of it cooking clinging to his nostrils. "The demon...used her. I wouldna eat, so it came one day with her. I dinnae ken where it got her, but it threatened ta eat her in front of me if I dinnae eat what it brought me."

"That's....Graces," Barrett swore. The frost under his hand popped with a sharp sizzle. "I—"

"How long was I down there?" Kyran interrupted. He could hear the apology coming on the tip of Barrett's tongue, and he was tired of it. An apology could not take away the torture he had suffered down there, the helpless fear, or the madness eating at his mind. It would not make him forget what that thing had done to him, and it certainly would not prevent the demon from doing it again.

"Near a month? And you were sick for...three months after that?" The hunter sounded unsure, but it definitely felt like winter outside.

Four months. Kyran calculated the time in his head and realized it must be near the end of the year now. The Long Night could not be far away. It had been one of the few feasts he had always celebrated on the sides of Cairngorm. He liked to spend it outside, enjoying the peaceful silence of the snow blanketing world as he watched the new year slowly rise.

Barrett tugged his coat over and knelt on it by the cell, careful to find a dry spot. Most of the frost evaporated without a trace, but in the worst places, close to the cell, where Kyran's cold had been the deepest, the thick ice melted and gathered in murky pools of water on the boards.

"Was time different there?" Barrett asked. "Was there a way to tell?"

Kyran shook his head. "It was dark. Nothing ever changed except when the demon was and wasna there."

"I remember how dark it was," Barrett murmured. Something caught the hunter's eye, and he leaned along the cell and snatched up something out of view behind a barrel. It was the doll, the one Effie had been holding since Barrett had bought it for her. He brushed the doll off and wrung the water from its dress before handing it to the lass. "It's a small wonder I found her down there."

"Where did you find her?"

"She was in that enormous building above the hole you were in. If she hadn't come out, I never would've seen her."

So the lass had come back. Kyran was not sure how to feel about that revelation. He had climbed that wall and walked as far as he could from the hole to keep her safe from the beast. But he had not been able to figure out how to escape the realm, not before the demon had tracked him down and—

Watch.

Kyran closed his eyes against the vivid memory of the demon eating his leg. It somehow managed to still be awful, even after everything the beast had done to him afterward, when it tore his mind apart. His hand moved to where his left leg should have been, where he still felt its phantom sitting against the hard floor.

Barrett noticed. "I'm sorry again. For everythin'. And I promise to do whatever it takes to—"

"It doesna matter now," Kyran cut him off again. "It's done."

"But—"

"It's done." He squeezed the wee lass's fingers and let them slip from his hand, trying not to hear her soft mewl of concern as he settled back in his cage.

"She really likes you, eh?"

Kyran lifted his head, but Barrett was looking at Effie, his eyes and mouth soft and wan.

"I'm no good with babes myself," the hunter continued. "Only seem to upset 'em." He shifted onto his backside, drawing his knees up to his chest and resting his chin on them. "Is your pa a good man?"

The question caught Kyran off guard with its strangeness. "Aye. Better than most, I would say."

"Wish I could say the same about mine." Barrett rolled his head so his cheek rested on his knee. His eyes drifted along the floor, staring at nothing. "I always said I would never be like him, but I think my sister might be right: I've made the exact same mistakes." His gaze sharpened, focusing on Kyran as he added, "I bet you'll get to see your pa soon."

The twin sensations of his pulse thudding against his ribs and his stomach clenching sent a roil of nausea through Kyran. Stars above, he wished he could see his da and his family. But not like this.

"I'm sorry if I seem like I'm pryin' or sayin' too much," Barrett continued. "I guess I let myself get carried away. I just...missed this. Missed bein' able to talk to you. I know we didn't talk an awful lot before everythin' happened, but it was a lot harder to see you lyin' there, starin' at nothin', not sayin' a word, than I ever would've thought."

Something stirred in Kyran at Barrett's words, more than surprise. Barrett had spoken with such unexpected sincerity and kindness that Kyran felt compelled to ask if it was all a gaff. But the hunter had never been the sort to make a gaff at his expense—not maliciously.

Pain bit sharply into him, and Kyran looked down to see spots of blood welling beneath his fingernails where he had dug the skin open on the back of his hand. He had not even realized he'd been scratching at it again. He clasped his other hand over the wound, squeezing until his hand throbbed.

"Graces, I'll just shut my ramblin' mouth," Barrett said quickly, sitting up. "Let me get a rag for that."

"It's fine," Kyran tried to assure him, but Barrett was already on his feet, rushing for the stairs. Kyran let out a slow breath as the sound of the hunter's boots disappeared into the creaking of the ship. He tried to listen to the paranoid warning at his ear that he was only staring at grey walls and talking to himself. That none of this was real. But curse the Graces if there wasn't a faint and dangerous hope coiling up in his chest.

He looked to Effie, reaching through the bars to take her hand again, as solid and soft as it had been in their cage. "Just more proof I've gone utterly mad."

Chapter Forty-Two

Barrett rubbed his aching eyes. He hadn't slept more than a few unwilling snatches since boarding the ship, fighting against the long, dull hours while Kyran slept fitfully. He told himself he was keeping watch for anymore of the mage's slips in power, but it was an obvious lie. Even while travelling with the wagon—Graces, even while he had been at the guild—he had only managed a few hours at a time, halfway convinced that if he fell asleep, he would wake up and realize it had all been a dream. Or a nightmare.

He hadn't realized until now how badly Kyran was hurt. It was more than his leg and his skeletally thin body. The mage had nightmares now, and he always seemed confused and scared when he was awake.

And his magic. Graces, it was powerful. It had been strong before, but now, if Kyran regained his strength and remastered his control, he would be nearly as strong as some of the oldest hunter families. Which would only make him even more tempting a target for demons like the one that had kidnapped him. Or at least for the ones that disregarded the threat of the Old One that Barrett's own demon had warned against.

There was a heavy *thump* on the stairs, and Barrett recognized the footfall of the sailor that had brought them their meals, and anything else Barrett had requested, for the duration of the three-day journey.

"Kyran," Barrett called gently, trying not to startle the mage. "Kyran, someone's comin'."

The mage opened his bleary eyes, peering up at Barrett in confusion before seeming to blink himself awake. Effie, curled opposite him outside the bars, gave a tremendous yawn, squeezing Kyran's hand as she did. They had slept that way for days, comforting one another in a way Barrett couldn't, despite whatever assurances he offered.

It hurt. He wanted to make Kyran feel safe that way, wanted to help him feel better, but the other two seemed to share something after their time in the demon realm.

There was a metallic jangle at the base of the stairs. "We have arrived, sirs," the sailor announced, holding up a ring of keys as he approached them, effortlessly plucking the correct one for the cell from their midst.

"Thank you, Sibu," Barrett murmured

"Are we in the Isles?" Kyran asked.

"I think so," Barrett said. "Can you stand?"

Kyran nodded, pushing himself up onto his elbow, and Effie did the same. Barrett grabbed the walking stick from where he had stashed it between two crates to keep it from rolling away, and slid it between the bars. Taking the stick, Kyran righted it and wrapped his other hand around the bars. Heaving himself to his knee, he slid his hand farther up the bars with the intent to get the rest of the way up. But as he started to pull, his arms began to shake, his face straining with the effort, and Barrett felt his heart sink. Kyran had barely eaten anything, only pecking at the ship's biscuits with the meals and sipping at the tepid water the sailors provided him, and it was showing.

Barrett let him struggle a second longer before he got to his feet to help. He just could not stand there and watch the man fight to simply stand. "I'm just goin' to touch your elbow to help you up," he said in warning, giving Kyran a couple of seconds before he reached through the bars to cup his limb.

Kyran flinched at the touch, but Barrett held his arm gently, pushing up until Kyran had his leg under him and his staff planted. Gripping the bars of the cell and the walking stick, he swayed in place as Barrett removed his hand.

His face was even more gaunt than when they had boarded, though Barrett was not certain how; there did not seem to be any place left for him to lose weight. He was nothing but bones beneath his clothes. He could not survive much longer like this.

Stepping aside so Sibu could unlock the cell, Barrett took a moment to pull his coat on and haul his pack up onto his shoulders. "We'll be up as soon as we can."

Sibu stepped back, pulling the cell door open. "I am to escort you, sirs, to ensure there is no chance of you getting lost."

Barrett snorted. It was a fairly straight shot to the deck. More likely he wanted to make sure they did not wander off into places they were not welcome.

Slowly, Kyran lifted his walking stick and set the end before him, making a small, shuffling hop forward. He had to stoop quite far to get out of the cell, even leaning on the walking stick. As soon as he was clear of the cell, Effie flung herself around Kyran's leg in a tight hug. Barrett started to reach for the staggering mage, but Kyran caught himself on the bars, giving the girl a wry smile and murmuring something in Isleish as he ran his hand over her hair.

If—*when*, Barrett corrected himself—*when* all of this was done, he swore he would learn Isleish.

With an encouraging nudge from the mage, Effie let go of his leg and stooped to pick up her doll in one arm, grabbing a fistful of Kyran's empty pants leg with her other hand. It was still strange to see the mage in ill-fitted Tennebrumian clothes, but there had hardly been a chance to give Kyran back his kilt. It was little wonder Myles had been unable to sort the thing. It seemed to just be a giant piece of cloth. How it transformed into the charming garment was a mystery Barrett was keen to know. Perhaps when Kyran was better, and this whole sordid mess was only a bad story.

Despite his weakness, Kyran made it to and up the first few stairs before he had to stop, his breathing coming hard. Sibu was mercifully silent, picking at his nails with the tip of a short knife.

Cold wind buffeted his face as they emerged onto the top deck, and he pulled his coat closer, drawing on his magic to warm himself. But even the cold could not dampen the relief of being under the sky after being cooped up in the damp, stuffy hold. The sky was a sullen grey, but, mercifully, it did not seem to be raining yet.

The deck was a flurry of activity, men hurrying this way and that while the white-haired hunter—the captain's first mate—barked out orders. Sibu stepped ahead of Barrett, gesturing for him to wait a moment. Barrett halted, watching as several ropes went flying over the edge of the ship.

That was when he caught his first sight of the Isles.

The ship had pulled up to a wooden pier that jutted out into the water from the steep, craggy coastline covered in every shade of green Barrett could imagine. Small houses and what must have been shops seemed to sprout in clusters among the rocks, connected by a narrow road that wound between them down to the rocky shore, where another line of buildings marched down to the pier itself.

Left and right, the shore seemed to stretch on endlessly. He wondered what the terrain looked like past the coastline, if the villages and towns were different from Tennebrum. "It's beautiful here," he murmured.

There was a deep rattling under the shouts of the men as the gangway was lowered to the dock and Sibu gave Barrett the go-ahead. "If you'll just head down and wait, your companions will be along shortly."

"Understood." Barrett gestured for Kyran to go first, falling in behind him.

He let out a sigh of relief when his boots hit the pier. The journey had been smooth, but it felt good to be on land again. He looked for a place to stand out of the way and wait for the captain and guardsmen, and finally noticed that the men on the dock were all Isleish, shouting and laughing to each other and the men on the ship in a fluid mix of Isleish and Common.

And, of course, each wore that distinctive Isleish kilt, their arms bare to the cold as if it were nothing more than a spring day.

"Need to learn some Isleish," he sighed aloud as he and Kyran took a place to one side of the gangway. "Then I'd be able to tell when you're makin' fun of me, too."

When Kyran didn't respond, Barrett pulled a face at him, but the mage's eyes were on the men too, his expression set in a deep furrow of concentration,

"What you lookin' at?" Barrett asked, trying to follow the mage's gaze.

"The tartans," Kyran said quietly.

Barrett frowned in confusion before realizing Kyran was watching the men's waists and legs. "Their kilts?" he asked, wondering what that had to do with anything.

"Aye. The patterns on them."

The answer, far from alleviating Barrett's confusion, only served to further it until some sluggish part of his brain began to work. It was something he had heard a long while ago, after he'd met his first Isleman at the capital. He had been baffled by the sight—a man wearing a woman's skirt. But as the day wore on, he found himself admiring the look, especially the way he had been able to catch glimpses of the man's very well-defined legs when he moved. He had asked some patron at the tavern that night everything he could think of about kilts. One of the odder points of fact the man had summoned, under Barrett's endless barrage of questions and payment of drink, had been that the different colors of the kilts seemed to denote different clans. Which meant....

"You're lookin' for the colors of the men we're takin' you to?"

Kyran nodded stiffly. "It will look like the one I wore."

It took a moment for the import of that statement to make it through to Barrett. If the man that wanted to try Kyran wore the same colors as him, then they were of the same clan. Kyran's own people—his own clan—turned on him. Barrett didn't know enough about Kyran or the Isleish to know if that was significant to the mage, but it sounded awful. "If I see anythin', I'll point it out."

Kyran simply nodded again, his hand dropping from his staff to reach for Effie, pulling her close. The girl hugged her doll against her chest and leaned her head against Kyran's leg.

The mage looked nervous, every muscle in his body stiff, his eyes darting around the pier. Barrett wanted to keep talking, to distract Kyran, but was not sure what to say. Talking had never been his strong suit. He was better at doing.

"Barrett."

Barrett looked up at the same time as Kyran to find Captain Griswold approaching the gangplank, the three guardsmen following behind, and the ship's captain watching them from the deck.

"The guardsmen will bring the horses. Are you both ready?" Captain Griswold said as he drew close.

Barrett nodded curtly, pointedly looking away from the guardsmen, who stayed several feet away, still talking and laughing with one another. "How far are we traveling tonight?"

"Just here in this town." The captain gestured to the buildings behind them. "We are to meet our escort at the inn either tonight or in the morning. The captain was good on his word for delivering us directly."

Graces, everything was happening so quickly. "Let's get movin', then, so we can get settled in and get somethin' warm to eat."

Captain Griswold gestured up the pier. "This way, then."

They wound their way up the road, garnering plenty of stares. Barrett couldn't understand a word of what was said around them, and Kyran kept his head ducked, his expression set, giving nothing away.

It took quite some time to reach the inn following Kyran's slow, halting pace. The inn was quaint, even by Barrett's considerably provincial standards. It was made of stone, crouched between the road and the steep, rocky hillside where the land fell away into the sea below. The rooms were small, with a single, narrow bed beneath the window that overlooked the sea, a washbasin, and a small nightstand with only a candle to light come nightfall. Barrett's gut tightened at the sight of it. A candle—not a lantern or a lamp, but a candle—against the dark of nightfall. What Kyran said about the Isles must have been true: they were untouched by the demon plague.

"I might have to ask for more candles," he murmured quietly, pinching the wick and igniting it with his magic. "What should we eat? I'll get you whatever you want."

Kyran only shrugged, hobbling to the bed and nearly falling down onto it. Effie joined him, flopping onto her back on the bed next to him with a delighted sigh, her doll at her side.

Barrett snickered. "Me too, lass. Me too."

Placing the candle back on the bedside table, he poured out a measure of cold water into the washbasin. Slipping a hand into the water, he stirred it with his power until it was steaming. "If you wanna wash up first, I'll step out to get lunch. There are clean bandages in my pack."

"Aye."

Barrett dropped the rag on the basin's lip into the steaming water, then searched the stand until he found a sliver of soap that had an oddly strong herbal smell, with small purple flowers dotting its surface. He thought it might be lavender, but it did not quite have the right smell for that.

He held it out for Kyran. "Don't think I recognize those."

Kyran glanced up at him, and Barrett thought he saw a trace of color glowing in his cheeks as he held his palm out for the soap. A flutter started low in Barrett's belly, and he quickly dropped the soap into Kyran's palm and found someplace else to look.

"It's heather soap," Kyran explained. "The innkeeper probably makes it herself." He rubbed it between his fingers, releasing more of the pungent yet pleasant scent.

"It smells good," Barrett remarked, fidgeting. "Do you...want me to move the basin closer?"

"I can manage."

"Alright." Hesitantly, Barrett excused himself

He was careful to knock when he returned to the room, waiting until he heard Kyran's soft summons to come in. To his surprise, the mage was not in the bed, but standing at the window, his walking stick under his arm, gazing out at the Isleish Sea. His damp hair curled against his neck and shoulders, and he was dressed once more in his kilt. Barrett smiled to see it, kicking the door shut behind him.

"One day you'll have to tell me how it is you get that on."

"You lay it out, fold it, and belt it on," Kyran said simply, turning from the window and lowering himself to the side of the bed next to where Effie lay curled up.

"Somehow, I don't believe it's as simple as you're making it seem." He held out one of the platters of food and drink to Kyran, waiting as the mage pinched the edge of his kilt to take it.

Effie lifted her head, her eyes fixing on the steaming food. Barrett picked up a bowl of porridge and held it out to her as she crawled over, dangling her legs off the side of the bed. "How is your leg?"

"Dinnae you mean what is left of it?"

Barrett winced. "I more meant if it's gone off any. The chirurgeon—"

"It doesna look ta have gone off."

Barrett's shoulders eased. "Good." He watched Effie as she put her mouth to the lip of the bowl, slurping the porridge. She chewed a little, making a quizzical expression before she started to smack her mouth, and Barrett laughed. "It's thicker than soup, little one."

"She may na like it plain," Kyran said. A shadow of a smile turned the corner of his mouth as he looked down at the girl. "It isna very good without something in it."

"I was thinking the same thing," Barrett confessed. "What do you normally put in yours? I'll go see if they have anything."

"I dinnae ken if they will have them." He chuckled, his voice cracking drily. "I used ta pick snowberries while I was on Cairngorm. Bright red and verrah wee." He held up his fingers, pinching them so there was a tiny gap between his forefinger and thumb. "But the sweetest taste of anything I ever had."

Barrett smiled at Kyran's sudden burst of speech. It was more than he had said since waking that wasn't the raving of a soul lost in waking nightmares. "I'll ask the kitchen, in any case."

"You dinnae hafta."

"No, but I want to. I think Effie will like it better with somethin' in it, like you said." And perhaps Kyran might as well. If there was even the faintest chance he might get the mage to eat something, it was well worth the small effort. "I'll be right back."

Not waiting for any other protest, he ducked into the hall and returned to the tavern at the front of the inn, asking the woman working there about snowberries. She gave him an odd look and replied that he was not likely to find those outside of the kirk or the sides of Cairngorm itself.

"Kirk?" he asked, not recognizing the term. "What is a kirk?"

"Oh, bless the stars," the woman laughed. "I forget. I think you Tennebrumians call them Houses down there."

"Oh. Well, then, is there anythin' else I can get?"

"Well, if you are just looking for preserves, I have a mighty fine red currant jelly. Best I've made in years. Autumn was beautiful this year."

"That sounds fine."

It took a little back and forth, but eventually, Barrett got the woman to sell him a tiny jar of the currant jelly for a reasonable price. He thanked her and headed back to the room, though not before he caught her telling someone about how the Tennebrumian had asked for snowberries.

He knocked at the door and waited again until he heard Kyran answer, then let himself in. "She had red currant," he announced, holding up the little jar.

Kyran looked up from his platter, amusement glittering in his emerald eyes, and Barrett got the feeling he'd known what the woman would say about the snowberries.

Barrett merely rolled his eyes and opened the jar. Picking a spoon from the tray, he scooped a tiny mound of the jelly into Effie's bowl, then stuck the spoon in his mouth. It was tart and sweet, and reminded him strongly of his short-lived days as a baker with his mother. The innkeeper was right; it was good.

Effie poked at the colorful blob in her porridge with her spoon, then lifted the utensil to her mouth, suckling at the sweet preserve.

"Here." Kyran leaned over, taking the girl's spoon hand in his, and stirred the porridge until the dark lump melted into the oats. "That's better, aye?"

She made an excited "mmh" noise, and scooped up another bite, her face lighting up at the taste. She kicked her feet against the side of the bed, taking another bite and scrunching her face up in obvious delight.

"There's a lass. Dinnae choke now," Kyran laughed hoarsely, shaking his head when Barrett held up the preserves.

"You should eat a little before they get here," Barrett chastised him gently.

"And what of you? I havena seen you touch a thing since you brought it up here."

"I'll be fine," Barrett insisted, but he did not miss the dry look the mage gave him. "Alright, fine." He picked up a piece of bread from the platter and bit into it. It was heartier than the bread in Avonmouth had been, but softer than anything that had been served on the ship except the stewed vegetables. "There," he said after swallowing the bite. "I'm eatin'."

Kyran's expression did not shift from the flat stare, but he gingerly picked up a cup of water from the tray and settled it in his lap. Then, pinching the fabric of his kilt in one hand, he wiped the rim of the cup. Barrett stared. The motion was so small and ultimately insignificant, but he had not seen Kyran do it since bringing him back, and it just felt so...normal.

Chapter Forty-Three

BARRETT STARTED FROM his half-doze, wincing at the painful crick in his neck. He peered up at the bed, where Kyran lay, leg tucked beneath his kilt, eyes open. There was another knock, and Barrett slowly got to his feet, massaging his neck as he made his way to the door.

Captain Griswold was waiting calmly outside. "They are here," the captain told him simply. "Bring Kyran and your things."

Barrett glanced stiffly back at the window, where the sky still showed light. "We only just got here."

"As have they."

Barrett ground his teeth. "We won't be long."

The captain excused himself, and Barrett shut the door harder than was necessary. He turned back to Kyran, who was sitting up, smoothing his clothes into place over his painfully thin frame. "So much for rest," he remarked, trying to make light of it.

Kyran didn't reply, only reaching for his walking stick propped against the wall and hauling himself to his feet. Effie rolled into the space he left, mumbling sleepily as her eyes fluttered open, and Barrett managed an amused chuckle.

"Me too, lass."

Slinging his pack onto his sore shoulders, Barrett got the door, holding it for Kyran as they made their halting way to the front of the inn, Effie following drowsily behind.

There were a few more patrons than had been there earlier, though it was by no means crowded. Captain Griswold was near the front, speaking to an Isleman with curling brown hair and a few days' unshaven beard.

The man stood a bit shorter than the captain, but he was built more like Barrett, with wider shoulders strung with thick bands of working muscle, though he had a more tapering waist. Barrett could not help his gaze dropping to the man's kilt as he and Kyran approached. It was the same colors and pattern as Kyran's.

They were nearly to them before Captain Griswold and the Isleman paused their conversation to take note of their approach. Barrett did not miss the way the Isleman's head jerked when he laid eyes on Kyran, as if he had been slapped.

"Is that proof enough?" the captain asked, sounding uncharacteristically peeved.

"Aye," the man answered, looking Kyran over again, but this time Barrett noticed the way the man's face paled, the corner of his mouth twitching. He was afraid. "Though I can promise you he willna be a moment without someone's eyes on him."

"We'll be keepin' an eye on him," Barrett said as calmly as he could manage, even as his hand curled into a fist at his side—Graces give him the strength not to strike that man for talking about Kyran like that.

The man's attention switched to Barrett, and his eyes narrowed critically beneath the wisps of escaped curls. "Oh, aye? And who might you be?"

"That is my subordinate, Hunter Barrett," Captain Griswold said before Barrett had a chance to reply.

To Barrett's astonishment, the man's eyes widened in surprise. "Is he now? I dinnae take him for one of your kine." He nodded in deference to Barrett. "Begging your pardon, but I just dinnae think the mage was still alive after.... Well, I thought you all were mistaken."

Barrett narrowed his eyes at the man as a cold chill rolled over him. He glanced at Kyran. The mage's normally closed expression was colored with something dark. Just what had happened between the two of them? Had they known one another before all this?

"How long is our journey ahead?" Barrett asked instead, turning his attention back to the curly-haired Isleman.

"It isna far—about four days, if we get moving now." He shot a glance at Kyran again and muttered something in Isleish. Barrett felt the temperature in the air drop a degree.

He glanced at Captain Griswold, but the captain was staring pointedly at the Isleman.

"Shall we get goin', then?" Barrett prompted impatiently.

The captain gestured to the door. "The wagon is just outside."

"Then let's go."

The Isleman pressed his lips together, then exited ahead of them. Barrett had started to turn to Kyran when Captain Griswold stepped forward. "Out. Now. And mind your tongue."

Barrett fixed the captain with a firm glare, biting his tongue so he would not say everything he wanted to. As if the man would even listen to him.

Shifting his pack against his back, he followed the other man out, and was met by a chorus of nervous whinnies. A cart had been pulled up alongside the inn's door, and the horse in its harness whinnied anxiously at their approach, dancing in place. The driver shushed the beast, tugging firmly at the reins to quiet it. Five other men loitered in the street beyond, mounted on heavy, powerfully built horses that shifted and snorted impatiently. The men all wore the same tartan as the curly-haired man. These were the people that Kyran had fled from, the ones that treated him like he was something less than human.

"Bastards," Barrett spat under his breath before turning to hold the door for Kyran, hearing the mage's stilted gait approaching.

Kyran squinted into the grey light of the day as he hobbled out of the dim tavern, lifting an arm to shade his eyes. The horses went stock still, their ears pricking sharply towards him, eyes wide and nostrils flared, their hides twitching. The riders tightened their grip on the reins when without warning, the closest horse let out a shriek and bolted, tearing down the street. The others balked at its sudden start, a few almost jumping straight up, snorting and neighing in fright. Another started to bolt, its rider fighting its reins, and the cart jumped forward as the horse bucked in the tresses.

Barrett stared, transfixed in fascinated horror at the horse's reactions as he remembered he was not dealing with the guild's trained beasts. Someone was shouting over the fray, and he turned to find the curly-haired man yelling in Isleish at Kyran, who spat venomously back. The other man stepped closer to the mage, hands balling into fists, when Captain Griswold exited the inn and interceded, physically stepping between Kyran and Isleman, and began speaking—to Barrett's surprise—in halting Isleish. It was nowhere near as fluid and effortless as Kyran's, and Barrett recognized a few of the words or syllables that tended to repeat, but he still could not understand a word of it.

"What's goin' on?" he demanded.

"Nothing," Captain Griswold said quickly in Common, then continued in Isleish, but the other man interrupted him, speaking in Common and jabbing a finger towards the horses.

"That isna nothing—that mage has made a pact with a demon!"

"That is ridiculous," Barrett argued. "You don't know what you are talkin' about."

"The horses seem ta ken it verrah well," the Isleman snapped back. "I saw that mage get taken by a demon! If he dinna make a pact, then you have brought something else inta my country, Graces help you!"

Realization dawned on Barrett like a sledgehammer, and before he could stop himself, he was moving towards the man. "You son of a whore!" he snarled, shoving the guild captain out of the way and lunging at the Isleman, grabbing him by the front of his shirt. "You! You were there!"

The man slugged him across the jaw. Barrett's mouth stung sharply, and he tasted blood, but he didn't let go. "Get off of me!" He swung again, but Barrett reared back out of reach, then shoved the man hard and drove a fist into his stomach.

The man staggered, clutching his gut, and Barrett hit him again, catching him high on the cheek. "You bastard!" he roared.

"Barrett! Stop. Now!"

He didn't. He couldn't. Everything that had happened—it was all this man's fault. He had chased Kyran across two entire bloody countries and right into the demon's grasp.

Barrett smashed his fists into the man's face again, and again, following him down as he fell and beating him into the dirt when, without any warning, his lungs seemed to seize. He froze, his anger rapidly turning to panic as he struggled just to breathe. The Isleman swung upward, catching Barrett's jaw again, and he sprawled sideways on the ground, making ugly sounds as he choked on the air, clutching at his throat.

"Don't." The captain's voice cut through the noise as the Isleman reared up over Barrett, fist back. "Leave him."

Barrett flicked his eyes up at the captain. The man had his hand extended, fingers spread, his face a mask of perfect calm and concentration. He was using his magic. He was suffocating him.

He tried to tell him to stop, that he could not breathe, but the words would not come: he did not have the air. His chest hitched, his back arching against the ground as his lungs began to burn for air.

"Stop it! You're goin' ta kill him!"

Barrett twisted on the ground, his eyes finding Kyran as the mage limped towards the captain on his walking stick, his teeth bared in naked rage. But if he used his magic against the guild captain, Barrett had no illusion that the captain would not hesitate to use his power on Kyran, too.

Barrett's chest heaved as he tried to shout, to call out to the mage, but it came out only a hoarse wheeze. "Kyran. No," he mouthed, spittle running down his cheek. He smacked his fist on the earth, trying to get the mage's attention as he snatched up the captain's shirt.

"I am not going to kill him," Captain Griswold said in the same cool, even tone he used when speaking about who was to light the campfire, his gaze shifting slowly to Kyran. It was intensely unsettling, even beyond the rising panic as Barrett's vision began to fade at the edges, his lungs burning like fire.

A wave of cold air rolled over him. "Then let him go," Kyran growled.

The guild captain looked from Kyran to the curly-haired Isleman. Mouth pressing into a thin line, he let his hand drop.

The effect was instant, as if someone had taken their hand from his throat.

Air, sharp and cold, flooded Barrett's lungs, and he sucked it down greedily in deep, ragged gasps. It felt like needles in his chest, and he clawed at his throat, coughing and sputtering as he struggled to control his frantic breaths. He heard the sharp tap of Kyran's stick before the mage dropped to his knee beside him.

"Are you alright?"

Barrett managed something like a nod, feeling the cold grit of dirt under his cheek. It took him several more seconds before his breaths began to slow and he did not feel quite so desperate for air. He blinked up at Kyran, but everything had a hazy blur over it, and his head throbbed at the slightest effort. Captain Griswold was speaking with the other Isleman, who was near shouting, but Barrett could not catch the words over the pounding of his pulse in his ears. Kyran half-turned away, saying something in Isleish to the other two.

"What—" He coughed again, letting his head fall back to the ground, swimming dizzily.

"My apologies for my subordinate's behavior," Captain Griswold said. The street was eerily quiet but for the sounds the horses' unrest. "I believe it is in our best interest to leave as soon as possible."

The Isleman spat a long curse in Isleish that changed jarringly at its tail to Common. "This whole business is cursed. Dunbar is a fool."

Something like a wheezing laugh came from Barrett at the comment. Cursed. Kyran had said almost the same thing about himself. But that was not true. No, if there was a curse, it was this laird and his son, and the fact that even the laird's men could see that tickled Barrett far more than it had a right to.

Instead of arguing with him, Captain Griswold simply waited until the Isleman seemed to surrender, muttering as he walked away and called to the other men. The others called back, mixed with the horses' nervous whinnies.

Barrett tried again to push himself up, but his muscles were not listening. He felt heavy. All his body seemed to want to do was lie on the ground and pass into blissful sleep. He grit his teeth, pushing harder, but his muscles only quivered uselessly.

"Put him in the cart for now," Captain Griswold instructed. "He will ride when he has recovered."

Boots crunched on the dirt behind Barrett, and two sets of arms lifted him off the ground as if he were little more than a ragdoll.

"Let go," he growled, trying to get his feet flat on the ground, but his knees kept buckling under his weight. One of the guardsmen approached Kyran with another Isleman, this one with blond hair streaked with iron, and a length of rope in his hands. It did not take much to guess what that was for.

Barrett jerked in the men's arms, twisting back to try to see what was happening, and caught a glimpse of someone reaching for the mage. "No! Kyran! Let go of me!"

The two men only tightened their hold on him, dragging him to the cart. With a heave, they tossed him up into the back, then pushed him the rest of the way in and left him to lie unceremoniously in the wet hay. The others' voices raised in an argument. Clear amongst them was Kyran's, shouting in Isleish.

Barrett struggled to push himself upright, desperate to get up and help, to keep them from hurting Kyran, but his body did not cooperate. He'd just gotten an elbow under himself when the cart lurched violently, knocking him back down.

"Curse it all!" he swore as the cart jerked and rocked. Up front, the driver spat his own curses at the horse. The bit jangled loudly over the beast's anxious pawing. Barrett managed to grab the side and haul himself up over the edge, gripping tightly to keep from falling out, and was surprised to see Kyran limping towards the cart, his hands bound in front of him and his eyes ablaze with fury. He had his walking stick still, clamped between his arm and his side, moving it in an awkward hunching motion as he made tiny hops forward.

He made it all the way to the side of the cart, but hesitated. The horse let out a wild bray and lunged in the tresses, pulling against its bit and sending the cart jolting forward. The driver yanked at the reins, wrestling the horse to a stop, but the beast continued to pace, the cart rolling forward and back. Barrett did not see how Kyran could get in like that, not with his hands bound and only the one leg.

Kyran shuffled to the side of the cart again and, to Barrett's surprise, pulled his walking stick from beneath his arm and threw it into the cart, grasping the side of the cart to keep his balance. Then, before the horse could flee, he jumped, planting his foot on top of the wheel, and hauled himself over the edge. He tumbled into the wet hay, landing next to Barrett with a sharp, pained hiss, grasping at his amputated leg through his kilt.

"Are you alright?" Barrett asked, but before Kyran could reply, there was a sharp cry from beyond the cart.

"*Kee-rin! Kee-rin!*"

Kyran bolted upright at Effie's plaintive wails and lurched to the sideboard, thrusting his bound hands over the edge. Barrett caught a glimpse of a tiny hand reaching up and grasping the Kyran's ropes. He leaned back, bracing his knee against the side as he pulled the little girl into the wagon with them. She clung to the mage, shaking, and buried her face in his shirt. With his hands tied, Kyran could only murmur soothingly to the girl, resting his cheek atop her hair.

Barrett smiled. It was so...different, the way Kyran treated the girl. It was a side of him Barrett had never really considered. The Kyran he knew was stubborn and proud and didn't let anyone close. But when he was with Effie, he was patient, gentle, careful.

The cart jolted again, but this time started away up the road.

Four days, Barrett reminded himself. Just four more days until they were at the laird's castle and this whole mess came to a head.

Chapter Forty-Four

Kyran leaned against the corner of the cart, watching the light fading out of the clouds with a growing sense of dread. It had been a long, slow day. The weather had broken over them barely an hour outside of town. It started as a cold drizzle, but as they slowly zigzagged into the hills and away from the coast, it turned to ice, then steadily thickening flakes of snow. The cold didn't bother Kyran, but Effie had started shivering against him until Barrett had pulled his long coat off and draped it around her. It smelled pleasantly of leather and smoke, colored by notes of something warm and musky underneath.

Not long after the poor weather began, the laird's men made Barrett get out and walk, citing that having the both of them back there was making the cart horse too skittish to handle. Barrett did not look pleased, but after glancing at Captain Griswold, who stood watching the exchange nearby, he slunk out.

The men stopped a few times to water the horses, but as the day began to turn to night, Kyran began to worry, as they showed no signs of stopping to break camp for the night. There would be no lanterns or candles to light the darkness—not in the Isles. They didn't believe in the danger the darkness brought. They didn't know. They had never seen the demons that could come crawling out of the shadows between the trees, or, the beast he knew was hunting him.

And if by some perverted miracle he was *not* trapped in some wretched, hallucinated nightmare, then he had no doubt that the demon was spending every moment of every day hunting him. Stars above, but if this was real, then he was locked in a race to see who would kill him first—the demon, or Dunbar.

"I willna let it take me, dream or no," he hissed, tugging at the ropes on his wrists, but they were tight. Despite his best efforts, the knots had not budged all day. He peered at the sky again, at the night bleeding down through the treetops. It could not be long before the sun would set.

"Effie," he whispered, nudging the girl. "Effie, the knots."

She sat up beneath the coat, grasping his hands when he nudged them towards her. "*Kee?*"

"No. No." He pulled his hands free and pushed the ropes against her fingers. "The knots. Can you undo them?"

She made another noise and ran her fingers over the ropes, latching onto the first knot and tugging, but it did not let loose. The Isleman that had tied his hands had known what he was about. She kept picking at it though, and after a few anxious minutes, her finger slipped through one of the knots and tugged. The rope's bite softened on one of his hands. He pulled hard, and his hand began to slip before the rope tightened down again, catching on his bony wrist.

An Isleish curse slipped off his tongue, and he twisted against the ropes, using Effie and Barrett's coat to hide his fidgeting, but the hemp only seemed to grow tighter again. It was not going to come free. He made himself stop, pushing his hands towards the girl again, when the cart rocked to a sudden halt.

He stopped squirming, listening for anyone that had noticed, but the men were too far, their voices muffled by the snow. The driver of the cart let out a heavy sigh, and Kyran heard him drop to the ground, the horse's tresses jangling as the beast danced in place. Effie continued to pick at the rope, struggling to loosen it as he twisted to try to see what was going on. The jangling of the cart's harness continued until he realized the horse's eager snorts and the muffled thump of its hooves were moving away, towards the sound of barked orders and laughter. They must have been breaking for camp at last.

But the sky grew darker, and still no one came to set him free. Soon he could barely see the inside of the wagon, and the heavy-boughed oaks overhead faded into black. Kyran pressed his back harder into the side of the cart, feeling the dig of the hard, straight lines of the boards against his spine, his heart racing faster and faster as he strained to see into the dark. He tried to hold still so Effie could keep picking at the ropes, but the knots refused to come loose.

Then he heard the crunch of boots approaching. He held his breath as the slow, deliberate steps stopped, and the wagon tipped at the weight of someone climbing in.

Barrett appeared from the gloam, and Kyran could not help a sigh of relief. "It's you."

The hunter gave him a wily grin and pressed a finger to his lips before crouching next to Kyran. "We've stopped for the night," he whispered, pulling a wad of fabric from beneath his arm. "Got some bread and..." He set the meal down and reached into his pants pocket, pulling out a flask. "Some whiskey off one of 'em."

"Did you steal that?"

Barrett's grin widened. "Maybe. They wouldn't let me come back all day to check on you. I don't know if they'll 'preciate me sneakin' up here, so let's hope they don't notice." He tucked the flask between his knees and set the bundle at his feet, then gestured to Kyran's wrists. "Let me see those."

Hesitantly, Kyran held his hands forward, fighting the urge to shrink away when Barrett drew his ornate dagger from his hip.

"It's alright," Barrett murmured, apparently noticing. "I'm just cuttin' these off." He slipped the blade into the miniscule gap between Kyran's wrists and began to saw at the tough hemp. It took only a few passes before the rope parted with a snap.

The relief was instantaneous. Kyran muttered an Isleish prayer as he tugged the rope off his wrists, rubbing at the raw places it had left on his skin. "Thank you."

Barrett nodded, sheathing the blade, then pointed at the pocket of his coat laying over Kyran's lap. "There's a kerchief in there you can use. It's not in the best repair, but it'll serve."

The consideration surprised Kyran. Nudging the pocket open, he pulled a wadded piece of linen from the very bottom. It looked old, the edges ragged, and it was nearly worn through in places, but it was clean. He smoothed it over his knee, running his fingers over a frayed bit of embroidery stitched in one corner. *KB*.

"'Bout the only thing I've got left of my mum," Barrett remarked. "But I know you'll treat it well."

"Are you certain I—"

"I said I know you'll treat it well," Barrett repeated, unfolding his bundle and lifting free a bannock. Effie appeared from beneath the coat, barely more than a pair of eyes and a reaching hand. Barrett tore off a piece to placate the lass, then held the rest out to Kyran.

Kyran's stomach squirmed at the thought of food. He had eaten since waking, if only because of his standing oath that he would live to spite the demon, but he couldn't fend off the lingering revulsion every time he tried. Still, he had sworn.

Laying the kerchief over his palm, Kyran took the bannock, cradling it in the cloth. "*Tapadh leat.*"

Barrett cocked his head, then chuckled. "I take it that was a thank you?"

"Aye," Kyran assured him, pinching off a piece of bannock and popping it in his mouth. It was cold, but the familiar taste was a small comfort. His stomach agreed, growling loudly in anticipation.

Effie started, staring at his belly, and Barrett snickered. "You're welcome, too."

Kyran swallowed a few more pieces of bannock until the dry bread was too much, but before he could ask, the hunter held the flask out for him. "Thank you," he said again, making the effort to reply in Common this time as he accepted the flask with the kerchief. He wiped the outside, pulled the cork, and wiped the lip as well before tipping it back. The whiskey was cold and bitter, burning all the way down into his belly, where it built a pleasant furnace.

He sighed, tilting his head back to look at the sky again, but there were no stars, only the snow still drifting down around them—silent and near invisible in the faint twilight gloom. "They are na goin' ta let me out of this cart, are they?"

Barrett glanced towards the camp. "The captain's been arguin' with them for nearly an hour over it. They don't have lanterns or candles. They finally stopped so we could make a campfire when he broke out his guild authority, and the Crown's men stood by it."

"They dinnae ken the danger," Kyran explained, taking another sip of whiskey. "There are na any demons here—or there were none." He shifted his gaze to Barrett, barely able to make out his features. "Whatever stopped the other demons... I dinnae ken if it will stop this one. Not after it worked so hard ta...ta *care* for me."

Barrett's expression hardened. "If it does come, I won't let it take you again. You're goin' to be okay, Kyran, you hear me?"

Kyran knew Barrett was trying to comfort him, but the hunter's words only made him angry. They had the hollow ring of desperation about them, as if they were something Kyran might mumble to himself while lying bleeding on those grey bricks, trying to convince himself that he might escape.

He looked past Barrett into the dark, watching the thick, white flakes of snow drift down into the wagon. It reminded him so strongly of his nights on Cairngorm. But the peace he had felt there was gone. The night was no longer empty; it was waiting.

"Aye, I hear you," he said at last, downing another swallow of drink that burned the whole way down.

"Good," the hunter continued, "because I'm goin' to figure out a way to get you out of this mess. I'm not goin' to let any demon or laird get you. You understand?"

"No," Kyran replied, his tone flat and cold. He fixed his gaze on Barrett again. "I dinnae ken you. You canna kill this beast that's hunting me. Neither of us can, or we would have done it by now. And Dunbar has you and the guild both tied 'round in laws so tightly, I am certain your king could hang you for not delivering me ta him." A muscle in his jaw flexed as his power pressed against his grip of control. "*If* I am talking ta ye, and na raving inta the dark. So what is it I am supposed ta feel when you tell me it is all goin' ta be okay?"

"I *am* real, Kyran," Barrett insisted, leaning forward until Kyran could make out his eyes again, wide and earnest. "You need to trust me. I don't care what it takes. I've come this far. I won't give up."

"You should," Kyran spat, his voice rising.

"No," Barrett snapped back. "I won't. I can't, even if you've given up on yourself."

"Dinnae be so daft." Kyran leaned forward to meet Barrett's glare, his balance wavering as the whiskey loosened his limbs. "I dinnae plan ta lay down for that beast."

The hunter's eyes narrowed and his lips twitched. "Then why would you tell me to give up?"

"So it isna your corpse the demon climbs over ta get ta me."

The fire died in Barrett's eyes, and Kyran instantly wished he had swallowed those words. Stars, what had he been thinking?

Barrett ran a hand up through his hair, grimacing as he looked away from Kyran. "You don't need to worry after me. That won't happen."

"Because you said?" Kyran asked, the venom gone out of his voice. He leaned back against the wall before his wobbling balance could give out, and lifted the flask to his lips again. Why had he said that?

"Because I'm...." Barrett's reply faltered. He laced his hands together and propped his arms on his knees. "Because I have you," he almost whispered.

Kyran almost choked on the drink, coughing and sputtering. Of everything Barrett could have said, that had been the last thing he'd expected. "You what?" he managed to gasp between coughs.

Barrett's face colored. "Because I...I *know* that together, we can kill it. And I know—" Barrett pressed on through Kyran's soft scoff. "I know right now you're weak from your leg and near starvin' to death, and you hate it. Your magic is strong, so much stronger than it was, but you can barely sit upright. Just...let me protect you. Let me do this until you're better, and then we can take that demon down like it deserves. Together."

Kyran felt the color rise in his cheeks, and he shook his head to clear it. He was being daft himself. This was in his head. Barrett was somewhere else. Even if he was here, he would not be saying things like this. He would be shouting and storming off to drink. "I dinnae need you ta protect me."

"Maybe not," Barrett allowed. "But I'm not goin' to just sit back and watch, either. I owe that thing."

Kyran's argument died on his tongue. He had forgotten Barrett's personal stake in the matter. *Raleigh*. Kyran ducked his head, picking at the bannock. "I meant no offense."

Barrett took in a long breath, sitting down in the snow gathering in the back of the cart. "I know. None taken." He pulled a second bannock from his pocket and held it out to Effie, who snatched it from his hand and stuffed it in her mouth. Smiling wanly, Barrett set his elbow on his knee and rested his cheek in his palm, his gaze directed outside the wagon as the sounds of conversation came closer, then faded with a bit of laughter.

Kyran ate his bannock, washing every bite down with more of the whiskey until he was so thoroughly sotted, he could barely hold his head up. He hadn't had this much drink since he had last seen his brothers. Clasping his hands in his lap, he let his head fall back against the wooden boards. The snow had grown heavy again. Flakes as big as Effie's palm drifted out of the dark and landed on his face and hair. He let his eyes slip shut, trying to recapture that feeling of peace and quiet from before all of this—before the demon, Tennebrum, and Connal. It felt so long ago now, but it could not have been more than two years.

"You should get some rest while the wagon is still," Barrett said in a low murmur. "I can try to find a lantern for you. I don't want you and Effie in this dark."

"If you or the captain doesna have it, the others willna have one ta give you," Kyran slurred in reply, his tongue thick. He started to lift his head, but the cart seemed to roll and sway beneath him like the hold of the ship, and he relented, reclining against the back again. "A torch is the best you will be able ta manage out here."

"I'll find something," Barrett said, then sighed. "They might come to take Effie in the middle of the night, or morning. I heard them talking to Captain Griswold about it. They don't want anyone around you. If they do, I'll keep her close."

"*They can try*," Kyran said in his native tongue.

The hunter snorted softly. "What did you say?"

Kyran picked his head up just far enough to peer at Barrett with one eye. "I said they can try."

"I really need to learn some Isleish." Barrett gave him a light grin.

Kyran let his head drop back. "You keep saying that."

"How do you say 'good morning?'"

Kyran slurred the Isleish phrase, shifting against the hard boards.

"Awh, come on," Barrett murmured. "I'm bein' serious. Your lil' lass seems to react to it better than Common, anyway."

Kyran rolled his eyes, and repeated the phrase more slowly. "Tha' good enough for you?" Barrett repeated the phrase back to him. The pronunciation was decent—for a Tennebrumian. "They'll at least understand you."

Barrett nodded and crouched again, shuffling to the edge of the wagon. "I'll see about that light and be right back."

The wagon rocked slightly as the hunter made his way out, leaving Kyran with just Effie tearing into her bread. He could hear the lulling conversations outside the wagon, stories about better days and bold actions, and he caught himself smiling absently, thinking of his brothers, Duncan and Murray. How often had those two kept him up, feeding him drink and telling him all about what they had been up to since last he'd seen them? He wondered if he would see them while he was here, if he would even have the chance, and then if he even wanted them to see him like this.

Effie crawled across his lap, and curled up against his thigh, her doll clutched close, breaking him from his thoughts. He smiled down at her and clumsily pulled the borrowed coat over her again. It sent up a strong waft of woodsmoke and leather, and he allowed himself a small moment to enjoy it. Stars, he was sotted.

Chapter Forty-Five

THE JOURNEY THROUGH the Isleish countryside seemed to stretch into a horrible sort of monotony. At night, Barrett and Griswold traded off watches, vigilant for any demonic activity, since the Islemen would have no way to sense the beasts, or even defend themselves should one appear. During the day, unengaged in conversation with the captain, guards, or Islemen, and unable to openly approach or speak with Kyran, Barrett had nothing to help while away the hours. He managed a few snatched conversations with the mage, whispered in the first hours of night and the small hours of the morning, but it was not until the morning of the fourth day that he actually had an opportunity to speak at length with him again.

"Barrett."

He cracked his eyes open to Captain Griswold kneeling over him. He grunted to let the man know he was awake, even if it was only barely. It had taken him a long time to fall asleep, and what few hours he managed had been far from peaceful.

"Dawn should break soon," the captain whispered. "You should see to Kyran while you can. Here." He slipped one of the dense, round loaves of bread the Isleish had given them from into Barrett's hand. "They'll be awake soon," he urged.

With another grunt, Barrett pushed himself up onto his elbow, wincing at the dull throb in his head. His cheek felt tight, and when he pressed his fingers into it, he found it still swollen. That Isleman had a good swing.

He slowly got to his feet, shivering as he crawled from his warm bedroll into the frigid air. The fire had died down to just a few feeble flames, but it was enough to see that the snow had not ceased. Everything was covered by several inches of white powder except for the impression of his head against his bedroll.

Stepping lightly to muffle the crunch of snow underfoot, he crept over to the cart, only to find Kyran and Effie both wide awake already. The girl was wrapped tightly in Barrett's coat on Kyran's lap as the mage stroked her hair, and Barrett caught the faintest note of a melodic hum. But it was not Effie humming.

Before Barrett could hear more, though, Kyran picked his head up. His mouth drew into a wan smile.

Barrett cleared his throat as quietly as he could manage, suddenly feeling a bit awkward. "Ah, *good morning*," he greeted him.

Kyran gave him a quizzical look at his admittedly terrible Isleish, then snorted dryly. "I dinnae ken if you would remember that."

Barrett felt his cheeks heat more than he would have expected. "I remembered the first couple syllables, but I couldn't remember the whole thing. I asked Captain Griswold for help." Rather reluctantly, but he had not about been to ask the Islemen.

"That explains some of your accent."

Barrett chuckled, rubbing at his face as he felt it go even darker red. "I kept hearin' it every morning. Recognized it from the others." He fished in his trouser pocket and pulled out one of the potatoes from dinner they had roasted over the fire. It had been a welcome change from the same bread, water, and whiskey.

He passed it and another bannock to Kyran once the mage shook his borrowed kerchief free. Kyran gave the bread to Effie and picked at the potato until he got a nail beneath the skin to peel it.

"We'll be reachin' the estate today," Barrett continued, folding his arms against the side of the wagon and setting his chin on them. "Not sure when I'll get a chance to talk to you again."

"You willna hafta wait long," Kyran assured him. He broke off a piece of the potato and dropped it into Effie's hands. The girl seemed a bit puzzled by the crumbly vegetable, but quickly ate it without complaint. "Dunbar isna a man ta let things lie too long."

Barrett sighed, setting his forehead on his arms. "The captain better pull through on this plan of his. It's probably the only reason I haven't throttled him in his sleep just yet." He peered up at Kyran, but the mage's expression had closed again, the faint smile gone. "I haven't pushed, because I know it isn't—"

"Can I ask a favor?"

Barrett blinked, his trail of thoughts unraveling. "Of course," he replied earnestly. "Anythin'."

The mage lifted a hand and settled it over Effie's head. "The lass here. She shouldna stay at the castle."

Barrett glanced around the camp again and leaned in closer so he could speak more quietly. "I'll watch her. She'll be alright."

"No. I....." Kyran hesitated, looking uneasy. "I dinnae want her anywhere near Connal."

"Who?"

"Laird Dunbar's son."

Barrett's argument died unspoken. That was the man mentioned in the warrant. "He would hurt her?" His stomach twisted at just the thought.

"I dinnae ken if he will, but if he thought it would hurt me...." Kyran trailed off, letting Barrett fill in the gap with his growing suspicions.

"That bastard," Barrett snarled. "That sick, sick bastard."

"Take her ta my kin," Kyran insisted. "They'll keep her safe. And...tell my da when you see him that I am well."

"Hey," Barrett said gently, wishing more than anything that he could take Kyran's hand or even touch his shoulder to reassure him, but he knew the mage would not welcome the contact. "You'll see your family before you know it."

Kyran's mouth twitched into something like a smile, but it didn't touch his eyes.

"Do they live close?" Barrett pressed. "I don't want to leave you in that castle alone."

"They live on the laird's land, just outside the castle."

"I'll make sure she gets there."

"Barrett," a man said behind them.

Barrett started, swiveling on Captain Griswold, who had appeared from nowhere. "What?" he snapped.

The guild captain jerked his head pointedly towards the Islemen, who were all beginning to get up and make ready to press on for the day.

"I know, I know." He turned back to Kyran. "I have to go, but I'll get you out of this mess. I promise, and I'll make sure Effie is safe."

Kyran grimaced, rubbing at his wrist where the rope had chafed him raw, but he nodded before Barrett retreated to his bedroll to pack and make ready for the day.

There was a comfortable sort of order to how the Islemen went about breaking camp, much in the same way as it had been when Barrett traveled with the hunters to Avonmouth. But instead of having someone handing out tasks, as Captain Griswold had, the men all seemed to know what needed to be done and did it without having to be told. One man kicked out the fire, while another two tended to the animals, and one came sauntering out of the woods—their own watchman—cutting up and laughing with his still-waking companions.

They seemed normal like this. Ordinary men just like any other. But these were the same people who found it so easy to treat Kyran like some diseased animal, who saw nothing wrong with starving him and tying him up. They wanted to kill him because he was different, for reasons he could not control. It made Barrett sick. The sooner this was resolved and they were back in Tennebrum, the better.

It took longer than the Islemen had predicted, however, to reach the estate. After four days of snow, the narrow road they had been following through the hills became choked by almost a foot of powder, obscuring the ruts and holes and making it far more treacherous for the cart and horses. To save the beast's legs from finding a hole by accident, one of the men dismounted and, holding the reins of his horse, broke through the snow ahead of the others. It looked exhausting, but he set to it steadily, trudging ever forward. Barrett and the other Tennebrumians trailed behind the cart, riding where the snow had mostly been tamped down by the others.

They met a few forks in the road, and soon the Isleman that had been breaking the trail was able to remount as, despite the miserable weather, they met others upon the road who had already cleared the way. The other travelers moved to the side when the men and cart approached, and murmured to one another when they spied the Tennebrumian trailing behind. Apparently a Tennebrumian this far north was news in the Isles.

Barrett did not spy the castle until they had almost reached it. The enormous edifice of grey stone loomed suddenly out of the weather behind tall, thick walls. Their party made its way through the gated entrance, the horses' hooves clopping along as the dirt road turned to cobbles. The open courtyard was alive with activity, people moving to and fro, laughing and calling to one another.

"Hey! Ewan!" one man called, running up to take the bridle of the curly-haired Isleman's horse. "I see you made it back. Is that the mage back there in the cart?" He leaned sideways, peering at the cart for emphasis. "I thought he was dead."

"Well, he isna," the curly-haired man said, sliding out of his saddle. "I'm off ta tell Dunbar we've brought him what he asked. No one is ta get near tha' cart unless Dunbar himself or Connal says so."

"Aye, I'll see what can be done about tha'."

"Good. Summon Mrs. McCrory. We've guests for her ta see about, and the lads'll need feeding when the mage has been put away."

"Very good then."

The curly-haired man, Ewan, glanced back over the party, but he did not look so sure as he sounded. Pushing his hair out of his face, he left them, disappearing under an archway into the castle proper. The man holding Ewan's horse turned and shouted in Isleish, and several other people scurried from the room.

It was a bit before a stout woman in green skirts came hurrying in, her iron-colored hair pulled up into a knot. Wisps of curls that had escaped clung to her neck and face.

"Good mornin' ta ye!" she said, going to the first man and swatting at his leg. "Roy! How have ye been? Seems I havena seen your face about here since summer."

"Ah, I have been busy, mistress," the man said, flustered. "Was out on that bloody mountain almost 'til the end of autumn before I got sent ta the port."

"Is that so? Well, I'm sure that wife of yours will be glad ta see ye again. She's been nigh inconsolable the last few weeks, certain you'd never be coming back."

The man groaned. "Aye, tha' woman. She'll worry herself inta the ground at this rate."

"That she will," Mrs. McCrory agreed sagely. "I told her na ta fret—that her husband was made of stern Roche stuff—but she dinnae want ta listen ta me. I mean, what would I know?"

The man muttered in agreement, and Mrs. McCrory went down the line of them, with something hearty and pleasant to say to each, whom she knew all by name, until she got to the hunters.

"You must be our guests. A pleasure ta meet you both. I am Mrs. McCrory." She bobbed into a curtsey, shaking more strands loose from her knot of hair.

"And a pleasure to meet you. I am Captain Griswold, and this is Hunter Barrett," Griswold replied, politely dismounting.

Barrett belatedly mimicked him. He simply could not wrap his head around the woman. She seemed so...pleasant—cheerful, even—and not at all what he had expected of the people set upon executing Kyran.

The woman's eyes lit up, her broad face blushing bright pink. "Hunters, are ye? Well, blessed be the Light, no one told auld Mrs. McCrory the castle was expecting hunters, now." She fussed with her hair briefly, tucking stray strands behind her ears before she curtsied again, this time more deeply. "Well, come with me, then. You men as well," she added, gesturing to the guardsmen. "Let's get ye out of the snow and cold and get ye something hot ta eat. I'll have a talk with Ewan later about letting a lass know when she has important guests."

"Ah, just a moment," Barrett called as the woman turned to lead them into the castle. She stopped and turned back, her face creased in puzzlement. Barrett passed Griswold his reins and hurried to the cart, ignoring the men's uncomfortable shifting. "I'll take Effie with me," he told Kyran quietly. "I'll take her to your pa."

Kyran nodded, gathering Effie into his arms. He murmured to her in soft, quick Isleish and pressed her close. The girl clung to his shirt and buried her head into his chest, whimpering as if she knew what was coming. She whined as Barrett took her, reaching for Kyran and straining out of Barrett's arms even as the hunter shushed and soothed her. Kyran didn't look at her, staring down into the cart, his expression closed off as he simply handed them her doll. The girl threw it on the cobbles, again reaching for Kyran.

Wincing at the crack of wood on stone, Barrett stooped to collect the doll, careful to keep a firm hold on the girl, who wriggled ferociously the entire time.

"Your coat," Kyran prompted when Barrett started to turn away, handing out the heavy leather garment. "I willna need it."

It was true. Barrett had yet to see the mage shiver, even when covered in snow in the back of the wagon. Shifting his hold on Effie, he draped the coat over his arm and offered Kyran his thanks. The mage only nodded.

Mrs. McCrory was watching when Barrett turned around, her expression troubled, but it brightened the moment she realized he was looking at her again.

"Oh, what a sweet wee *bairn*," she cooed. "I bet she's freezin' out here in all this. Well, right this way, then. The lad here will take your horses to the stable. We'll get you all warmed right up."

She led them to a long, narrow hall. The walls were adorned with tartans and banners carrying what must have been the heraldry of the Roche clan. A long table ran down the center, with another against one wall. The interior wall was largely taken up by an enormous fireplace over which a pig was spitted, tended to by a young girl.

"Now, you just warm yourselves, and I'll be right back with somethin' hot for ye ta eat."

"Ah, thank you, ma'am," Barrett murmured awkwardly, shifting his arms around Effie, who hadn't quite given up trying to squirm out of his grasp. "That's awful thoughtful of you."

"Oh, it's nothin'!" she laughed. "Just a wee bit of Roche hospitality, dears. Now I'll be back in just a nip."

Barrett watched her rush off, frowning to himself. "This is unnerving."

Captain Griswold raised an eyebrow at Barrett, then wandered over to the fire and held his hands out to it while the other men found places at the table to sit together. "What is so odd about it?"

"These are the people that think Kyran is a monster and want to try him for a crime he isn't even guilty of," he explained in a low voice.

"And?"

"It just...doesn't feel right, how hospitable they are."

"They are people, Barrett. Not demons."

"I'm better at dealin' with one than the other," Barrett admitted gruffly.

"That is why Selah sent me."

Barrett sighed and adjusted Effie in his arms as he sat down next to the guild captain, balancing the girl on his knee. She let out an unhappy huff. "What about Kyran?"

"What about him?"

"Well, we're here. At the castle. We're runnin' out of time to help him."

"I still have not heard from Kyran what happened between him and the laird's son."

Barrett's jaw flexed. "You *know* what happened."

"No," the captain corrected, rubbing his hands together. "I have *inferred* what Kyran has *hinted* might have happened."

Barrett pinched the bridge of his nose, restraining the urge to shout at the man. "Then what are we goin' to do?"

"We will speak with him after we have spoken with the laird. He will doubtless summon us after that other man, Ewan, finishes speaking with him."

Effie squirmed again, kicking, until Barrett had to set her doll aside to hold her more firmly.

"It is probably best we find a nurse that can watch her while we attend matters," Captain Griswold remarked.

Barrett shushed the girl when she let out another doleful wail. "Kyran asked me to take her to his family."

"Are they here?"

"He said they live just outside the castle."

The captain gave him a thoughtful glance. "Perhaps that is something you can attend to while I meet our host."

Barrett's eyes narrowed. "Is there somethin' you don't want me there for?"

"This meeting will largely engage politics far above your stature within the guild. I believe it would be a better use of your time to meet Kyran's family."

Barrett was about to call the captain out on his blatant attempt to get rid of him when the full import of his words suddenly fell into place. Kyran's family might know more about what happened, and taking Effie was a good excuse to go see them—one the laird couldn't readily deny, even if he didn't want anyone to talk to the family. Such as if he were trying to hide something.

Mrs. McCrory reappeared shortly with two other girls, carrying food and drink to the long table closest to them. "Here ye are, dears. I got you a nip of whiskey ta warm ye after your trip out there in the snow. Anythin' else I can get ye?"

"Yes," Barrett replied, nodding down at Effie. "Kyran asked that I take this little one to his family. He said they live just outside the castle."

"Kyran?" The mistress pursed her lips. "You mean the mage?"

Barrett contained his flash of ire to a cutting look, and the woman immediately mollified her expression, clasping her fingers below her bosom. "Yes."

"I dinnae ken if that would be the best place for the lass, given the circumstances," she replied, her tone much gentler than before. "I could watch her for ye, if ye need."

"It would only be a temporary measure," Captain Griswold cut in before Barrett could respond. "We plan to take her with us on return to Tennebrum, but it would offer us an excuse to speak with the mage's family in regards to his development while he was young. The guild is curious to know more about such things."

"I ken your meaning," she replied carefully, "but are you certain you want a lass around folk like them?"

"It would only be temporary," the captain repeated calmly—much more calmly than Barrett was feeling. Here it was, right in his face. The same ugly bigotry that had convinced Kyran that his power was a curse and sent him fleeing to another country for safety.

"I'll take your words ta Dunbar," she finally agreed. "Is there anythin' else?"

"No," Captain Griswold replied, smiling politely. "Thank you for your hospitality, ma'am."

Her broad face blushed dark, and she swatted at him. "Aye. It's my pleasure, lad. If ye need anything, just ask Glenna here. She'll come fetch me if she canna get what ye need herself."

"Thank you," Barrett murmured to her, watching her bustling away in retreat. He didn't understand it, how such a sweet woman could say such things about Kyran while so politely serving two hunters.

Because she didn't know, he reminded himself. Nobody knew the hunters' secret. The guild had made sure of it, after the riots. If she knew, she would likely have run screaming from the room.

He cherished that image for a moment before a finger of guilt slipped through. He wasn't a monster, and neither was Kyran. Kyran was innocent, and Barrett was going to prove it, or Graces help him, he was going to make sure the mage wasn't there to be found guilty.

Chapter Forty-Six

DESPITE SPENDING MUCH of his time isolated in the back of a wagon, both in Tennebrum and then here in the Isles, Kyran hadn't felt quite as alone as he did now, in that courtyard. There were the laird's lads standing close by to make sure he didn't try to escape, and the other people that lived in the castle moving about and chatting, but they were nothing more than a muted noise at the edge of his awareness. He had spent so long sitting in the dark alone, and lived so many years on Cairngorm before that, that he should have been immune to this feeling. This isolation.

Yet it plagued him still, the growing sense that he was stranded in a vast gulf, waiting only for it to swallow him.

A hot stab of pain lanced through his spiraling thoughts, and he clenched his fingers, forcing his hands to his lap as blood welled fresh on the back of his fist. By all the Graces in the Isles, he was getting worse. He was going out of his head. When was this going to stop? When was he going to wake up?

The curly-haired Isleman—the one that had put an arrow through his leg in that alley in Tennebrum—appeared at the edge of the courtyard, moving purposefully towards the others. "He's ta go ta the dungeon," he told them, refusing to look at Kyran.

Kyran had never seen Castle Erchleis's dungeon, but he knew immediately that it was not a place he wanted to be. He considered for more than a second resisting the men when they ordered him out of the wagon. He could. He could use his magic and walk out.

Aye, his reason whispered to him, he would walk out—but to where? Back to Cairngorm? He would starve well before he reached the mountain, if the demon did not find him first. And there was the guild captain's promise to consider as well. If he escaped, no doubt Barrett and the guild captain would give chase, and he was not strong enough to resist them as well.

More than that, he was not a demon, monstrous blood or not. Killing any of them with his magic would make him no better than the beasts that preyed on *weans* like Effie and the lad he had saved beneath Oareford. It may have been foolish to cling to that thin belief now, but it was the last thread in his mind he could see left of his connection to humanity, and he was not certain he wanted to know what he would become if he let it break.

"You," one of the men said, pointing at Kyran. "Come on. Let's go."

Taking up his walking stick, Kyran painstakingly climbed out the back of the wagon. The curly-haired man took the lead, and Kyran followed, his pace slow and stiff after sitting in the cart for so long, but he felt steadier. Some of his strength seemed to have seeped back into him with the scant food he had taken. The others fell in before and behind him, careful to keep their distance, as if mage blood were catching.

They took the most circumspect route, Kyran was certain, through the less used halls of the castle. They only met a few people, and the men escorting him ordered them back the way they came. They hurried to comply.

At last they came to a small room down a flight of stairs. There was a table in the middle with a few dirty platters and mugs strewn about it, and a bench on either side, but that was not their destination. The men lead him to a heavy, oak-timbered door set beneath the stairwell. They parted, letting Kyran to the front as one of their number pulled the door open to a narrow, steep stair that led down into a waiting pool of black.

A rank draft rolled up out of the darkness, sliding along his skin and face with a cold, greasy touch. He shivered, though not from the cold. He did not want to go down there.

"Go on," one of the men prodded. "Get movin'."

Kyran shook his head faintly, gaze fixed on the darkness. He could not go down there. He would never come back up.

"What's the problem?"

Kyran's heart froze. He had clench his control around his magic as his blood flared bright and cold. He had not heard that voice in two years, but he would never mistake it.

Behind them, Connal stepped off the stairs. The man had his father's stature, though he had filled it out more thickly. He had his mother's raven-black hair, which he kept long, pulled back in a low tail. He had been handsome. There had always been more than a few lasses swooning after the man, though he had yet to be wed when Kyran had last known him.

Kyran doubted they were swooning now.

As he faced Kyran, the mage saw for the first time the ruin wrought to the once-handsome features of the man's face, and likely beneath his clothes. Guilt twined with the fear and anger already twisting in his gut, and he hated it. He hated that he felt guilty for hurting Connal when the man had done so much worse to him. Yet he couldn't banish the feeling entirely.

"I asked what the problem is," the man drawled, his words hampered by a faint lisp. As he crossed the room, Kyran noticed his limp.

He didn't make it more than halfway across before he stopped, his one good eye fixed on Kyran—or, rather, on his leg—in open surprise before his face split in a wide grin.

"You...." He let out a loud guffaw. "Look at you! I hafta say, the Graces do hear our voices. Get your foot caught in a snare, *connie*?" Connal jeered, closing the distance between them.

Kyran had to fight not to back away. He was taller by a head, but he felt small and frail before the laird's son. His stomach turned in knots just looking at him.

"It's nothing more than a beast like you deserves," Connal said.

"I am na a beast," Kyran bit back, but his voice sounded thready and hoarse.

Connal snorted. "No. You're even lower than that, cur." He drew closer, and Kyran caught himself leaning back. "If it were up ta me, there wouldna be a hall. Na for something like you. You shoulda been put in the trough a long time ago. If anyone should stand at that hall, it's your da, for not doing it himself in the first place."

Kyran's nails dug into his walking stick, and he drew himself upright. "Dinnae speak about my da that way."

"Or what? You touch me, and you're dead where you stand, mage. There'll be no formality."

"If I touch you," Kyran replied, baring his teeth, "you'll be dead first."

The mocking smile vanished. "Is that a threat?"

"It is the truth."

Connal tilted his head just enough to look the nearest man in the eyes. "Make yourselves busy."

They all went silent, staring at Connal or glancing between one another. Then a smile came over one of their faces.

"I think I hear someone in the hall," he said. "Would be a shame if they were lost." He started for the stairs, and the others followed shortly after, that same smile passing among them. Only Ewan hesitated, staring at Kyran, his eyes burning.

"Go on," Connal said. It was not a suggestion. Ewan hesitated a moment longer, then tore his eyes from Kyran, barely glancing at Connal as he followed the other men upstairs.

The air in the room grew taut as the door at the top of the stairs swung closed, and the skin along Kyran's arms and the back of his neck prickled. Oh, Stars, what was he planning?

Connal fixed his good eye on Kyran again. Kyran's stomach churned: he knew that look. That almost sickly gleam.

"You dinnae ken how hard I tried ta convince my da ta keep this matter just between us," Connal said, his voice eerily calm. "But he insisted that it was important we punish you publicly, so they would ken that the cur that did this ta me couldna escape justice, no matter where it scurried off ta hide."

"Justice?" Kyran spat the word. "How is it justice, after what you did ta me?"

"After what I did?" Connal's smile was empty of anything but malice. "I only came ta speak with you about those terrible rumors I heard, but when I mentioned them, you attacked me. I was lucky ta get away with my life."

Kyran's snarled. The air snapped deadly cold as he let his magic slip a measured amount, and Connal's eye widened. "You—"

Connal's boot connected with his walking stick, knocking it out from under his arm, and Kyran fell onto the unforgivingly hard stone.

Pain shot through his knee and elbow, but it was dwarfed by the white-hot agony in his mutilated leg as it connected with the stone. He bit down on a scream as spots of light burst before his eyes, and clutched at his injured leg, pouring his magic into it until the pain began to loosen its grip.

"See. This is what I was talking about," Connal continued, circling Kyran. "You are dangerous. You are na human like me and other folk. There's no telling what sort of lies you may try ta concoct when my da brings you in front of the hall. But we both know what really happened." He kicked the walking stick away.

"You bastard," Kyran hissed through his teeth, panting.

Connal tilted his head at Kyran, as if he had not heard him properly. "Maybe I dinnae make myself clear." He crouched just out of Kyran's easy reach, his fingers toying with the obvious handle of a knife protruding from the top of his boot. "Dinnae make this harder than it has ta be. You let them bring you before the hall and keep your mouth shut, and our conversation here is done. Then, after Hall ends and the servant's are scrubbing your filthy blood out of the stone, the problem that's been sitting between my da and your da all these years will have finally passed."

He leaned forward, resting one elbow on his knees. "But let's say you *did* get it inta your thick head ta try telling a story. Well, then things would start ta get pretty messy, since it was only you and me there when it happened. Only, we both know you werena supposed ta be there in the first place. You were supposed ta be left for the wolves when you were a *bairn*, before you could hurt anyone. Instead, your family hid you, lied about you for years until it was obvious you were still alive."

He shrugged, sighing. "My da—he wanted to let it go. He likes your da, see. Been fast friends since they were *weans*. But now you've gone and hurt someone—bad—and ta ignore the fact that your da kent what you were, and how things like you are supposed ta be taken care of, would be negligent of a laird with so many people counting on him for their safety. You ken?"

So those were the choices. Go quietly, without telling anyone what Connal had done to him, or the man would make certain the laird punished his family too. Die alone and silent, or drag his family with him.

Kyran's eyes narrowed. Looking up at Connal, he weighed the price of killing the man.

"I ken what you're thinking," Connal said quietly. "But dinnae think for a minute that killing me will protect you or your family from the law. My da willna let his brotherhood with your da stop him from doing what is right."

He got back to his feet with a heavy grunt and limped away, leaving Kyran with the slowly sinking realization that he was trapped and fast running out of time. Cruel illusion or real, it didn't matter anymore: it was all coming to its end tomorrow, and there was nothing he could do to stop it.

There was a sharp clatter, and Kyran jerked from his thoughts as his walking stick slid into him.

"There," Connal said, pacing back to him. "I trust you ken where I am coming from now. There's no need ta make all of this messier than it has ta be."

Kyran grasped the piece of silverbark, pushing himself up on his other hand. The faint flicker of desire to strike anyway, to be rid of that ugly leer and the ghost of coarse fingers clutching the back of his neck, burned through Kyran—before fading.

Connal would deserve it, without a single doubt, but not his family. He couldn't do that to them.

He closed his will around his magic and laboriously pulled himself upright, wedging his walking stick beneath his arm. Connal nodded towards the open dungeon door.

Kyran looked at the darkness beyond the archway and, despite everything, still dreaded slinking down there without a light.

"Go on," Connal said, stepping up behind him. "Dinnae draw this out."

Chapter Forty-Seven

A YOUNG WOMAN met Barrett in the great hall and introduced herself as Aggie, explaining that she had been sent by the laird to accompany him to Neil's—Kyran's pa—house. She seemed about Kyran's age and pretty, her face sweet. Her dark hair had been gathered into a pair of braids, and her hazel eyes were framed by thick lashes.

They left immediately, heading out over the frozen ground.

"That's him there," she said as they came over a rise, pointing to a small house that sat hunched against the white field, almost blending into its surroundings. Like most of the buildings Barrett had seen at the Isleish port, its walls were made of stacked stone, its roof thatched. A lone figure was splitting firewood outside, his face indistinct in the poor weather.

The young woman shivered beneath her shawls and the tartan draped over her, sending flakes of snow fluttering off of the fabric and into the increasingly bitter wind. "Begging your pardon, sir, but this weather doesna do me any good."

"I think I can manage from here, if you want to head back," Barrett offered, pulling his coat more closely around Effie, who was tucked against his chest, as he felt a shiver perch at the top of his own spine.

He frowned, realizing he had been growing steadily colder since they had stepped out of the castle. Usually his magic kept him comfortable without him even having to think about it. In fact, as far as he could recall, this was the first time since he'd become a hunter that he had actually felt cold. It was especially strange after the last months in Tennebrum, where he had felt so warm that he had barely suffered wearing clothes.

Barrett reached for his power to warm himself, but it was oddly resistant. His frown deepened. He reached again, and a pulse of warmth spread through him. That had never happened before.

"Thank you," Aggie said in obvious relief. "But are you certain you can find your way back in this? It's getting ta be a proper storm out here now."

"I'm certain. This shouldn't take long. Thank you again for your help."

"Well, if you're certain." She shrugged her shawls closer. "I suppose demon hunters face down worse things than a nip of winter."

"That we do, miss."

She flashed him a shy smile and began to trudge through the snow back towards the distant outline of the castle, barely visible through the white haze and wind-driven snow.

The man splitting wood glanced up as Barrett approached but did not slow his work, even when the hunter stopped several feet from him. He was not remarkable in appearance. He looked to be of an average height and build, though Barrett imagined his arms were corded with muscle beneath his long, woolen coat, by the way he swung the axe so precisely. Between his thinning chestnut hair, broad cheekbones, and high forehead, Barrett had difficulty imagining the man shared blood with Kyran.

"Are you Neil Roche?" he called over the wind.

"Aye," the man replied, picking up another log and setting it on the wide, flat stump before him. "And who might you be?"

"I'm Barrett. I'm a hunter with the guild in Tennebrum."

The man seemed to hesitate at that as he reared back to swing, his eyes flicking up to Barrett, then back at his log.

"Aye, is that so?" he asked, bringing the axe down hard. The log split neatly in two, the two pieces tumbling off the stump into the piles of split wood on either side. Neil left the axe embedded in the stump and reached for another log. "And what brings a hunter ta my doorstep? As I am certain you have noticed," he wedged the axe free, "there are na any demons here in the Isles."

Barrett watched him swing again, suddenly nervous and irritated. He didn't like being brushed off so casually when he was trying to help. Whatever welcome he had been expecting after Kyran had described his father, this was not it. The man looked less than pleased to see him.

"I've been working with your son Kyran."

The man swung again, but appeared to bring the axe head down with too much force, burying it straight through the wedge and into the stump. He seemed to contemplate the axe a moment before looking up again. "He isna here. Has na in years."

Barrett swallowed nervously, looking at the axe. "I know. I'm here at his request."

The man set a hand to his hip, his fingers drumming at something Barrett could not see beneath the shadow of his coat. "What do you mean by that?" he asked carefully.

"We worked together in Tennebrum," Barrett tried to explain, hoping the man wouldn't try to take a swing at him.

The man's brows rose, the corners of his dark blue eyes crinkling in confusion. "My son was working with a hunter?"

"Yes. He....He was good at it."

The man's deep scowl softened, and Barrett finally saw the first glimpse of the protective father beneath his gruff exterior. Neil wasn't angry; he was afraid. For Kyran.

Barrett licked his lips, suddenly shy for words, but he forced himself to keep going. "But it came to the guild's attention that there was a warrant out for him from the laird, Dunbar. One that had been issued to the Crown."

Neil's expression hardened again, his mouth curling in a snarl. "So you brought him here? Ta the people tha' wanted his ma ta leave him in the woods for the beasts when he showed the signs?"

Barrett's eyes widened in horror. Kyran had never told him that. "I...We...." he stumbled to explain. "We're tryin' to help him."

The man leaned over and spat in the snow. "My son dinnae do anything more wrong than be born."

"We're trying to prove that, but everyone in that castle is a superstitious git."

Neil snorted thickly. "Aye, tha's the truth of it." A small grin pulled at Barrett's lips at the man's tone. Now Barrett could see the relation. The man glanced up at the sky, then to the pile of wood he had been chopping. "Come inside. Get that *wean* out of the cold."

"I'm sure she would 'preciate that," he agreed. "The winter is cold in Tennebrum, but nothin' like this."

"It isna usually this snowy either, at least this early," the man remarked, bending to gather some of the split logs into his arms. "I suppose I shoulda guessed Kyran was back, then."

Barrett laughed, caught off guard by the man's casual reference to Kyran's magic. With his arms full of wood, Neil led them around to the front and let them in the house, latching the door behind them.

Barrett near groaned in relief. Graces, it was so much warmer inside. Effie squirmed beneath his coat, and he eased her down to the floor, keeping careful hold of one of her hands. She clung to his leg, shivering still.

"Barrett," Neil said, crossing the small room to stand behind a woman seated near the fireplace, a half-mended shirt in her lap. Barrett had to do a double take. She was slender beneath her layered skirts, her features fine-boned and delicate. Her hair was a burnished auburn, twisted up off her long, graceful neck, and her skin, flushed from the heat of the fire and colored by a sprinkle of freckles, was the softest tint of peach. She smiled up at them, soft age lines showing around eyes the color of sun-baked earth.

"This is my wife, Sorcha."

Barrett was at a loss for words. This couldn't be anybody but Kyran's mother.

"Afternoon ta ye," she greeted him, setting aside her mending, and Barrett nodded dumbly in return. "My apologies for my rudeness, but I dinnae expect guests."

"Aggie brought them 'round," Neil answered before Barrett could. "He works for the hunter's guild in Tennebrum."

Instead of the surprise and curiosity that most of the Isleish had shown, Sorcha's face went dead pale. "Oh?" she asked, her voice wavering as she made an obvious effort to hide her initial reaction, smiling nervously. "And what brings a hunter this far inta the Isles?"

Again, Barrett opened his mouth to explain, but Neil answered her first. "He brought Kyran ta Dunbar."

Her smile evaporated. "Kyran is....Right now?"

Neil nodded.

She looked at Barrett again. Her nervous fear hardened into a cold glare. "Why?"

"There was a warrant," Barrett tried to explain, "through the Crown. We had to. But my captain said if we could prove Kyran's innocence, he could help clear his name. Kyran won't tell us what happened, though."

"My son dinnae do anything ta that bastard he dinnae deserve!" Neil snarled, but he looked more than angry—physically ill. "You dinnae see him when I found him hiding, blood all...." He seemed to stop himself, the cords of his neck standing out as he ground his teeth.

The room went silent except for the crackling of the fire. Barrett had to hold his breath to keep from vomiting. The more he learned about what had happened, the sicker it made him.

Slowly, Sorcha looked up at her husband and reached to touch his arm. "Neil," she said softly.

His arm flexed under her touch, and he turned his hand to take hers. "I'd like some tea, *mo chridhe*," he said at last, leaning down to kiss her hair. "I am certain our guest would like a cuppa as well."

"Aye," she said, almost too quiet to hear. She squeezed his hand and got up, adjusting her shawls and pulling one up over her hair. "I'll just fetch some fresh water for the kettle." Picking up a wooden bucket from the table, she quietly let herself from the house.

Neil raised his head and glared at Barrett. "Connal deserved what happened ta him."

"If he's alive, he deserves worse," Barrett agreed. "But my captain insisted the only way he can help Kyran is if he knows the whole of what happened. But Kyran won't tell us." Barrett sighed, frustrated and sick at heart. "Even knowing it's the only way the guild can help him."

"You canna blame the lad," Neil spat, shifting on his feet. "Let me talk ta him. I can explain it ta him. But"—he jabbed a finger at Barrett—"I want you ta swear that if he tells you what happened, you willna let Dunbar kill him."

"I swear," Barrett said without hesitation. "Graces curse the rest."

Neil held his gaze, measuring the worth of his words before heaving a sigh. "How is he?"

Tell my da when you see him that I am well.

"He's gotten stronger since I first met him," Barrett admitted softly, wincing at what he needed to say next. "But he's...strugglin' right now."

The man's head tilted, brows furrowing. "Struggling? Is he ill?"

"He is recoverin' from a...surgery."

Neil's lips parted in a silent gasp. "He was hurt?"

"Yes." Barrett hesitated to say more.

Neil spat another short, Isleish curse, dropping his head into his hand and rubbing at his eyes. "Curse the Graces. Curse them all."

It could have been worse, Barrett added silently.

"Where are they keeping him?" Neil asked.

"I don't know. He was gone when I came out."

"It'll be the dungeons," Neil growled. "Dunbar wouldna show him real courtesy." He rapped his knuckles against the table, bowing his head as if drawing strength before he asked his next question. "What favour did he ask of ye?"

"Oh," Barrett started, realizing he had never even begun to explain the real reason for their visit. "This is Effie," he said, directing his gaze down at the girl. "Kyran has been carin' for her. It was his wish that I bring her to stay with you all."

The man's drawn expression widened in surprise. "Did he now? And where did Kyran come across a *wean* such as this?"

"It's...complicated to explain," Barrett answered vaguely. Now was not the time to bring up what had happened with the demon realm. "But she's an orphan. She doesn't speak much, but she responds well to Isleish. Isn't that right, lass?" He smiled as the girl picked her head up to look at him. "Kyran is the one that gave her the name Effie."

The first glimpse of a smile appeared on the man's mouth at that. "He would."

The click of the latch sounded behind them, and Barrett stepped out of the way as Sorcha returned. Snow clung thickly to her shawls and trailed behind her in mushy boot prints as she carried the heavy bucket of well water to the fireside.

Neil murmured something to her in Isleish that made her look up, a sweet smile on her lips, before he continued. It was all in Isleish, but he could tell by the way Neil was gesturing, and the way Sorcha's eyes kept flicking between them and her husband, that he must have been explaining the situation. She nodded, asking him something, but he shook his head and gestured to Barrett.

"Does she have anything warm ta wear?" she asked Barrett in Common.

"Just what she has now," Barrett admitted.

"Aye, well, I should still have some of Isobel's wee things. If na, there's plenty of things about I can make something from. She willna be cold while she stays."

Barrett smiled gratefully. He had a good feeling about leaving Effie here. Kyran was right about his family. They were good people that cared a lot for one another and their children. Effie would be alright.

He slowly eased the girl from his leg, shushing her gently when she began to whine. "It's alright," he said, running a hand over her dark hair. It had gotten frizzy and tangled over the last few days of travel, and there were bits of hay stuck everywhere in it. She looked up at him, her eyes open as wide as they could go, her little mouth trembling. "We'll get Kyran back soon."

"*Kee?*" she whispered.

Barrett's chest stung. "That's right. Kyran."

"Anythin' ta ken about her?" Sorcha asked, coming to kneel in front of the girl. Effie hid behind Barrett's arm, pressing against his leg.

"She's good at sneakin' around. She'll do almost anythin' to get back to Kyran."

"I promise I keep an eye on all my *weans*," Sorcha assured him, leaning to peer around his arm at the girl. "She looks ta be a wee bit younger than my Isobel. She and Tavish are at the stables right now mucking out. Perhaps the lass would like ta meet them?" She said the last bit in a soft, childish tone as she looked down at Effie, offering the girl a warm smile as she extended a hand to her.

The nervous expression on the girl's face softened, but she did not move from Barrett's side.

"It's alright, *wean*," Sorcha murmured softly to her. "I'm just goin' ta fix you a nice hot meal. How does that sound, hm? Are you hungry?"

Effie glanced up at Barrett uncertainly, and he towed her forward until Sorcha caught her beneath her arms. The girl squirmed in her grasp as the woman swept her up into her arms, whimpering in distress. Barrett's heart ache to hear it.

"She'll be alright," Sorcha assured him. "You both should get going."

Neil stepped towards his wife, wrapping an arm around her waist to pull her against him and press a kiss into her neck, murmuring something in soft Isleish that made her laugh before she kissed him back until his tight shoulders relaxed, never letting go of Effie.

Barrett's cheeks heated at the display. There had never been an abundance of affection between his parents. The majority of their interactions had started and ended with shouting. It was hardly a wonder he and Kyran saw so little eye to eye. They had grown up in completely different worlds.

With obvious reluctance, Neil let his arms slip from around her waist, and started for the door. "Aye, let's go."

Chapter Forty-Eight

The moment Barrett stepped from the sheltering side of the house, the wind slapped him. It howled over the fields like a thing alive, driving icy needles of snow before it. He pulled his coat collar up around his face, hunching his shoulders in an attempt to shield himself from the stinging wind, but the cold seemed to cut right through him and his magic, even as he drew more to keep from shivering. Graces above, he had never seen such weather before.

"It's getting worse," Barrett shouted over the wind.

"Aye," Neil agreed, tugging at his tartan until a swath of it came free, and flipped it up over his shoulders. "Glad I brought the horses in. Even they couldna stand ta be out here by night."

"Wouldn't bother Kyran one bit, I bet," Barrett chuckled, more to himself, but he knew Neil heard him by the way the man smiled and shook his head, mumbling in Isleish as he started forward.

Barrett watched his boots kick up snow as they walked, keeping his head ducked against the wind, and remembered the peace on Kyran's face when it had begun snowing. Despite everything that was happening, he had never seen Kyran so calm. Soon, he would have that peace back. Barrett would make sure of it.

He was glad Neil was coming with him, or Barrett wasn't certain he would have made it back to the castle. He couldn't even see Erchleis anymore, but Neil led them unerringly through the weather back to the castle's courtyard. Barrett let out a relieved sigh, brushing the snow from his shoulders and head, surprised it had not melted from his magic. They were still out in the open air, but, cut off from the wind by the walls, it felt infinitely warmer.

Neil, on the other hand, merely dropped his tartan from his shoulders, the snow falling out of it. His skin was flushed, his hair thickly covered in white, but he did not seem bothered by the weather at all.

"You said Kyran was being kept in the dungeon?" Neil asked, watching a pair of women hurry across the courtyard, picking their skirts up to avoid the trampled slush on the stones.

"I think," Barrett confirmed, keeping his voice low. "Do you know the way?"

"I've never been ta the keep's dungeon," Neil confessed quietly. "And I'm not taken by the idea of everyone knowing where we're headed."

"I might have an idea," Barrett offered, focusing his attention inward, on the constant, faint press of magic that had reached out to him upon entering the castle. "This way."

"Where are we goin'?"

"Just follow me," Barrett assured him, leading the man into the maze of halls towards one of the two sources of magic he sensed. It gave him a general direction, more or less what he usually worked with in Oareford, but, unfamiliar with the layout of the castle, he kept running into dead ends and looping halls that forced him to double back.

"Graces above," he swore as they came to the same staircase for the second time. "Who built this place?"

"'Ey! Hunter!"

Barrett looked up at the voice as a young man came jogging from around the corner behind them, barely out of boyhood, his face flushed from exertion.

"Pardon, sirs," he greeted them, folding in half in a sloppy bow, "but Dunbar needs ta speak with Neil there."

"It can wait," Neil growled, starting to turn back down the hall again.

"Ah, Dunbar said it couldna," the young man disagreed, straightening. His red hair stuck out in every direction. "Says he needs ta see you now."

Neil grumbled something in Isleish which turned the young man's ears red.

"You dinnae hafta come too, hunter," the young man quickly stammered. "He said he only needs ta see Neil."

Except that Barrett needed Neil to speak with Kyran, and Barrett was not certain the laird was calling on the man for a simple, friendly chat. "I'll come too, if it's all the same."

The young man nodded, smiling uncertainly, then started down the hall in the opposite direction they had been going.

Neil sighed behind him, muttering in more Isleish, but Barrett caught his tone amply well.

Me too, he thought sourly.

The laird received them in a room at the top of a set of stairs on what felt like the far side of the castle. There were two male voices on the other side, speaking indistinctly to one another within, and while Barrett was certain one must be the laird, he did not recognize the other. The young man leading them knocked gently, and the two people quieted.

"Aye?" one called from within.

"I've brought Neil, as you've asked. The other hunter was with him, and came as well."

"Verrah well. Let them in."

The young man turned the latch, pushing the door in as he stepped to one side, and gestured for them to go in.

The hard stone floor was softened by a thick, plush-looking bear pelt laid over an intricately woven rug like nothing Barrett had ever seen. Ijeichon, he would guess, but he had not the faintest where in the empire it might come from. The walls, too, were covered in woven tapestries of hunting scenes and the same heraldry he recognized from the hall. Other ornaments and well-oiled weapons lay or hung scattered about the place, on hand-carved tables and shelves, amongst books and parchments. A roaring fireplace drove off the winter chill, and several candles in iron brackets fixed to the walls kept the dark at bay.

And standing behind a desk at the center of it all was the laird—the man who had issued the warrant that had led them here. The father of the man that had hurt Kyran, and who was willing to stand behind that son, even if what he'd done was monstrously wrong.

He was not an outstandingly large man, as the ship's captain had been, but he was far from the slight build Kyran professed. He stood at perhaps a handspan shorter than Barrett, and while the red-blonde of his long hair had gone almost entirely grey with age, his features were still strong-boned and handsome beneath a neatly trimmed beard.

Captain Griswold stood at the corner of the desk where Dunbar was seated.

"Evening," Dunbar greeted them with a polite smile. "My apologies for not standing. If you would come in, please. You stay just there by the door, Jock."

Graces, it was warm in here. Barrett slipped his hands out of his coat pockets, rubbing them together as he eased towards the hearth, but stopped when he realized someone was already standing at the fire, his back to the room as they warmed their hands. This man was younger than the laird and possibly even Barrett himself, with long black hair held in a tail at the base of his neck, and a frame heavy with muscle. He must have been the second voice, as it definitely hadn't been the guild captain he'd heard. Barrett squinted at the man, but he could not make out whether he recognized him.

"So, did you plan ta tell me my son was here, in your dungeon?" Neil growled at the laird, instantly bringing Barrett's attention around. "Or were ye hopin' ta have him in the ground before I could get here?"

"I was planning ta send a messenger 'round in the morning if word hadna reached you," Dunbar replied evenly.

"In the morning?" Neil banged his palms on the desk. "Did it ever occur ta ye that I might want ta speak ta my son after he has been gone for two years?"

Two years? Barrett frowned. That didn't match up with what Kyran had told him. The mage had never given him a number, but by the way he acted, Barrett had presumed he had not been in Tennebrum more than a few weeks when he met him. Had he remained in the Isles before that until he was finally forced to leave the country? Graces above, if that was true, then Kyran would have been only sixteen or seventeen when all of this had happened.

"Aye, it did," the laird agreed. "But do you intend ta just speak with him?"

"And what do ye mean by tha'?"

"I mean ta say that I am na entirely an auld fool, Neil, and I ken what lengths you would go through ta protect your family. But you ken Kyran is dangerous, dinnae ye? Ye saw what he did ta my son."

"And you dinnae see what he did ta *my* son!" Neil shouted, spittle flying past his lips as he slammed his palms against the desk again. "I willna let ye hurt my lad ta cover what he did!"

"Did what, Neil?" Dunbar argued back louder, standing to match Kyran's father. "Do ye have an accusation ta bring before the hall?"

"Ye know what he did! There's no way ye're tha' blind or tha' daft ta na hear what Connal's been about!"

"I've heard what you've said, and what Connal's said. And I ken that Kyran ran off for near two years before I could find the lad—in Tennebrum, no less. Now, why do you suppose he went and did that?"

"Because we both ken he would have met the sword for it anyway. Stars above, there were folk at the house the next day looking ta drag him inta the road right in front of my wife and *weans*."

"And I sent the lads over ta deal with them."

"You sent them over ta bring Kyran ta ye."

"Neil...." Dunbar stopped, lowering his head a moment as he took a deep breath through his nose. "You are angry, but you are right. I am na daft, nor am I blind, nor have my senses left me yet. I let this issue in your family go because I dinnae have the heart ta make an auld friend kill his son, mage or no. But I have learned the hard way that the auld laws exist fer a reason."

"No—no, that's just an excuse ta hide behind! Kyran is a good lad!"

"Maybe once," the laird agreed, glancing at Barrett and Captain Griswold. "But he is a mage, and the demon in their blood always outs."

"They're not *demons*," Barrett snapped, unable to hold back any longer. This was why they wanted to kill Kyran—superstitions and fear. A curse indeed. A curse of ignorance."

Dunbar looked past Neil to Barrett. "I dinnae say they were, but they are na human either, and they are dangerous."

"Kyran isna like that!" Neil barked.

"Tell tha' ta Connal," Dunbar reminded him.

"After he—"

"Neil." The laird looked the man in the eyes, his expression set. "I ken that I canna make you see reason on this, but I canna let you see him."

Neil's head jerked as if slapped. "What? You canna—"

"I can," Dunbar said firmly, cutting him off again.

Barrett felt a shock of panic begin to overtake his anger. Dunbar couldn't do that. This was their last chance to get Kyran to open up, to tell them what had happened so they could save him. He couldn't keep Neil from seeing his own son. Barrett shot a glance back at the captain, to see if he had anything to rebut the laird with, but the captain only gave him a tiny shake of his head. He either could not, or would not, do anything.

"You care for the lad," the laird continued. "He is your family, but the truth is that I canna be blind ta this any longer. This clan looks ta me ta protect them, ta lead them. How can they trust me if I dinnae keep my word? If I dinnae uphold our laws? If there was proof of what you say happened, I would let you speak in the Hall, but there isna any, and it would only serve ta stir things up and remind people that I ignored the auld laws in favor of a friend."

"Dinnae call me that," Neil hissed.

Dunbar bowed his head again with a tight sigh before lifting his gaze to look Kyran's father in the eye. "Go home, Neil. Go home. Be with your wife and *bairns*, and let this be."

Neil's hands clenched into fists. "I canna do that."

"You're as stubborn as you have always been, but this isna like before. If ye willna leave, I will have the lads help ye out."

"I'd wager they might take a few minutes ta get here."

Barrett's jaw ached as he ground his teeth to keep silent, but his hands twitched at his sides. He wanted nothing more right then than to lunge across the desk and grab Dunbar by his shirt and drag him to the floor, and he could see Neil thinking the same. Curse Dunbar, and curse Captain Griswold for doing nothing. He was supposed to be helping Kyran, and instead, he was doing everything in his power to aid the laird instead.

"Neil." All three of them turned at the captain's quiet voice. "It is better you go. My subordinate and I will speak with Kyran. We will tell him you were here."

The man looked from the captain to Dunbar. The anger in his eyes slowly faded into a haunted anguish as he realized he was not going to see his son before the trial, and maybe not ever again. But he drew himself upright, holding the laird's gaze. "Graces hear me, but I hope ye find everything you deserve, Dunbar."

The laird said nothing, only held the man's gaze until Neil turned away and stomped out of the room, throwing the door open so hard that it smashed into the wall and rebounded.

Jock let out a soft squeak, jumping in place. Dunbar waited until the young man looked back at him, then nodded towards the open door. Jock quickly bobbed into a bow and scurried after Neil.

Slowly, Dunbar let out a long sigh and sank into his seat. "I...apologize for that," he said as he reached into the desk drawer and pulled out a half-empty bottle of dark brown liquid and a small horn cup. He pulled the stopper from the bottle and began to pour a very full cup for himself. "The last few years have been hard on Neil."

"I can't imagine why," Barrett spat.

The laird tilted his head without looking up from his drink, and Barrett forced his teeth shut before he could say anything else. But he could not stop his hands from shaking as his nails bit into his palms.

"It was never mentioned in any of the letters I received from His Majesty, King Kaiden, or your guildmaster," Dunbar remarked evenly, "that Kyran had formed allies amongst your hunters." He set the bottle down on his desk and lifted the cup, looking over the brim at Barrett. "It begins to make sense to me now how he remained hidden for two years."

"I assure you, that is not the case," Captain Griswold said mildly before Barrett could respond. "It is my understanding that my subordinate here met Kyran some six months ago, when the mage assisted him with a demon that was attacking a village he was staying in. Per our guild's law regarding mages, Hunter Barrett had sent in the appropriate application, whereupon we at the guild realized there was a warrant out for a mage of his description."

"Assisted?" The laird lowered his cup. "The mage was helping a hunter?"

"Yes. Mages are uniquely suited to assist hunters in their work, given their ability to use magic without a hunter's blessing."

Dunbar seemed to consider this. Taking a drink, he said, "I see."

"It was never our intent to interfere with your affairs," the captain continued. "Only to ensure we knew all of the facts for His Majesty."

The laird nodded slowly. "I suppose auld Neil and his son have told ye their side of things, then. It isna a pretty story, ta be sure, but tha' isna the whole of it." He tilted his cup and let out an exhausted sigh. "Connal."

The man by the fireplace turned his head towards the laird.

The scent of scorched leather stung Barrett's nostrils. He was here. The man Kyran had fled his home to escape had been standing there in the room all along, and Barrett had not even known.

"Come here, lad. I want the hunters ta ken the full story."

The man turned from the fire, and despite everything, Barrett's breath caught. One half of Connal's face was a near mirror of his father's, though perhaps with a bit stronger line to his jaw. The other half, though, was a craggy, pitted ruin. His hands, hanging by his sides, showed the same cruel destruction, with fingers missing from each. He moved with a noticeable limp as he approached, and Barrett could not help but wonder if the scarring went farther than he could see.

He stopped next to the laird's desk, folding his hands behind his back. Dunbar took another sip. "This is my son, Connal. I dinnae need ta explain what I am asking you ta see."

Barrett lifted his chin. The muscles beneath his eye and along his jaw fluttered as he fought not to raise his hand and let the fire itching beneath his skin go.

A breeze blew across the back of his neck, and his skin tightened at the sudden pull of magic next to him. The captain.

He slid his eyes to the man, his lips twitching at the obvious threat. *Bastard. Utter, rotten bastard.* Graces, if they were alone, he would not have hesitated to hit him.

"I gather ye were friendly with the mage, much like me and Neil," Dunbar said when Barrett and Captain Griswold remained silent. "But, much like us, you canna let that blind ye ta the truth. I am bloody lucky my son is alive at all."

Barrett made himself look back at the laird and force his teeth apart. "The entire time I have known Kyran," he said, making his words slow and even so as not to shout, "he has never harmed anyone. He works actively to keep his magic contained. He has more discipline than I've seen from any hunters or other mages. There....There has to have been a reason for all this, but we can't get any more of the story if you...get rid of Kyran."

The laird frowned over his drink, and Connal shifted on his feet, sharing a glance with his father.

"Barrett." It was Captain Griswold that spoke. "We are not here to interfere with the way the laird runs his court."

No, apparently they were there to bow to his every whim, even if that meant letting him kill Kyran. He glared at the captain, hating his ever calm, neutral stare. "Oh?"

"We are here as representatives of the guild," the captain explained, as if to a child, "to offer our assistance should Kyran attempt to use his powers against the people here, or should he lose control." He leaned closer to

Barrett and muttered, "Be quiet and control yourself before you make this even more difficult."

Barrett's fist twitched at his side, his skin flushing before he felt another breeze stir his hair. He swore, if Captain Griswold tried to suffocate him again, he would break his nose.

"Perhaps it is best if your subordinate doesna visit the mage or remain in attendance at the Hall tomorrow," Dunbar said in a tone that clearly indicated it was not a suggestion.

The heat of Barrett's magic dissipated, and the blood drained from his face. "What? No." He had to be there in case things went wrong, so he could get to Kyran.

Captain Griswold let out a long sigh. "I think that might be best, to avoid a scene."

"No," Barrett replied firmly. "I won't be kept from this."

"I ken you are right," Dunbar agreed without even acknowledging Barrett. "He will be confined ta a room until the Hall is over. Then, you will both be free ta leave at your discretion."

Barrett could not believe what he was hearing. "No! I should be there. So should Neil. It's his son, for the Graces' sake."

But the laird didn't seem to see him anymore, his eyes going straight through him. Barrett whirled to the captain, searching his empty face for some sign, some morsel of understanding, but it was utterly vacant.

"I have to be there," he pleaded.

"I think it is the laird's decision, and I will uphold whatever that may be," the captain said without hesitation, his dark eyes flicking past Barrett to the laird.

"You bastard," Barrett spat. "You utter bastard."

If the captain heard him, it did not show. "I do not mean any offense," he said to Dunbar, "but if we are to have enough time that I may write up my notes for you this evening, I must set about my work."

Dunbar raised his hand in dismissal. "Aye," he said, draining his cup. "I will speak with the lad outside. He will see ye ta your rooms. Mrs. McCrory has had them prepared and your things brought ta them."

The captain bowed his head. "Thank you, sir."

The laird rose from his desk, and Barrett did not even bother to hide his sneer. This was wrong. This was so utterly wrong, and Captain Griswold was helping them. He wanted to scream at the captain, wrap his hands around his throat, to shake him and ask him why. Ask him how he could do this to someone he knew was innocent. But he knew the answers he would get—about laws and representing the guild and proof. The captain was more concerned with upsetting someone than with Kyran's life.

Fine, Barrett told himself as he and Captain Griswold followed the laird into the hall. *If no one is going to do anything, then I will.*

Chapter Forty-Nine

It was dark. Oh, stars, it was as if Kyran had never left that black prison. The truth pressed against him there in the dungeon's dark, unraveling the edges of his delusion. The light of his blood only blended into the nightmares outlining the stone walls around him. The madness that had been growing in him must have finally hatched.

At least there wasn't much longer to wait. It would all be over soon, by Connal's hand or the demon's. He wished he could see its face, *know* that it was the beast raising the sword over his head. Then he could at least stand against it, knowing only his own neck was at risk. But he couldn't gamble his family's lives. They didn't deserve to suffer for him. Not any longer.

There was a loud clack, and Kyran near started out of his skin before realizing it was the heavy lock turning at the top of the stairs. It couldn't be morning already....Could it?

The door creaked open, the faintest glow of light appearing. He pushed himself upright, not willing to be seen curled up and miserable—not if it was Connal coming to mock him further. Voices murmured indistinctly, then the door shut again.

He waited, listening as whomever was on the stairs began their descent, but he didn't recognize the footfalls. It was neither Barrett's heavy-footed shuffle, nor Connal's stilted gait. He squinted into the dungeon as the faint light resolved itself into the flickering glow of a shuttered lantern, and was surprised to see Captain Griswold stepping down onto the moldy straw-strewn floor.

"Good evening," the man greeted him, approaching his cell.

Kyran offered him a short nod in return, his attention divided by the flickering light. He could feel it against his face, like a warm touch brushing away the phantoms that had been haunting him.

"How is your leg?"

Kyran's mind focused on the guild captain again at the question. "It isna rotting yet, if that is what you are asking," he replied warily.

"I suppose that is the most I could ask of it at this point." The captain's eyes moved past him, taking in the cell behind Kyran. "I hope you will forgive me for not bothering with mincing through niceties, but I trust you understand that time is short for you. What happened between you and Connal?"

The muscles along Kyran's neck and back went rigid. The smell of the damp hay turned cloying in his nostrils. "Why?"

The man's wandering eyes shifted back to Kyran. "I know the laird and his son are not telling me the whole story, but I cannot do anything to protect you unless you tell me your side of things. I cannot work with supposition. Not in this matter."

"And how do you propose ta protect me, hm?" Kyran snapped. "It isna goin' ta matter what you say up there. Who is goin' ta believe the word of a mage over the laird's son? You've seen him by now, have ye na? Who would believe that he...." He choked on the words as the terror and pain bubbled up with them.

"That he what?" the captain prodded gently, but Kyran shook his head, his fingernails finding the bloody furrow he had scratched into his other hand.

The man seemed to watch him for a moment, the whites of his eyes casting the firelight back like ghostly moons. "Have you been threatened, Kyran?" he asked quietly.

Kyran did his best not to react, not to show anything, but he saw the way the captain's eyes narrowed in thought.

"I think I see now," Griswold mumbled, half to himself.

A knot of panic clenched in Kyran's gut. "See what?" he blustered, anxious the man might say something to the laird, to Connal.

"The truth that no one will tell me."

The blood in Kyran's veins turned to ice water. Were it anyone else, Kyran would say the man was bluffing, trying to scare him into revealing something, but the guild captain had proven himself not to be the bluffing type when he'd strangled Barrett.

"Ye canna tell anyone," Kyran babbled, lurching towards the bars until he was almost pressed against them. "Do you ken? Ye canna breathe a word!"

"That would be a grave injustice to my purpose here," Captain Griswold replied in turn. "I came to the Isles not simply to safely carry a mage under warrant, but to make certain there was no miscarriage of justice in a matter involving the Crown."

Kyran could hear his family's futures being sealed. "No, ye don—"

"I believe you when you say you are innocent," the captain continued over him without raising his voice in the slightest. But he did not need to. The words alone silenced Kyran. "I always have, even if I did not understand why you would not speak up for yourself. What could they threaten you with that would make you willing to die after escaping a demon?" He shifted closer, bringing the lantern up between them. "What was threatened? Or who? If you tell me, I can protect them. That is what the law is for."

Kyran wished he could grab the man by his shirt and make him understand. "It is the law he aims ta use."

"How?" the captain emphasized. "I understand there is little precedent for you to trust me, but I ask you to consider your family before you decide to simply give up. For that matter, you should consider Barrett. I have known him for a long time, though not intimately. He may be a stubborn fool, but he has been more himself these last weeks than he has been in a long while. He cares for you, more deeply than he probably realizes, and I ask that you consider what it may mean for him if you decide not to fight."

The protest on Kyran's tongue failed him. He had been ready to argue his family would be better without him; if he were gone, there would be nothing the laird could hold against them.

But Barrett....That was different. It didn't seem to matter what Kyran did or said, or that they hardly knew one another, because Barrett was there anyway. Hot-headed and stubborn, but with a deep compassion for the people he helped, despite whatever jaded air he feigned. Barrett was willing to throw his life away for almost any stranger. For him.

Laughter from far above cut through the damp air. Kyran glanced up the stairs towards the door that stood between him and the guards that were supposed to be watching him, lads loyal to Connal. "How did you convince them ta let you down here alone?" he asked the captain.

The man shrugged one shoulder. "I negotiated with a bottle of whiskey from the kitchen."

Kyran couldn't help a small chuckle. That would do it.

As the laughter from the men receded, the silence of the dungeon closed in again. Captain Griswold did not try to prod him, apparently set on simply waiting for him to make a decision, but Kyran was not certain anymore what he wanted to do. The man seemed so sure that he could help him. But even if he could protect his family, Kyran was not certain if he could bear telling the man what had happened—what he had let happen—especially if that meant the captain would have to explain it in front of the Hall.

Kyran's stomach turned at just the notion. Stars, he would pass of shame right there. But if he said nothing, he would die. They would kill him.

"Captain, I don—" He was interrupted by a loud, elongated gurgling from his stomach. Kyran's face flushed.

"They haven't given you anything to eat since we got here, have they?" Captain Griswold asked, and Kyran shook his head, looking down at his noisy stomach with embarrassment. The man reached into a pocket of his long coat and pulled out a bannock. "Hold out your hand."

Kyran pulled his borrowed handkerchief from his pocket, and the captain set the bannock in his palm, then dug out another, then a third.

"I also got these while I was in the kitchen," he explained as Kyran wolfed down the first bannock. "I suspected they would not be accommodating while you were down here."

Kyran grunted in dry amusement.

The dungeon door swung open again, admitting more raucous laughter. "'Ey!" called a thickly accented voice in Common. "Captain! Ye still down there?"

Captain Griswold's shoulders tensed for a brief moment before he called back, "I am."

"Ye about done then?"

"Just a moment, yes."

"Good. Dunbar is askin' after ye."

Captain Griswold pressed the heel of his hand to his forehead. "I understand." There was a moment of silence in which he was obviously waiting for the Isleman to take his leave, but the door remained open. Sighing, the captain pulled his hand from his head, catching Kyran's eye again. "I apologize. I promised the laird I would speak with him this evening, and it seems he deems it necessary now."

"You are na going ta tell him anything, are you?" Kyran pressed.

The captain's mouth pursed in thought, and Kyran's stomach knotted again. "I will make you a proposal," he said slowly. "I will say nothing to Dunbar, but I want you to seriously consider what I have told you while I am detained."

Kyran frowned, confused by the man's open terms. He nodded, slowly, and Captain Griswold bowed his head in acceptance.

"I will return as soon as I can, but I implore you to remember that you are not alone. You do not have to face this on your own."

But is that better or worse? Kyran asked himself silently as the captain climbed the stairs, taking his lantern with him and leaving Kyran to his dark prison.

Chapter Fifty

BARRETT KEPT HIS hand pressed against his eyes, suppressing the urge to vomit. Graces, why had he drunk so bloody much?

He had to give the Isleish credit: their whiskey was strong, stronger than any of the ale or mead he had favored in Tennebrum. He reached for the bottle on the floor next to him, giving it a shake. It was near half empty.

"Graces preserve me," he moaned, peeling his hand from his eyes. He had fallen asleep at the foot of the bed, watching the fire in the fireplace. After the laird had declared him barred from the Hall and from seeing Kyran, he had been locked in one of the castle's guestrooms. It was a nice enough room, with its own fireplace and a wide, arched window, and furnished with surprisingly refined taste. His things had even been brought up and left for him. But it did not disguise the fact that it was to be his prison.

But that must have been hours ago now. The room was dim; the fire had bedded down, and the candles the serving girl had lit were now barely flickers drowning in their pools of wax. The lantern was still lit, its shutters drawn close so it let out only a small pool of light. A thread of panic had begun to worm through his nausea. He leaned forward, cautious of his roiling stomach, until he could see out the window. But despite the disconcerting sound of the wind howling and what must be snow pelting the glass, it was black as the Inbetween outside, and he had no idea what hour it was.

How long had he been out? He'd only been planning to wait until it was dark to break out of the room. He'd tried the door the moment he had been left alone, despite hearing the lock turn as it was shut. He could melt a lock. But a man's voice had called from the hall beyond for him to settle down; they'd set a guard.

"Kyran, what am I doin'?" he groaned. He had only made it that much harder to help the mage by giving into his drinking. Why was he always doing this? Why did he always run away to drink when things got hard? "Graces, just let me get through this. Let me help him, and I swear I'll—"

A loud bang rattled his door in its frame, and he nearly jumped out of his skin, a violent throb stabbing through his temples. "What the...?" He caught the muffled impacts of flesh against flesh, and his door rattled in its frame again. Someone was fighting out there.

He got to his feet, swaying a moment as his head throbbed painfully again, and his stomach joined in the chorus. He pressed the back of his hand to his mouth and waited for the nausea to pass. The hall beyond the door suddenly went dead quiet.

Then the latch at his door rattled quietly, and the lock turned over. Barrett drew his power in readiness. The door slowly swung open.

An Isleman who couldn't have been much older than him peered inside, grinning when he spotted Barrett. The young man set a finger to his lips to shush him before pushing the door open the rest of the way. Behind him was another young Isleman tying off the wrists of the guard who had been sitting watch.

"By the...." Barrett trailed off as the first man waved a hand at him to be quiet.

Looking back at the other man on the floor, he said something quick in Isleish. The other nodded. Together, they lifted the guard by his shoulders and feet and dragged him into Barrett's room, kicking the door shut behind them.

"Get his feet now," the first man told the other as they set the guard down on the floor. The second Isleman grunted, pulled another length of rope from his shoulder, and started to bind the guard's feet.

"What's going on?" Barrett demanded.

The first Isleman grinned at him. "Name's Murray," he said, thrusting a hand out, which the hunter took reluctantly. He was the lankier of the two, and while the man on the ground had dark, almost chestnut-brown hair cut short, the one shaking his hand had golden-brown locks he'd let grow just a bit too long. His face had several days of scruff grown over it, but it looked oddly familiar to Barrett, though he was certain he'd not seen either man before.

Murray broke the handshake and jabbed a thumb at the other Isleman. "That's Duncan. You're Barrett, aye?"

"Ay—yes," Barrett confirmed. "But who are you?"

Murray snorted, glancing back at the other man. "I just said."

"We're Kyran's kin," Duncan intervened, tying off the guard's feet. "Da said you could help us."

Kyran's brothers. Of course; Barrett recognized their names now. "I hope you've got a plan," he said, watching them make quick work of the guard.

"Aye," Murray answered, sweeping his gaze over the room. "You've a washbasin?"

"Ah, yes. Why?"

The man held out a hand. "I need the cloth."

Barrett fetched the rag from the basin and tossed it to Murray, who then knelt next to the trussed-up guard and stuffed it into his mouth.

"That should buy us some time," he announced. "We should move him ta the other side of the bed, and...." He frowned at Barrett a moment. "Stars, you're green as the heath."

"M'fine," he groused. "I've just had some whiskey." A lot of whiskey.

The brothers laughed. Duncan leaned over and snatched the half-empty bottle off the table. "I think I found the culprit." He pulled the cork from the top and held it out. "How about a wee bit of the hair of the dog?"

Barrett waved him off. "I won't be drinkin' more if we're gettin' Kyran. Now, what's the plan?"

Duncan lifted the bottle, taking a long swig, and Murray nodded at the guard. "Tell ye when we get out of here."

Barrett nodded and moved to help drag the guard to the opposite side of the room. He debated putting his heavy coat on, but it would cause more noise than it was worth while they were moving around the castle. He set his hand on his hip, making sure his dagger was still there. He hoped he wouldn't have to hurt anyone, but he would do what he needed to get Kyran out of here.

Once they were in the hall, Duncan shut the door behind them, produced a key from someplace on his person, and locked the room.

"Can you get us ta the dungeon?" Murray whispered to Barrett as they started down the hall.

"Yes," Barrett replied. "I can—" He had not taken three steps out of the room when he felt a new source of magic erupt from somewhere in the castle below. He'd felt something like that before. In Willowvale and Oareford, when he'd left Raleigh and Kyran alone.

"Something's wrong," he said, breaking into a run past the brothers and down the hall. It was the demon. It had to be. Kyran was in danger, Barrett was sure of it.

"Graces, no," he swore as he turned a corner and someone stepped out in front of him.

He raised his fist, ready to barrel through them, when he felt another pulse of magic and a cold breeze rushed past his face—Captain Griswold.

Barrett set his teeth as he slowed. "Get out of the way!" he hissed. "Kyran's in trouble!"

The captain looked past Barrett to the two Islemen with him. They came to a halt on either side of Barrett, their hands balling into fists as they looked from him to the captain, ready to fight. The captain shook his head but turned, beckoning Barrett to follow.

"Who are they?" Griswold asked as they broke into a run down the hall.

"Kyran's brothers. Do you know where you're going?"

"Yes. I was there earlier, as promised."

"And who is he?" Murray prompted, easily keeping pace.

"My captain," Barrett answered.

"Can we trust him?"

Barrett looked from Murray to the captain. As much as he had come to loathe the captain for every action he'd taken to seal Kyran's fate here in the Isles, he was not so foolish as to turn the man's help away now. If it was either of the demons that had shown an interest in Kyran down there, he would need another hunter's help.

"Yes. He'll help us."

And Graces above, if Captain Griswold tried to stop them from getting Kyran out of there after the demon was dealt with, they would have it out once and for all.

Chapter Fifty-One

Kyran's head snapped up as the air tightened against his skin. The darkness squirmed, pressing the circle of light from his blood closer, smaller. Then something brushed across him—across his thoughts—like the whisper of a familiar voice.

The demon. It had found him again.

His magic flared beneath his skin, but the fey light could no longer even reach the wall opposite his tiny cell. "No...." He wasn't ready. He didn't want to wake up. Not when there might be hope still.

He snatched his walking stick, scrambling to stand as the light shrank, and the whisper through his mind became steadily louder and louder until it was a vicious howl. He clamped his hands over his ears, but the sound was deeper than that, scraping along his thoughts.

"No! Get out! " he screamed, releasing the last restraint over his magic and shoving the foreign thing from his mind. The whispers faded, and instead, he felt the noise as a horrid pressure, an almost physical weight against him.

The darkness rolled over the stone beneath him like a black tide, lapping up around his ankle, his knee, his hip, hot and smothering, until it closed over his head, and he was submerged in that dark vastness of the Inbetween. The wall at his back disappeared, and he could no longer feel the stone beneath his foot. It was gone. He resisted the urge to turn in place, to look around him. It was useless. There was nothing left—only endless, smothering darkness. The illusion was finally falling apart.

"*There* you are, pet."

Kyran flung his arm out at the voice, his power screaming out of his blood. But there was nothing there.

"You've grown," the demon purred into his ear

He flinched, his magic lashing at the place it should have been. But there was still nothing.

Kyran swore again, clenching his control around his magic, reining it in even as it fought him. He would need every drop to make this beast hurt—

if he could catch it. He might be in the demon's prison, but he would not surrender to it. He would not go quietly. If it meant to take him, it would have to kill him.

But where was it? It had never been this coy before. Every time it had confronted him before now, it had simply snatched him up in its claws and done whatever it was going to do. Why this game of hiding in the shadows? What was it playing at? What was it afraid of?

He glanced at his hands. His blood glared bright beneath his skin even in the thick darkness of the Inbetween, and the answer struck him like a fallen stone. It was his magic the beast feared. It *was* stronger, but it was finite. The demon didn't intend to give him the opportunity to face it. It wanted to hide, to force him to use his magic until his blood went dark. He would be easy enough to recapture if he were unconscious.

As he touched his hip, he missed the comfort of feeling of his amulets hanging there.

An idea occurred to him. How hadn't he thought of it before?

Wary of the beast's next attack, he shaped his will around his magic and reached out into the space around him the same way he did when touching one of his amulets. Only this time his focus was broader, like casting a net into the sea. Something resisted him, and he narrowed his focus upon the sensation until, like a fish taking the line, there was a tug at his attention, pulling his eyes to a spot in the darkness to his left.

For the first time in a long while, a fearsome smile stretched across Kyran's mouth. He extended his hand and let his power go.

The demon screamed, its body flashing bright in the dark. It dropped to the ground, writhing. Kyran didn't let up as its flesh steamed and cracked. He had promised he would make it pay dearly for taking him, and he meant to keep that promise.

"You half-blooded beast!" the demon shrieked. Its skin burst into scarlet and black flame with a howling gale, shielding it from Kyran's deep, wintery cold.

"Dinnae call me that," Kyran snarled over the deafening bay of the wind.

The demon laughed, its mouth gaping obscenely. "That is all you will ever be. A beast. Fodder for your greater kin. Now, *submit.*" The demon's power slammed into him, hard enough to stagger him, but it was nothing compared to any time before. He could endure it. He was stronger.

"Never!" he shouted, gathering his will around his magic, shaping it. Then he cast it at the demon, using that same reaching sensation he had used before, only this time, he did not aim blindly.

He felt the demon's resistance crumble as his magic speared through not its flesh, but its very essence.

Images and sensations flooded his mind. He saw the demon pinned beneath another beast that tore into its belly, swallowing mouthfuls of ashen flesh. As his gaze flickered downward, he saw not his own body, but the demon's spidery limbs. Movement caught his eye, and he turned to see himself staring up from a pile of rubble, wide-eyed and filthy, begging.

"No." The word growled involuntarily from his throat, and he began to eat. He jerked his head, tearing loose a mouthful of meat. Blood splashed over his tongue.

"Graces, no! Raleigh!" someone shouted.

Kyran lifted his head, licking the blood from his chin to see Barrett at the doorway, his face clean-shaven, his eyes wide in horror.

"Barrett...." the man beneath him rasped, and Kyran spared him a simpering glance. He looked young. Blood and sweat plastered his curling black hair to his head. His dark eyes were nearly closed, and his skin had gone ashen with blood loss.

Kyran lifted his gaze again, and met Barrett's eyes—only it was no longer Barrett. It wore his clothes, his hair, but his skin had turned utterly black, and stretching from his back were what he could only describe as two enormous, featherless wings.

And his eyes....The whites had turned the same, lightless black as his skin, their rings of summer blue transformed into a molten, fiery red.

"What would you, a hunter's pet, want with a half-breed, anyway?" he asked the winged figure.

Its wings shifted as crimson, and black fire kindled along its hands. "To take it away from you."

The scene lurched dizzily, and Kyran blinked as he found himself standing not in a stone courtyard, but in the empty darkness of the Inbetween, staring down at the demon as it shuddered and staggered on all fours. He was breathing hard, his extended hand trembling, but he had done it. He knew beyond reason that what he had seen was the demon's memories. He had not just fended the beast off, but broken it, the way it had him.

Kyran frowned, the import of the realization slowly dawning on him. The demon would never have shown him something like this. It would never have let him see it as weaker than him. It was too proud for that deception. But it couldn't mean....No, it had to. This...was *real*. It had to be! Barrett *had* found him, and he was in the Isles. And he was strong.

Terribly strong.

The demon shook itself, its skin leaping with flames as it rounded on Kyran. He clenched his shaking muscles, focusing his will around his power again.

This was it. No more running. No more staring at the walls in the dark, waiting to hear the click of nails on stone. He was not going to let this thing escape to hunt him down again. If he was free, he was going to make certain he stayed that way.

But before he could loosen his magic again, the demon's body began to glow, the pressure of its magic pushing against Kyran. He squinted as it glowed brighter and brighter, until he had to close his eyes and look away.

The beast's light seared through his eyelids in a blinding flash. Dazed, he blinked as the light and magic faded, but he could see nothing around bright specks of color filling his darkened vision. *By the stars above, what was that?*

He heard the demon indulge in one of its ugly, hissing laughs, and he sent his magic blindly lashing out in its direction. Something else collided with him, knocking him to the ground. Pain seared through his mangled leg, and he screamed, clutching at his thigh, only to have his wrists caught in the demon's crushing grip and pinned over his head. He blinked frantically, trying to clear his vision, his magic boiling out of his blood as he thrashed against the ground, his shoulders wrenching painfully.

"Such a fragile creature."

He could see its outline above him now, its skin gone dark.

"Your blood is stronger, but your body has weakened," it continued.

He tried to focus, to shape his thoughts as he had before, but a third hand came down on his thigh, and a second, identical demon appeared above him. Kyran blood turned to ice water.

Stars above, why were there two of them?

They sneered down at him, drool dripping from their long teeth. The second demon reared back and struck.

A scream tore its way out of Kyran's throat. His body went rigid with pain as a hundred red-hot needles plunged through his shoulder with an ugly hiss of steam. He arched against the ground, thrashing, kicking, trying to rip free. But the demon's teeth only bit down harder, its grip on his wrists tightening.

No. He couldn't die like this. Not now. Not after he finally got out, finally realized he was awake.

Chapter Fifty-Two

Barrett wanted to scream in frustration. Every second they took getting to Kyran was another second he was alone with that demon. But the corridors just kept going, and he was starting to wonder if the captain actually knew where he was leading them when they stopped outside a door. There were voices beyond, laughing and talking. The dungeon had to be just beyond. The sense of magic was almost overpowering. But the captain was blocking the way.

"Why have we stopped?" Barrett demanded.

"Let me handle the guards," Captain Griswold began. "We cannot risk—"

"Move your arse!" Murray interrupted, and before the captain could respond, Duncan snatched him by the back of his coat and sent him sprawling out of their way. Murray grabbed the door and flung it open, bellowing in Isleish, taking two running steps, and leaping from the top of the stairway leading down into the room. Duncan, face split in a broad, fearsome grin, charged after his brother with a roar of his own, dropping down amongst the unsuspecting guards.

Barrett started after them, but Captain Griswold snatched the back of his coat. "Don't."

"We don't have time for your politics!" Barrett snarled, yanking his coat free. "Kyran needs us now!"

"Barrett, wait!"

He didn't look back, launching himself over the edge of the stairs after the brothers. He landed hard; the drop as farther than he'd anticipated. His knees popped loudly and pain shot up his thighs, but he didn't slow, barreling towards the nearest man.

"Hunter—here!"

Barrett whipped around as Duncan flung a ring of keys his way. He swiped at them, missing, and scrambled after them as they clattered across the floor.

"Stop this!" Captain Griswold's voice boomed through the room, echoing off the stones unnaturally and startling several of the Islemen from their fighting. Barrett snatched up the keys, looking for a second door, and found one in the wall beneath the stairs. *The dungeon.*

"There is a demon in your dungeon," Captain Griswold. "Please leave so we may deal with it."

Barrett flipped through the keys. He jammed one into the lock, but it didn't turn. "Na likely," one guards hissed, drawing a knife from his hip. "Ye'll na be helping tha' mage esca—"

There was a rush of wind, and the man's eyes went wide as his voice cut off. He clutched his throat, his shoulders heaving, but only ugly little choking noises came out. Barrett's stomach turned at the sight. The others looked on in obvious terror, though some hid it behind a mask of defiant anger.

Barrett didn't care for these men and their unbridled hatred for Kyran, but he didn't like the captain's underhanded magic either. That crossed a line.

"Let him go, witch," snarled one of the men.

"I am not a witch," the captain replied calmly. The breeze playing about the room died, and the man who was choking gasped a ragged, wheezing breath. "Now leave."

They didn't hesitate, hastening for the stairs, the one man still clutching his throat as he coughed. They edged warily past the captain, who watched them file out, then shut the door behind them.

If Barrett didn't need the captain to help bring this demon down, he would have clocked him. "You didn't have to do that," he growled, shoving another key into the door.

"They will go to the laird," Captain Griswold said, ignoring Barrett's remark. "There will be more men here when we come back."

The violent press of magic reminded Barrett there wasn't time to argue. They could do this later, after Kyran was safe.

"Duncan. Murray," Barrett called to the brothers, who stood frozen, their expressions a conflicted mixture of awe and fear. He called again, and they seemed to come to. "Watch the door, and do *not* come down here after us."

"Stars above," Murray swore, glancing aside at Duncan. "Ye're demon hunters, ye say?"

"Yes," Barrett replied.

"Ye are na planning anything funny with our wee brother, now are ye?"

"And just what do you mean by that?" Barrett asked, jamming another key into the lock, to no avail.

"Enough," Captain Griswold interrupted. "The two of you will watch the door. Slow anyone that tries to come down here."

"But Kyran—" Murray started to protest.

"Will not be helped if you are taken by this demon," the captain finished. "We will bring him back, but only if we can get to him in time."

The brothers looked at him incredulously. Any other time, Barrett might have understood their reluctance, but now, it was only delaying them further.

Duncan finally nodded. "You had better bring him back."

Barrett was taken aback for a moment at the man's manner. It was uncanny speaking with the two of them, like seeing different facets of Kyran. "I will," he assured them.

"Give me the keys," Captain Griswold said, holding his hand out. "I know the one we need."

He glared at the captain, then slapped the keys in his palm with a frustrated huff. But there wasn't time to be stubborn. The captain selected a key from the ring without hesitation and stuck it in the lock. Barrett waited for the lock's protesting *click* of a wrong choice, but, to his surprise, it turned over with a shrill squeak on the first try.

"You *were* down here," Barrett murmured.

"That is what I said," the captain replied, pulling the door open. Thick, murky blackness pooled beyond, tugging at Barrett's awareness. The Inbetween.

He tried to summon his flame to light the way, but just like before, his magic refused to come. "Graces cursed beast," he hissed, pulling harder, but still, he reached nothing.

"What's wrong?" Captain Griswold asked as he pulled the door to behind them, sealing them in the darkness and cutting off the hushed Isleish passing between the two brothers.

Barrett ground his teeth, fighting the panic building quickly in his chest. He couldn't do this now. Kyran needed help, and needed it *now*. "My demon. It won't....I can't use its magic."

"Has it done this before?"

"No. Not like this. I don't know why."

He is near, his demon growled, its presence swelling within him. It was almost familiar now—disquietingly so. But it had done him no lasting harm so far. In fact, it had only been helpful, and if he didn't need it so badly just then, he might have been inclined to suspect it of currying favor for something down the road. But he needed its magic. Now.

"Who is?" Barrett demanded.

"Barrett? Is it—"

The Old One, and he is angry.

The bottom dropped out of Barrett's stomach. "It can't be. The demon from the guild?" But this didn't feel like that one. It didn't have that overwhelming crush to its power.

Yes. He is coming.

"Then we have to hurry. Kyran—"

No.

Barrett's lips curled from his teeth. "Coward!"

His demon's ire flared through him. *Wisdom is not cowardice.*

There wasn't time for this. "Captain, have you been in the Inbetween before?"

"Of course," the man replied, his own power swelling beside Barrett, stirring the air.

"Take me with you."

The demon uncoiled within him like a snake disturbed from its nest. *I will not let you.*

"But your demon—" Captain Griswold protested.

Barrett yanked his dagger from his hip. "I still have this, don't I?"

The captain laid a hand on his shoulder. "Well, enough."

Do not cross me, human.

They slid into the Inbetween's waiting throat until the walls and stairs fell away, deeper and deeper, until a piercing scream ripped through the dark with the sense of magic, powerful and wild.

Barrett's heart plummeted into his stomach. "Kyran!" he shouted, but when he tried to move, his body would not react.

"What...?"

Human, his demon growled. Its presence filled him, crowding his brain until he almost couldn't think. *I warned you.*

Barrett strained to move any part of him, but even breathing was growing difficult. "Let...go."

Leave this place.

"No."

Hunter, you do not understand the danger.

"Then we do this fast." He pushed harder, fists curling. "Get Kyran before the Old One gets here."

That is not—

"You think you can't handle that toothy bastard this time?" His arm flexed, bending ever so slowly. "Is that what's wrong?"

You mock me, his demon growled.

He dragged one foot in front of the other. He was not going to let his own demon stop him. Not here. Not now. "You would do the same."

Hunter....

"You're afraid," Barrett accused, dragging his other foot forward, his chest beginning to move more freely.

The demon writhed within him, but its presence was shrinking. *What are you...? Cease this!*

"If you won't give me your power, then I'll do it without you."

I will take you again!

"You can try!" He broke into a staggering jog. "I'll fight you every step of the way. We're getting Kyran, and you won't stop me."

You are a Graces-cursed fool!

"And you're stuck with me. So either help, or get out of my way!"

His demon fought him, dragging at his limbs, but Barrett kept moving, fighting.

You are going to get us both killed.

"Then fight with me, and we'll take down this bastard in no time."

The demon growled, its voice shivering through Barrett's middle, but its weight disappeared. He stumbled, nearly falling as his limbs came free, his lungs expanding in a sudden gasp.

He had won. "Finally," he snarled, summoning fire and illuminating the captain's face.

"Are you...?"

"Myself," Barrett assured him, breaking into a run. He didn't care what awaited him. Nothing was going to stop him from getting to Kyran in time.

Chapter Fifty-Three

THE DEMON CLUTCHING Kyran's wrists snarled, lifting its head to the impenetrable dark. "Hunters...."

Kyran's pulse thrilled through the pain. *Barrett and the guild captain!* They had come for him.

Setting his teeth, he wrenched with every ounce of strength he could summon and tore one of his hands from the beast's grip. He grabbed the demon, still embedded in his shoulder, its teeth grinding against bone and muscle, and shoved his magic into it.

It let out an inhuman shriek into his flesh. Images flickered through Kyran's head of *weans*, small and scared.

"*You monster!*" Kyran snarled in Isleish before his hand was yanked back into place.

"It appears there will be no time to savor you," the demon above him sneered, gripping his wrists with crushing strength. Its body began to glow white-hot again, forcing Kyran to squeeze his eyes shut.

There was a surge of magic from someplace in the dark a split second before the roar and searing heat of fire rolled over Kyran. The grip at his wrists vanished, the blinding light with it, and he didn't hesitate.

He shoved the demon still lying atop him, but it was still fastened to his shoulder by its teeth. Its body was dark when he peeled his eyes open, the flesh hard and pocked by black crystals of blood where it had split and torn, covered in steadily thickening scrawls of silver ice.

But it lived. It let out a whimpering growl and sank its teeth in deeper as Kyran shoved at it again, the pain flaring bright and new even beyond his magic.

"Captain! Don't let the other one get away!"

Kyran's gaze snapped to the familiar voice. Barrett, eyes wide in terror and golden hair loose about his face, appeared from the Inbetween. Kyran's heart soared at the sight.

"Get off of him!" the hunter bellowed, plunging his dagger into the demon's back. It flinched and groaned, its teeth vibrating in Kyran's shoulder before it began to turn to ash. Kyran sighed in relief, slumping against the ground as his magic dulled the pain in his shoulder to nothing.

"Kyran?"

The mage pushed himself upright with his good arm. "I'm fine. I—"

Another blinding light cut through the murk of the Inbetween, slicing through Kyran's vision like a hot knife before he could close his eyes. He threw his arm over his face, his balance teetering dangerously. He knew that light.

"There's more of 'em," he warned. "It can make more of itself, somehow."

Barrett growled a dark curse. "It did this before. Are you—"

"I'm fine," Kyran assured him, pushing to his knee again. "My walking stick. We canna let the bastard get away again."

Barrett's expression fluttered between confusion and surprise. "But you—"

"I can kill it," Kyran insisted, lifting his chin as a sneer of a smile drew his lips back from his teeth, "if you can keep it from laying a hand on me."

Barrett blinked, taken aback, before a smile split his face. "I can do that."

"Barrett!" Captain Griswold's voice came from the distance. "You need to get over here!"

"Curse it," Barrett swore, searching the dark. "There!" He disappeared, and Kyran worried for a split second that he'd only invented a vision before Barrett reappeared again, a glittering length of wood in his hand. "Here."

"Thank you." Kyran took the stick, hissing as he settled the crook beneath his injured shoulder. But he was grateful to have it nonetheless. He would take the pain to be able to walk.

"Barrett!" the captain called again with a note of urgency.

"Go!" Kyran urged him. "I'll be right behind you."

The hunter hesitated a moment longer, then took off running in the direction Captain Griswold's voice had come. Kyran didn't know how they could hear the man. It was impossible to hear anything in the Inbetween. Already, Barrett's footfalls had faded to silence. But that was a matter for later. He didn't have to hear or see to find them now.

Following the press of magic in the dark, he leaned into his walking stick, wincing at the throb of his left shoulder even through his magic as he hurried. He could not let the demon escape, no matter what. He would *not* be made its pet again.

A strange wind began to stir fitfully around him, tugging at his hair and clothes, when out of the dark, the guild captain suddenly appeared. Griswold was expertly deflecting fire from one of the demons, sending crimson gouts left and right. Kyran reached out with his power past the deep, potent well of the guild captain's power and touched the demon. This beast felt different than the one Kyran had been facing before, no longer the overwhelming crush of power that had demanded he submit. It was weak.

Gathering his will around his power, he thrust it at the beast as he had the first.

It broke before him. Images swam through his thoughts again, some familiar, some different, all distinctly horrid. But as he watched, the images blurred in his mind's eye, going double before another blinding light cut through his vision.

He clapped a hand to his eyes, rubbing at them as the light dissipated. Stars above, but that was an aggravating trick.

"Captain!" Barrett called, and a powerful gust of wind nearly knocked him from his feet as the captain lashed out at something. The second demon must have come around him after the split.

Kyran rubbed at his eyes, trying to feel through the darkness around him for the beasts, when there was another glare of light he could see through his palms and a surge of magic from his right, where he had heard Barrett.

"Stay close," he heard the captain's voice at his side above the shriek of wind. "I can protect you."

"I can fight them!" Kyran called back, forcing a tight breath out. He didn't need to see. He left his eyes shut and stretched his awareness into the void of the Inbetween. Magic whirled around him, pushing and pulling at his attention, but as he focused, he found he could pick its sources apart. They had...almost a flavor to each of them, a depth of power he could read as they drew upon their stores. He sifted through the shifting directions, narrowing his attention until he drew his arm back, and thrust it into the dark with a surge of frigid magic.

There came a shrill squeal of pain, and the wind around him raged, threatening to knock him over before the demon's voice went silent, its well of power disappearing beneath the captain's strength. That was another one down.

Kyran reached out, feeling for the next demon when. There was a sudden, overwhelming burst of magic where he had felt Barrett fighting. Then nothing. No demons, no Barrett. Nothing but a terrible vacuum.

Chapter Fifty-Four

BARRETT SEEMED TO fall through the air forever, as if he were sinking into a pool of water, before he landed—hard—skidding across the ground. He let loose a burst of fire from his body, and the demon that had collided with him let out an earsplitting shriek, its grip vanishing. But before he could even sit up, there was another flash of light from behind him. Fingers clutched at his arms and hair, digging into his skin and making his scalp burn.

"Get off!" he shouted, forcing out another burst of fire that swallowed the demons clinging to him. Their touch turned brittle, their bodies falling to ash, but he could hear others chuckling in chorus elsewhere in the dark.

He clenched his fist, but his stomach dropped as his fingers closed on nothing; he'd dropped his dagger. Panic swelled in his gut as he peered around him, but he didn't see it before another clap of light forced him to shut his eyes. Graces, but they were multiplying faster than he could keep up with. He needed to get to his captain's side before he was overwhelmed.

"Captain," he shouted, rubbing at his eyes. No one answered. "Kyr—"

Another beast drove into the middle of his back, knocking him to the ground. Others fell upon him, grabbing his arms and hair again, and hauled him to his knees, where another of their ilk leered down at him, its thicket of teeth only inches away.

"I learned something about your kind, hunter," the demon sneered, its empty sockets boring into Barrett's eyes. An ache filled his head. "You lash out when you're afraid to die. Waste your resources."

He reached for his magic, but felt it slip through his control with a lurching sensation like missing a stair. "Not now," he snarled at his demon. Of all the times to fight him over its power....

The toothy demon reached for his chest, tracing the tips of its claws along his shirt. The fabric began to smoke, the edges burning away at its touch.

"You can't burn me," Barrett growled, wincing as one of the demons behind him yanked on his hair.

"Not well, no," the one before him simpered. Its power practically radiated against him. It had gotten so much stronger. The hand on his chest dragged down, making him shudder in disgust. He felt the first fingers of control over his magic return, and he pulled as hard as he could when the demon's long digits wrapped around the amulet he always wore.

"Here it is," it murmured.

Panic shot through Barrett's middle. If the demon took that....He floundered for his magic, but when the demon looked him in the face again, his control slipped away from him.

"Oh Graces…"

The demon. Was it doing something? Something to interfere with his connection to his own demon? Or were they both toying with him?

"I could never get close enough. But this"—it lifted the amulet, turning it so he could see the stone—"is where the rest of me is. Where *they* are." It yanked at the chain, and Barrett let out a cry as it bit into the back of his neck and then broke with a metallic ping.

"Give that back!" Barrett shouted.

"Your demon feeds from this, does it not?" the demon purred, stroking the pendant lovingly as it began to pace around him. "What happens when you are separated? Does your demon feed on you?"

"Give it back!" With a furious wrench of his will, Barrett found his magic again. Fire erupted from his skin, wringing another chorus of screams from the beasts holding him, but they didn't crumble, their grips never lessening.

A smothering chill rolled over him. His fingers went numb, and he was reminded of when his demon had last taken control. *No*, he begged silently. *Please, not yet.*

"At last," the demon purred, its nails clicking against his stolen amulet. "I knew my pet would figure out how to come to me if I gave it the proper motivation."

Barrett gasped as he realized what the demon meant, surprised by the fog of breath that came out. He was not going numb; the air was growing cold. Kyran was coming through the Inbetween.

Chapter Fifty-Five

Kyran searched the Inbetween for any sense of Barrett, but the hunter had disappeared. "Captain? Barrett—"

"I felt it," Captain Griswold replied, at his side again with another burst of wind. "He's moved deeper."

Deeper into the Inbetween, closer to the demon realm. Kyran tried to assure himself that Barrett might have simply been pursuing the demons to keep them from escaping, but he could not deny the horrible twisting feeling in his gut that Barrett was in trouble. Before he could ask the captain how he might follow it, though, there was another flash of light in the dark, though dimmer this time, as the remaining demon split again. Beside him, the captain let out a tight sigh.

"I will handle these," he said above the rush of his wind as it grew in intensity once more. "You go to Barrett. Use your magic to pull yourself deeper. If you cannot, I will take us when I have finished these." He did not wait for Kyran to respond, but took off into the dark, moving so fast that he almost looked to be flying over the ground before disappearing.

Kyran stared after him in awe, then shook his head and turned to the place he had felt Barrett. *Pull himself deeper....*

Reaching out with his magic, he searched for a way. He could feel the captain and the two demons at his back, their magics clashing, but nothing before him. Only the endlessness of the Inbetween. Only, it was *not* endless. Somewhere, this void ended, at the edge of the demon realm. But how did he go deeper?

Kyran tried using his magic and heard the blood seeping from his shoulder crack and pop, the wound stinging, but he moved no deeper. He growled in frustration, pressingly aware of every second that trickled by as he fumbled blindly for the solution.

He forced his mind to calm, to find that place he had made in his thoughts when first learning to control his magic. The Inbetween, the press of magic, *everything* faded from his attention except his own power. He had first begun to bring his magic to heel by imagining fences keeping it in check, and he had figured out how to sense and hurt these demons by using the same abstract process by which he touched his power to his amulets. It was all in how he used his thoughts and will to direct his magic. If he wanted to *pull* himself deeper, as Captain Griswold had phrased it, then he needed to shape his magic to do so.

Kyran imagined his magic stretching into the dark, angled downwards like a length of rope, its end tying him to Barrett. Then, straining to hold his power to that image, he slid his walking stick forward and made a tentative hop. The darkness seemed to slide past him in a tangible current, and he dared to hope he might have discovered the necessary secret. He took another slow, shuffling step, then another. The sense of the captain and the two demons faded behind him until they disappeared, and he found himself adrift in the Inbetween.

He hurried, lengthening his awkward hops so that he might move faster, but the farther into the Inbetween he went, the harder it became to keep his magic trained to the task. It fought him every inch of the way, desperate to be free of his control. His head began to throb in earnest at the effort of fighting to keep it trained to task.

Still the darkness stretched on. He could sense neither Captain Griswold nor Barrett, only that he was moving ever deeper. The current of the Inbetween grew stronger with every step, and so did the pounding in his skull, until it began to grow unbearable. How much farther must he go? He had no way to gauge how far he had come, or how much farther Barrett must be. He could only keep moving, forcing his thoughts to remain locked around the image of the rope, even as the throbbing in his skull began to make his vision blur, the light of his own magic glowing beneath his skin like a hammer blow through his eyes.

He let out a sickly moan, pressing the heel of his hand to his temple, as the first touch of the demon's magic brushed against his awareness. His grip of control wavered at the sudden sensation, nearly breaking his concentration, and he had to force himself to focus, clinging to the image like an outstretched hand in a storm. If he lost that, if he fumbled and could not hold his power to this task, he would never find Barrett.

Dragging his walking stick forward, he kept moving, the pull of the demon's magic growing stronger with every step until he was no longer alone.

Before him, mere feet away, was the demon, its body aglow with molten lines, and three identical beasts lurked behind it. Between them was Barrett, forced to his knees, their vile claws clutching his throat, his arms—every place they could reach. The hunter's fingers flexed, his body straining against their tight hold. His gaze bored into Kyran's as he mouthed a single word: *run*.

Kyran's jaw clenched. Not a chance. He had done enough running. This was ending here.

He dropped the rope in his mind, gasping in sheer relief as the pain in his head lessened, then snapped his hand up. His blood's magic surged down his arm and towards the beast.

Black flames licked over the demon's flesh as it dropped to all fours and darted behind the others, placing Barrett squarely between them. Kyran wrenched his magic back, snarling an oath as the beast laughed.

"I have been inside that fragile mind of yours," the demon sneered from between the its brethren. "I know what it would do to you to see this hunter's blood on your hands."

"You canna manage tha' if you are dead first," Kyran growled.

Barrett made a strangled noise, fire flaring along his limbs as he thrashed against the demons' grip. But before he could get free, before Kyran could react to help him, the demons shoved the hunter forward, pinning him flat and grinding his face into the hard ground.

"I could snap his neck," the demon threatened, and Barrett's heavy pants cut off with a gurgle. "Slit his throat."

Kyran's nails dug into his walking stick, and he had to bite his tongue to keep from snarling at the demons. But his hands were tied. If he tried to take them all on now, while they were ready and waiting, it was likely Barrett would get hurt. But if he had help....

"Now," the demon continued, its black tongue lolling between its teeth as it hissed in laughter, "you remember how to beg for someone's life, don't you, pet?"

Kyran raised his chin, a cold fury igniting under his skin. Stars above, when he got his hands on that beast, he swore he would not let go until it was dead this time. But for now, he still had to draw this out.

Leaning heavily into his stick, he let his good leg fold beneath him, and knelt.

There was a choking noise behind the demon, and Barrett jerked on the ground, his mouth opening and closing, struggling to breathe, to speak, to even move—but the demons held him fast.

"Yes," the demon purred in delight, "and you know it will take more than kneeling for me to spare him. Will you beg for him?"

Kyran barely restrained himself from lashing out at the beast, terrified it might change its mind and strangle Barrett to death before he had bought enough time. *Graces be damned, but this had better work.*

Chapter Fifty-Six

Barrett watched in horror from the corner of his eye as Kyran bowed his head and said, "Let him go. Please."

Kyran—proud, stubborn Kyran—was begging. For him. This was all wrong. How had it all gone so wrong? How did everything always get so far out of his control?

I can save him.

Barrett jerked in the demons' grip, his mouth gaping in a silent, breathless gasp of surprise at the sound of his demon's voice. *You? But I thought—*

Would you prefer I not?

He almost agreed right then. What it offered was a naked temptation. He had seen how much power his demon had—more than he himself could ever even dream of. But it would mean surrendering his body again, possibly even his mind. There was no telling what the demon might do then. And Kyran.... Kyran would see him. See his body twisted into an abomination.

"You will always submit to me, pet," the toothy demon crooned, sauntering towards the mage. "I know you better than anyone else."

Barrett squeezed his eyes shut, his fists clenching impotently. He wished that he would wake up in the Drunken Wind, that all of this would simply dissolve into an awful nightmare that he could drink away. He wished he could undo everything that had happened, not just to Kyran, but to Effie, and Raleigh. But there was no such magic. Still, he could keep anything worse from happening.

He opened his eyes, fixing them on the beast as it reached to run its claws along Kyran's cheek, dragging a shudder from the mage. "Ah, my proud little mageling. I wish you could know how very much I am going to enjoy this after all the trouble you have caused."

Do it, Barrett snarled at his demon.

The effect of his consent was instant. Magic boiled up from deep within him and burst from his skin, unguided and raw. The demons holding him squealed in pain, but did not release him, crushing him into the ground.

Kyran shouted.

The fire demon roared in agony, "You will both die today!"

"NO!" Barrett bellowed.

Get up! You have my strength, now get up!

Screaming with the exertion, Barrett wrenched his arms under him, then his legs, fighting to stand against the weight of the demons. He would not be stopped. They were nothing now. He fixed his rage on the beast standing over Kyran. "You will not hurt him!"

"Kill—"

Whatever the demon had been about to say was drowned out as a gale howled through the Inbetween, raking over Barrett. He dug his feet into the ground, holding steady, intent on getting to Kyran. Whatever this new beast was could be hanged. The demons holding him began to lose their grip, their claws biting into his arms and neck, desperately clinging to him as the wind threatened to peel them off.

Kyran swung his walking stick, knocking something from the beast's hand into the dark.

The amulet! his demon hissed at Barrett's ear, but the hunter didn't turn away to follow. He was almost to them. He almost had the demon.

The beast snatched the walking stick from Kyran's hands and heaved the mage into the air.

Then they vanished.

"No!" Barrett roared at the empty space where the demon had been only moments before. "Curse you! Where did you go?"

The gale grew in intensity, and Barrett yanked one arm away from a demon, pulling it free. The demon reached for him again, but he twisted and slammed his palm into its chest. The hunter pushed his magic forward, but rather than the power conjuring into raw fire, he watched in horrid fascination as his power flowed right into the demon, cooking it from the inside out. Its chest glowed where he touched it, and it screamed, clawing at him, trying desperately to get away.

The other two demons dropped from his body, and Barrett snarled, feeling his control shift as his demon guided its power. There was so much of it. With a breathless whimper, the demon went limp, a glow like a white-hot coal spreading through its flesh. It began to flake away in the roaring wind. Graces, but this power!

A flash of movement caught his eye. He turned, swiping blindly at it, and nearly caught Captain Griswold as he rushed past after the last beast.

He tried to shout after him, but Barrett's demon pulled on his will, and he followed its directions, his eyes sweeping through the darkness until they fixed on a seemingly random place. Without his permission, his legs began to carry him towards it.

There on the ground, chain gone, was his amulet. He bent and scooped it up, staring at the ornate filigree and its mercurial stone with an enormous sense of relief. Then he turned again and walked until he found his dagger as well.

"Kyran," Barrett reminded his demon. "We have to find—"

Deeper, his demon rumbled, already summoning power to draw them farther into the Inbetween. *It always likes to take its prey deeper.*

Chapter Fifty-Seven

Kyran could barely draw breath around the blackness pressed so thickly against him.

The demon stopped, at seemingly the very precipice of its realm. He'd recognized the smothering, suffocating feeling of the Inbetween growing thick against his skin as the beast dragged him deeper, away from Barrett and Griswold.

"It appears there will be no time to savor you," it snarled down at him.

Its power came down on him again as he struggled to reorient himself, a sudden hammer blow that sent stars sparking through his vision. His breath caught in a silent scream of pain.

"You cannot fight me," it growled. "Do not make me break you again."

"No," Kyran forced past his lips. "You willna." The sound of ice breaking grinding through his numb flesh, Kyran drove his left arm up and grabbed the demon behind its head. He yanked as hard as he could and, snarling in defiance, sank his teeth into the beast's neck.

It squealed, viciously tearing him from its throat. Its flesh ripped free in Kyran's teeth as it threw him to the ground. He swallowed the mouthful of awful, bitter meat and rolled onto his knee, gathering his will and focus for one last assault.

Its snarl shifted into a raspy laugh. "You are more like us than you realize, half-breed."

"No," the mage panted, his vision swimming dangerously, but he felt his magic bend beneath his control, shaping as he commanded it. "I am na."

With a shout, he thrust every mote of power he could hone into the beast.

The demon shattered before his magic, its mind cracking open to him. Images and memories flooded through him.

But he did not simply observe this time. He pushed deeper into the beast, driving his magic before him, carving into it from the inside as it had him. It screamed, not only from its throat, but from every fibre of its being. He could hear its shriek in his ears and in his head His own voice joined it, full of his own pain and rage—not only for those months of imprisonment and torture, but for the years wasted believing he had to hide, that he was not human. That he was a monster. His magic tore into the beast that had made him less than human, ripping it apart.

Then, without an ounce of warning, his connection to the beast severed.

He blinked heavily, disoriented. The Inbetween swam back into view, and the demon's screams trailed into harsh whimpers.

He had reached the end of his stores.

"No," he slurred, lifting his hands. The already dim light of his lines faded to nothing, his strength draining with it. "No, no, no."

"You...." the demon croaked, shuddering weakly as it crawled towards him on all fours, its dark sockets burning with hatred, "will pay for that, half-breed."

Kyran fought to stay awake, to force his blood to answer him, but his thoughts were drifting apart. He touched his hip, a swear slurring past his lips as he remembered he still had no amulets.

"Oh, no," the demon laughed as Kyran's body slumped sideways. "You will not escape that way. You will suffer for this."

It was all he could do to keep his eyes from shuttering closed as the demon rolled his limp body over. It leered down at him, running its fingers along its throat before indelicately shoving its claws past his lips. The bitter taste of the beast's blood filled his mouth again, and he gagged as the barest measure of strength returned to him.

"There," the demon sneered, removing its fingers before Kyran could collect himself enough to bite down on them. "Now it is my turn."

It reared back, its maw opening wide, and Kyran stared in horror at his fate, remembering keenly the sensation of its teeth tearing his thigh open.

"No!" Kyran threw his hands up as the beast lunged at his shoulder, catching it about the throat.

He dug his nails into the open wound on its neck with feral snarl. It hissed in pain and slapped him across the face, but he did not let go, burying his nails in its flesh. Its hot blood ran freely down his arm. He would not give up. He would fight until he died if he had to, and buy whatever time he could so the hunters could catch this beast once and for all. No more *weans* like Effie. No more mages like Raleigh. No more.

But the demon was no weakling, and it had no plans to surrender. Wrapping a hand about his wrist, it peeled his fingers from its throat with a terrible strength. Its other hand found his injured shoulder and sank its claws into his flesh.

Kyran screamed, his magic flaring to protect him. But he fought back, clenching his will around it. If he burned up the last of his borrowed power, he would be helpless once again.

"Give up," the demon taunted him, it claws digging ever deeper, following the marks of its own teeth.

Kyran's lips peeled back. He would never, not to it or anyone else.

Another surge of magic rolled through the Inbetween, and Barrett tore through the darkness with a furious bellow, dagger raised above his head. The demon flinched and tried to get out of the way. But Kyran threw his arms around its neck, clinging with every inch of strength he had left as Barrett buried his blade in the beast's back.

It arched against him. Its furious screech faded to a whimper, and it collapsed atop Kyran in a heap, limp and still. He held his breath, not letting go as he waited, panting, for it to try something—anything.

But its body began to dissolve into ash.

"Thank the stars," Kyran wheezed, letting his arms drop.

Barrett lifted his head, settling back on his knees. "Kyran? Are you...?"

"Drew too much power," the mage croaked weakly, watching the ashes dissolve. "It's dead."

"It's dead," Barrett repeated. He sounded as surprised and exhausted as Kyran. All that struggle, all that horror, and it was gone. Dead. Kyran was nearly giddy at the thought.

"You killed it."

"*We* killed them," Barrett corrected him. "I couldn't have—"

A breeze whistled past, and the captain emerged from the dark, his coat flapping like a sail in a stormy gust. His clothes were torn and singed, and he had a nasty cut below his eye, but he looked otherwise unscathed. He had Kyran's walking stick in one hand and his dagger in the other. He raised both defensively as he turned to face Barrett.

"Who am I speaking to?" the captain asked, his tone unusually cautious.

Barrett looked from the man to the dagger and back. "Barrett," he replied sharply, but the captain did not lower his guard. "There isn't time for this."

"Captain?" Kyran croaked, struggling to push himself up. "What is this—"

Power such as he had never felt slammed into Kyran, knocking him back to the ground. His senses reeled as the darkness was torn apart by a blinding, blue-white star.

The air shrieked as a cold deeper than that even Cairngorm's most brutal winters instantly sank into Kyran's bones. A long, eerie wail filled the void as he stared up into the light, awed and powerless to even move beneath the thing's mere presence. It let out another, softer wail, and the light faded until he found a face gazing back at him. One he recognized from long ago.

Chapter Fifty-Eight

Barrett caught himself on all fours as the demon's power battered against him, wheezing in the too-cold air. Griswold made a pained, choking noise beside him, and Barrett forced some measure of heat into the air around them with his magic. But the relief it provided was minimal, dwarfed by the power crushing down against them—one Barrett had felt before.

The Old One.

The light dimmed against his eyelids, and he pried his eyes open to look upon the strange beast, though he had to squint against the vicious cold. It looked as it had in the guildhall—an enormous beast carved of ice, its limbs long and fragile-looking, with a face that blended the elegance of an elk with an uncanny resemblance of human features. It stood over Kyran, its long neck bent to examine him with one crystalline socket.

The mage gazed back at it with an expression of utter rapture. "You were real," he whispered, and the demon let out a soft, almost plaintive noise. Kyran collapsed to the ground, unmoving.

"Kyran!" Barrett tried to scream.

As if in response, the demon's mouth opened, emitting an eerie, harsh wail. It spread its forelimbs and fixed him and the captain with its wide stare.

Barrett had felt demons try to pry into his mind before. Usually, his own demon countered it before he even noticed. But the moment the Old One met his eyes, he was locked in its gaze. Graces, but he could not even comprehend the amount of power that thing held. Not even the fire demon came close—or even his own. He was an insect pinned beneath it. It could kill them all without the faintest effort.

It cried out again, and Barrett's skull seemed to split open. Things filled his mind—thoughts, whispers, emotions. He saw his own memories, fragments of his life—terrible and wonderful moments aligned next to one another in chaotic collages. Kat when she'd learned that their father had died. Sweet Raleigh, naked and gasping in a shadowed corner of the guildhall. The dizzying sensation of alcohol, then the heat of a woman bearing down on him. Blood, and a last, dying gasp. Guilt. Relief. Then fire. So much fire. Kyran, fierce, calm, and beautiful. A slurry of nostalgia and desire. Then fear. Loneliness. Kyran, lost.

The thoughts became more fragmented, rotating. He remembered his father, fleeting and stern. His mother, baking, then, one morning, gone. He remembered finding Kyran, veiled by the demon in their realm. He remembered the rain falling on the burnt ruins of a house—his house. The rain when escaping the demon realm. It went back to his father, sickly and bedridden. Barrett tried to look away, to close his eyes, his mind. But it simply kept coming—his entire life, his entire person, broken down into a tumult of experiences.

Then it stopped. Barrett let out a hoarse sob. His heart throbbed in his chest with the raw agony of feeling everything all at once. But there was more—something foreign left behind, threaded through his mind—a sensation of caution and fear not his own. A warning. But against what?

Barrett picked his head up, but he could not look at the demon. He found Kyran instead, still lying beneath the beast. His aching heart squeezed beneath his ribs, but the demon was not hurting him, its gaze fixed outward upon the hunters. It was protecting him. Just as Barrett had been trying to do since he had met the mage. Graces, how he had failed.

The demon watched him for a long moment more, its cold no longer touching him. He felt frozen and empty, a husk that even the sun could never warm again. Then, snorting a misty breath from its nostrils, the ancient demon withdrew, its light fading—and with it, the crushing power of its presence—until it was gone.

Barrett didn't hesitate a moment longer. With the cold fading and all sense of the demon gone, he staggered to his feet and forced his tired body to run to the limp body before him.

"Kyran?" he called, fearful the mage might have gone over the edge again, that he would simply lie there, staring at nothing. Dropping to his knees at the mage's side, Barrett could only his breath until he noticed the mage's runelines shining faintly beneath his skin.

"Please say somethin'," Barrett begged.

Kyran's eyes flicker faintly, and the hunter almost could not breathe.

"Barrett?" The mage's eyes drifted up to his, heavy with exhaustion, but clearly focused as they met. "You're alright."

"Yes." He nodded, relief filling his chest at the clarity in Kyran's voice. "Yes, I'm fine."

"The demon...." Kyran started, trying to get up. "We have to—"

"It's gone. We should get out of here, though, before somethin' else comes along."

Kyran's gaze flickered away, the faint light in his cheeks brightening ever so slightly. "I...canna stand," he murmured.

Barrett extended his hand without hesitation. "Here, let me help you up."

"I will help as well."

Barrett looked over his shoulder as Captain Griswold knelt down next to him. He looked nearly as ragged as Barrett felt, but he cast a wary eye at Barrett. He knew what Barrett had done to save Kyran. Barrett could only hope the captain wouldn't say anything more about it.

"We will all need to be close so I may pull us out again," the captain continued, and Barrett groaned at the reminder that they still were far from safe.

Still, he nodded to the captain, the movement alone making his head ache. Graces, he felt awful. But at least he had Kyran back, and the demon that had taken him would never be able to hurt him again. As far as he was concerned, everything else could hang.

Chapter Fifty-Nine

It was warm. The smell of woodsmoke and unfamiliar bitter herbs filled his nostrils. Kyran lay still, allowing himself the pleasure of comfort a moment longer before he dared to open his eyes and break the illusion with whatever awaited him.

But when he finally opened them, he discovered he was not in the dungeon or the demon's barren stone prison, but in a bedroom, tucked beneath the covers of an enormous four poster bed. And, of course, Barrett sat at his bedside. The man seemed to have become a permanent fixture of his waking, ever since dragging Kyran from that infernal pit.

The hunter looked rough. His skin was pale and clammy, as if he were ill. His throat was purple and black with bruises, and there was a bandage wrapped around his head. He sat hunched over, elbows propped on his knees, blinking owlishly as Kyran shifted on the bed. Then he smiled.

"Evenin'," he said, his voice hoarse. "Didn't think you'd wake up so soon."

"How...." Kyran's own voice caught, Wincing, he cleared his throat. "How long was I sleeping?"

"Most of the day, after they finally let us bring you up here. They tried to send me back to my room. Told me I could see you in the mornin'."

"I convinced the laird he was not, in fact, a dangerously possessed criminal," Griswold's voice joined in.

The mage picked his head up to see the captain seated near the roaring fireplace across the room.

"I have a feeling Guildmaster Selah will be less than pleased with the guild's work here," Griswold continued.

"She knew what she was getting into when she let me come," Barrett groused, rubbing at his eyes until he gave up with a sigh. "How're you feelin', though?" he asked Kyran.

Kyran wasn't certain how to answer that. He took stock of himself, of his various pains, as he pushed himself up in the bed. His clothes were missing, he realized belatedly, and pulled the quilt more securely into his lap.

His hand and left shoulder were swathed in bandages. It was there the herbal scent was emanating from, likely some poultice to prevent the wound from going off. He could tell by the way he ached that he would be covered in bruises. But he was alive, and the beast that had imprisoned him, tortured him beyond his breaking point, was not.

"I am...." He hesitated, not willing to call himself well. Taking advantage of the silence, his stomach let out a noisome gurgle.

Barrett chuckled weakly. "Hungry?" he finished. "I can get you somethin'."

"Mrs. McCrory assured me we need only tell the men outside, and something will be brought," Captain Griswold interjected again.

"As you like," Kyran answered tentatively, picking at a loose thread on the quilt top.

Barrett started to get up, groaning quietly, but the captain stood instead.

"I'll get it," he said, going to the door. Barrett let out a grunt of what might have been assent or defeat, but he settled heavily back without arguing the man down.

Kyran gingerly shifted on the bed, pulling the quilt closer, and took in the room. It was fine compared to the inn rooms in Tennebrum, or any of the places he'd lived growing up in the Isles. A bedroom somewhere in the castle, and likely meant for guests of some importance. He ran his hand over the quilt, examining the indents and lines made by the threads, but try as he might, he couldn't piece together an answer to the question his surroundings brought to mind. "How did I...get here?"

Barrett lifted his head, the dullness in his eyes quickly turning to concern. "How much do you remember?" he asked slowly, as if Kyran's answer might mean trouble.

"Everything," Kyran replied without hesitation. He remembered every detail—the long, desperate fight in the black void washing over him in its entirety again, and even the final, strange confrontation with the beast he had long believed a mere fever dream from his youth. "I remember Captain Griswold taking hold of us and starting back, but I dinnae remember seeing the dungeon again or how I came ta be here."

The tension coiled in Barrett's shoulders unknotted at Kyran's reply, and he slouched back, his eyes slipping closed. "You fainted on the way out and missed the best bit. When we got to the top of those Graces-cursed stairs, there was a whole room of furious Islemen waitin' for us."

"It was a near thing," Captain Griswold interjected, closing the door again and returning to his seat. He looked haggard, his clothing irredeemably rumpled, and shadows beneath his eyes. "I believe the inroads I made with the laird are the only reason we are not all three spoiling in separate cells, and we've your brothers to thank for preventing an even larger disaster."

"My brothers?" Kyran interrupted. "What do my brothers have ta do with this?"

"They showed up here last night," Barrett replied. "Broke me out of my room so we could rescue you from the dungeon." He chuckled, scratching at his unkempt beard. "They said it was your pa's idea to get me out before they went for you."

Kyran felt a well of gratitude for his family. They had come for him, regardless of the circumstances, indifferent to the risks. They had come to try to save him, as had Barrett once again.

Stars above, but now that Kyran realized that the past few weeks had been real, it dawned on him just how much the hunter had sacrificed to bring him to this moment. Barrett had managed to find him in the demon realm and drag him out, get him to the guild and its chirurgeons, and then come with him all the way to the Isles, where he'd chased him back into the Inbetween when the demon had reappeared. Kyran owed the man more than gratitude. He owed him his life.

"As I was saying," the captain continued, breaking the line of Kyran's thoughts. "Your brothers stayed in the dungeon while we were in the Inbetween. When Laird Dunbar sent men to see what was going on, they prevented any of them from following us and potentially becoming lost in the Inbetween.

"Once we returned, I did my best to explain the circumstances to the laird, and made apologies for our manner. There was some persuasion involved, but our injuries seemed to convince him of the truth of the matter. For now, the Hall is to be put off to allow us time to recover and, I believe, in deference of observing the Long Night—may our lanterns keep us and see us through."

"Stars above," Kyran muttered. It was the Long Night—the Lumen observance of the longest night of the year? It had been a full two seasons since he'd stepped off the ship in Tennebrum. But, more than that—"There is still to be a Hall?" It felt so unfair. After fighting so hard to survive in that crushing darkness, to wake and find he was still to stand before the court was a stinging blow.

"The crimes you are accused of still stand, in the laird's eyes," Captain Griswold reminded him.

"You got the information you need for this trial?" Barrett asked, resting his head on his fist as he looked at the captain.

"As of this moment, no."

"I thought you said you'd talked to Kyran."

The captain met Kyran's eye. "We spoke, but we were interrupted. I did promise you I would return, though. My apologies for not making it sooner."

Kyran offered him a weak smile in return, shaking his head. But his stomach twisted painfully as he recalled their brief conversation. "No, I....We dinnae talk *about that*."

"Did—"

All three of them jumped at a series of sharp raps at the door.

"I'll get it," Barrett volunteered, already getting stiffly out of his seat, joints popping.

A man Kyran didn't recognize handed Barrett a large, wooden tray, which the hunter carried carefully back to the bed. To Kyran's surprise, it seemed to be made to be used in bed, with legs to hold it over his lap. He looked over the food, pleased to discover a steaming bowl of pottage and a plate of bannocks. But it was hardly enough for two people, let alone three.

"Are you na eating?"

"We ate earlier," Barrett answered. "Been awake a while."

"Aye, you've that look about you," Kyran said quietly, and the hunter gave a huff of laughter at his own expense.

"I suppose I do," he agreed, rubbing at his eyes again.

Pinching the edge of the quilt, Kyran picked up the spoon from the tray and wiped it clean before scooping up a bit of the pottage. The texture of oats and a variety of green things met his palate, and he let his eyes slip closed in bliss. He had eaten the stuff before—it was a staple in the Isles—but it was as far removed from the savory bitterness of demon flesh as it could be. And, for the first time since waking in the back of that wagon, he was confident it was what it appeared to be.

The room fell into a strange quiet while he slowly ate. Barrett seemed to have drifted off again, his gaze slack, and Captain Griswold simply watched the fire. Despite his efforts to resist it, Kyran found his thoughts drifting back to the Inbetween. They had finally killed the demon, the one responsible not only for every evil it had wrought on him, but Barrett and his lover before.

Stars, Kyran couldn't even begin to comprehend what that meant. The beast that had haunted his every hour, waking or sleeping—that had torn his mind apart, starved him, hurt him in ways he could not have even begun to imagine—was gone.

Or the strongest part of it was, anyway, an uneasy voice in the back of Kyran's mind reminded him. After what he had seen of the beast's abilities and persistence, it was not entirely unreasonable to believe it might have left some sliver of itself behind in the demon realm, hidden safely away in that vast kirk it nested in. It could very well reappear one day, powerful again from feasting, and boiling with wrath.

Kyran suppressed a shudder. He didn't want to dwell on that now. Couldn't he be satisfied with its death? The death he had seen with his own eyes?

But even as he wished it, he knew that sort of reasoning would never comfort him again. Not after what the demon did to him within his own mind. By all the Graces, despite whatever confidence he boasted, there was still a lingering doubt that what he saw was anything more than an illusion, and he knew with the terrible weight of truth that he likely never would rid of it.

Kyran set his spoon down and folded his hands in his lap. But without the distraction of eating, he soon caught his fingers worrying along the bandages on his knuckles as his thoughts turned from the demon to what was to come next.

He had to tell them what had happened. He wasn't going to survive this demon only to let Connal have his head for his pride. But even thinking about what Connal had done—even trying to find a place to start to explain it—made him nearly sick.

"Kyran?"

Barrett's voice made his eyes flicker up.

The hunter was watching him, worry etched into his every feature. "You look ill." When he did not respond, Barrett straightened in his seat. "What is it?" he asked gently. "Are you alright?"

Squeezing his eyes shut, Kyran locked his fingers together. He needed to do this. The captain had reminded him that he wasn't alone in this—that he didn't have to face Connal alone this time.

"Captain," he started, looking up at the man. Stars, he couldn't believe he was saying this. "Can you really do as you promised? Can you protect my kin?"

"So Connal did threaten you?" Captain Griswold asked, turning to face him as Kyran nodded jerkily. "What did he say?"

"He said if I speak at the Hall and tell them what happened, he would make certain ta remind Dunbar that my family sinned first by sparing me. He would see my kin buried with me."

"Your family did nothin' wrong," Barrett interjected sharply. "*You* did nothin' wrong."

"Maybe na in Tennebrum, but things are different here," Kyran reminded him, though the words were bitter on his tongue as he spoke them. "It is the law—dinnae suffer a mage ta live."

"That's just bullshit."

Kyran felt a flicker of warmth for the man. Barrett had staunchly disapproved of the Isleish notions of mages since they had met. While Kyran had initially found the hunter's inability to understand what growing up surrounded by those beliefs had been like irritatingly ignorant, he was slowly finding the man's uncompromising opinion that mages were just people like anyone else almost reassuring, even if he doubted himself.

Kyran didn't have any answers for the things that happened in that prison—why his magic had grown, what the demon meant in calling him a half-blood. But the truth was there, lurking in the suspicion that the Isleish were right. He still wasn't certain how to contend with even the idea of what that truth meant about him—about his family. It was something he would have to face one day. But for now, he was more than willing to pretend to live in ignorance. It was just more than he could think about right now.

"Let it be, Barrett," Captain Griswold cautioned. "He is right; this is not our country. The laws are different here."

"It's still ridiculous," Barrett maintained, crossing his arms stubbornly. But he didn't press the argument further.

The captain shifted his attention back to Kyran, waiting until the mage looked up at him. "Now, I cannot speak for any actions Connal may take outside of the law, but should he try to bring your family into this in the manner he described to you, I would without doubt be able to protect them from any retribution."

"No matter how this ends?" Kyran pressed.

"No matter how this ends," Griswold swore solemnly.

Kyran closed his eyes, murmuring a near-silent prayer of thanks. After everything his kin had gone through trying to protect him, he could finally offer something in return. His family would be safe.

Which left only his tale to tell.

He took a deep breath, squeezing his hands together until his fingers ached, and began.

Chapter Sixty

He had been in the stable, the horses all turned out and the stalls empty. The hayloft had always been one of his favorite places on the farm—a place he could be alone, surrounded by the gentle animal sounds of the horses and the pleasant, pungent smell of their hides and hay.

But it had offered him no solace that day. Head cradled in his hands, he sat amongst the bales and tried to take comfort in the familiar, but he simply hurt too much. Ben was gone. It had not been an easy couple of years. The burden of trying to keep everything a secret had taken its greatest toll on Ben; he was such an honest lad. He had tried to end it so many times, but Kyran had always convinced him not to give up, that what they had was worth it. But not this time. This time was the last.

"Kyran, there ye are."

His head snapped up to see Connal peering over the loft ladder. He quickly got to his feet, turning his back to the man and wiping the tears from his eyes and cheeks as the laird's son climbed up into the loft.

"What's wrong?"

Hearing the man's feet crossing the hay, Kyran quickly turned to face him. He backed towards the wall.

He and Connal had never gotten on. In Kyran's estimation, it was because Connal was an enormous prick who liked to harass him whenever he had the chance, especially if it meant it would end in a fight. Connal, being older and much larger than Kyran, usually won. If Kyran were to use his magic, he would make short work of the man, but he would also hurt him quite badly, something the laird would not take kindly to. It would mean trouble for his family, especially with the tension already so thick between the laird and his da—all over him—so he suffered the man's constant harassment in silence when he visited his family's home.

The fact that Connal was there asking after Kyran as if he gave a whit was suspicious at the very least.

"What do you want?" Kyran bit back, sidling along the wall as Connal walked right up to him.

The man stank of ale and sweat. His clothes looked rumpled, as if he had only just left the alehouse after a long night, and his dark hair, shorn short, was disheveled and oily.

"You've been crying," he slurred, his face split in a leering grin Kyran was all too familiar with. "Was it Ben?"

The bottom of Kyran's stomach dropped into his feet, and he felt what little color he had in his face drain.

Connal laughed, an ugly, thick sound. "Yeah. I heard all about that. It's kind of disgusting, innit?"

"You shut your mouth," Kyran barked back, but Connal only laughed again. How did he know? If Connal told anyone....

"Or what?" The man leaned closer, caging Kyran against the wall with his bulk. He was not nearly so tall as Kyran, but he was at least twice as broad, and corded with thick, heavy muscle.

Kyran tried to move away from him, but Connal put his hand to the wall, blocking Kyran, and the mage glared up at him. Connal leered back.

"Get out of my way," Kyran told him.

"Or what?" Connal repeated.

Kyran didn't like the look in Connal's eyes, a kind of sick gleam. He was up to something.

It happened faster than Kyran could react. He turned to force his way around Connal when the bigger man snatched a fistful of his hair and shoved his mouth against his. Kyran froze, too surprised to remember how to act. Then, a tongue roughly pushed its way into his mouth, bitter with alcohol, and Kyran jerked his head, crying out when the hand yanked his hair again. Connal's mouth pushed harder against his, tongue plunging into his mouth, but when he shoved against Connal, the man broke the kiss with a low chuckle.

"Stop!" Kyran demanded, wiping his mouth with the back of his hand and spitting. His magic tugged at him, and he clenched his will around it. If he lost control, he could kill Connal. He had to rein it in. "What is wrong with ye? Let go of me!"

"What? I thought you liked it like this?" Connal cupped one big hand between Kyran's legs, and Kyran jerked back against the wall, breath catching in a sharp hiss.

He grabbed the man's thick wrist, trying to push it away. "What are you—stop!"

Connal's eyes narrowed in satisfaction as his hand started move, stroking, and, to Kyran's horror, he felt himself respond.

"Stop!" he shouted again, but Connal yanked at his hair again, hard enough that Kyran thought he saw stars for a moment. The familiar touch of frost crawled down his skin.

"Stop shouting," Connal said, eerily calm. "We both know you like it. You let Ben touch you like this, dinnae you? Maybe if you're quiet, I willna have ta tell anyone."

Kyran's lips pulled back from his teeth at the threat, and his magic pushed hard against his control. He almost let it loose. "Let go of me before I—"

Connal's fingers tightened between his legs, and a moan slipped out of Kyran before he could stop it, his knees going weak beneath him. "Before you what?" His hand slipped higher, pulling Kyran's kilt up, and he pressed against him so Kyran could feel something hard against his leg. "Tell me what you want ta do, you disgusting wee animal."

He rubbed against Kyran, and the mage wanted to simply vomit as he felt the man move against his thigh. "If you stay quiet, I willna tell anyone what you and Ben have been doing."

Kyran felt himself weigh it. He actually weighed the consequences for him and his family and for Ben if Connal made it known that Kyran and Ben had been together as more than clansmen. It would be a disaster—all their careful secrecy shattered in an instant. All he would have to do was bear the humiliation and let Connal grope him.

He smashed his fist into Connal's jaw, and did not stop swinging. The bigger man, caught off guard, staggered back, spitting a curse, but he didn't go down, and his hand in Kyran's hair tightened painfully. He raised his other hand and clubbed Kyran across his face, knuckles catching him in the temple like a brick. Kyran's skull exploded in pain, and his vision went abruptly black, his body crumpling limply. Distantly, he felt the straw under his cheek before a boot caught him in the gut. He gagged on a mouthful of bile and spit, his gasp of pain cutting off in a choking little sound.

"Like it rough, huh?" he heard Connal say over him. The man spat, and a wet glob hit Kyran's cheek. He tried to move to wipe it off, to crawl away, anything, but his body was not working. He struggled just to breathe, but he only made sucking, gasping sounds. His magic strained against him, and it took almost all of his concentration to keep it from escaping.

"That what gets your demon blood hot? Huh? Ye need someone ta just give it ta ye on the ground like an animal?"

Another boot connected with Kyran's stomach, and he vomited in the hay.

Connal laughed. "Ye disgust me."

Shapes started to form in front of Kyran's eyes again, and he made out Connal standing over him, one hand under his kilt. The man moved to stand behind Kyran, and the mage felt a sudden horrible surety at what was about to happen. But why? He couldn't understand why this was happening. Connal had always been an ass, but he had never done anything like this. Why was he doing this?

"Stop," Kyran gagged, spitting out more bile, the smell stinging his nose. He forced himself to uncurl, his aching guts threatening to send more vomit up as he clawed at the hay, dragging himself away.

A hand clamped around his ankle, yanking him back. He twisted on the ground, lashing blindly up, and caught another hammer-like fist under his eye. His head snapped back, bouncing off the loft's wooden floor, and his thoughts seemed to burst in his skull. His eyes rolled and slid over nothing. He felt Connal roll him back onto his belly as he grabbed his legs, dragging him backwards over the straw.

"Look at ye," the man said, voice rough and thick in his throat as he pawed at Kyran's kilt, pulling it up over his backside. "You dinnae even have any hair. Skin as smooth as a lass." His hand ran over Kyran's thigh, and Kyran clawed at the hay again, trying to make his limbs crawl away, but Connal's hot, heavy weight leaned down over his back, and his big, calloused hand pressed down on the back of Kyran's neck. Straw bit into his cheek and knees, and, as his thoughts began to come together again, the first wild fingers of panic seized him. This was happening. This was really happening.

"Hold still," Connal growled, spitting loudly. "Quit squirming. I know you canna wait. I got your blood all up." One of those heavy hands yanked at his belt, pulling his hips up, and Kyran kicked as hard as he could, hitting nothing, his legs forced too far apart by the man's knees. Bucked against the hand pushing his face against the ground, he felt his hips rock back into something hard and wet, and his breath caught in the terrified realization of what it was.

"Eager beast!" Connal laughed again, his breath hot and stinking on the back of Kyran's neck as he leaned farther over him. "Da was right. Ye're nothing more than a demon-blooded animal. Just hold on, I'm going as fast as I can."

Kyran felt a hand fumble at his backside, and he struggled harder. "No! No! Stop! Don'!" he shouted, but the man wasn't listening. "Stop. Stop. Stopstopstop..."

That hard wetness pressed against him again, and then a big hand grabbed his hip and pulled. The pain took his breath away, a fire that split him in half all the way to his core. Kyran screamed, and his magic ripped out of his control, tearing into Connal. The man howled in pain, shoving Kyran away before collapsing to the loft floor.

Kyran couldn't move, his face streaming as he struggled not to scream again. He'd never hurt so badly.

"You bastard!" Connal howled, curled on his side and clutching between his legs. "You demon-blooded, mongrel bastard! I'll kill ye!"

Someone was going to hear. Someone would find them. He had to move.

Slowly, Kyran crawled onto his hands and knees then got unsteadily to his feet. The ground seemed to swim beneath his boots, and the walls looked as if they were moving around him, tipping and whirling. He couldn't stand straight—only hunched over, clutching his middle, his stomach aching and his head pounding as if someone were driving nails into his skull. But nothing hurt more than his backside. He could feel something wet running down his thighs, and when he pulled his kilt down and touched his leg, his fingers came away red with blood.

He tried to take a step and strangled a pained whimper. By all the mercy in the Isles, it hurt. He looked at the ladder on the other side of the loft and let out a soft swear, his breath catching in a frustrated sob. It was so far away.

"I'll kill ye," Connal was still howling. "Ye willna get away with this! You hear me?"

Kyran tried to ignore him, tried not to look as the man spat curses at him from the floor, but he couldn't help it. He looked, and saw the ugly white and black patches of frostbitten flesh on Connal's face and arms and the large, white blisters that had formed and burst. It didn't take a great deal of imagination to picture what it looked like under his kilt where he was clutching himself. Kyran grimaced through his own pain. They would know. There was no denying what had happened. Anyone that looked at Connal would know.

And they had.

The room was utterly silent when he finished his tale. Kyran was no longer sitting upright, but had slowly curled into himself as his story had poured out until he was hunched over his middle, clutching his arms.

He didn't blink, didn't move, staring down at the quilt without seeing as the memory he had tried hardest to forget—that had instead clung, rotting, within him—played out as vividly as if he were still there. He could still smell the spice of dried hay, the bitter stink of alcohol and bile. Could still feel Connal's hand wrapped in his hair, pressed at the back of his neck, grabbing his hip, ghosting along his leg. His skin fairly crawled at the man's touch, and no matter how he scratched or rubbed or washed, he still couldn't forget it.

"Well, captain?" Barrett asked, his voice sharp. The fury on his face when Kyran lifted his eyes was undeniable.

Captain Griswold inclined his head at Barrett's words, touching his steepled fingers to his lips. "I am...sorry you had to go through something like that. I know it was difficult for you to talk about. You do not need to worry. The guild has more than reasonable cause to act here."

"Like I said from the beginnin'." Barrett turned to Kyran again, though his eyes wouldn't quite meet his. "Connal got what he deserved. You know that, right?"

He did, or at least part of him did. But even after all this time, after everything he had seen and overcome, he still felt scared and guilty about what had happened. He knew it wasn't his fault. Connal was a monster that had used him and hurt him. But that didn't stop him from feeling as if he were still a frightened, wee lad.

He took a shaking breath, nodding as he shut his eyes. He pushed the memories back into their corners where he had left them rotting, where he didn't have to think about them. When he opened his eyes, his breathing was steadier, and he could pry his fingers from his arms. He folded them in his lap and sat up, lifting his chin to meet Barrett's eyes. "Connal will never get what he deserves, but he got close enough."

Barrett's lips curled in a smile, his eyes flashing with fire. "I can't wait to see the look on his face, though I'd like it better if I could beat it in for him." He leaned back in his seat again with a huff, though his smile did not dim. "Dunbar barred me from the Hall before 'cause I couldn't keep my mouth shut."

A smirk tugged at the corner of Kyran's lips. "I dinnae ken where he might have gotten tha' idea."

Barrett laughed, then winced, touching his darkened throat. "I wouldn't know," he said softly.

Chapter Sixty-One

"Kyran ban Neil Roche. You stand accused of assaulting my son, Connal ban Dunbar Roche, by the use of your magic. An attack tha' has left a permanent scar upon him, after which you fled the country. What have you ta say for yourself?"

A black murmur went through the Hall, and Kyran squared his shoulders, keeping his chin raised even as his fingers played a staccato on his walking stick. The day of the Great Hall came faster than he could have imagined. He stood at the center of the hall in borrowed clothes, the enormous dining tables pushed to the walls to clear the space for the assembled men to watch the proceedings. Boughs of evergreen graced the walls and hearths, their potent fragrance and touches of color a reminder of the celebrations that had been held only a night ago. Kyran heard some of it, even up in the room he was confined to with the hunters. Barrett had caught him humming at the window. Kyran didn't enjoy crowds, but as his countrymen raised their voices in familiar song, he'd wished he could be down there. Murray would have said it was the Isleish in him.

Now, before him on a raised section of the floor, sat the laird, dressed in his finest, his long, red-gold hair freshly washed and tied back with a velvet ribbon, his beard neatly groomed.

To his left and slightly behind him stood Connal. His thick black hair had been secured back as well, showing well the ruined half of his face for the gathering bystanders. His one good eye was fixed on Kyran, and the side of his mouth not dragged into a permanent scowl by his scars was fixed in a sly smirk. Kyran pointedly ignored him—and the guilt that looking at his scars still sent crawling through his belly.

He had been protecting himself, he reminded his conscience. He had done nothing wrong.

"My laird," came Captain Griswold's calm voice from behind Kyran as the captain stepped up to speak on his behalf, as they had discussed beforehand. For his benefit, the Hall was being held in Common instead of Isleish. "As a representative of the hunter's guild, and given leave to speak on behalf of Tennebrum's Crown, I wish to speak in the defense of Kyran."

Another murmur went through the crowd, this one of surprise. The same surprise flashed over Connal's face right before his expression darkened. The laird, however, seemed to be expecting the captain's interference. He raised his hand, allowing him to continue, but Kyran could have sworn he could see a smile hiding at the corner of Dunbar's mouth.

Captain Griswold drew up to Kyran's side, nodding respectfully to Dunbar. "Thank you, my laird. As you are aware, I have spoken with both of the parties affected by these accusations while here in Castle Erchleis. I have received a conflicting set of events from either side, both of which prove somewhat disturbing, and which I would rather not repeat in polite company if it is not necessary. It is of my opinion, however, after hearing these two explanations, that Kyran is innocent of the crimes of which he has been accused."

The murmuring in the crowd grew in volume as men voiced their dissent, some even shouting or booing. Connal's face had gone pale—not in fear, but in white-hot rage. Dunbar's own mein had gone very still in his seat. He allowed the Hall to go on for a moment before raising his hand again, calling in Isleish for order to be restored.

"Is that so?" he prompted the guild captain, his voice tight with restrained anger.

Griswold bowed his head once more. "It is. I can relate what I have been told, if I must, but I recognize that proving which set of events truthfully occurred is impossible, given we have only each of their words to go by. Therefore, I offer you restitution for Kyran's crimes in the form of—" Here he listed the amount of currency he was authorized to pay on Kyran's behalf, and the mage nearly choked. Stars above, that was more money than he had ever seen.

Dunbar seemed to consider the offer, reaching to stroke his beard. The crowd had grown loud again, openly dumbfounded at the sum, many furious at the suggestion that a mage could be found innocent. Connal bent over his da's seat, whispering angrily with the man, who listened with his own head bent. Kyran didn't know what to make of any of it. That was a lot of money, but what if Dunbar turned it down? Could he do that? He glanced at Captain Griswold for some indication, but the captain stood as perfectly composed as ever, his gaze on the laird.

At last, Dunbar waved Connal back to his place, and the crowd shushed as he raised his hand again. "I find your offer amenable, captain. You will come to speak with me when this is done."

The crowd exploded, shouting in Common and Isleish alike.

"He is a demon-blooded cur!" someone shouted.

"He'll kill someone else!"

"Monster!"

"Half-blooded bastard!"

Kyran clenched his fingers around his staff to keep from clapping them over his ears. It was just as he'd feared.

Dinnae suffer a mage ta live.

Even though the guild captain had convinced Dunbar not to take his head today, Connal or any one of the others here in the Hall would do it for him, and Kyran's da would be next. He shouldn't have told them. He should have bowed his neck under the blade.

They pressed closer, looking as if they meant to tear his head off right there, when Dunbar raised his voice over them. "*Silence in my Hall!*"

Their voices fell to a disquieted murmur, and they glanced amongst one another, casting dark glares at Kyran and the captain.

The laird's gaze swept over the room. As it turned to Kyran, the mage felt his spine straighten a little more. "Let it be known tha' upon delivery of the agreed-upon sum, Kyran will be forgiven all crimes."

There was an instant uproar, voices rising with the excitement of the moment.

"Those that are tempted ta cross me," Dunbar continued over them, "ken that you will be crossing the hunter's guild in this matter, and if you try ta resolve things your own way you will find the edge of my blade is verrah sharp."

Kyran's mouth went dry. He didn't know what to say. In a hundred years, he never would have thought he'd hear those words from the laird's own mouth. But it was done. He was free.

Then his eyes met Connal's across the hall, and the hatred burning behind the man's glare. No. It was not quite done yet.

"Captain," he called quietly, "what of my kin?"

"A moment," the man replied, calmly waiting as the storm of voices raged around them.

At last, Dunbar appeared to notice his patient stare, and raised his voice to quiet the crowd again.

"My laird," the captain said when it was quiet enough to be heard. "I am also aware that there are certain accusations lingering over the young man's family. If I may offer...."

Dunbar actually chuckled. "Aye. You may," he replied, and named another sum, this one much smaller than the last.

Captain Griswold bowed his head. "The guild will pay that amount in addition to the previous sum."

"Are there any other of my clansmen you would like ta pay for?" Dunbar jested, sending a round of uneasy chuckles through those watching, but it didn't hide the suspicious murmurs of the rest.

"No, my laird."

"Then I believe you and I have business ta discuss. We shall adjourn ta my office."

Chapter Sixty-Two

It was fiercely cold out, the air biting and crisp, but it seemed the worst of the storm had passed. Snow blanketed the ground as far as Barrett could see, and while there was no more falling at the moment, heavy grey clouds threatened more to come. He snuggled his leather coat closer, trying to trap what heat he could within it while he chewed over his thoughts.

He had watched the Hall from one of the balconies overlooking the proceedings at the laird's request. He hated being so far away, so useless. It had taken every measure of his control not to leave his place and force his way into the Hall proper. It had offered a good vantage of the hatred Kyran had grown up surrounded by when the laird accepted Captain Griswold's outrageous sum of money. It was a small wonder Kyran thought of his magic as a curse, after hearing what they'd shouted at him.

"Bloody backwards bred arseholes," he snarled to himself.

But the laird had accepted the restitution and cleared Kyran's name. It was a hollow victory. Kyran was free, but so was Connal. Barrett swore if he ever saw that man's face again, it would be the last time.

He tucked closer to Sweetheart's neck, grumbling again when the mare jumped skittishly, tugging at her reins. They had left the castle almost immediately after whatever had proceeded in the laird's office. Kyran had insisted.

"My *'crimes'* were paid. Dunbar canna make me stay under the same roof as his son, or any of the other folk here that would still like ta see my blood on the stones. If I am free ta go, I am goin' ta see my family."

Barrett grinned at just the memory. That was the Kyran he'd come to know.

Kyran didn't seem to notice the cold at all. Clothed at last in his kilt and a borrowed shirt, he didn't even have gooseflesh on his exposed skin, nor did his breath fog in the frigid air. But despite that, the mage looked...worried. He kept looking in Captain Griswold's direction as if expecting something from the man.

It went on long enough, until Barrett finally asked, "Somethin' on your mind?"

Kyran glanced at Barrett, a bit of color rising in his cheeks. "Aye," he admitted, looking to the captain again. "I dinnae mean ta sound ungrateful. I ken I wouldna be walking free like this if it werena for you. But what was tha' paper I had ta sign? You said you would explain it."

"I did," the captain replied, shrugging deeper into his coat. "The first one was a legal contract stating that the guild had paid your and your family's sum to Dunbar."

"I remember," Kyran said warily. "We all signed that one."

The captain nodded. "The second paper was a statement of your debt bondage to the guild for the outstanding balance of your restitution."

Kyran frowned.

"In other words, you are bound by your debt to render services to the guild until such time as you are able to repay it."

Barrett was stunned. How could the captain...?

"Until I—? You tricked me!" Kyran snarled.

Sweetheart danced sideways away from the mage, ears halfback as she tugged on her reins, and Barrett tightened his hold beneath her chin.

"I did no such thing," Captain Griswold said mildly.

"You sold me inta servitude!"

"I did what was necessary. You had no other options available." He raised a hand as Kyran made to shout again. "You may be a bondsman, but by your service, the guild will be able to offer you its protection and its own services in turn. You will have access to our chirurgeons, teachers, the library—whatever you so please. And, if you choose, you may even become a full member once you have recovered your health. Your application will have to be reviewed, but, given your...circumstances, it is likely to be mere formality. You would be able to earn wages, as a member, though they would be garnished to continue paying your bond."

Kyran was not mollified by the captain's explanation. His lips peeled back from the tips of his teeth. "You're a bastard."

Barrett felt his lip twitch in agreement as he wrestled with his mare, but the captain's explanation brought to light something Barrett had not even thought of yet. Somehow, he had assumed now that Kyran was no longer being accused of any crimes, that everything would return to normal—that he, Kyran, and Captain Griswold would return to Tennebrum and pick back up where they had all left off. But now that he had the chance to consider it, he realized that was never going to be the case. Though improved, Kyran was still recovering from his time in the demon realm. He needed time to heal more than just his body.

More than that, if it were not for the guild's sudden demand of Kyran, it was just as likely the young man would have wanted to stay here, with his family. He was not from Tennebrum; he had only fled there to escape the laird. Now he was being forced to leave his homeland and his family again until he was able to satisfy the guild.

And what did Barrett have to offer, anyway? What was he even returning to? He had left the last of his family with no intent of going back. But he had finished what he'd come to do. Kyran was safe, the demon dead. What was he supposed to do now?

"Does he have to pay this debt himself, or are others free to help pay?" Barrett asked with faint hope.

"That would be a matter to take up with the guildmaster," the captain supplied. But it wasn't a no. Maybe there was something for him, after all.

They continued through the snow, the quiet between them awkward, but not as impenetrable as it had been those long weeks travelling here. Barrett looked around as they started up the base of a hill, certain he recognized it despite the snow, when a piercing whistle sounded from the top of the rise, nearly startling Barrett out of his skin.

Beside him, Kyran lifted his head, a boyish grin spreading over his face. Pursing his lips, he blew a sharp, trilling call in return and cocked his head to listen. After a pause, several short, high chirps responded, and Kyran chuckled. "Wee Tavish has spied us."

Barrett grinned. He heard a holler and a shout in the distance. He was pretty sure he knew who they belonged to. "You've got a wild set of brothers."

"You dinnae ken the half of it," Kyran sighed.

A moment later, three figures came down off the rise, the smallest—wee Tavish, Barrett presumed—racing ahead of them and straight for Kyran, head down, arms pumping. He looked somewhere in that nebulous era of boys just beginning to come of age, all gangly limbs, specks of hair on their chins, and voices prone to cracking. The end of a scarf flapped behind him like a grey tail, matching the knitted cap pulled down over his hair and ears. He let out a squawk of a battle cry as he neared, and flung a snowball straight for Kyran's chest. It exploded in a puff of white powder.

"Ha!" he laughed, pointing at Kyran as the mage dusted himself off. "That's what you get for making it snow again!"

"I dinnae do anything of the sort," Kyran defended himself mildly.

"Aye, you did. It snowed the last time you visited, too."

"Nay, that was the summertime."

"Before that, then." The boy walked over to his brother, staring down at the empty space where his left leg had once been. "Murray told me about your leg," he said, "but you look awful. You forget how ta trap up there on the *ben*?"

"Aye. Had ta eat the bark off the trees ta keep from starving."

Tavish rolled his eyes. "Sure ye did. Is that silverbark?"

"It is."

"What are you doing with that?" the boy asked with alarm. "The wee folk are going to put splinters up your nails for taking one of theirs."

Kyran bent conspiratorially towards his brother. "What do you think I've really been trapping and eating on the *ben*?"

Tavish's jaw dropped in horror. "You wouldn't!"

Kyran only grinned in reply.

Finally, Murray and Duncan finally strolled up—Murray with one black eye, and Duncan with two.

"'Lo again," Murray greeted Barrett and Captain Griswold, shaking his long hair out of his eyes. "Fine weather we're havin', no?"

Barrett shook his head, a twinge of guilt touching his conscience at their appearance, but they really had helped prevent a disaster by keeping the laird's men out of the dungeon until it was safe. "Thank you both, for the other day," he said quickly. "I hope you're not too beat up."

They both grinned.

"This is nothing," Murray insisted.

"Says the man who hasna gone home ta see his wife yet," Duncan chuckled.

"Wife?" Kyran cut in. "You got yourself married, Murray?"

"Aye, he did," Tavish answered for his brother. "And—"

"And there's a *bairn* on the way," Murray finished, scowling at Tavish. "I told you *I* was goin' ta tell him."

"Well, you were too slow." The youngest brother grinned up at Kyran, his previous alarm gone without a trace. "Duncan's got another one, too. Just a few months old."

Duncan merely shrugged.

"Well," Kyran shook his head, "I see what you two have been up ta since I've been gone."

"You canna say 'no' good anymore," Murray said loftily, raising his chin in a fair imitation of Kyran. "I have a wife that needs looking after."

"More like one that looks after him," Duncan added, snorting when Murray threw him an exasperated look.

"Can you believe this is my own brother? Talking about me in such a way?"

"Aye," Duncan replied, patting Murray on the shoulder. "I think it comes rather expected. Now, if you're done with your whinging, we've got ta take the prince here ta see the rest of his kin, if you havena forgot."

Murray beamed. "Oh, aye. I had forgotten we were in the presence of royalty." He swept forward in a dramatic bow to Kyran. "Please excuse our behavior, your royal highness."

Kyran stared at his brother, his eyes narrowing. "What is this about?"

"Oh, you dinnae have ta feign ignorance in front of us, your Highness," Murray continued, prancing backwards when Kyran started to lift his walking stick. "Dunbar's man told us how much money the Crown paid for you. A king's ransom by the king himself. We figured that must mean you're royalty now."

"Is that so?"

"Aye, so it is, your Highness."

"Dunbar sent someone here?" Barrett interrupted.

"Aye," Duncan responded. "He sent one of his lads running ta the house just a few hours ago ta tell our da what came of the Hall, and ta likely make certain ta account for all of us." He glanced sideways at Murray, who grinned and shrugged in reply.

"We dinnae get caught."

"What did you do?" Kyran asked in exasperation, as if already expecting some wild tale.

"He was my distraction," Tavish answered, puffing his chest out proudly. "He made sure ma and da couldna find me while I crept inta the Hall."

"You *what*?" Barrett blurted out before he could stop himself.

"Aggie let me in," he proclaimed, smirking.

"He's sweet on the laird's lass," Duncan explained, and Tavish turned scarlet. "She let him play at being a serving lad."

"Aggie?" Barrett frowned, thinking of the dark-haired girl that had led him and the captain to Neil's home. That had been...?

"Dunbar's daughter," Kyran filled in, apparently noticing Barrett's confusion, before leveling Tavish a look. "You're still on about her?"

"Sh-shut it, already!" the boy stammered. "Just be glad I was there! If they had tried anything, I would have got you out."

Barrett shook his head incredulously. This family. They were willing to do almost anything for each other. It was a small wonder Kyran spoke so well of his father. Barrett was almost jealous. What he would have given for a family like this. Things might have turned out differently.

"Alright, alright," Duncan sighed, waving his hands between them all as if calling a truce. "Back ta the house, eh? Before ma comes lookin'."

The four of them nodded in agreement, the threat apparently serious enough to put a stop to even their shenanigans. Sorcha really was a force to be reckoned with. They started up the hill again, matching Kyran's stilted pace as they started chatting again, Tavish filling his older brothers in on Kyran's eating habits, and Barrett with Sweetheart and Captain Griswold fell in behind them.

Kyran seemed so much more animated than Barrett had ever seen him. His eyes were bright, and he was quick to smile at whatever his brothers did or said. He looked happy. It was like seeing another person, one Barrett had only caught rare glimpses of beneath the proud, cold exterior, but one that did not fail to capture his attention any less as he found himself wondering what it would be like to get to know this part of Kyran better. He imagined the two of them at the Drunken Wind, sitting at a table in their room, drinking and chatting as Kyran's face lit up with rare laughter, his cheeks flushed with drink. The thought alone made him smile fondly. A not-unpleasant heat crept into his belly.

The small, thatched house came into view as they crested the hill. Neil was outside, sitting on the stump he had been chopping wood on the last time Barrett had visited. As they started down towards him, the man lifted his head and got to his feet to meet them. Murray and Duncan hung back as they got close, allowing Kyran to draw ahead of them, and Barrett slowed beside them with the captain.

Tavish dashed past, aiming for the door, likely intent on telling the rest of the family they were back, when the door flew open. A tiny shape bolted out into the snow with an excited shriek, ignoring the sharp Isleish calling after her. Effie ran straight for Kyran. The mage quickly dropped to his knee, flinging his arms out before she threw herself into him full speed, her arms wrapping around his neck as he toppled backwards into the snow.

"She missed you," Neil chuckled, shaking his head down at the pair of them as Sorcha hurried out the door, her face set in a scowl.

"Lassie, this is the last time you—" She stopped short, her eyes widening as she recognized Kyran. He pushed up on his elbow, his left arm curled awkwardly about Effie as the girl began to wail against his chest.

"Hello, ma," he said quietly.

She started at his words, as if they had broken some spell that had come over her, then blinked rapidly until her composure crumpled. "Oh, Kyran," she sobbed, flinging herself down beside him and wrapping him and Effie in her arms, pulling them tight against her.

Barrett flushed and found somewhere else to look, as did the rest of them. He could hear Sorcha saying something in Isleish between sobs, and Kyran murmuring in reply, comforting her.

After a moment, Neil bent over them, speaking in a low tone Barrett couldn't make out and offering her his hand, his other gentling against her back. She sniffed, looking up at him, and then the rest of them standing around, her face blotchy. Wiping at her eyes with her sleeve, she regained her composure and accepted his hand, straightening her skirts as she stood.

"I made an early supper," she announced, her voice broken by a sniffle.

"And there's plenty of drink ta share if you would like ta get out of the cold."

There was a chorus of agreements, and the brothers went ahead inside, stomping the snow from their boots before entering.

Sorcha raised her eyes to Barrett, their rims red and swollen, and smiled tearfully. "Of course, you both are more than welcome in this house, as well. I canna thank you enough for what you've done for us."

"It was nothing," Barrett assured the woman, uncertain how to take her brimming gratitude.

"No. It wasna," Neil replied quietly. "But we can leave that talk for later."

"Aye, after you've had a good meal," Sorcha agreed, squeezing his hand before she stooped over Kyran and gently but deftly disentangled Effie from him, scooping the girl up into her arms. Effie broke into another wail, reaching for Kyran as the mage slowly got up.

Sorcha shushed her, murmuring a long string of Isleish. "Tavish, take the hunter's horse to the stable."

"Aye, ma," the youngest brother said, bounding up to Barrett for his horse's reins.

"The rest of you, come and find a seat," Sorcha said, shooing them towards the door. "I've the kettle on."

Chapter Sixty-Three

IT QUICKLY TURNED into a much more lively gathering than Barrett had experienced in a long time. There was hot food, a warm fire, good company, and more than enough strong drink to loosen everyone's tongues. And the stories. It seemed there was an endless number of them. Murray took great pride in recounting any he could remember that involved Kyran, much to the mage's embarrassment. Apparently, Kyran had had quite the mischievous streak in his youth.

During the telling of a tale involving Tavish and a lost goat, Barrett realized there was a face he didn't recognize watching him from the doorway at the back of the house. When he asked Kyran, the mage belatedly introduced his youngest sibling—his sister Isobel. Barrett lifted a hand to wave at the brown-haired girl, and she wrinkled her nose at him before disappearing through the doorway.

As the sun set outside and the drink poured even more freely, Barrett struggled to understand a thing being said as the Islemen began to lapse into their native tongue, their accents so thick when they did remember to speak Common that it was rendered all but incomprehensible. It was amusing to listen to anyway, their expressions and wild gestures telling their own tale. But, mostly, Barrett found his eyes wandering over to Kyran, who had fallen asleep with his head on the table, Effie snuggled against his hip with her head in his lap.

There were more than a few jests over it, and a few sly suggestions from his brothers of what they might do to punish him for passing out after so little drink, but his mother fended them off with a sharp look and draped a homespun blanket over the mage's back and shoulders. His hair had fallen into his face, the copper strands bright against his pale skin, and Barrett's fingers twitched with the need to brush them back before his face warmed at such a thought. He blamed the drink, which he took another long pull from to hide his embarrassment.

Graces above, where was his head at?

He finished his drink a hair before Duncan leaned over and filled it again, encouraging him to drink up. Barrett didn't resist. Clearly he hadn't had enough.

The next thing he knew, though, he was in front of the fire, jolted awake by a sense of magic and a frigid breeze. He picked his head up, still muzzy with drink, and caught a glimpse of pale starlight reflected on snow before the front door closed.

"Oh," he slurred heavily to himself, slumping in his chair. It was only Kyran.

His eyes flicked open again, and he sat up as his drink-addled mind finally managed to churn into wakefulness. Kyran had gone outside.

Pulling the blanket from his lap, he managed to get to his feet, but walking to the door turned out to be quite the endeavor. He was still dreadfully drunk. He fumbled with the latch, his fingers clumsy, until he managed to push the door open. The cold was like a slap across his cheeks, jarring his brain fully awake.

The night was pitch dark, heavy clouds hiding the stars and moon, but that was not to say there was no light. Kyran's runelines glimmered against the snow, illuminating the flakes drifting around him like wisps of faerie fire as he walked away. Where in the world was he going in the middle of the night?

Without hesitation, Barrett pulled the door shut behind him and followed Kyran out into the snow.

They didn't go far, stopping at the top of the rise opposite the way they had come to the house. Barrett hesitated at some distance, not wanting to startle the mage, until he saw Kyran's head tilt towards him in acknowledgement.

"Cold out," Barrett remarked as he joined Kyran, rubbing his arms and beginning to regret not grabbing his coat.

"I suppose," Kyran replied, still only dressed in his kilt and borrowed shirt, but apparently untouched by the cold.

Barrett eyed him enviously, waiting, but the mage did not offer anything more, his eyes fixed on something in the dark. Barrett tried to follow his line of sight, but it was far too dark with the clouds above. He could make out a stacked stone fence buried in snow next to them, but that was all.

"You alright?" he asked at last.

"I couldna sleep."

"Nightmares?" Barrett guessed, more than familiar with sleepless nights himself.

A flicker of the hollow-eyed stare Kyran had worn when Barrett found him in the demon realm passed over his face like a shadow. His jaw clenched, his grip tightening on his walking stick. "Aye," he said quietly.

"I know what that's like," Barrett sympathized, wishing yet again there was more he could do to comfort him. "I'm here if you need anythin'. You know that, right?"

The faintest smile lifted just the corner of Kyran's lips. "Aye."

"Good." He followed the mage's gaze back out into the dark, squinting, but he couldn't make out anything but the faintest shadows of drifting snow. "What is it you see out there?"

Kyran shook his head, finally peeling his eyes away. "When the weather is clear, you can see Cairngorm from here."

Barrett looked out over the distance again. So that was why Kyran had chosen this spot. "You'll have to show me in the mornin', when the weather passes."

"It isna likely ta before we leave."

"Then maybe later, when you come back here."

Kyran scoffed bitterly. "If the guild ever lets me."

Barrett winced with guilt. "You're not a slave, Kyran. You'll be able to see your family again. I'm goin' to talk to the Guildmaster. Whether she allows it or not, I'll find a way to help you pay off your debt. Then you can do whatever you want. You could come back here. You could become a hunter." He licked his lips, the cold stinging them as a pounding started behind his ribs. "If you wanted, we could even work together again. You're good at it. Graces know, you're better than me."

Kyran didn't reply right away, his head still bowed, and Barrett worried suddenly if he had been too forward.

"It's just a suggestion," he added. "I know you probably don't want anythin' to do with me after...after everythin'." His voice broke into an awkward chuckle, and he silently cursed himself. Graces, what was he asking? Of course Kyran wouldn't want to work with him.

The mage made a soft sound like a laugh and finally looked up from the snow. "I should be asking you tha'."

"Eh?"

"After you crossed inta their realm ta find me, brought me ta the guild ta heal me, then came all the way ta the Isles ta face down that Graces-cursed demon and...." Kyran hesitated, drawing a breath before adding, "And Connal, are you na sick of the sight of me yet?"

"Not at all. Why would you think that?" When Kyran looked away, Barrett stepped around the mage, forcing him to look at him. "Why?"

"I havena brought you anythin' but trouble since we met."

"You—?" Now it was Barrett's turn to laugh, though it was harsher than he'd expected. "The demon I failed to kill took you and hurt you—not once, but twice." The bitter pain and guilt that had crawled into Barrett's middle two years ago when he'd held Raleigh's cold body against him stirred in its nest. "I don't even know how you can look at me."

"It wasna your fault."

Barrett lifted his head from his misery, caught off guard by the mage's reassurance, but his guilt only rose again, this time in his throat. "But if I had killed it—"

"It would have been another." The mage's nails clicked against his walking stick. "You said yourself mages call to their kine. But you came for me. I dinnae know if anyone else would have."

They wouldn't. Barrett was the first to ever set foot in that realm and return to speak of it. He hadn't considered just what that meant for Kyran, though. If it had been anyone else, he would still be there. Unless...."You would have handled any other demon."

"You canna be sure of tha'."

"You're strong," Barrett insisted. "Any other demon wouldn't—"

"I dinnae even ken what a demon *was* before I met ye," Kyran interjected sharply. "I slept in the dark on your country's soil. If I'd escaped the first, there would be another ta take me. I'm na untouchable." He wrapped his second hand around his walking stick, squeezing until his knuckles went white. "Far from it. And if I'd managed ta escape every demon, Dunbar's men would have still found me and dragged me back here, alone, ta stand in the Hall. If they dinnae kill me first."

Barrett wanted to disagree, felt he had to, but he had no argument. Reluctantly, he had to admit Kyran was right. He still felt he was responsible, that he could have done something to prevent all of this, but he couldn't deny that he had done everything in his power to rectify it—more than anyone else might have.

"Alright, alright. You're right," he conceded with as much grace as he could muster, scuffing at the snow with his boot.

"Of course I am."

Barrett shot him a look, catching the mage's impish grin. "You...." Barrett shook his head, running a hand over his face to hide his own smile. "Your brothers were right about you. You're a brat."

"Oh, aye?" Kyran snickered.

"Aye. Have your *gaff*."

Their laughter faded into the snow, and Kyran's gaze drifted back to the mountain. "What about you?"

Barrett cocked his head at the question.

"Are you goin' back ta Oareford?" Kyran clarified.

Barrett flicked a heavy flake from his lashes. "Well, I'll have to go to the guildhall and write whatever report the captain is goin; to want on what happened here." He groaned at the mere thought. The scribes were sure to have dozens of questions for him, too. "Oareford is my territory, but I can put in to have it changed."

Kyran tipped his head to look at him. "Dinnae you have kin there?"

Curse it, the mage had a good memory. "Not anymore. She's rejoined the guild."

"Dinnae you have any other kin?"

"No. Just her. My pa....He died years ago, and mum left even before that."

Kyran made a soft hum of acknowledgement, ducking his head, and Barrett flushed with embarrassment. He didn't like airing his family business, especially not after having met Kyran's family. They were everything he could have ever dreamed of a family being. He was almost jealous.

"I could stay at the guild. Maybe get you to teach me how to throw knives." Kyran grinned, and Barrett ducked his head to hide his own pleased smile. He shrugged and kicked at the snow with his boot, watching the dry flakes turn to glittering dust in the ring of Kyran's light. "They may make me go back anyway, but I can write you while I'm away, if you like."

There was a long pause between them, long enough that Barrett started to regret the admittedly sentimental offer. Then Kyran quietly admitted, "I...canna read."

Barrett's head snapped up in surprise, and Kyran looked away in embarrassment. It suddenly made sense how Kyran hadn't known what he was signing with Captain Griswold, or why he hadn't read the letters Barrett had handed him in Oareford.

"There are teachers at the guildhall," he offered, and Kyran let out a tired groan. "You'll learn fast," Barrett assured him, smothering a laugh at the man's uncharacteristic chagrin. "I'm certain. I'll write you e—"

A sharp, mewling whine called from the dark, and both men nearly started out of their skins before Effie darted into view, clinging to Kyran's leg. "What are you doin' out in the cold, lass?" Kyran asked the girl, stroking the top of her head.

"Same reason as me, I imagine," Barrett teased, grinning when Kyran looked up at him. "Makin' sure you weren't runnin' off into trouble."

"Is that so?"

"Aye."

Kyran gave him an even look, though his eyes betrayed his amusement at the gentle rib.

Barrett grinned. "We'd better get the little one back in the house before she gets too cold," he said, rubbing his own frozen hands together as he thought of the warm fireplace waiting for him.

"Aye, but...wait just a moment."

The mage's tone voice caught Barrett's attention immediately—earnest and more than a little nervous. Vulnerable.

"Yes?" Barrett prompted.

The mage fidgeted in place, his fingers tapping lightly against his walking stick again as he seemed to gather the words he needed. "I wanted ta say... that I ken that I have...that I havena been in my right mind in some time, and I dinnae know if I will....well...." He sighed, his mouth tightening with a grimace of what looked like embarrassment. "I was too mad ta say it before, but...."

With another deep breath, Kyran lifted his hand and extended it to Barrett. "Thank you. For everything."

Barrett looked at the outstretched hand in amazement. Slowly, he reached out, and took Kyran's hand, smiling when the mage's fingers curled over his, cool and soft as the falling snow.

"Of course," he murmured back, meeting Kyran's gaze. The mage's eyes flickered nervously, but he could see the determination there as well in their bright, emerald green.

Barrett eased a half step forward, and Kyran's fingers tightened around his before Barrett caught himself, uncertain what his nervous mind had been about to do.

Barrett looked down at their hands and saw Effie still clinging to Kyran, her face buried in his kilt as she began to shiver in earnest.

"We should hurry and get her inside," he murmured, giving Kyran's hand a last squeeze before he let go and folded his arms back over his chest. "If you still can't sleep, though, you can sit with me by the fire. I'll tell you what I know about the guild."

A small smile curved the corner of Kyran's lips as he took up his walking stick. "Aye," he agreed. "I think I will."

Authors' Note

Thank you so much for reading Frostfire, the first installment of our first series, The Dark Inbetween. It's been a long road getting here, one that was not without difficulties. But not as difficult as the challenges Kyran and Barrett faced. If you enjoyed their story, and would like to see more, we would be forever grateful if you left a review wherever you purchased the book to let us know.

If you would like an exclusive look into our current writing projects, we do have a monthly newsletter. You can also find us on social media.

www.thorneandivey.com

thorne.and.ivey

thorne.and.ivey

thorneandivey

CPSIA information can be obtained
at www.ICGtesting.com
Printed in the USA
BVHW030912210521
607713BV00017B/293